Stephen Parkinson

An elementary treatise on mechanics

Third edition revised

SALZWASSER
VERLAG

Stephen Parkinson

An elementary treatise on mechanics

Third edition revised

Reprint of the original, first published in 1863.

1st Edition 2022 | ISBN: 978-3-37500-801-7

Verlag (Publisher): Salzwasser Verlag GmbH, Zeilweg 44, 60439 Frankfurt, Deutschland
Vertretungsberechtigt (Authorized to represent): E. Roepke, Zeilweg 44, 60439 Frankfurt, Deutschland
Druck (Print): Books on Demand GmbH, In de Tarpen 42, 22848 Norderstedt, Deutschland

AN ELEMENTARY TREATISE ON MECHANICS

WITH

A Collection of Examples.

BY

S. PARKINSON, B.D.

THIRD EDITION REVISED.

Cambridge and London.

1863.

PREFACE TO THE THIRD EDITION.

In preparing a third edition of this work I have kept the same object in view as I had in the former editions,—namely, to include in it such portions of Theoretical Mechanics as can be conveniently investigated without the use of the Differential Calculus, and so render it suitable as a manual for the Junior Classes in the University and the Higher Classes in Schools. With one or two short exceptions, the Student is not presumed to require a knowledge of any branches of Mathematics beyond the elements of Algebra, Geometry and Trigonometry.

Motion on a Curve, which is treated of in the last Chapter of the Dynamics, does not seem to admit of any complete discussion without the aid of the Differential Calculus; but in consequence of the present requirements of the Senate-House Examinations, I have put together those theorems respecting cycloidal oscillations and curvilinear motion which admit of a tolerably simple Geometrical exposition.

Several additional propositions have been incorporated in the work for the purpose of rendering it more complete:—and the collection of Examples and Problems has been largely increased:—to most of them I have annexed results, which I hope will render the collection more useful both to tutor and pupil.

St John's College,
Nov. 1863.

CONTENTS.

STATICS.

CHAPTER I.

CHAPTER II.

CHAPTER III.

CHAPTER IV.

CHAPTER V.

CHAPTER VI.

DYNAMICS.

CHAPTER I.

CHAPTER II.

CHAPTER III.

CHAPTER IV.

CHAPTER V.

STATICS.

CHAPTER I.

INTRODUCTION.

1. MECHANICS is the science which treats of the laws of rest and motion of *matter*.

A general notion of the meaning of the term *matter* is acquired in the daily experience of life, since matter in various forms and under various circumstances is perpetually affecting our senses: we shall therefore assume that the notion of it is familiar to the student.

A *particle* or *material point* is a portion of matter indefinitely small in all its dimensions; so that its length, breadth, and thickness are less than any assignable linear magnitude. A *body* of finite size may be regarded as an aggregation of an indefinitely great number of particles; and the dimensions of any given *body* being limited in every direction, it will consequently have a determinate *form* and *volume*.

A body or system of bodies all the points of which are held together in an invariable position with respect to one another, is said to be *rigid*.

2. When a body or particle constantly occupies the same position in space, it is said to be *at rest;* and when its position in space changes continuously in any manner whatever, it is said to be *in motion*. All matter is capable of motion, but we can only judge of the state of rest or motion of a particle

by comparing it with other particles; for this reason all the motions which we can observe are necessarily *relative* motions.

When a great number of objects maintain the same relative position, our first impression is to consider them as at rest; and if one of them changes its position relatively to the others, it is to it that we ascribe the motion. Thus for instance, the earth was for a long time considered to be fixed in space, notwithstanding the motions of the sun, moon and stars relatively to objects on the earth's surface with which the observer compared them. The motion was ascribed to *them* whilst the earth was assumed to be fixed. A careful study of natural phenomena may modify this first impression, but we can never arrive at absolute certainty in this respect; and the conclusions respecting absolute motions, to which we are led by the observation of relative motions, can only be regarded as inductions which may have indeed a high degree of probability, but which have always need of being verified by the accordance between the logical consequences to which they lead, and the phenomena directly observed.

3. The following principle we assume as being in accordance with experiment and observation, viz. a particle which is absolutely at rest will continue so, until some cause, extraneous to itself, begins to operate so as to put it in motion. This principle asserts that matter at rest has no tendency to put itself in motion, and that any motion or tendency to motion which it may possess, must arise entirely from some external cause. To such causes we give the name of *forces*, and we give the following definition:—

Any cause which excites motion in a particle, or which only tends to excite it when its effect is prevented or modified by any other cause (or which tends to modify existing motion), is called *force*.

And the *line of action* of the force is the line in which the particle would begin to move in consequence of the action of the force, if the particle were at rest and perfectly free.

When several forces act simultaneously on a free particle or on a system of connected particles, the forces will modify each other's effects: if they are so related that no motion of the particle or system takes place, the forces are said to be in *equilibrium*.

That part of Mechanics which treats of the conditions of equilibrium of forces (applied to matter) is called *Statics:* the other part which treats of the conditions of motion is called *Dynamics*. The two combined constitute the whole subject.

4. Forces are brought into action by various causes, and different terms are applied to them in different cases. Thus, for example, if one body press against another, each body is subjected to a force acting at the point of contact,—such force is frequently called *pressure;* again, when a body is pulled by means of a string, or pushed by a rod, the force exerted by the string or rod is called *tension;* again, experience teaches us that if a body be let free from the hand it will fall to the surface of the earth in a certain definite direction,—however often the experiment be tried the result is the same, the body strikes the same spot on the ground in each trial, provided the place from which it is dropped remain the same:—this unvarying effect must result from some cause equally unvarying.

This cause is assumed to be an affinity which all bodies have for the earth, and is termed the force of *attraction*. It is found to prevail at all parts of the earth; and is, in fact, included in the general law of gravitation established by

Newton, viz. that every particle of matter attracts every other particle of matter according to a certain law. The name *weight* is given to the force which the earth's attraction causes a body at rest to exert downwards. The term *gravity* is frequently used in the same sense statically.

5. We have a simple example of the simultaneous action of two *equal* forces when a body rests on a horizontal table, or is supported by the hand. The pressure of the table in the former case, or of the hand in the latter, exactly counterbalances the weight of the body, and is equal to it.

If a body be suspended freely by a string, the tension of the string, which is the force it exerts on the body, is exactly equal and opposite to the weight of the body.

6. The question may suggest itself to the student whether the weight of a body remains the same at different times. The answer to this must necessarily depend upon experiment, since we have no means of determining, *à priori*, whether the attraction of the earth remains the same: but if we can ascertain that the mechanical effect of the weight of the body is unvarying (for instance, if it deflect a spring through the same space under precisely similar circumstances), the answer would be in the affirmative. But it would be very difficult to ascertain whether the spring were under exactly similar conditions at the different times, and so no reliance could be placed on the result of the experiment. We are able, however, to assert from dynamical considerations that the weight of the same body at the same place of the earth's surface is invariable. We may also here state, as a result of experiment, that the weight of a body is not altered by altering its figure. It depends solely upon the volume and material. Thus, for

example, a cubic inch of iron requires the same effort to support it, whatever be its form.

This of course we could not know except from experiment; for we could easily conceive it to have been otherwise, as, for instance, if the attraction of the earth had been of a kind similar to magnetic attractions which do not influence all substances, and which besides do not exert equal influence over those which are subject to them.

7. *Mass.* Common experience makes us acquainted with the fact, that the constitution of all material bodies is not the same. Equal volumes of different substances are differently affected by equal forces applied to them. A cubic inch of wood and a cubic inch of lead require different efforts to support them in the hand. Equal weights of different substances occupy different volumes. We are thus led to consider a quality of matter to which the term *mass* has been given. So long as the volume and constitution of a given portion of matter remain the same, this quality *mass* remains the same. The *mass* of a body has been sometimes defined as the *quantity of matter* in it: but this vague definition does not assist us in forming a distinct conception of it. The notion of *mass* is one as completely *sui generis* as those of *space*, *time*, *weight* are so:—and as in these cases, so in that of mass, our principal business must be to establish some mode of measuring or comparing *different* masses.

Our only means of measuring mass are derived from dynamical considerations, and we shall have occasion hereafter (in Dynamics) to consider this subject again. For the present, if necessary, the student may assume that the masses of bodies are proportional to their weights at the same place on the earth's surface.

8. *Method of estimating and comparing forces.*

When a force acts on a material point, there are three things necessary to be known in order to render the force perfectly determinate, viz. the *intensity* of the force, the *direction* in which it acts, and the position of the point where it is applied, in other words, *its point of application.* These three things may be called the elements of the force: and when the two latter are assigned, i.e. the point of application and the direction, the line of action becomes determinate,—that is, the line in which the particle would begin to move by the action of this force only, if the particle were perfectly free.

If two forces be applied in opposite directions to a point which is free and at rest, and constitute an equilibrium, they are said to be *equal forces.* The notion of the equality of two forces will readily lead to the conception of forces having any proposed ratio to one another: thus if two equal forces be applied in the same direction to the same point, we shall have a *double* force; if in the same way we combine three equal forces there results a *triple* force, and so on; so that, in general, to measure forces we have only to adopt the same method as when we measure or compare any homogeneous quantities: i.e. we must take some known force as unit and then express in numbers the relation which the other forces bear to this unit.

For example, if F represent the unit of force (the weight of a given body for instance), PF will represent a force the intensity of which is P times that of the unit: or we may speak of a force P simply, in the same sense,—the unit of force being understood.

9. We have seen that the gravitation of bodies to the earth is unceasing, and, as has been observed, the gravity

or weight of the same body is invariable; so that weight affords a very useful means of estimating all statical forces. The tension of a string may be measured by the weight (the number of *pounds* if we please) which it will sustain; the force exerted by a string under constraint may be measured by the weight which will just hold it in its constrained position; the force of attraction of a magnet may be measured by the weight it would support:—and so of all statical forces.

The standard of weight in England is the *pound Troy*, consisting of 5760 *grains*; and it is stated that a cubic inch of distilled water weighed in air by brass weights at 62° Fahrenheit, the barometer being at 30 inches, weighs 252·458 such *grains*:—the pound Avoirdupois contains 7000 such grains.

5° GEOR. IV. c. 74.

10. We proceed to explain how forces may be represented *geometrically* and *algebraically*.

The three things necessary to render a force perfectly determinate are (as we have said) its point of application, the direction in which it acts, and its magnitude or intensity. Now if there be two forces P, Q acting at the points A, C in the directions AB, CD respectively, we may take the lengths of the lines AB, CD such that

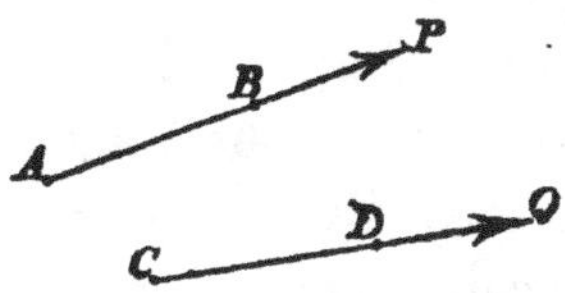

$$AB : CD = P : Q.$$

Or if we take Q for our unit of force and CD for our unit of length, then the force P will be represented *geometrically* by the line AB; for this line is drawn in the *direction* of the force AP, from the *point of application* A, and also represents the force in *magnitude:* the convention in this respect being understood to be that the line contains as many units of length as the force contains units of force.

The student must be careful to observe the *order* of the

letters which indicate the line; thus AB expresses that the force acts in direction of the arrow from A towards B; a force represented by BA would indicate a force of equal magnitude, but acting in the opposite direction, i.e. from B towards A.

The force P would be represented *algebraically* by expressing in algebraic symbols, the magnitude and position of the line AB which represents the force geometrically: thus its direction would be assigned by assigning the angle θ at which it is inclined to a known fixed line Ox in the same plane with AB: its magnitude will be assigned by assigning the numerical value of P, the *number* of units of length; and the point of application A will be assigned by assigning the position of A with respect to the fixed lines Ox, Oy in the same plane with AB.

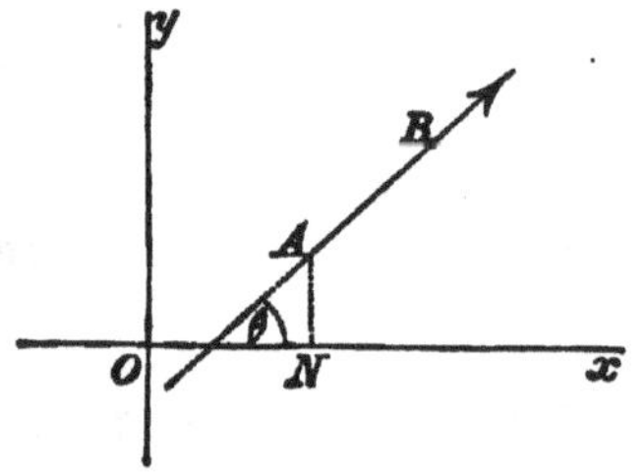

11. This mode of representing forces by lines is of great utility, as we shall see more particularly in the next chapter. We may illustrate it here by supposing several forces as P, Q, R to act simultaneously at the point A in the same direction: if they would be separately represented by AB, AC, AD, they will when acting simultaneously be together represented by a line AD', the length of which is equal to the sum of $AB+AC+AD$.

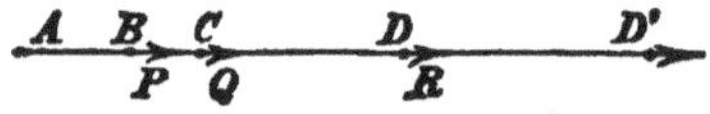

If one of the forces as R, acts in a direction opposite to that of the others P, Q, we shall have to subtract the line AD from the sum of the others

AB, AC, and the three would be represented by a line AD' equal in length to $AB+AC-AD$. This is still the algebraic sum of the lines AB, AC, AD, if lines in one direction from A be considered positive, and lines in the opposite direction negative; and generally if any number of forces act simultaneously at a point and be affected with the sign + or − as they act in a given direction or the opposite, they will be equivalent to a single force represented by the *algebraic* sum of the several forces; and if this sum be affected with a positive sign, the equivalent force will act in the direction which has been considered *positive;* and if it be affected with a negative sign, it will act in the opposite direction.

12. From the definition which has been given of *equal forces* (in Art. 8), it is obvious that two equal forces applied at a point in opposite directions will be in equilibrium. Further, it will readily be granted that two equal and opposite forces P, Q applied at the extremities of a straight rigid rod AB and acting in direction of the rod will be in equilibrium;—for there is no reason that the rod should move in one direction rather than in another;—and this result will be true whatever be the length of the rod: from hence we infer that P will balance Q at whatever point of the rod Q be applied: in other words the effect of Q is the same at whatever point of the rod B, C,... it be applied, the direction remaining the same.

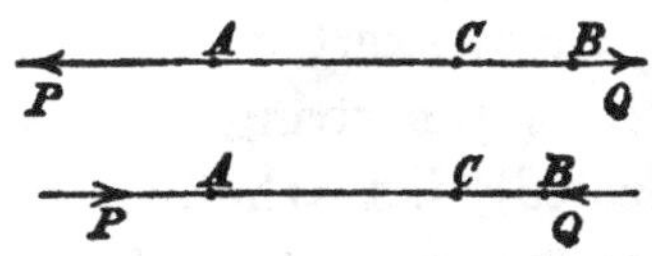

These considerations lead us to the following principle, called the *principle of the transmission of force*, which we shall hereafter find to be of great utility.

The effect of a force on a particle to which it is applied will be the same, if we suppose the force applied at any point we please in the line of action, provided the point be rigidly connected with the original particle.

This principle—which is the fundamental one of the science of Statics—will hold whether we consider the particle as isolated, or as a constituent element of a body of finite size; and we shall find it of great use when we wish to transfer the point of application of a force from one point to another for convenience of calculation. We shall not think it necessary in every case where the supposition is required, to state that the system is supposed to be rigidly connected, but in any instance where this is not done the student will understand it to be so.

13. As an illustration of the above principle we may give the following. If a weight be supported by the hand by means of a string, the effort which the hand must exert will be the same whatever be the length of the string (the weight of the string being neglected), i.e. whether the force, which the hand exerts, be applied at A, or B, or C, or any point in the line of action of the force.

Obs. In this example the student will observe that the connection between the points A, B and the weight is not a *rigid* one, and in general when the force Q (fig. Art. 12), which we transfer from the point C to B, acts as in the upper figure, i.e. tends to draw C towards B, the connection between C and B need not be *essentially* rigid; but the two points may be otherwise connected, as for instance, by a fine inextensible thread; when however (as in the lower figure) the force tends to thrust B towards C, the connection must be a rigid one.

14. We have called the example above an *illustration*, and not a *proof* of the principle of Art. (12), for as this principle has been enunciated with reference to a *particle*, and since particles *as such* cannot be subjected to experiment, it would be vain to look for or expect a direct proof of this, or in fact of any other physical law. The student must be prepared to admit its truth as established by evidence similar to that by which other physical laws are established.

CHAPTER II.

OF FORCES ACTING IN ONE PLANE.

15. WHEN a system of forces acting on a particle at rest is not in equilibrium, the particle will begin to move in some definite direction, but a single force might be found of proper intensity which when applied independently to the particle and acting in the same direction would cause the particle to move in exactly the same manner; such a force is called the *resultant* of the system of forces; and the constituent forces of the system, with reference to this resultant, are called *components*.

In other words, the single force which is capable of producing the same effect on a particle or system of particles as would result from the combined action of several other forces, is called their *resultant*.

We do not enter into the question what the dynamical effect might be if the system of forces were not in equilibrium—but *whatever* it may be, the *resultant is equivalent to the components*.

When a system of forces acting on a particle or body is in equilibrium, the particle has no tendency to motion, and the resultant is consequently *nil*. Hence when a system of forces (as P, Q, R,...) is in equilibrium,

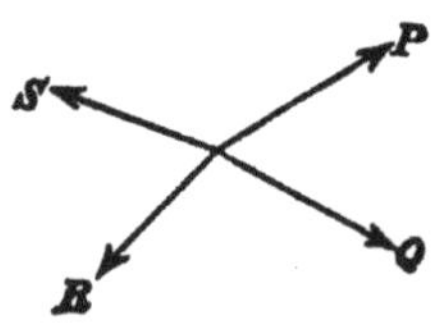

one of them (as P) may be regarded as counterbalancing the combined action of all the rest, Q, R, S. It appears then that the remaining forces (Q, R, S) produce the same effect on the particle as would result from a single force equal and opposite to P. We infer then, that when a system of forces acting on a body is in equilibrium, *any one* of the forces is equal and opposite to the resultant of all the rest.

Again, since the resultant of a system of forces in equilibrium is *nil*, such a system of forces has no tendency to excite or prevent motion; we may therefore (in any case where we find it convenient) suppose such a system of forces to be annihilated without altering the state of rest or motion of the body upon which they act; or stating this principle more generally, any system of equilibrated forces may be applied to or withdrawn from a body without affecting its state of rest or motion. The student, however, must bear in mind the observation of Art. (13) whenever this principle is employed in dealing with a system of bodies not in *rigid* connection.

16. We now proceed to deduce the rules for the *composition of forces*, that is, to find the resultant of two or more forces acting simultaneously; and it will then be easy to ascertain the conditions of equilibrium of a system of forces.

We shall confine ourselves in the present chapter to the discussion of forces acting in one plane.

The case of forces acting in the same straight line has been already considered in Art. 11.

When two forces P and Q are applied at the same point A in directions inclined to each other at any angle whatever, it is easy to see that some third force R properly applied at the point A would constitute an equilibrium with P and Q: for by virtue of the combined action of P and Q the point A

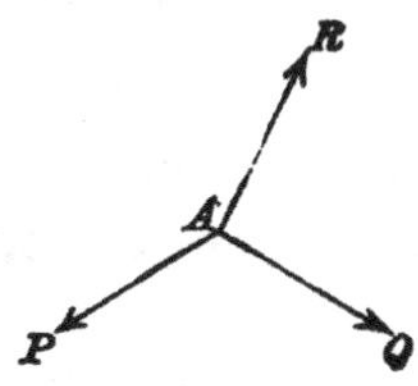

tends to leave the position in which it is; but since it could move in one direction only, it follows that if we apply a proper force R in a direction contrary to this in which it would move, the point could not move at all, i.e. would be at rest. The three forces P, Q, R acting on the point A would be in equilibrium, and the force R is equal and opposite to the resultant of the other two. *Two forces then, whose lines of action meet, have a resultant.*

Again, it is obvious that this resultant must lie in the plane which passes through the directions of the two components AP, AQ; for no reason can be assigned in favour of this resultant's lying in any proposed position *above* the plane PAQ, which would not hold with equal validity in favour of the resultant's being in a perfectly symmetrical position *below* the same plane.

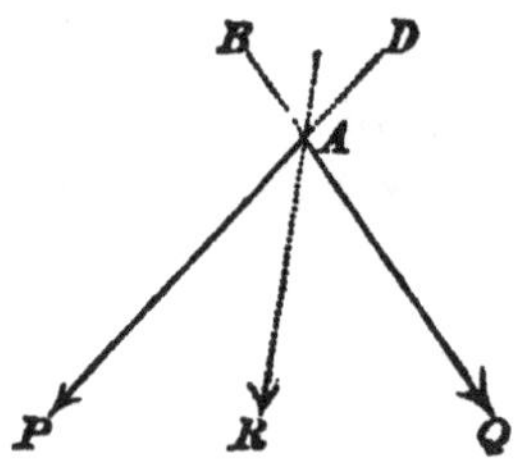

Further, the resultant must lie within the interior angle PAQ ($<180^\circ$) contained by the directions of the two forces, for it is clear that the point A could not by the action of the forces P, Q move in the plane PAQ, on the side of AQ remote from P and towards D; and similarly, it could not move on the side of AP remote from Q and towards B: consequently it could only move within the angle PAQ, the direction therefore of the resultant R must lie within this angle.

17. There is one case in which we can see *à priori* what will be the direction of the resultant: viz. when the two forces P, Q are equal; it is clear in that case that the direction of the resultant bisects the angle between the direction of the two component forces P, Q: for there is no reason

why the resultant should make with one of the component forces an angle different from that which it makes with the other.

Obs. The student may remark that the conclusion of the preceding article is based on reasoning *ex absurdo:* instances will have come under his notice, in which the elementary theorems of a subject do not admit of a *direct* demonstration, but he will regard the proof as equally valid though the demonstration is indirect. The general principle involving all such proofs as this: If under assigned circumstances, *one* issue or conclusion and *one only* can result, and the arguments in favour of two hypothetical issues or conclusions A and B are of equal value, then that hypothetical issue must be the true one in which the two hypotheses A and B coalesce.

18. We proceed to establish an important theorem which enables us to determine the resultant of any two forces acting at a point: the theorem is called *the parallelogram of forces*, and may be thus enunciated.

If two forces acting at a point be represented in magnitude and direction by two straight lines drawn from that point, and if a parallelogram be constructed having these two lines for adjacent sides, then that diagonal of the parallelogram which passes through the point of application of the forces will represent their resultant in magnitude and direction.

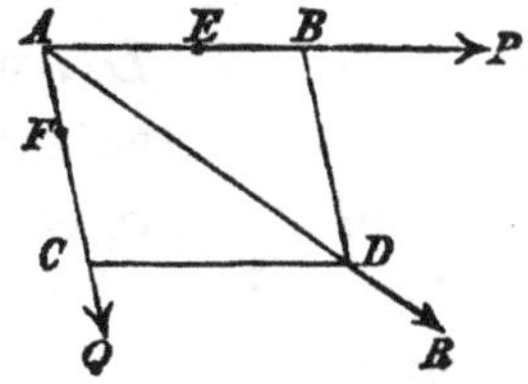

That is, if the two forces P, Q be represented by AB, AC, and the parallelogram BC be completed, their resultant R will be represented by the diagonal AD. The same is true if P, Q act at points E, F, provided their directions meet in some point A. We shall divide the proof of this proposition into two parts; and

(i.) To prove that the resultant acts in direction of the diagonal, the forces being *commensurable.*

We have seen (Art. 17) that when the forces are equal ($AB=AC$), their resultant bisects the angle between the directions of the forces, and therefore acts along the diagonal AD; that is, this first part of the proposition is true for two equal forces.

Let us assume (α) for the present that it is also true for two sets of forces P and Q, P and R—*equal* or *unequal*;—we can then prove that it is true for the forces P and $Q+R$.

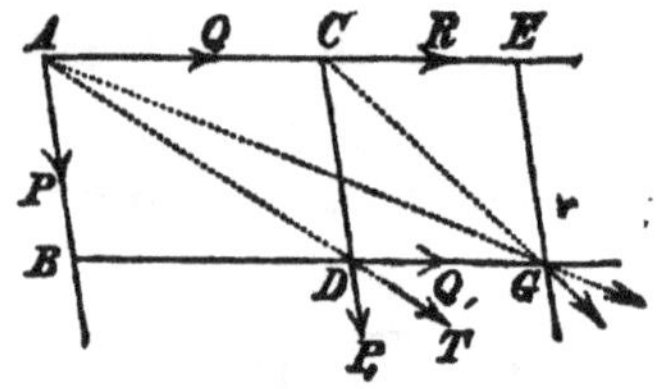

Let P act at A in direction AB, Q and R in direction ACE, and let AB, AC respresent P, Q in magnitude; and since R may be supposed to act at any point in the line ACE which is rigidly connected with A, let R act at C, and let CE represent R. Complete the parallelograms BC, DE.

Then since by the hypothesis (α) the resultant T of P, Q acts along AD, let them be replaced by their resultant, and let this resultant be applied at D—which may be done without altering its effect (Art. 12).

Now this resultant T acting at D may be decomposed into two forces P_1, Q_1 (equal respectively to P, Q) acting at D in directions CD, DG which are parallel to AB, AC.

Let T be replaced by P_1, Q_1, and let the point of application of P_1 be removed to C and that of Q_1 to G.

Again P_1 and R acting at C have a resultant acting in direction CG; let them be replaced by this resultant, and let its point of application be transferred to G.

{The student may suppose all the points A, C, D, G, rigidly connected together, Art. (12).}

We have thus shewn (on the hypothesis α) that the forces P, Q, R which are applied at A, may be supposed to be applied at G without altering their combined effect,—that is, AG must be the direction of the resultant of P and $Q+R$ in any case in which the hypothesis (α) holds true.

But this hypothesis is true when P, Q, R are each equal to any the same force f, therefore the conclusion is true for two forces f and $2f$, and again, (making $Q=2f$, $R=f$, $P=f$), it is true for f and $3f$, and so by induction it is true for f and mf. Again, putting $P=mf$, $Q=R=f$, our conclusion is true for two forces mf, and $2f$, and again for mf, and $3f$, and generally for mf and nf:—if m, n be any integers whatever.

Now any two commensurable forces may, by assigning a proper value to f, be expressed by mf, nf.

Hence proposition (i) is proved.

19. (ii.) To prove that the resultant acts in direction of the diagonal, if the forces are *incommensurable*.

Let AB, AC represent two such forces. Complete the parallelogram BC, and if AD be not the direction of the resultant, let it be some other line, (AV suppose). Let AC be divided into an integral number of equal parts each *less* than DV,—which is always possible; and mark off from CD portions equal to these,—the last division E clearly falling between D and V. Complete the parallelogram CF,—then the resultant of AC, AF will be in direction AE, and we may suppose this resultant to be substituted for them.

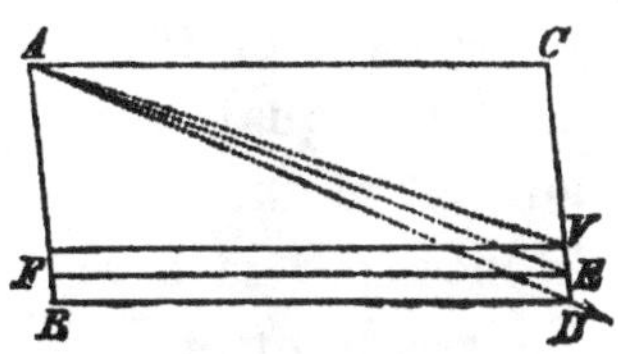

The resultant then of AC and AB is equivalent to the resultant of some force in direction AE, together with FB which acts along AB: and this resultant must lie *within* the angle BAE. But by hypothesis it acts in direction AV, *without* the same angle,—which is absurd.

In like manner it may be shewn that no direction but AD can be that of the resultant of the forces AB, AC. The theorem is therefore completely proved so far as the direction of the resultant is concerned: it will be easy now to prove that

20. (iii.) The diagonal represents the *magnitude* of the resultant.

Let AB, AC be the directions of the given forces, AD that of their resultant: in DA produced take AE of such a length as to represent the magnitude of the resultant. Then the forces represented by AB, AC, AE balance each other. Complete the parallelograms BE, BC: then AF will be the direction of the resultant of AB, AE, and therefore since each of the three forces AB, AC, AE is equal and opposite to the resultant of the other two,—AC, AF are in one straight line. Hence FD is a parallelogram, and $\therefore AE = FB = AD$; i.e. the resultant of AB, AC is represented in *magnitude* as well as in direction by AD the diagonal of the parallelogram.

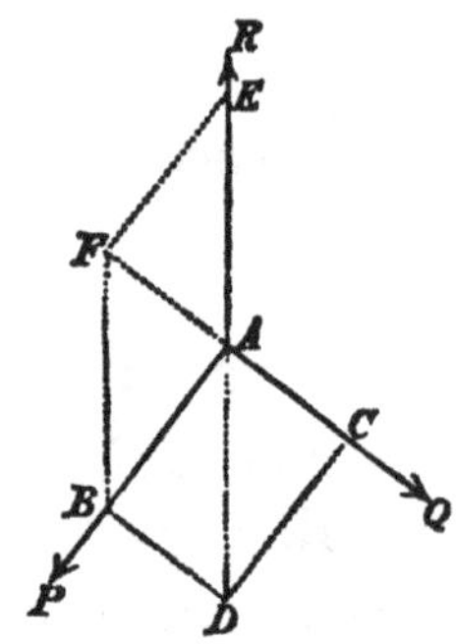

21. The theorem which we have just proved is of so much importance that it may fairly be considered *the fundamental proposition* of Statics. It was enunciated in its present form by Sir Isaac Newton, and Varignon the celebrated

mathematician, in the year 1687,—probably independently of each other: since that time various proofs of it have been given by different mathematicians, several of which have been reviewed by Jacobi.

The proof given above is due to M. Duchayla.

Several very interesting theorems can be readily deduced from the *parallelogram of forces:* the first we shall give, called the *triangle of forces*, was announced in the year 1586 by Stevinus of Bruges, without any strict proof of it.

22. *The Triangle of Forces.* If three forces acting at a point be represented in *magnitude and direction* by the sides of a triangle *taken in order*, they will be in equilibrium.

Let ABC be the triangle whose sides taken in order represent in direction and magnitude three forces applied at any point, (A suppose).

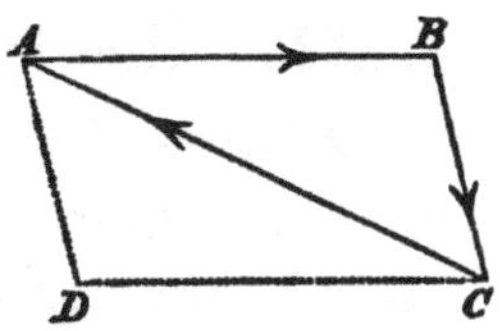

Complete the parallelogram BD.

Then the forces AB, BC applied at A are expressed by AB, AD—(since AD is equal and parallel to BC).

But the resultant of AB, AD is a force represented by AC.

Therefore the three forces represented by AB, BC, CA, all applied at A, are equivalent to AC, CA, which will clearly balance one another.

Therefore the three forces represented by AB, BC, CA, applied at any point A, will be in equilibrium.

The *converse* of this is also true, viz. If three forces acting at a point balance one another, and any triangle be constructed having its sides parallel to the directions of the forces, the sides of the triangle will be proportional to the forces.

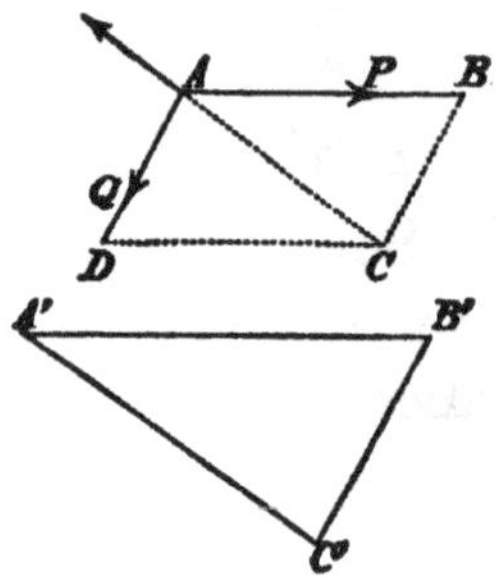

Let P, Q, R be three such forces acting at any point A, and let AB, AD, represent P, Q, then will the diagonal CA of the parallelogram BD represent R.

And if $A'B'C'$ be any triangle whose sides are parallel to the sides of ABC, we shall have by similar triangles:

$$A'B' : B'C' : C'A' = AB : BC : CA$$
$$= P : Q : R.$$

23. From the parallelogram of forces we can easily deduce the following theorem first stated by Lami, in 1687.

If three forces acting at a point are in equilibrium, each force is proportional to the sine of the angle contained between the directions of the remaining two.

For referring to the fig. of Art. (20), if P, Q, R, the three forces, be represented by AB, AC, AE, and the parallelogram BC be completed, since $AE = AD$, we have

$$P : Q : R = AB : AC : AD = CD : AC : DA$$
$$= \sin DAC : \sin ADC : \sin ACD.$$

But $\sin DAC = \sin QAR$,

$\sin ADC = \sin DAB = \sin PAR$,

$\sin ACD = \sin DCQ = \sin PAQ$;

$$\therefore P : Q : R = \sin QAR : \sin PAR : \sin PAQ \ldots\ldots(\alpha);$$

or, we may express these relations in the form

$$\frac{P}{\sin(Q, R)} = \frac{Q}{\sin(R, P)} = \frac{R}{\sin(P, Q)},$$

(Q, R) meaning the angle $(< 180^\circ)$ included between the directions of Q and R,—and so of (R, P), (P, Q).

We can readily obtain the equivalent formulæ

$$P^2 = Q^2 + R^2 + 2QR \cos(Q, R)$$
$$Q^2 = R^2 + P^2 + 2RP \cos(R, P)$$
$$R^2 = P^2 + Q^2 + 2PQ \cos(P, Q),$$

by which any one of the three forces P, Q, R is expressed in terms of the other two and the angle between them.

24. The student will observe that this result is still true if the direction of any one of the forces be exactly reversed; for example, it would hold if we took a force R' $(= R)$ represented by AD instead of AE, for we should then have

$$P : Q : R' = \sin R'AQ : \sin PAR' : \sin PAQ,$$

but the three forces P, Q, R', would not be in equilibrium; in fact, the resultant of P, Q being R', the resultant of the three would be $2R'$.

Hence the *converse* of the theorem of this Article is not true without some additional condition,—such as that each force lies *without* the angle $(< \pi)$ formed by the other two.

The student however will have no difficulty in proving the following:

If each of three forces acting at a point be proportional to the sine of the angle between the directions of the other two, either the three forces are in equilibrium, *or* they have a resultant double of some *one* of the forces.

25. We may now give a theorem which is an extension of that contained in Art. 22, and is called the *Polygon of Forces.*

Polygon of Forces. If any number of forces acting at a point be represented in magnitude and direction by the sides of a polygon taken in order, they will be in equilibrium.

If the forces be represented in magnitude and direction by the sides of the polygon $ABCDE$, joining AC, AD we see that forces represented by AB, BC acting at A are equivalent to a force AC, which may therefore replace them. Again, AC, CD acting at A are equivalent to AD; i.e. AD is equivalent to forces AB, BC, CD all acting at A. Again, AD, DE are equivalent to AE; and therefore AD, DE, EA will balance. (Art. 22.)

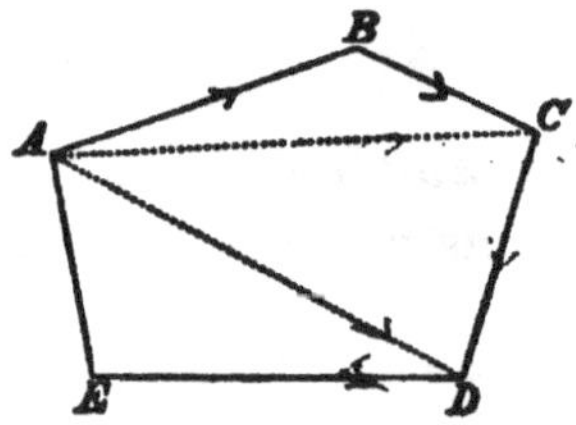

Hence the forces represented by AB, BC, CD, DE, EA will be in equilibrium. Q.E.D.

The same mode of proof will hold whatever be the number of the forces, and the student will observe that there is no necessity for all the forces to be in the same plane:—the polygon whose sides represent the forces may have re-entering angles, or some of its sides may intersect each other. The only condition is that the polygon must be a *closed* one.

By drawing a line parallel to one of the sides of the polygon, as BC, we might form a new polygon whose sides are parallel to those of the former, but the sides of the two polygons are not in the same proportion.

Hence the *converse* of the proposition of this Article is not necessarily true.

26. Cor. From the proposition of the previous Article

we can obtain at once a theorem given by Leibnitz for determining geometrically the resultant of any number of forces acting at a point.

From any point A draw a straight line AB to represent one of the forces in magnitude and direction; from the extremity B draw BC to represent the next force; from C draw CD to represent the third force, and so on; and let E be the extremity of the line representing the last force.

Then if E coincide with A the resultant is *nil*, and the forces are in equilibrium; but if not, AE will represent the resultant in magnitude and direction. The student will easily deduce this from the preceding Article.

27. We have seen in Article (18), that if BC be a parallelogram, the two forces AB, AC acting at a point A are equivalent to a single force AD acting at the same point; which single force might be substituted for the two component forces: *vice versâ* if a line AD represent a force, and *any* parallelogram as BC be constructed having AD for a diagonal, the single force AD may be replaced by two forces represented by AB, AC, i.e. AD may be *resolved* into two forces AB, AC.

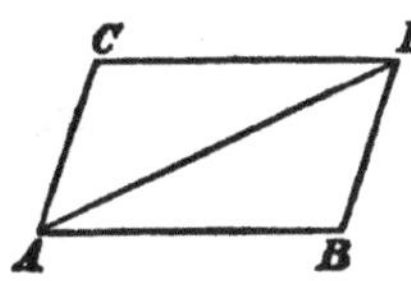

Also, since the number of parallelograms which can be constructed with AD as diagonal is unlimited, it follows that a single force can be resolved into two others equivalent to it in an unlimited number of ways.

Further, each of the forces AB, AC, may be *resolved* into two others, in a way similar to that by which AD was resolved into two, and so on to any extent; so that we arrive at the conclusion that a single force may be resolved into any number of forces we please, the combined action of which is equivalent to the original force.

On comparing the sides of the triangle ADB in which $BD=AC$ we readily obtain

$$AB=AD\frac{\sin CAD}{\sin BAC},$$

$$AC=BD=AD\frac{\sin BAD}{\sin BAC};$$

or if AD represents a force R, we conclude that a force R acting in a direction AD is equivalent to the two forces

$$\begin{cases} R\dfrac{\sin CAD}{\sin BAC} \text{ in direction } AB, = P \text{ (suppose)}, \\ R\dfrac{\sin BAD}{\sin BAC} \ldots\ldots\ldots\ldots\ldots AC, = Q. \end{cases}$$

Hence if we put $BAC=\alpha$, $BAD=\beta$, $CAD=\gamma$, we have

$$P=R\frac{\sin\gamma}{\sin\alpha},\quad Q=R\frac{\sin\beta}{\sin\alpha};$$

$$\text{and } R^2=P^2+Q^2+2PQ\cos\alpha,$$

formulæ which enable us to find the resultant of two forces, or to resolve a single force into two others.

N.B. We shall hereafter meet with instances of the resolution of one force into two others equivalent to it; perhaps the most frequent case which occurs, is when the angle $CAB=90°$, or the parallelogram becomes a rectangle: in this case a force P acting in direction AD is equivalent to the two forces

$$\left.\begin{array}{ll} & P\cos DAB \text{ in direction } AB \\ \text{and} & P\cos DAC \ldots\ldots\ldots\ldots\ldots AC \end{array}\right\}.$$

28. We may now proceed

To find the resultant of any number of forces acting in one plane at a point.

We may proceed geometrically thus,

Let AB, AC, AD,... represent the forces P, P', P''... Take any two forces AB, AC, complete the parallelogram BC; and AQ, the resultant of P, P', may be substituted for them.

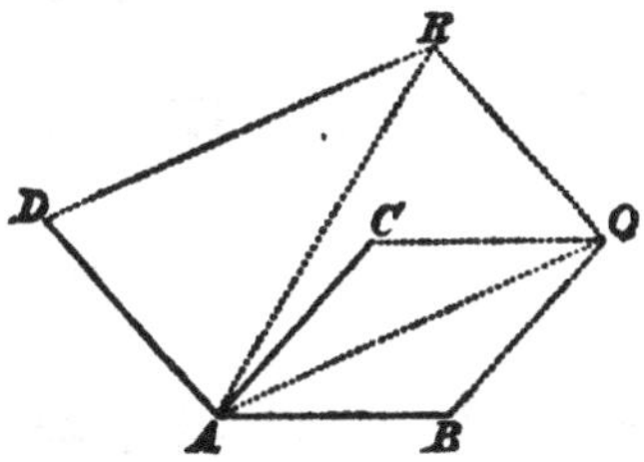

Find the resultant of AQ and AD (or P'') in a similar way; then the three forces P, P', P'', are equivalent to AR, and so on, till the resultant of all the forces is obtained.

Or we may proceed thus by the aid of trigonometry.

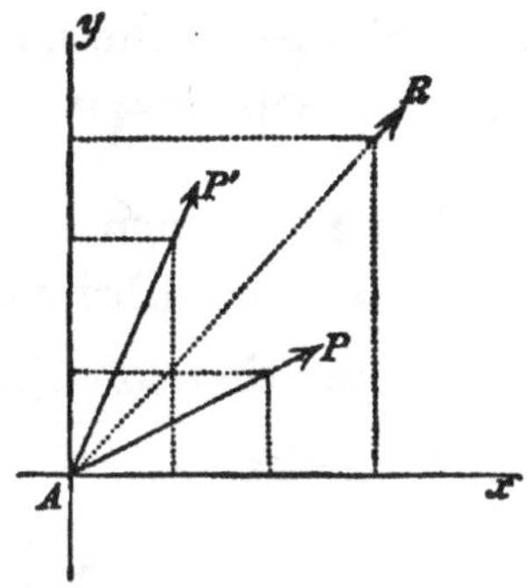

Through the point draw two lines Ax, Ay at right angles to each other in the plane of the forces, and let the directions of P, P',... make angles α, α',... with Ax.

Then since P, P',... are equivalent to

$P\cos\alpha$ in direction of Ax, and $P\sin\alpha$ in direction of Ay,

$P'\cos\alpha'$ .... $P'\sin\alpha'$ ....

all the forces P, P',... are equivalent to

$$P\cos\alpha + P'\cos\alpha' + \dots \text{ in direction of } Ax,$$

$$P\sin\alpha + P'\sin\alpha' + \dots \dots\dots\dots\dots\dots \; Ay.$$

Or as we may write it $\Sigma\,(P\cos\alpha)$ in direction of Ax,

$\Sigma\,(P\sin\alpha)$ .... Ay.

If then R be the resultant making an angle θ with Ax, we must have

$$R\cos\theta=\Sigma\,(P\cos\alpha),$$

$$R\sin\theta=\Sigma\,(P\sin\alpha).$$

Whence $R^2=\{\Sigma\,(P\cos\alpha)\}^2+\{\Sigma\,(P\sin\alpha)\}^2$...... (i),

$$\tan\theta=\frac{\Sigma\,(P\sin\alpha)}{\Sigma\,(P\cos\alpha)}\ \text{.................}\ \text{(ii)};$$

the results (i) and (ii) determine the magnitude and direction of the resultant.

COR. 1. If the separate forces P, P'... be resolved *in direction* of their resultant R and *perpendicular to it*, the *algebraic sum* of the former resolved parts will be $=R$, and of the latter will be $=0$.

COR. 2. If such a system of forces as is considered in this Article is in equilibrium, the resultant must be zero; i.e. $R=0$;

and therefore $\{\Sigma\,(P\cos\alpha)\}^2+\{\Sigma\,(P\sin\alpha)\}^2=0$,

which requires that

$$\Sigma\,(P\cos\alpha)=0,\ \text{and}\ \Sigma\,(P\sin\alpha)=0,$$

that is, the sum of the forces resolved in any two directions at right angles to each other must be severally *zero*.

29. *To find the resultant of two forces whose directions are parallel.*

Let A, B be any two points in the lines of action of the two

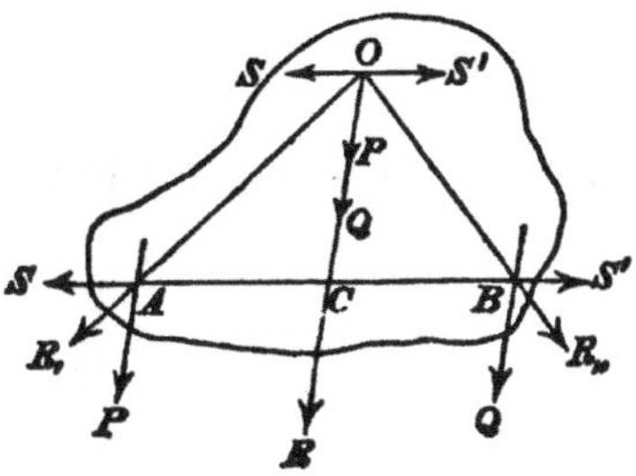

forces P, Q, which act in the parallel directions AP, BQ.

At A apply any force S in direction BAS, and at B apply an equal force S' in the direction ABS', — this will not modify the combined action of the other forces.

Now S, P acting at A, are equivalent to a single force $R_{,}$ acting in some direction $AR_{,}$.

And S', Q acting at B, are equivalent to a single force $R_{,,}$ acting in some direction $BR_{,,}$.

Let these two pairs of forces be replaced by $R_{,}$, $R_{,,}$, whose directions will meet in some point O; let the points of application of $R_{,}$, $R_{,,}$ be transferred to O.

Draw OCR parallel to AP or BQ, and SOS' parallel to AB.

Now let $R_{,}$ acting at O be resolved into two components in directions OS and OC, which will clearly be S and P, and let $R_{,,}$ acting at O be resolved into two components in directions OS' and OC, which will be S' and Q.

Then S and S' being equal in magnitude and opposite in direction, will balance each other, and may therefore be removed, and there remain P and Q acting at O in the line OCR.

Hence, if R be the resultant of P and Q,

$$R = P + Q \qquad \text{(i)}.$$

Again, in the triangle ACO, the sides are proportional to S, P, $R_{,}$, and in the triangle BCO the sides are proportional to S', Q, $R_{,,}$. Hence

$$\frac{P}{S}=\frac{OC}{AC}, \text{ and } \frac{S'}{Q}=\frac{BC}{OC};$$

therefore multiplying together, and remembering that $S=S'$, we get

$$\frac{P}{Q}=\frac{BC}{AC} \text{..................} \text{(ii)}.$$

Hence the point C in the line AB, through which the resultant acts parallel to each of the forces, divides the line AB into segments which are inversely proportional to the forces.

(i) and (ii) determine the resultant completely.

30. If the two forces act in opposite directions the method is very similar: the point C lies outside AB;

and $R=P-Q$............(iii),

$$\frac{P}{Q}=\frac{BC}{AC} \text{...............} \text{(iv)}.$$

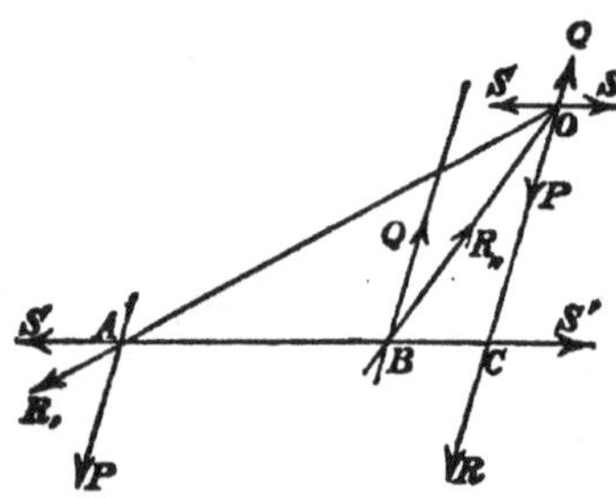

It will be observed that (iii) and (iv) are the same as (i) and (ii), if the sign of Q be changed, so that algebraically (i) and (ii) comprise both cases.

Cor. 1. The position of the point C does not depend upon the direction of the forces. Hence if the directions of the forces be turned through any the same angles in the same direction about the points A, B, the position of C will not be changed.

Cor. 2. In the case of Art. 30, we have from (iv),

$$\frac{P}{Q}=\frac{BC}{AC}=1-\frac{AB}{AC}.$$

If now $P=Q$, we get $\frac{AB}{AC}=0$, or $AC=\infty$, and $R=0$.

A system of two equal forces acting in opposite directions and not at the same point is called *a couple*;—and the results $R=0$, and $AC=\infty$ with reference to such a system indicate that a couple cannot be replaced by *any single finite force* acting at a *finite distance.*

31. *Moment of a Force.*

The *product* of a force into the perpendicular distance of its line of action from a given point is called *the moment of the force with respect to the point*, or *the moment of the force about the point.*

If an *axis* be drawn through the point at right angles to the plane which contains the point and the direction of the force, this product is called *the moment of the force about the axis.*

Further, The *moment of a force about any line* is defined to be the product of the resolved part of the force perpendicular to the line into the perpendicular distance between the line and the line of action of the force.—This perpendicular distance is the shortest distance between the two lines.

The student will be careful to observe that the force and distance here spoken of are expressed *numerically* in terms of their respective units; and the *moment* consequently is the product of two numerical quantities. Thus if AB represent a force P, and O be any given point,—

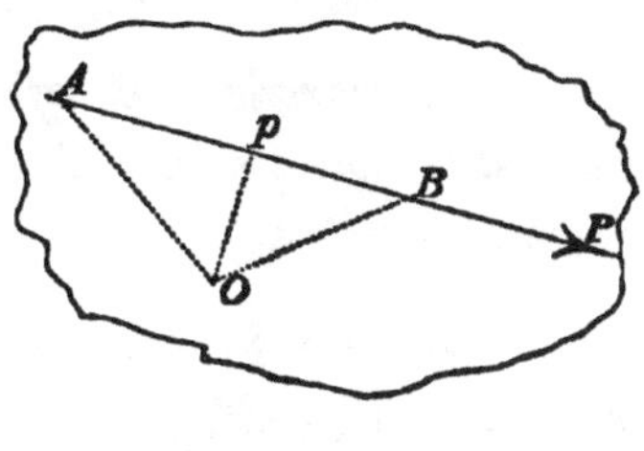

Op perpendicular to AB, and if m, n be the number of linear units in AB, Op respectively, then will mn be the moment of P about O, or about an axis through O perpendicular to the plane ABO. Also since the area of the triangle $ABO = \frac{1}{2}AB \,.\, Op$, it is obvious that $mn =$ twice the number of units of area in the triangle ABO. We *may* then represent moments geometrically by areas, and the moment of P about O would thus be represented by twice the triangle ABO: the unit of moment (i.e. the product of a unit of force into a unit of distance) being represented geometrically by a unit of area.

Further, the force P would tend to *twist* the body on which it acts in one direction or the reverse, according as O is on one side of AB or the other. We shall for convenience consider the moment of a force negative or positive, according as it tends to twist the body in the same direction as the hands of a watch revolve, or the contrary.

If P, Q be two equal forces acting in parallel but opposite directions—constituting a couple—if C be any point in the plane of the forces, and CBA be perpendicular to their lines of action (fig. Art. 30), we have the moment of the two forces about $C = P \,.\, AC - Q \,.\, BC = P \,.\, AB =$ constant; i.e. the moment of a couple is the same about any point in the plane of the couple.

32. The following proposition is important.

The algebraic sum of the moments of two forces acting in one plane about any point in the plane is equal to the moment of their resultant.

When the forces are not parallel it admits of a simple geometrical proof.

Let AB, AC represent the two forces P, Q, and complete the parallelogram BC, and through the point O draw rOs parallel to AC; then taking those moments to be positive which tend to twist a body in a direction opposite to that of the hands of a watch,

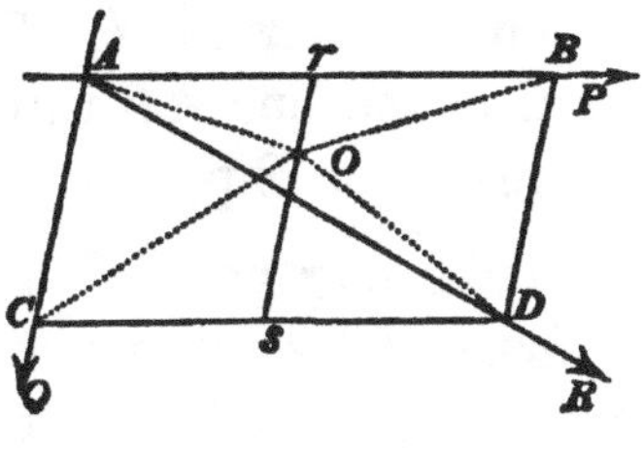

sum of moments of P and Q about O

$= 2\Delta AOC - 2\Delta ABO$
$=$ parallelogram $Cr - 2\Delta ABO$
$=$ parallelogram $BC -$ parallelogram $rD - 2\Delta ABO$
$= 2(\Delta ABD - \Delta BOD - \Delta ABO)$
$= 2\Delta AOD$
$=$ moment of R the resultant of P and Q.

The above construction will apply if the point O lie within the angle BAC, or the vertically opposite angle. If O lie within either of the supplemental angles of BAC, as in fig. 2, draw Ors parallel to AC, then

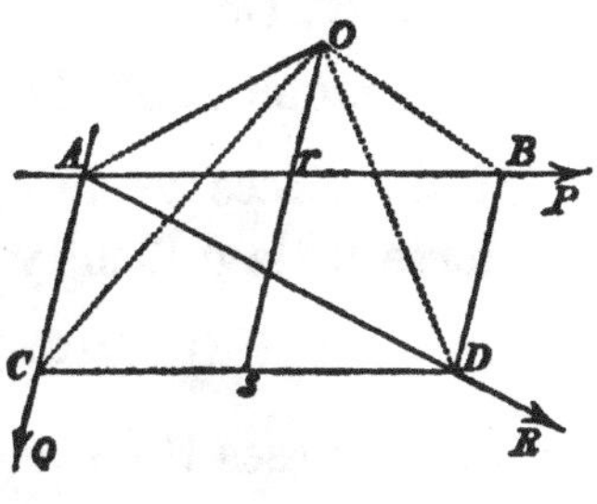

sum of moments of P, Q about O
$= 2\Delta AOC + 2\Delta AOB$
$=$ parallelogram $Cr + 2\Delta AOB$
$=$ parallelogram $CB -$ parallelogram $Bs + 2\Delta AOB$
$= 2(\Delta ABD + \Delta AOB - \Delta BOD) = 2\Delta AOD$
$=$ moment of R the resultant of P and Q.

33. It remains to prove the proposition for two parallel forces.

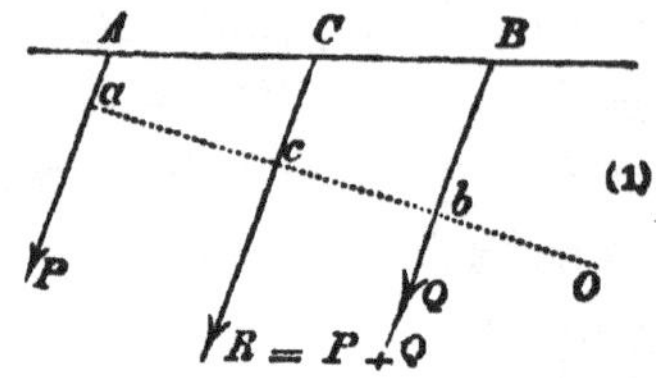

Let A, B be two points through which the forces P, Q act, C a point in the line AB through which the resultant R passes.

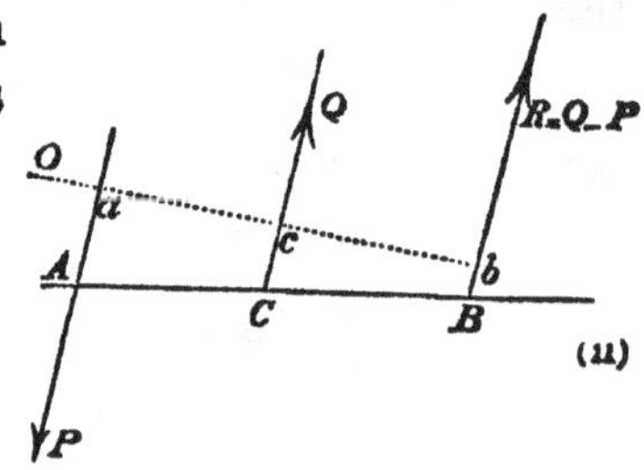

Take any point O and through it draw $Obca$ at right angles to the directions of the forces; then since the resultant of P, Q passes through C,

$$P \cdot AC = Q \cdot BC,$$

and $\therefore P \cdot ac = Q \cdot bc$;

when the forces P, Q act in the same directions (fig. 1), we have

sum of the moments of P, Q about the point O

$$\begin{aligned} &= Q \cdot Ob + P \cdot Oa \\ &= Q(Oc - bc) + P(Oc + ac) \\ &= (Q + P)\, Oc \qquad \because Q \cdot bc = P \cdot ac \\ &= R \cdot Oc \end{aligned}$$

= moment of the resultant about O. Q.E.D.

If the forces act in opposite directions (fig. 2), the student will have little difficulty in proving that

$$Q \cdot Oc - P \cdot Oa = (Q - P) \cdot Ob,$$

which expresses the same proposition in this case.

Obs. The point O has been taken in such a position that the moment of the resultant is in each case positive. The proposition is readily proved for any other position of O.

COR. 1. If the point O be taken anywhere in the line of action of the resultant R, the moment of R vanishes, and we conclude that *the moments of two forces about any point in the line of action of their resultant are equal in magnitude and opposite in direction.*

COR. 2. We can readily extend the proposition of Art. (32) to any number of forces in one plane. For since the sum of the moments of two forces is equal to the moment of their resultant, we may substitute the resultant for the two forces; we may now combine this resultant with a third, and suppose them replaced by their resultant, and so on whatever be the number of forces. Hence

The moment of the resultant of any number of forces in one plane, taken with respect to any point in that plane, is equal to the algebraic sum of the moments of the several forces with respect to the same point.

When the moment of the resultant vanishes, we conclude either that the resultant is *nil*, or that the resultant passes through the point with respect to which the moments are taken.

34. *The sum of the moments of two parallel forces about any line at right angles to their direction, is equal to the moment of their resultant about the same line.*

Let Opq be any line in the plane of the paper—and let R be the resultant of two parallel forces P, Q acting perpendicular to this plane,—their directions meeting it in the points R, P, Q.

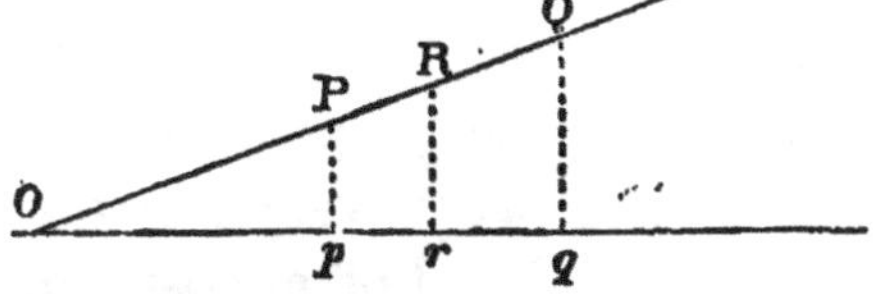

Draw Pp, Rr, Qq perpendicular to Opq—then if the line Opq is parallel to PQ, these perpendiculars are equal, and—since $R = P + Q$—the moment of R about pq is equal to the sum of the moments of P and Q.

But if Opq is not parallel to PQ, let them meet in O—then taking moments about O,

$$R.OR = P.OP + Q.OQ;$$

but by similar triangles,

$$\frac{Rr}{OR} = \frac{Pp}{OP} = \frac{Qq}{OQ},$$

whence we get

$$R.Rr = P.Pp + Q.Qq,$$

which proves the proposition.

Obs. The proposition may easily be extended to any number of parallel forces.

35. Let two forces P, Q act in one plane at points A, B of a rigid body, and let O be a fixed point of the body about which it *might* turn freely; if the two forces P, Q balance about O, the force arising from the reaction of the fixed point (which of course passes through the point) must with P, Q constitute a system of forces at equilibrium: in other words, the reaction of the fixed point is equal and opposite to the resultant of P and Q.

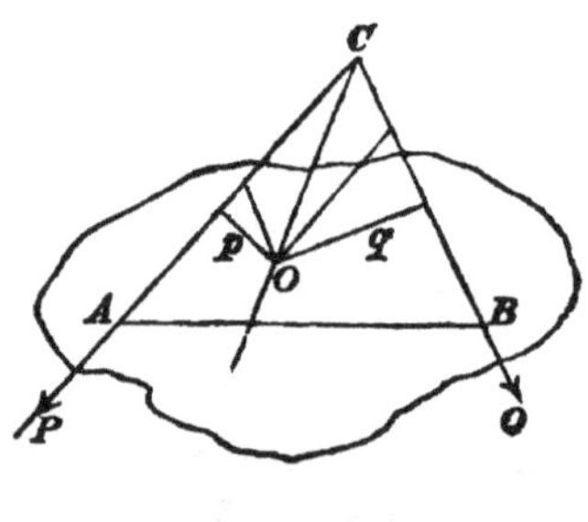

If p, q be the perpendiculars from O on the lines of action of P and Q, we have, since the moments of P, Q about O must be equal and of opposite tendency, $P.p = Q.q$.

And the pressure on the fixed point O

$$= \sqrt{(P^2 + Q^2 + 2PQ \cos PCQ)}.$$

Such a fixed point as O is commonly called a *fulcrum;* the rigid body, whatever be its form, is called a *lever.*

COR. If more than two forces act on the body in one plane, and balance about a fixed point or fulcrum O, the resultant of the forces must pass through O, and the *algebraic sum* of the moments of the forces about O must be *zero;* or *in other words* the sum of the moments of the forces which tend to turn the body in one direction about O, must be equal to the sum of the moments which tend to turn the body in the contrary direction.

36. Further, *any* point of a body at rest under the action of any forces may be regarded *hypothetically* as a fulcrum: for since the body is at rest, no point of it has a tendency to move; we shall not therefore disturb its equilibrium or the relations between the forces by supposing any point we please to be incapable of moving, i.e. by supposing it to be a fixed fulcrum.—Hence *the sum of the moments of the forces about any point whatever must be zero,—if the forces be in equilibrium.*

The principle of this article when applied to a rigid body in equilibrium is frequently referred to as the *principle of the lever.*

37. The theorem stated in Article (32) admits of the following simple analytical proof,—in the case of forces which are not parallel.

Let AP, AQ be the directions of two forces P, Q whose resultant R acts in direction AR. Let O be any point in the plane PAQ, join AO and draw Op, Oq, Or perpendiculars to AP, AQ, AR. If the forces P, Q be resolved in direction of AO and at right angles to AO, the

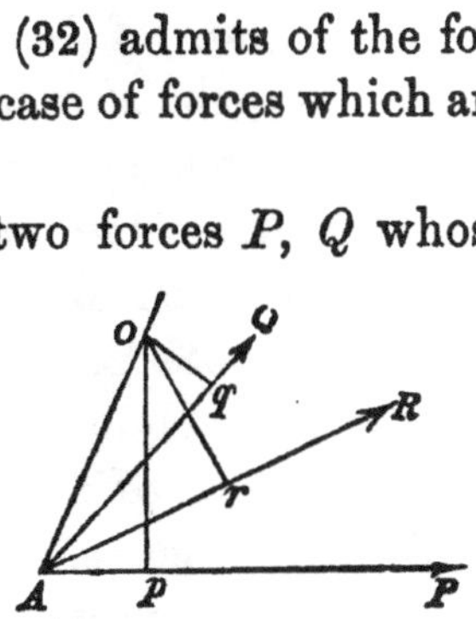

sum of the parts resolved in the latter direction will

$$=P.\sin PAO+Q.\sin QAO,$$

and $R.\sin RAO$ is the resolved part of R in the same direction; hence from the nature of a resultant

$$P.\sin PAO+Q.\sin QAO=R.\sin RAO.$$

Multiply each term of this equation by AO, then

$$P.AO\sin PAO+Q.AO\sin QAO=R.AO\sin RAO,$$

$$\text{or } P.Op+Q.Oq=R.Or;$$

a result which expresses that *the sum of the moments of two forces about any point in the plane in which they act is equal to the moment of their resultant about the same point.*

38. We are now in a position

To find the conditions of equilibrium of a system of forces acting in one plane.

We have seen (Art. 32) that the sum of the moments of a system of forces in one plane about any point is equal to the moment of their resultant. Hence if the sum of the moments of the forces about any proposed point A be *zero*, either the resultant is zero *or* the direction of it passes through A. Again, if the sum of the moments about another point B be *zero*, the resultant, if there be any, must pass through B; i.e. it must act in the line AB. If, further, the sum of the moments of the forces about a third point C (not lying in the line AB) be also *zero*, it would follow that the resultant, if any, would act in each of the lines AC and BC, which is absurd. Hence the *resultant* must be *zero*, and consequently the system of forces in equilibrium. The conditions of equilibrium then of a system of forces acting in one plane on a rigid body or system are these three: "*The sums of the moments of the forces taken with respect to three points in the plane (but not lying in one straight line) must be severally zero."*

Obs. There are then *three* and *only three* mechanical conditions for the equilibrium of a system of forces acting in one plane.

39. The conditions of equilibrium obtained in the preceding article may be expressed analytically somewhat differently as follows:

Let the system of forces be referred to two lines Ax, Ay, at right angles to one another in the plane of the forces.

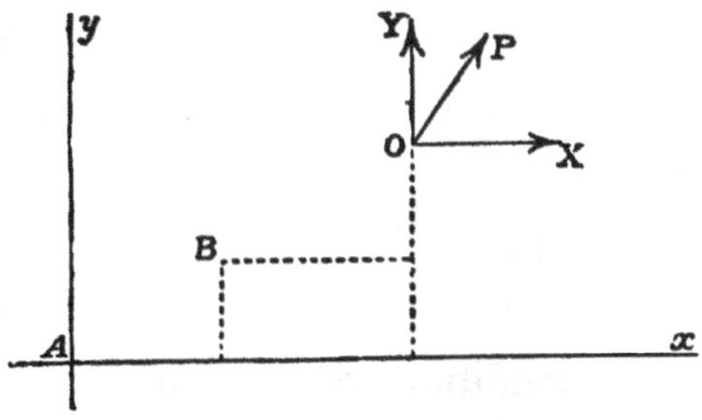

Let O be the point of application of any one of the forces P, and let P be resolved into two components X, Y, in directions parallel to Ax, Ay respectively.

If x, y be co-ordinates of O, and a, b of any point B, the moment of P about B

$$= (x-a)\,Y - (y-b)\,X.$$

And if similar expressions be taken for each of the forces of the system,

the sum of the moments about B

$$= \Sigma\,\{(x-a)\,Y - (y-b)\,X\}\ldots\ldots\ldots\ldots(\text{i}).$$

Similarly, if a', b' be co-ordinates of C, another point,

sum of moments about C

$$= \Sigma\,\{(x-a')\,Y - (y-b')\,X\}\ldots\ldots\ldots(\text{ii}),$$

and sum of moments about A

$$= \Sigma\,(xY - yX)\ldots\ldots\ldots\ldots\ldots\ldots\ldots\ldots(\text{iii}).$$

Now if A, B, C be three points not in a straight line, the conditions of equilibrium are that (i), (ii), (iii), must be severally zero;

$$\therefore \Sigma (xY - yX) = 0 \;\ldots\; \text{(iv)},$$

$$\Sigma \{(x-a)Y - (y-b)X\} = 0 \;\ldots\; \text{(v)},$$

$$\Sigma \{(x-a')Y - (y-b')X\} = 0 \;\ldots\; \text{(vi)},$$

(iv) and (v) combined, give $a\Sigma Y - b\Sigma X = 0$,

(iv) and (vi) .... $a'\Sigma Y - b'\Sigma X = 0$,

from these latter two we get (since $\frac{a}{a'}$, is not $= \frac{b}{b'}$, — the points A, B, C not being in one line),

$$\Sigma X = 0,\ \Sigma Y = 0,$$

which with (α),

$$\Sigma (xY - yX) = 0,$$

are the conditions of equilibrium;

or we may interpret (α) as follows:

In order that the forces may be in equilibrium, the sums of the resolved parts of the forces in two directions at right angles to each other must severally be zero, and the sum of the moments about some one point must be zero also.

40. The conditions (α) of the preceding article, might have been obtained directly from (i) by the consideration that if the system is in equilibrium, the resultant is *zero*, and therefore the sum of the moments about *any and every point* must $= 0$, i.e. the expression

$$\Sigma\{(x-a)Y - (y-b)X\}$$

must $= 0$ for any and every value of a, b—which can only be satisfied by having each of the conditions of (α) satisfied.

COR. 1. We may further interpret the equations of condition (α) thus,—$\Sigma X = 0$, $\Sigma Y = 0$, indicate that the body must have no tendency to move parallel to itself, (i.e. without rotation) in direction of Ax or Ay respectively, and the condition $\Sigma (xY - yX) = 0$ indicates that it must have no tendency to twist about the point A. That is, there must be no motion of *translation* or *rotation*.

COR. 2. If the system of forces be not in equilibrium, and a, b be co-ordinates of *any* point in the line of action of the resultant R, we must have

$$\Sigma \{(x - a) Y - (y - b) X\} = 0;$$

and regarding a, b as current co-ordinates, this will be the *equation to the line of action* of R, or if we use x', y' instead of a, b in accordance with the usual notation, we may arrange the equation (i) in the form

$$x' \Sigma Y - y' \Sigma X = \Sigma (xY - yX).$$

If ϕ be the angle which R makes with Ax, we should easily get $R \cos \phi = \Sigma (X)$, $R \sin \phi = \Sigma (Y)$,
and therefore $R^2 = (\Sigma X)^2 + (\Sigma Y)^2$.

41. *General Remarks.*

Before closing this chapter, we may make a few remarks which may be some guide to the student in applying the principles and results of this chapter to the solution of problems.

The forces which affect a body's state of equilibrium must arise from some agent external to the body, such as (i) the tension of a string attached to a particular point of the body; (ii) the action of a rod in contact with the body, and which may be a pulling or a thrusting action; (iii) the pressure arising from some other body in contact with it either at a point or over a finite surface; (iv) the attractive or repulsive force exercised by some external agent, and which may be conceived as acting like the tension of a string or the thrusting of a rod.

42. I. *Mutual Pressure of smooth and rough Surfaces.*

If two bodies be in free contact at one point C, there is a mutual action between them, the direction of which passes through that point. Draw the common tangent plane at C.

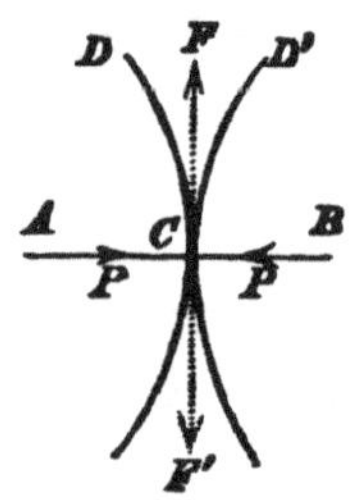

Then, (i) if the surfaces be *smooth*, they can exercise no *tangential* action on each other; the mutual force between them must therefore in this case be in the common normal, and the pressure on each body will tend within the body; for instance, the body A will exert a force on B in direction CB, and *vice versâ*.

(ii) If the surfaces be *rough*, the mutual pressure between the surfaces may be resolved into two, P and F, one in the direction of the normal, and the other in the tangent plane; the latter is counteracted by the tangential force brought into play by the roughness of the surfaces; each of these component forces (normal and tangential) which act on one body are severally equal and opposite to the corresponding forces acting on the other body.

If the full amount of friction which the roughness of the surfaces can give rise to is brought into exercise, then, as will be seen in Chap. III. (to which the student is referred), $F=\mu P$, $-\mu$ being some quantity found by experiment; and the direction in which the friction acts in the tangent plane is exactly opposite to the direction in which the point C would tend to slide if the surfaces were for an instant supposed smooth; of course the full amount of force which the roughness of the surfaces is capable of exercising will not in *every* case be brought into action; no more, in fact, will be exercised than is necessary to prevent a tangential sliding motion.

II. The same principles apply in the case of a rod in free contact with a smooth or rough surface.

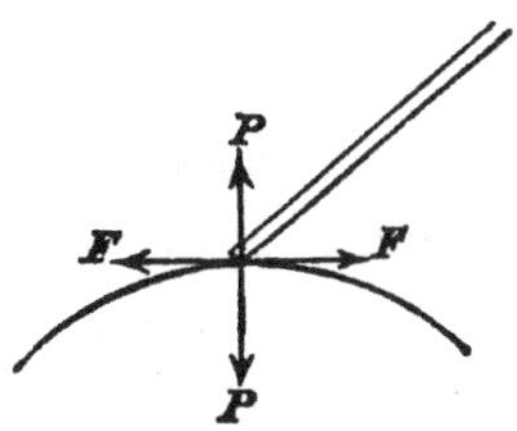

If a rod be connected by a free compass-joint or hinge with another rod (or with a body), there will be a force exercised on each rod equal in magnitude and opposite in direction.

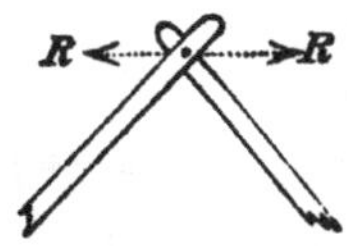

If we wish to find the magnitude and direction of this mutual reaction, we must assume some unknown force R acting in an unknown direction, and obtain equations for determining them by taking the conditions of equilibrium of each rod. It will not unfrequently be the case, however, that the symmetry of the parts of the system will enable us to assign at once the direction or magnitude of R, or both.

43. III. *Tension of Strings.*

If we consider a string as a line of consecutive particles, the force which binds successive particles of the string together is called the *tension*, and since each particle of the string is urged in opposite directions by the forces which the consecutive particles on either side of it exercise upon it, these forces must be equal and opposite; i.e. on each element of the string there are two tensions, equal and opposite. If we neglect the *weight* of the string, the tension at all points of the same rectilinear portion is the same: for if A, B be any two points of the string AB, it is obvious that the tensions at A and B must be equal, otherwise the string would move.

(i) Also the tension of the string is not altered if it pass over a *smooth* surface; for let pq be a small element of the string on the smooth surface,—pq may be regarded as a small arc of the circle of curvature at the middle point of pq, and we may consider pq as a rigid body kept in equilibrium by the tensions t, t' at p, q acting along the tangents pt, qt', and by the reaction of the surface R, which acts along the line OR bisecting the angle pOq,—since the arc pq is symmetrical with respect to OR, and the resultant pressure of the surface will therefore act along OR.

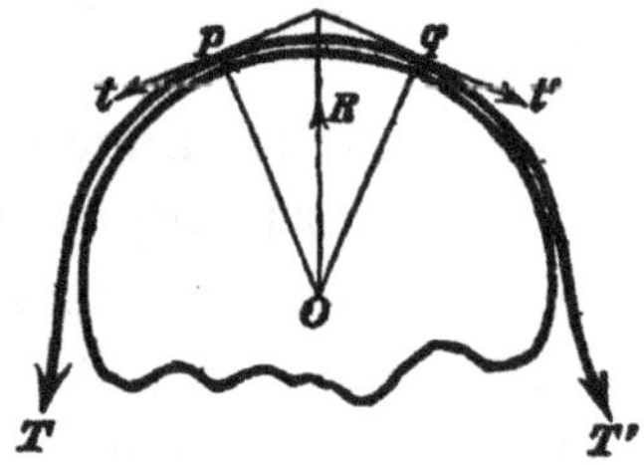

Since then t, t', R are three forces in equilibrium, we get by resolving them perpendicular to OR

$$t\cos pOR = t'\cos qOR; \qquad \text{but } qOR = pOR, \qquad \therefore t = t';$$

i.e. the tension at successive elementary distances is the same, and therefore it is so at finite distances. Hence if the string be pulled by forces T, T' at its two ends, we must have $T = T' =$ tension at any intermediate point.

A stricter proof of this result will be given hereafter, Art. (65, 66).

(ii) If a string pass over a *rough* surface, the tension at successive points will not be the same.

If P, Q be the tensions at the extremities of a string which passes in one plane over a rough curve or surface, and the string be on the point of motion in the direction in which P acts, then $P = Qe^{\mu\phi}$: where μ = coefficient of friction (see chapter on Friction) and ϕ is the *circular measure* of the angle included between the normals to the curve at the points where the string quits the curve. Art. (66).

(iii) *Elastic Strings.* If an elastic string whose natural or unstretched length is l be stretched to a length l' by the action of a tension t which is uniform throughout the length of the string, it is found by experiment that the *extension* $l' - l$ is proportional to the natural length l, and also to the tension t, so that

$$l' - l \propto lt = \frac{lt}{e} \textit{ say};$$

$$\text{or} \quad l' = l\left(1 + \frac{t}{e}\right),$$

where e—which is called the *modulus of elasticity* of the string—is some quantity depending upon the nature of each particular string. If $t = e$, then $l' = 2l$, i.e. if the string be subject to a tension equal to the modulus of elasticity, it will be stretched to twice its natural length.

N.B. In all the above cases the weight of the string is neglected.

44. When a system of bodies is at equilibrium under the action of any forces, no part of the system has any tendency to move; and we shall not affect the statical condition of the system, if we suppose any part or parts of the system to be deprived of the power of motion; as, for example, by supposing a body in contact with others to be *rigidly* attached to them. In accordance with this principle, which is of

frequent and useful application, when we are considering the equilibrium of *any* system, or part of a system of bodies, we may suppose the portion under consideration to be *rigid;* which supposition will enable us to lay out of account all mutual forces within the system. As an illustration of the application of this principle, suppose a system of bodies A, B, C, D kept at rest under the operation of a known system of forces; in considering the equilibrium of the body C (for example) we may regard the rest A, B, D as rigidly connected together, so that we thus avoid the introduction of the mutual pressures between A and D, and B and D.

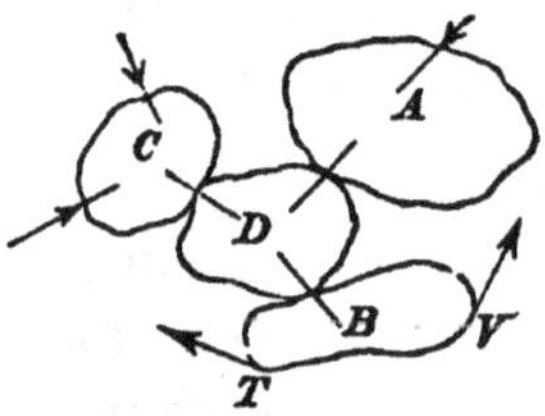

Again, if a string passes round a surface B, quitting it at the points V, T, we may suppose the string to be attached to the body B at the points V, T, which is equivalent to supposing that the portion of the string in contact with the body is *rigid* and *rigidly attached* to the body.

45. The case of a body kept in equilibrium by three forces acting in one plane, is of so frequent occurrence as to deserve special notice.

The conditions of equilibrium of a body kept at rest by three forces P, Q, R in one plane may be stated thus:

I. *If their directions are parallel:—*

(i) Their algebraic sum must be zero, or

$R = P + Q$, Art. (29).

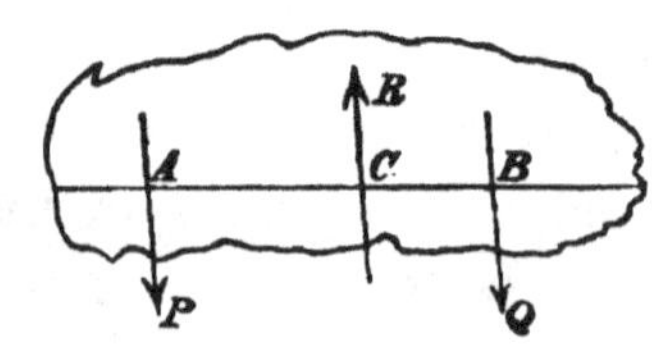

(ii) The moments of any two of the forces about a point in the line of action of the third must be equal and of opposite tendency, *or*

$P.AC = Q.BC$, or $P.AB = R.BC$, or $R.AC = Q.AB$, which are all equivalent to one another, Art. 33, Cor. 1.

II. *If their directions are not parallel:—*

(i) Their lines of action must meet in a point, Art. (22).

(ii) Each force is proportional to the sine of the angle between the other two, the direction of each force lying *without* the angle formed by the other two, Art. (23).

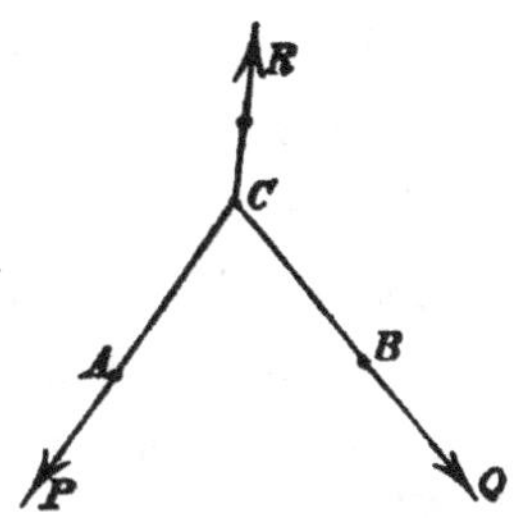

For this latter condition we may substitute the following; viz. each force is equal and opposite to the resultant of the other two,

$$\{\text{for example } R = \sqrt{(P^2 + Q^2 + 2PQ \cos PCQ)}\}.$$

Cor. In each case I. and II. we have *three*, and *only three* conditions from mechanical considerations. In I. the forces are parallel, which with (i) and (ii) constitute the three conditions. In case II., (i) gives one condition, and (ii) two independent conditions; three in all. If in any problem more than three quantities have to be determined, the subsidiary equations of condition must be sought for from geometrical considerations; and whenever the weight of a body is one of the forces to be taken into account it must always be supposed to act in a vertical line passing through the centre of gravity of the body. (See Chap. V.)

If more than three forces act on the body in one plane, the conditions of equilibrium given in Art. (38) or the equivalent forms given in Art. (39), will furnish all the requisite mechanical equations. Geometrical relations as stated above must furnish any additional data required.

These considerations would equally apply in the case of the preceding Article when only three forces act, and may be used by the student instead of them, at his discretion.

The following problems are worked out as examples:

46. I. *To find the conditions of equilibrium of a uniform heavy rod, which is suspended by two strings attached to its ends, the strings being of given length and attached to the same fixed point.*

If AB be the rod, G its middle point, AC, BC the two strings attached to a fixed point C, we have the rod kept in equilibrium by three forces, viz. the tensions (T, T') of the two strings and the weight of the rod which acts through G in a vertical line.

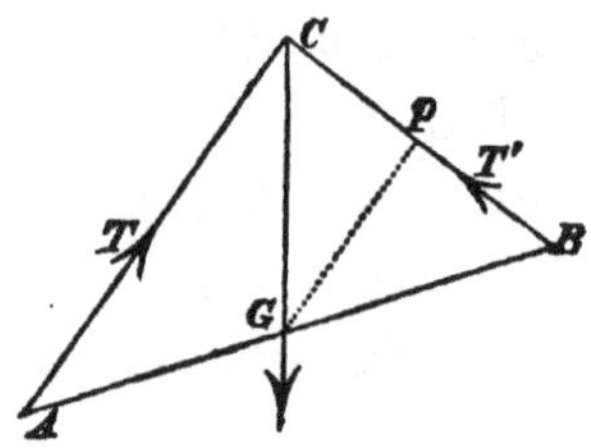

Since the two tensions act through C, the third force must also pass through C, and therefore CG must be vertical; this determines geometrically the position of the rod, and if we draw Gp parallel to AC, the sides of the triangle CGp taken in order, are in the directions of the three forces.

Hence, $T : T' : W = Gp : Cp : CG$....... (α).

Since the triangle CGp is geometrically determinate, the proportions (α) determine T, T'.

We may express T, T' thus analytically.

Let $ACG = \alpha$, $BCG = \beta$, then α, β are known quantities since all the lines of the figure are of known length.

Then, $T : T' : W = \sin\beta : \sin\alpha : \sin(\alpha+\beta)$;

$$\therefore\ T = W\frac{\sin\beta}{\sin(\alpha+\beta)},\quad T' = W\frac{\sin\alpha}{\sin(\alpha+\beta)}.$$

47. II. *Two spheres are supported by strings attached to a given point, and rest against each other: find the tensions of the strings.*

Let A, B be the two spheres, T, T' the tensions of the two strings, W, W' the weights of the spheres which may be supposed to act through their centres.

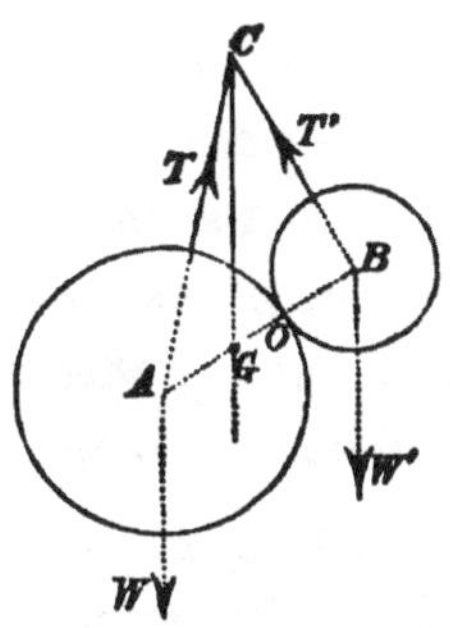

Then in considering the equilibrium of A, there are three forces acting on it, viz. the tension of the string T, the weight W and the pressure at the point of contact O: now the directions of the two latter forces pass through A, hence the third does so also; i.e. the direction of the string passes through A, or CTA is a straight line.

Similarly, $CT'B$ is a straight line.

Further, in considering the equilibrium of the whole, we may regard A and B as forming one rigid body, Art. (44); let G be the centre of gravity of the two spheres.

Hence, since the forces which keep the united mass of A and B at rest are T, T' and $W + W'$, of which the two former pass through C, and the latter acts in a vertical line through G, this vertical line must pass through C also, or CG must be vertical.

This determines the position of equilibrium geometrically, and the tensions T and T' might be found as in the last problem: the only difference being that G is not necessarily the middle point of AB.

If it be required to find the mutual pressure (P) between the two spheres, we have by considering the equilibrium of the three forces which pass through A,

$$P : W = \sin TAW : \sin TAB$$
$$= \sin ACG : \sin TAB;$$

a known ratio, since ACG, TAB, are known or easily found. Hence P is determined.

48. III. *A heavy particle (weight* W) *is attached to the middle point of a rod* AB *without weight, the ends of which rest against two inclined planes at right angles to one another: the vertical plane which passes through the rod being at right angles to the line of intersection of the two planes. Find the position of equilibrium of the rod, and the pressure on each plane.*

Let R, R' be the pressures which the planes exert on the rod at its ends A, B, then the only forces which act on the rod are R, R' and W, and therefore when the rod is in a position of equilibrium these forces must satisfy the conditions of equilibrium of three forces in one plane. Art. (45), Case II.

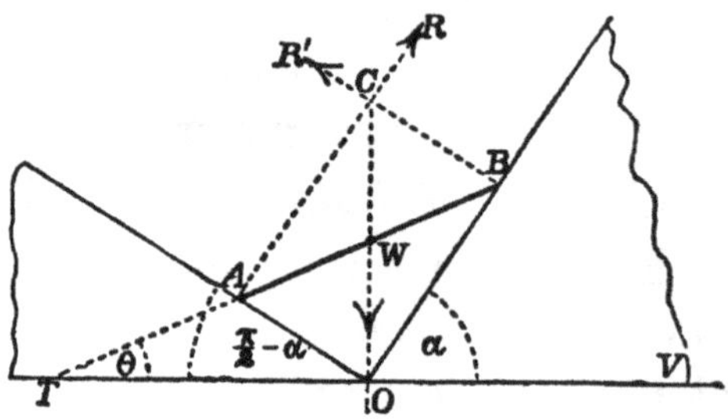

Let the normals to the planes at A, B meet in C, then the vertical line through C must pass through W; and therefore the diagonal CWO of the rectangle CO must be vertical.

Hence $\qquad \alpha - \theta = \angle TBO = \angle WOB = \frac{\pi}{2} - \alpha,$

$$\therefore \ \theta = 2\alpha - \frac{\pi}{2} \ \ldots\ldots\ldots\ldots\ldots\ldots\ldots\ldots (i).$$

Also,

$$R : R' : W = \sin R'CW : \sin RCW : \sin R'CR$$
$$= \sin \alpha : \cos \alpha : 1.$$

Since $R'CW = \pi - \alpha$, $RCW = \frac{\pi}{2} + \alpha$, $R'CR = \frac{\pi}{2}$;

whence $R = W \sin \alpha$, $R' = W \cos \alpha$............(ii).

(i) and (ii) express the complete solution.

If $\alpha < \frac{\pi}{4}$, i.e. if OB be that plane which is least inclined to the horizon, θ assumes a negative value, which indicates that the rod is inclined in the other direction to the horizon.

49. IV. *A rectangular picture-frame is suspended by a string attached to the ends of one side of the frame, the string passing over a smooth peg; determine the position of equilibrium.*

Let C be the peg over which the string ACB passes freely; we may suppose the weight of the frame to act at G, the point where the diagonals intersect, and which is the centre of gravity of the frame. Then the forces which must be in equilibrium are the weight W which acts in the vertical line through G, and the tensions which act on the frame at A, B in directions AC, BC; hence the vertical line through G must pass through C; i. e. CG must be vertical. Also, since the peg is smooth, the tension of the string is the same throughout its length.

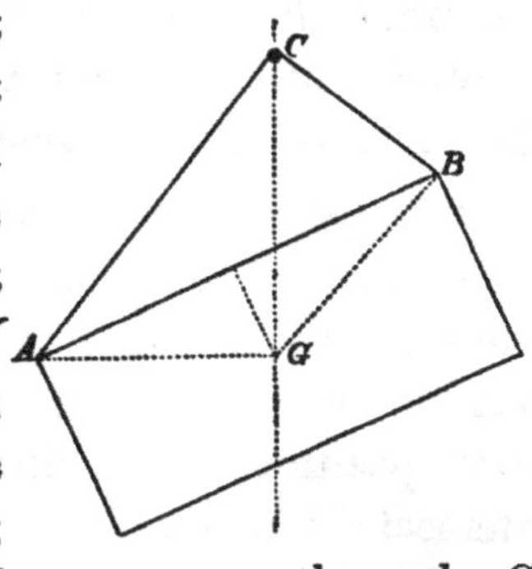

Since then of the three forces in equilibrium whose directions pass through C, two of them, viz. the tensions at A, B, are equal in magnitude, the direction of the third CG must bisect the angle ACB. The problem then is reduced to the following geometrical one.

To determine the position of the string ACB of given length in order that the line CG, passing through G a given point in the frame, may bisect the angle ACB. We may construct it geometrically thus,—with A, B as foci describe an ellipse whose major-axis equals ACB; also describe a circle round the triangle ABG. The points of intersection of this ellipse and circle (C and C') will determine the point C of the string, which must coincide with the peg; for the arcs AG, BG being equal, it is obvious that CG, $C'G$ bisect the angles ACB, $AC'B$, respectively.—There is a third position of equilibrium, viz. when the string is in the position $AC''B$, C'' being the extremity of the minor axis of the ellipse,—for in this case also $C''G$ bisects the angle $AC''B$.

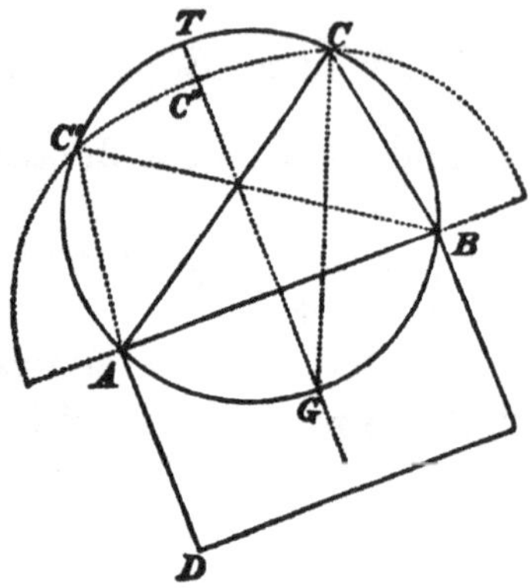

It appears then, that if the circle and ellipse intersect, there are three positions of equilibrium. But if they do not intersect, C, C' have no existence, and there is only one position of equilibrium. The condition that there may be three positions of equilibrium is that the two curves may intersect; i.e. the length of string must be < 2 chord AT. If $AB = a$, $AD = c$, the condition becomes

$$l < a\frac{\sqrt{(a^2 + c^2)}}{c}.$$

50. V. The determination of the action of a hinge or joint is well illustrated in the following problem.

Three rods, forming a triangle, are connected by free joints or hinges at their extremities, and the system is at equilibrium when certain forces are applied perpendicularly to the rods at their middle points—shew that

(i) *the force applied to any rod is proportional to the length of the rod;*

(ii) *the strain at each angular point is the same, and acts in the direction of a tangent to the circle circumscribing the triangle;*

(iii) *this strain is proportional to the radius of the circle.*

(i) Since the mutual action at any one of the hinges will be equal in magnitude and opposite in direction upon the two rods which meet at that hinge—the strains of the hinges may be left out of consideration when we are considering the conditions of equilibrium of the three rods *as one system*.

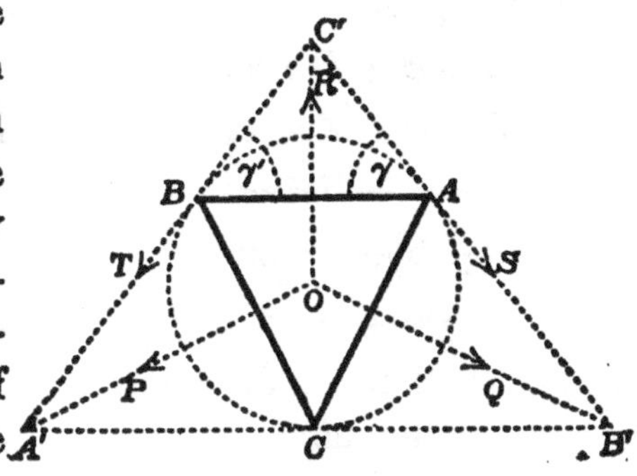

Now the directions of the forces P, Q, R meet in O the centre of the circumscribing circle;—and since P, Q, R are in equilibrium we must have

$$P : Q : R = \sin QOR : \sin ROP : \sin POQ$$
$$= \sin A : \sin B : \sin C = a : b : c,$$

which proves the first part of the problem.

(ii) Let us consider the conditions of equilibrium of one rod AB, and let S, T be the strains which the hinges at A, B exert upon the rod AB in directions making angles $\gamma\gamma'$ *say*, with AB respectively.

Since AB is in equilibrium under the action of the three forces S, T, R, the directions of these forces must meet in a point C' suppose—and since R bisects AB at right angles we easily infer that $\gamma = C'AB = C'BA = \gamma'$, and $S = T$. Similarly the strain at C is equal to S or T—therefore the strain at each angular point is the same.

Also the strains at A, B make equal angles γ with AB, similarly the strains at A, C upon the rod AC make equal angles—β *say*—with AC; and the strains at B, C equal angles—α *say*—with BC.

From the geometry we readily see that

$$\alpha + \beta + C = \pi,$$

$$\beta + \gamma + A = \pi, \quad \text{and} \quad A + B + C = \pi,$$

$$\gamma + \alpha + B = \pi,$$

$$\therefore \alpha + \beta + \gamma = \pi,$$

$$\text{and} \ \therefore \alpha = A, \quad \beta = B, \quad \gamma = C;$$

and it follows that the direction of the strain at any hinge is a tangent to the circumscribing circle. Hence the second part of the proposition is proved.

(iii) Since S at A, and S at B balance R, we have

$$2S \sin \gamma = R \quad or \quad 2S \sin C = R,$$

but if r be the radius of the circumscribing circle

$$2r \sin C = c;$$

$$\therefore \frac{S}{r} = \frac{R}{c} = \therefore \frac{P}{a} = \frac{Q}{b}.$$

Hence the strain at any hinge bears to any of the forces P, Q, R the same ratio which the radius of the circumscribing circle bears to the side to which the force is applied—which is the third part of the problem to be proved.

51. The following is an exercise on the parallelogram of forces.

VI. *Assuming the truth of the parallelogram of forces* (Art. 18) *for the* magnitude *of the resultant, prove it also for the* direction *of the resultant.*

Let three forces P, Q, R acting in one plane at a point A be in equilibrium, and let them be represented by AB, AC, AE respectively.

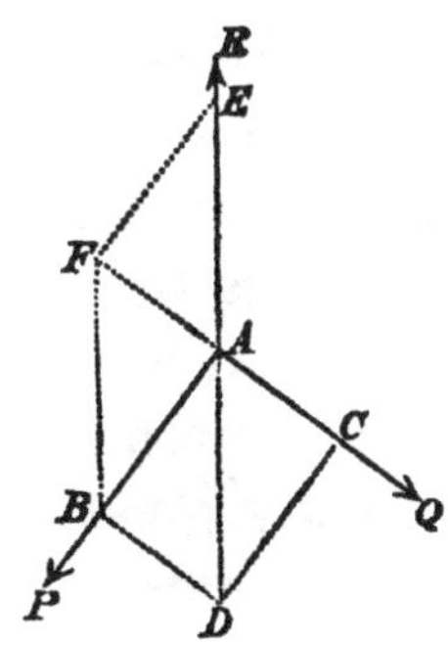

Complete the parallelogram BC; then by the assumption the diagonal AD represents the resultant of P, Q in *magnitude*:—and since any one of the three forces P, Q, R is equal in magnitude to the resultant of the other two, it follows that $AE = AD$.

Complete the parallelogram BE; then AF represents the resultant of P, R in magnitude, and therefore $AF = AC$.

Hence BF, AD are equal, since they are each equal to AE,

and AF, BD are equal, since they are each equal to AC,

that is, the opposite sides of the quadrilateral $AFBD$ are respectively equal to each other, and therefore $AFBD$ is a parallelogram.

Hence AD, AE being each parallel to BF are in the same straight line;—which proves the parallelogram of forces for the *direction* of the resultant.

CHAPTER III.

OF FRICTION.

52. WHEN a heavy body rests on a plane horizontal surface, on a table for example, and we wish to make it slide along the surface, we encounter a resistance to this motion; there exists between the particles of the body and the table an adhesion which resists their separation, and this adhesion is only overcome by applying to the body a force of traction sufficiently great. This adhesive force is called *friction*, and the magnitude of the force which is necessary to overcome the resistance to motion will be a measure of the friction.

More generally, when one surface presses against another, if the direction of this pressure be not normal to the surfaces in contact, there will be a tendency of one surface to *rub* or *slide* over the other; and no sliding motion will ensue, unless the resolved part of the pressure *along* the surface be sufficient to overcome the friction. When a body is *just on the point of sliding*, it is said to be in a state *bordering on motion*, and the greatest amount of friction which the surfaces can exert is then in operation. In other cases no more friction is called into action than is just sufficient to balance the part of the pressure resolved along the surface in contact.

In this point of view, friction may be called a *self-adjusting* force, since it adapts itself to the requirements of each particular case; no more being called into operation than is just necessary to prevent motion.

53. If R be the normal pressure between two surfaces in contact, F the friction when the bodies are just on the point of sliding over each other, i.e. the maximum friction which the substances can exercise, the ratio $\frac{F}{R}$ is called the *coefficient of friction*, and is commonly designated by μ:

$$\text{so that } F = \mu R.$$

If in any particular case the full amount of friction which the substances can exert is not called into action, the amount of friction which is *actually* in operation is one of the unknown forces which it is the object of the problem to determine.

54. The results of careful experiments made with the object of determining the laws of friction are thus given by Coulomb, and M. Morin: viz.

(i) *When the substances in contact remain the same, the friction varies as the pressure*; i.e. μ is the same for the same substances, but will vary for different substances. When the pressure is very great indeed, it is found that the friction is a little less than this law would give.

(ii) *So long as the normal pressure between the surfaces in contact remains the same, the whole amount of friction is independent of the extent of surface in contact.*

These two laws are true when the body is in a state bordering on motion, and also when actually in motion; only it is to be remarked that in the latter case the magnitude of the friction is much less than in the former. If we call the friction in the former case *statical*, and that in the latter *dynamical*, we may express the above by saying that the *coefficients* of dynamical and statical friction are severally constant for the same substances, but that the dynamical is less than the statical.

It is also found:

(iii) *That the friction is independent of the velocity when the body is in motion.*

55. The friction between two bodies will generally be diminished by smearing them with some unctuous substance, as oil, &c., and the friction when they are on the point of moving, or what we may call the friction at starting, is pretty nearly the same as during motion when the bodies are made of hard material, like stone or metal. But in the case of compressible substances like wood, the friction at starting is very considerably greater than during motion. When two bodies are placed one upon the other, one of them at least being compressible, the amount of friction at starting will partly depend upon the length of time they have been in contact. For wood sliding upon wood, the maximum friction is attained after a contact of a few minutes; but for wood upon metal it requires a much longer time, frequently several days for the friction to attain its maximum: but when it has attained this, the friction at starting is not altered by any continued duration of contact.

Further, it is found that *rolling friction* is much less than *sliding* friction: for example, when a cylinder rolls on a plane, or a cylindrical axis turns within a hollow socket (when there is simply a *line* in contact and not a finite area), the amount of friction is much less than would be given by the above laws (i) and (ii), for the same amount of pressure.

The fact that *rolling friction* is much less than *sliding friction* is taken advantage of in various contrivances for facilitating the transport of heavy bodies;—thus for instance, heavy blocks of stone or other material are often transported by placing them on a platform beneath which rollers are placed:—the wheels of carriages are examples of the same principle,—the most delicate application of which perhaps is that of *friction wheels*, such as those employed in *Atwood's Machine* (see Dynamics, Art. 82).

56. The values of μ for different substances have been determined by experiment, and arranged in tables; the following may be taken as approximate results in many cases for friction at starting:

wood upon wood	(without oil)	$\mu = \cdot 5$,
....	(with oil)	$\mu = \cdot 2$;
wood upon metal	(without oil)	$\mu = \cdot 6$,
....	(with oil)	$\mu = \cdot 12$;
leather upon wood	(without oil)	$\mu = \cdot 63$,
....	(wetted with water)	$\mu = \cdot 87$;
metal upon metal	(without oil)	$\mu = \cdot 18$,
....	(with oil)	$\mu = \cdot 12$;

When a cylinder of wood rolls upon wood so that there is a single line of contact only, $\mu = \frac{1}{12}$;—when the surface in contact is a physical point the statical friction is inconsiderable.

57. *To find the coefficient of friction between two substances practically.*

Let AB be the plane surface of one substance, upon which

is placed a mass M of the other substance with its plane face in contact with AB. If the plane AB be horizontal, no friction will be called into action, but if it be gradually inclined more and more to the horizon till the body M is just on the point of sliding down AB, then the full amount of friction between the two substances is called into action and only just prevents M from moving down the plane.

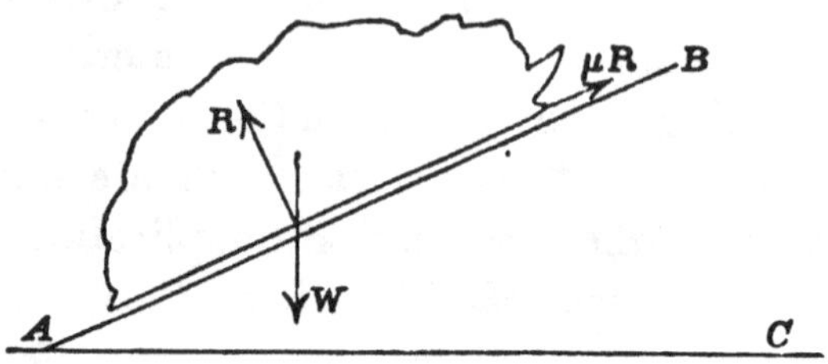

The forces which act upon M and balance each other are W the weight of M, R the pressure of the plane AB upon M normal to AB, and μR the friction *up* the plane AB.

If ϕ be the angle which AB makes with the horizon, the conditions of equilibrium give—resolving along the plane and perpendicular to it,

$$W \sin \phi = \mu R,$$
$$W \cos \phi = R;$$

whence $\tan \phi = \mu$. Hence if ϕ be observed, the value of μ is known. The angle ϕ is commonly called the *angle of friction.*

58. The above can only be regarded as an approximate method of determining friction. For a complete account of the refined contrivances which have been employed with this object, the student is referred to the memoirs of Coulomb and M. Morin.

Experiments have been made on a large scale by *Stephenson, De Pambour* and others for the purpose of determining the dynamical friction on railroads—by which the laws stated in Art. (53) have been substantially confirmed. In some of the more favorable cases detailed by Mr. Nicholas Wood in his *Practical Treatise on Railroads* the *rolling friction* from the contact of the wheels with the rails was about $\frac{1}{1000}$th part of the whole weight of the train,—and the friction at the axles about as much more—making the total resistance to the motion of the train arising from friction to be about $\frac{1}{500}$th part of the load.—But the results of different experiments differ considerably.

CHAPTER IV.

OF FORCES, THE DIRECTIONS OF WHICH MEET IN A POINT—TENSION OF STRINGS ON SMOOTH AND ROUGH SURFACES.

59. We proceed to discuss the resultant and the conditions of equilibrium of a system of forces whose directions meet in a point, but which do not lie all in one plane.

60. Theorem. *If three forces* X, Y, Z, *not in one plane, be applied at the same point* O *(in space) and be represented by the three lines* OA, OB, OC, *and the parallelopiped* OABCR *be completed, the resultant* R *of these three forces will be represented by the diagonal* OR *of this parallelopiped.*

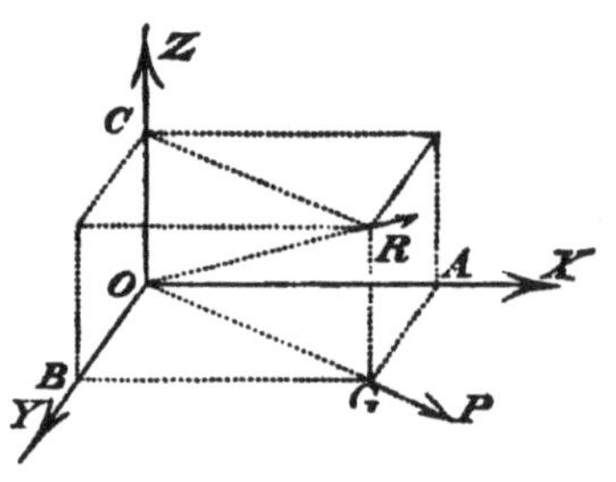

For the two forces X, Y, which are represented by OA, OB two sides of the parallelogram $OAGB$, are equivalent to a resultant P, which is represented by the diagonal OG of this parallelogram.

And since OC is equal and parallel to GR, the figure $OCRG$ is a parallelogram, and consequently the two forces P and Z represented by OG, OC sides of this parallelogram, will be equivalent to a resultant R represented by the diagonal OR.

Hence the resultant of the three forces X, Y, Z, is represented by the diagonal OR of the parallelopiped.

This theorem is sometimes called *the parallelopiped of forces.* It is an easy extension of *the parallelogram of forces.*

COR. 1. By the preceding theorem we see how a given force R may always be resolved into three others, severally parallel to three lines given in space: these three lines not being in one plane, and no two of them parallel.

For if we take OR to represent the given force R in magnitude and direction and draw through the point O, lines OA, OB, OC severally parallel to the proposed three lines, we have three planes XOY, YOZ, ZOX,—and if we draw through the point R three planes severally parallel to these three, the six planes will form a parallelopiped, three adjacent edges of which OA, OB, OC will represent the three components X, Y, Z.

COR. 2. If the parallelopiped be rectangular, we have in the rectangle $OAGB$, $OG^2 = OA^2 + OB^2$,

$$\text{and in the rectangle } OCRG,\ OR^2 = OG^2 + OC^2,$$

$$\text{whence } OR^2 = OA^2 + OB^2 + OC^2;$$

$$\text{and therefore } R^2 = X^2 + Y^2 + Z^2 \ldots\ldots\ldots\ldots\text{(i)}$$

$$\text{or } R = \sqrt{(X^2 + Y^2 + Z^2)},$$

the value of the resultant in terms of the three components.

61. If we wish to express each component in terms of the resultant, and the angles which they make with it, and if we denominate by α, β, γ the angles which the direction of R makes with the directions of X, Y, Z,

$$\text{i.e. } XOR = \alpha,\quad YOR = \beta,\quad ZOR = \gamma,$$

$$\text{we shall have } OC = OR\cos\gamma;$$

$$\left.\begin{aligned} \text{and therefore } Z &= R\cos\gamma \\ \text{similarly, } Y &= R\cos\beta \\ X &= R\cos\alpha \end{aligned}\right\}\ldots\ldots\ldots\ldots\ldots\ldots\text{(ii)},$$

comparing (i) with (ii) we get

$$\cos^2\alpha + \cos^2\beta + \cos^2\gamma = 1,$$

a well-known relation which holds whenever α, β, γ represent the angles which any given line makes with three rectangular axes.

If we multiply the three equations of (ii) successively by $\cos\gamma$, $\cos\beta$, $\cos\alpha$, we get by virtue of the relation

$$\cos^2\alpha + \cos^2\beta + \cos^2\gamma = 1;$$

$$X\cos\alpha + Y\cos\beta + Z\cos\gamma = R \text{............(iii)},$$

which expresses that the resultant is equal to the sum of the resolved parts of the components estimated in its direction—a theorem which is true for any system of forces which admits of a single resultant: for if each force be resolved into two parts, one in direction of the resultant and the other at right angles to it, these latter parts must be in equilibrium themselves, and there remains the sum of the former parts equal to the resultant.

62. We can now proceed:

To find the resultant of any number of forces whose directions pass through a point.

Let O be the point through which the directions of all the forces pass, and through O draw any three lines OX, OY, OZ mutually at right angles.

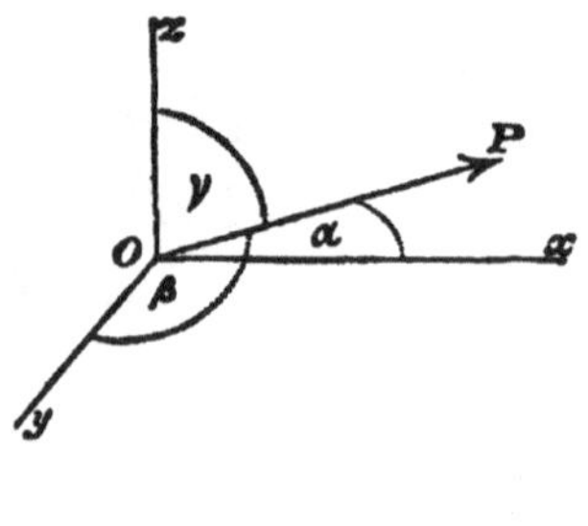

Let P be any one of the forces acting in direction OP, making angles α, β, γ with OX, OY, OZ, then P is equivalent to three components

$$P\cos\alpha,\ P\cos\beta,\ P\cos\gamma,$$

acting in directions OX, OY, OZ, respectively.

Similarly, if P' be another force, α', β', γ' the angles its direction makes with OX, OY, OZ, it is equivalent to

$$P'\cos\alpha',\ P'\cos\beta',\ P'\cos\gamma',$$

in direction of the same lines;

and so on whatever be the number of forces.

The system of forces is equivalent then to three components X, Y, Z, which are severally equal to

$$\left.\begin{array}{l} P\cos\alpha + P'\cos\alpha' + \ldots \text{in direction of } OX \textit{ or } \Sigma\,(P\cos\alpha) \\ P\cos\beta + P'\cos\beta' + \ldots\ldots\ldots\ldots\ldots\ldots\ldots OY \ldots \Sigma\,(P\cos\beta) \\ P\cos\gamma + P'\cos\gamma' + \ldots\ldots\ldots\ldots\ldots\ldots\ldots OZ \ldots \Sigma\,(P\cos\gamma) \end{array}\right\} \ldots \text{(i)}.$$

Now these three components (i) are equivalent to a single resultant R making angles λ, μ, ν with the line OX, OY, OZ, provided

$$R\cos\lambda = \Sigma\,(P\cos\alpha),$$

$$R\cos\mu = \Sigma\,(P\cos\beta),\ R\cos\nu = \Sigma\,(P\cos\gamma)\ldots\ldots\ldots\text{(ii)},$$

and remembering that $\cos^2\lambda + \cos^2\mu + \cos^2\nu = 1$,

these give us the magnitude of the resultant, i.e.

$$R^2 = \{\Sigma\,(P\cos\alpha)\}^2 + \{\Sigma\,(P\cos\beta)\}^2 + \{\Sigma\,(P\cos\gamma)\}^2;$$

and this being known, the equations of (ii) give λ, μ, ν, which assign the direction of the resultant.

This analytical mode of finding the resultant of a system of forces applied at a point is of course equivalent to the geometrical construction of Leibnitz noticed in Art. (26).

63. If the forces be in equilibrium the resultant is *nil*. i.e. $R = 0$;

and $\therefore \{\Sigma(P\cos\alpha)\}^2+\{\Sigma(P\cos\beta)\}^2+\{\Sigma(P\cos\gamma)\}^2=0$; which requires

$$\Sigma(P\cos\alpha)=0,\ \Sigma(P\cos\beta)=0,\ \Sigma(P\cos\gamma)=0,$$

the three conditions of equilibrium of a system of forces acting through a point.

That is, the sum of the forces resolved in three directions mutually at right angles must be severally zero.

Or we may reason thus:

In considering any system of forces whose directions pass through a point, if they be in equilibrium, we may (as has been observed before) regard any one of the forces as equal and opposite to the resultant of all the rest. Hence, in any case in which we are discussing the conditions of equilibrium of a body or system of bodies acted on by such a system of forces, we may resolve all the forces in a particular direction (any we please)—and perpendicular to the direction so taken: the conditions of equilibrium then will be

(i) The algebraic sum of the former resolved parts must be zero.

(ii) The resolved parts acting in a plane perpendicular to the direction taken, must be in equilibrium *inter se*,—and must satisfy the condition of equilibrium of forces in one plane: and we may apply the principles established in the second chapter in the same way as if these resolved parts had been the only forces acting.

And it will in general constitute part of the solution of the problem to shew that these resolved parts are in equilibrium.

64. The remaining articles of this chapter contain demonstrations of two results relating to the tension of strings passing over smooth and rough surfaces referred to in Article (43)—and some properties of a funicular polygon.

They may be omitted by a student whose previous reading has not prepared him for the consideration of *small quantities*.

65. *The tension of a string which passes in one plane over a smooth curve or surface, is the same at every point—the weight of the string being neglected.*

Let ps be any finite length of the string in contact with the curve, the normals to which at p, s include an $\angle\, \phi$.

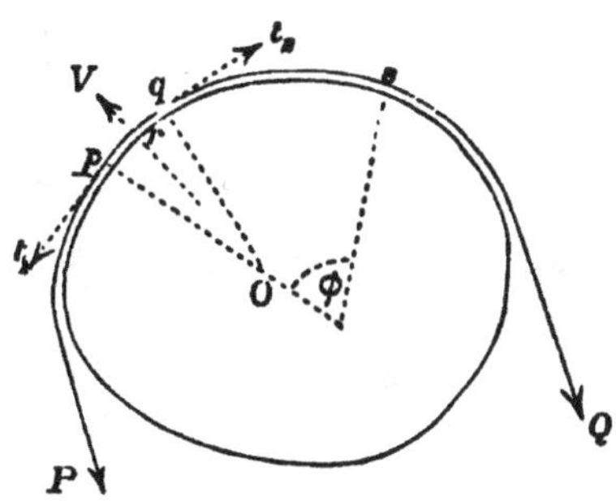

Let ps be divided into n parts, such that the normals at the extremities of consecutive parts include the same angle θ—so that $n\theta = \phi$.

pq the first of these parts, the normals at p, q meeting in O, t_1, t_2, ... t_{n+1} the tension of the string at p, q, ... s.

R the measure of the pressure on the curve at p—then we may regard the resultant pressure of the curve on the element pq of the string as equal to $(R + \kappa)\,.\, arc\, pq$, acting in some direction rV intermediate to Op, Oq, and making angles α_1, β_1 *say* with pO, qO,—so that $\alpha_1 + \beta_1 = \theta$, and κ is some small quantity which vanishes in the limit, when θ is taken smaller and smaller.

Considering now the equilibrium of the element pq of the string as a rigid body—resolve the forces upon it parallel and perpendicular to rV, and we obtain the equations

$$t_1 \sin \alpha_1 + t_2 \sin \beta_1 = (R + \kappa)\, pq \quad \text{.............(i)},$$

$$t_1 \cos \alpha_1 - t_2 \cos \beta_1 = 0 \quad \text{........................ (ii)},$$

equation (ii) may be written in the form

$$t_1 - 2t_1 \sin^2 \frac{\alpha_1}{2} = t_2 - 2t_2 \sin^2 \frac{\beta_1}{2} \quad \text{............. (1)},$$

and if we write down the corresponding equation for each consecutive element of ps, we shall obtain

$$t_2 - 2t_2 \sin^2 \frac{\alpha_2}{2} = t_3 - 2t_3 \sin^2 \frac{\beta_2}{2} \quad \text{................ (2)},$$

$$\text{.........} = \text{.........}$$

$$t_n - 2t_n \sin^2 \frac{\alpha_n}{2} = t_{n+1} - 2t_{n+1} \sin^2 \frac{\beta_n}{2} \quad \text{............ (}n\text{)},$$

adding equations (1), (2) ... (n), we obtain

$$t_1 - 2\left(t_1 \sin^2 \frac{\alpha_1}{2} + t_2 \sin^2 \frac{\alpha_2}{2} + \dots + t_n \sin^2 \frac{\alpha_n}{2}\right)$$

$$= t_{n+1} - 2\left(t_2 \sin^2 \frac{\beta_1}{2} + t_3 \sin^2 \frac{\beta_2}{2} + \dots + t_{n+1} \sin^2 \frac{\beta_n}{2}\right) \quad \text{.... (iii)}.$$

Now if τ be the greatest of the quantities t_1, $t_2 \dots t_{n+1}$, we see that

$$t_1 \sin^2 \frac{\alpha_1}{2} + t_2 \sin^2 \frac{\alpha_2}{2} + \dots + t_n \sin^2 \frac{\alpha_n}{2} < n\tau \sin^2 \frac{\theta}{2}$$

$$< n\tau \frac{\theta^2}{4} < \frac{\tau\phi^2}{4n}.$$

Similarly

$$t_2 \sin^2 \frac{\beta_1}{2} + t_3 \sin^2 \frac{\beta_2}{2} + \dots + t_{n+1} \sin^2 \frac{\beta_n}{2} < \frac{\tau\phi^2}{4n}.$$

If now n be increased indefinitely, ϕ remaining unchanged, and therefore θ being indefinitely diminished—the expression $\frac{\tau\phi^2}{4n}$ vanishes, and equation (iii) becomes

$$t_1 = t_{n+1} \text{ .... (iv)},$$

i. e. the tension of the string is the same at every point.

Further, from equation (i)—suppressing the suffixes—

$$t = (R + \kappa) \cdot \frac{pq}{\sin\alpha + \sin\beta},$$

and if ρ be the radius of curvature at p,

$$\rho = \frac{pq}{\theta} \text{ in the limit}$$

$$\frac{\text{arc } pq}{\sin\alpha + \sin\beta} = \frac{pq}{\alpha + \beta} = \rho, \text{ in the limit,}$$

in which case κ vanishes; whence

$$t = R\rho \text{ .... (v)},$$

a relation which gives the pressure on the curve at any point in terms of the tension and radius of curvature.

Hence in the same curve

$$R = \frac{t}{\rho} \propto \frac{1}{\rho}.$$

Obs. For simplicity we have supposed the string to be all in one plane—the demonstration might without much trouble be extended to shew that the tension is the same at every point in whatever manner the string passes freely along a smooth surface or tube of any form.

66. *A string passes in one plane over a rough curve or surface, the tensions of the extremities being such that the string is on the point of motion—to find the relation between these tensions, the weight of the string being neglected.*

Let P, Q be the tensions at the points where the string quits the curve—and suppose it to be on the point of motion in the direction in which P acts—then the friction at every point of the arc will act tangentially in the opposite direction.

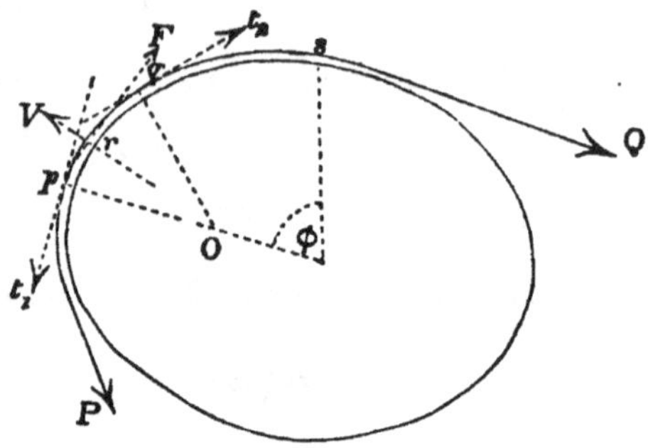

Let ps be any finite length of the string, the normals at p, s including an $\angle\ \phi$, let ps be divided into n parts—the normals at the extremities of successive parts including the same $\angle\ \theta$, so that $n\theta = \phi$, pq the first of these parts, the normals at p, q meeting in O, $t_1, t_2 \ldots t_{n+1}$ the tension of the string at $p, q \ldots s$.

R the measure of the normal pressure on the curve at p, μR that of the friction along the tangent at p.

Then we may regard the resultant of the normal pressure of the curve on the element pq of the string as equal to $(R + \kappa)\,.\,arc\,pq$ acting in some direction rV intermediate to Op, Oq, and making an $\angle\ \alpha$ *say* with Op,—and the resultant friction on the arc pq as equal to $\mu\,(R + \kappa')\,.\,arc\,pq$ acting in some direction inclined at an $\angle\ \beta$ *say* to the tangent at p—α, β being each $< \theta$, and $\kappa\,\kappa'$ small quantities which vanish in the limit when θ is taken smaller and smaller.

Considering now the equilibrium of the element pq of the string as a rigid body—resolve the forces upon it parallel and perpendicular to the tangent at p, and we obtain the equations

$$t_1 - t_2 \cos\theta = (R + \kappa)\,pq\,.\sin\alpha + \mu\,(R + \kappa')\,pq\,.\cos\beta \ldots \text{(i)},$$

$$t_2 \sin\theta = (R + \kappa)\,pq\,.\cos\alpha - \mu\,(R + \kappa')\,pq\,.\sin\beta \ldots \text{(ii)};$$

whence

$$\frac{t_1 - t_2 \cos\theta}{t_2 \sin\theta} = \frac{(R+\kappa)\sin\alpha + \mu(R+\kappa')\cos\beta}{(R+\kappa)\cos\alpha - \mu(R+\kappa')\sin\beta}.$$

Now the second member of this equation becomes $=\mu$ if θ and consequently α and β be taken indefinitely small, we may therefore write it $=\mu(1+\lambda)$, λ being some quantity which $=0$ when $\theta=0$,

$$\text{or } \frac{t_1}{t_2} = \cos\theta\{1+\mu(1+\lambda)\tan\theta\}$$

$$= \left(1 - 2\sin^2\frac{\theta}{2}\right)\{1+\mu(1+\lambda)\tan\theta\}$$

$$= 1 + \mu\theta(1+\lambda'),$$

where λ' is some quantity which $=0$ when $\theta=0$. Hence

$$\log t_1 - \log t_2 = \log\{1+\mu\theta(1+\lambda')\}$$

$$= \mu\theta(1+\lambda') - \frac{1}{2}\{\mu\theta(1+\lambda')\}^2 + \ldots$$

$$= \mu\theta(1+\lambda_1) \textit{ say, } \lambda_1 \text{ vanishing with } \theta.$$

Similarly,

$$\log t_2 - \log t_3 = \mu\theta(1+\lambda_2)$$

$$\ldots\ldots\ldots = \ldots\ldots$$

$$\log t_n - \log t_{n+1} = \mu\theta(1+\lambda_n)$$

$$\therefore \log t_1 - \log t_{n+1} = \mu n\theta(1+\kappa_1), \text{ if } \kappa_1 \text{ be the mean value of } \lambda_1, \lambda_2 \ldots \lambda_n,$$

$$= \mu\phi(1+\kappa_1).$$

If now n be increased indefinitely, ϕ remaining unchanged, and therefore θ being indefinitely diminished, each of the quantities $\lambda_1, \lambda_2 \ldots \lambda_n$ will vanish, and therefore κ_1 will do so likewise, and our equation becomes

$$\log t_1 - \log t_{n+1} = \mu\phi, \text{ or } t_1 = e^{\mu\phi}\, t_{n+1},$$

which expresses the relation between the tensions at any two points of the curve of contact.

If ψ be the angle between the normals where the string quits the curve, we have

$$P = Q\epsilon^{\mu\psi} \text{..............(iii)},$$

if ρ be the radius of curvature at p, we shall obtain from equation (ii) the result

$$t = R\rho \text{ .... (iv)},$$

Obs. The results of Arts. (65, 66) are true whether the string be elastic or inelastic—if it be elastic, we may remark that in Art. (66) every element of the string must be supposed to be simultaneously on the point of motion.

67. *The funicular polygon.*

If a series of n weights $P_1, P_2 \dots P_n$ be suspended by knots at given points of a string (without weight), and the string be attached to two fixed points A, B, it will when in equilibrium form a polygon in a vertical plane, and is called a *funicular polygon.*

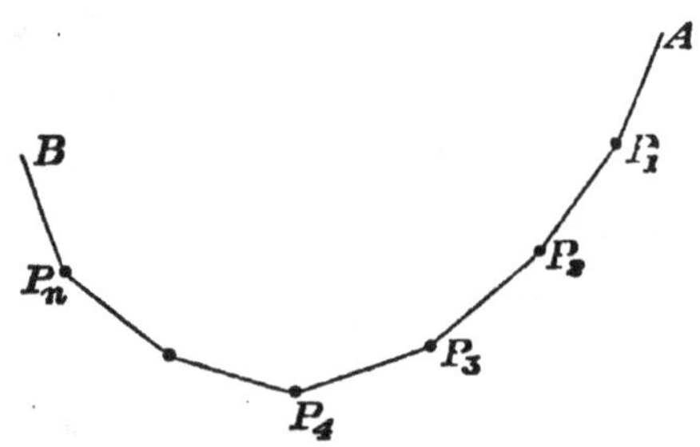

To find the conditions of equilibrium in such a system.

Let $t_1, t_2, t_3 \dots t_{n+1}$ be the tensions of the successive portions of the string $AP_1, P_1P_2, P_2P_3 \dots P_nB$, and let $\alpha_1, \alpha_2 \dots \alpha_{n+1}$ be the angles which these successive portions make with the horizon.

We shall have for the equilibrium of $P_1, P_2, P_3 \dots$ in succession the following sets of equations,

$$t_1 \cos \alpha_1 = t_2 \cos \alpha_2, \qquad t_1 \sin \alpha_1 - t_2 \sin \alpha_2 = P_1 \ldots\ldots \text{(i)},$$
$$t_2 \cos \alpha_2 = t_3 \cos \alpha_3, \qquad t_2 \sin \alpha_2 - t_3 \sin \alpha_3 = P_2 \ldots\ldots \text{(ii)},$$
$$\ldots\ldots\ldots\ldots \qquad \ldots\ldots\ldots\ldots$$
$$t_n \cos \alpha_n = t_{n+1} \cos \alpha_{n+1}, \quad t_n \sin \alpha_n - t_{n+1} \sin \alpha_{n+1} = P_n \ldots\ldots (n).$$

If $a_1, a_2 \ldots a_{n+1}$ be the lengths of the successive portions of the strings $AP_1, P_1P_2 \ldots P_nB$, and a, b the *horizontal* and *vertical* distance between A and B, we have from the geometry of the figure the following equations,

$$\left.\begin{aligned} a_1 \cos \alpha_1 + a_2 \cos \alpha_2 + \ldots a_{n+1} \cos \alpha_{n+1} &= a \\ a_1 \sin \alpha_1 + a_2 \sin \alpha_2 + \ldots a_{n+1} \sin \alpha_{n+1} &= b \end{aligned}\right\} \ldots\ldots (n+1).$$

The sets of equations (i), (ii) ... $(n+1)$ are sufficient to determine the $2n+2$ quantities $t_1, t_2 \ldots t_{n+1}, \alpha_1, \alpha_2 \ldots \alpha_{n+1}$, and contain implicitly a complete solution of the problem.

From the first column of equations in (i), (ii) ... (n) it appears that the tension of each portion of the string *resolved horizontally* is of the same magnitude, and if we put this $= c$, so that $c = t_1 \cos \alpha_1 = t_2 \cos \alpha_2 = \ldots$ we obtain from the sets of equations (i), (ii) ... (n) the following results,

$$\left.\begin{aligned} \tan \alpha_1 - \tan \alpha_2 &= \frac{P_1}{c} \\ \tan \alpha_2 - \tan \alpha_3 &= \frac{P_2}{c} \\ \ldots\ldots\ldots\ldots &= \ldots \\ \tan \alpha_n - \tan \alpha_{n+1} &= \frac{P_n}{c} \end{aligned}\right\} \ldots\ldots\ldots\ldots \text{(A)},$$

from which we may obtain the following relations connecting the angles $\alpha_1, \alpha_2 \ldots$

$$\frac{\tan \alpha_1 - \tan \alpha_2}{\tan \alpha_2 - \tan \alpha_3} = \frac{P_1}{P_2}, \qquad \frac{\tan \alpha_2 - \tan \alpha_3}{\tan \alpha_3 - \tan \alpha_4} = \frac{P_2}{P_3}, \quad \text{\&c. \&c.}$$

If we simplify the problem by supposing the weights $P_1, P_2 \ldots$ each equal to w, the equations (A) become

$$\frac{w}{c} = \tan\alpha_1 - \tan\alpha_2 = \tan\alpha_2 - \tan\alpha_3 = \ldots = \tan\alpha_n - \tan\alpha_{n+1},$$

which results shew that the tangents of the angles $\alpha_1, \alpha_2 \ldots$ are in Arithmetical progression.

68. Cor. If ACB be a heavy uniform string or chain suspended from two points A, B;—C the lowest point of the string, and ϕ the angle which the tangent to it at any point P makes with the horizon, we may obtain a simple relation connecting ϕ with the length of the arc CP $(= s)$.

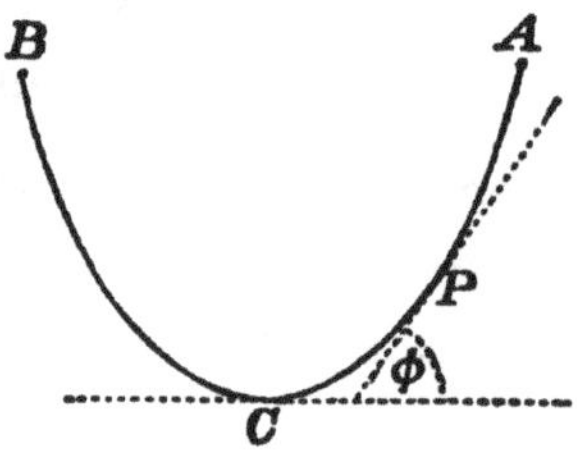

For we may regard the heavy string as made up of a series of small equal weights attached at small equal intervals, and so forming a funicular polygon:—and since the tangent at C is horizontal and the tangents of the angles which the successive elements of the string (taken from C) make with the horizon are in Arithmetic progression, $\tan\phi$ will for different positions of P vary as the number of the elements in the arc CP, *i.e.* $\tan\phi \propto s$.

And further, if c, t be the tensions of the string at C and P, we shall obtain for the conditions of equilibrium of CP (which for this purpose we may regard as a rigid body)

$$t\cos\phi = c, \quad t\sin\phi = s, \text{ and } \therefore \tan\phi = \frac{s}{c},$$

the weight of a unit of length of the string being here taken as the unit of weight.

CHAPTER V.

OF THE CENTRE OF GRAVITY.

69. THE attraction of the earth on any body would, if unopposed, draw it towards the surface of the earth.

The direction in which a particle would fall freely at any place is called the *vertical* line at that place. It coincides with the direction of a plumb-line, or the normal to the surface of standing water.

A plane perpendicular to this vertical line is said to be *horizontal*.

If we regard the earth as a sphere (which is very nearly the case), the vertical lines would all converge to the centre, and therefore the directions of the forces which the earth exerts on the different particles composing a body are not parallel, strictly speaking. But since the dimension of any body we shall have to consider is very small compared with the radius of the earth, we may consider these directions to be appreciably parallel, and the resultant attraction on the body or system equal to the sum of the attractions on the constituent particles; i.e. the *weight* of the whole equal to the sum of the weights of the several parts.

The object of the present chapter is to shew that for every body or system of particles there exists a point through which the resultant attraction of the earth may be supposed to act; i.e. a point at which we may suppose the weight of the body to be collected,—a point whose position depends only on the relative arrangement of the particles composing the body or system, and on the relative constitution of these particles. If this point then were in rigid connexion with all the parts of the system, all positions of the body or system would be positions of equilibrium, if this point were supported.

Such a point in a body or system is called the *centre of gravity* of the body or system, and we give the following definition.—The point at which the weight of a body or system may always be supposed to act, whatever be the position of the body or system with respect to a horizontal plane, is called the *centre of gravity* of the body.

70. We shall first shew that such a point exists in any system of particles.

PROP. *Every system of heavy particles has one and only one centre of gravity.*

First let us consider two heavy particles A, B, whose weights are P, Q, and suppose them connected by a rigid rod without weight. Now, since P and Q act through A and B in parallel directions and towards the same parts,

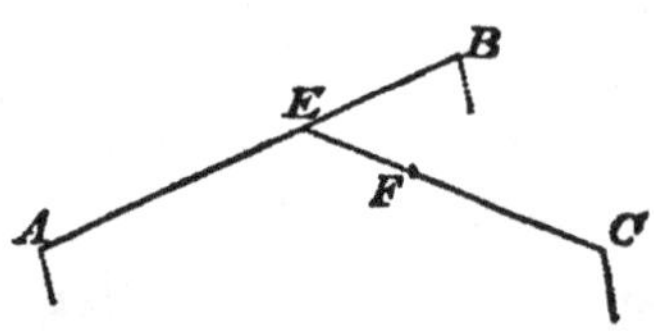

they are equivalent to a single resultant, the magnitude of which $= P + Q$, and which acts through a point E in the line AB, such that $P : Q = BE : AE$; and since the position of E in the line AB does not at all involve the direction of action of gravity, if this point E were supported, this system of two particles would balance about E in any position. E then is the centre of gravity of A, B, and the statical effect of P and Q will be the same as if they were collected into one particle and placed at E.

Again, if there are three particles A, B, C whose weights are P, Q, R, we can take E the centre of gravity of P, Q as before, and suppose $P+Q$ placed at E instead of A and B, and we then have two particles at E and C whose weights are $P+Q$ and R; these then, as before, have a centre of gravity at a point F in the line EC, such that

$$P+Q : R = CF : FE,$$

and we may suppose P, Q, R all collected at F so far as their statical effect is concerned. And so on whatever be the number of particles, so that every system of heavy particles has a centre of gravity.

Also a system of particles can have but one *centre of gravity.* For, if possible, let a system have two such points G and G', and let the system be turned about if necessary till the line joining G, G' is horizontal. Then we have the weight of the system acting in a vertical line through G, and also in another vertical line through G'; which is impossible, since it cannot act in two different lines at the same time.

We should arrive at the same point G in whatever order we may take the points A, B, C...

COR. 1. Since every continuous body is an aggregation of a great number of particles, every body has a centre of gravity through which the resultant weight of the particles acts: and we may suppose the weight of the whole body collected at its centre of gravity.

And we may proceed to find the centre of gravity of a *system* of bodies by supposing them to be a series of heavy particles, the weights of which are equal to the weights of the bodies, and which are in the position of the centres of gravity of the several bodies.

COR. 2. The determination of the successive points E, F, &c. in the previous proposition does not require the actual weights P, Q, R, but only their ratios. Hence if the weights of the several parts of a system be all diminished or all increased in any the same proportion, the *position* of the centre of gravity will not be altered.

COR. 3. Since the weights P, Q, R...are equivalent to a series of parallel forces acting at the points A, B, C..., and the position of the centre of gravity does not depend on the direction in which these forces act, but only on their relative magnitude and their points of application; it would therefore remain in the same position if the direction of these forces were turned about their points of application in any manner, still remaining parallel. Hence the point under consideration is sometimes called *the centre of parallel forces.*

71. *Having given the centre of gravity of a body and also of a part of the body, to find the centre of gravity of the remaining part.*

Let w_1, w_2 be the weights of the two parts of the body; G_1, G_2 their respective centres of gravity:—then G the centre of gravity of the whole body must be a point in the straight line which joins $G_1\,G_2$, such that

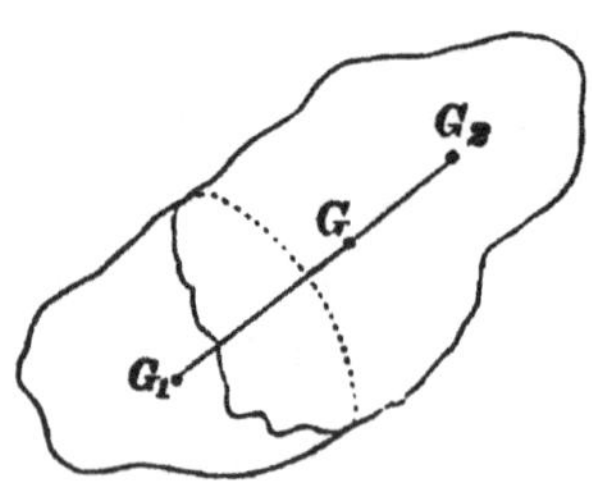

$$w_2 \,.\, GG_2 = w_1 \,.\, GG_1.$$

Hence if G and G_1 are given in position, join $G_1\,G$ and produce it to G_2 making $GG_2 = \frac{w_1}{w_2} \,.\, GG_1$, and thus the position of G_2 the point required is determined.

72. Before proceeding to give a general method of finding the centre of gravity of any system of particles, we will give a few examples of finding the centre of gravity,—premising that when we speak of a line, or plane, or surface as having a centre of gravity, we suppose it to be made up of equal particles of matter uniformly diffused over it: unless some other supposition is stated.

I. *To find the centre of gravity of a right line.*

Considering it as a line of equal particles uniformly arranged, it is clear that the middle point of the line is its centre of gravity. For we may divide the line into a series of pairs of equal elements, the particles composing any pair being equidistant from the middle point. Hence the centre of gravity of each pair is at the middle point, and therefore the centre of gravity of the whole is there also.

II. *To find the centre of gravity of a parallelogram.*

Let *ABCD* be a parallelogram regarded as a uniform lamina of matter, and draw the line *EF* parallel to *AB* or *CD* and bisecting *AD* and *BC*,—and also the line *HK* parallel to *AD* and bisecting *AB* and *CD*. The point *G* in which *HK*, *EF* intersect is the centre of gravity required. For by drawing lines parallel to *BC* and at equal distances from each other, we may divide the parallelogram *AC* into a number of equal small parallelograms whose lengths are all equal *BC* and breadths as small as we please; and we may take the breadths so small that each may be regarded as a line of particles, the centre of gravity of which is at its middle point,

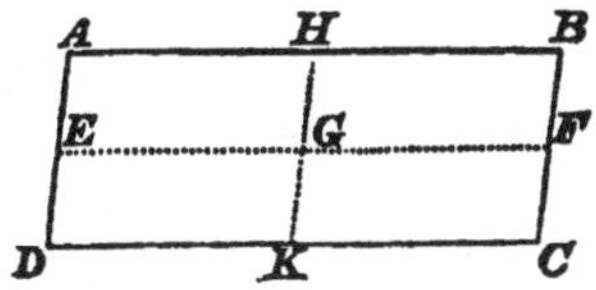

and which therefore is on the line EF, since EF bisects every line that is parallel to BC.

Hence the centre of gravity of the whole parallelogram lies in EF. Similarly it may be shewn to lie in HK.

Therefore G the point of intersection of EF, HK is the centre of gravity of the parallelogram.

III. *To find the centre of gravity of a plane triangle.*

Let ABC be a plane triangular lamina of matter. From any two of the angular points B, C, draw lines BF, CE bisecting the opposite sides in F, E and cutting each other in G. G is the centre of gravity of the triangle.

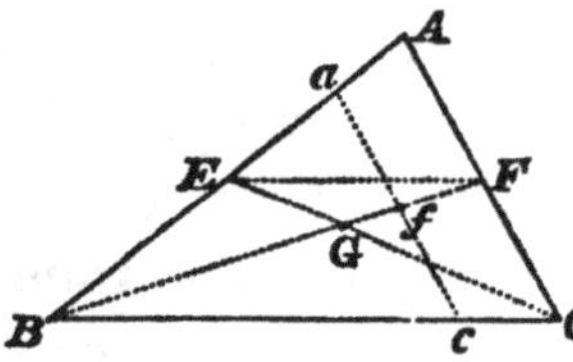

By drawing a series of lines parallel to one of the sides AC at equal distances, we may divide the triangle into a number of quadrilaterals, each of which, when their number is sufficiently increased, may be regarded as a uniform material line.

Let ac be one such line cutting BF in f; then we have

$$af : AF = Bf : BF$$
$$= cf : CF;$$

by the two pairs of similar triangles afB, AFB and cfB, CFB.

Hence $af : cf = AF : CF$

$$= 1 : 1;$$

$\therefore af = cf$; i.e. f is the middle point of ac, and is consequently its centre of gravity.

Hence the centre of gravity of each of the lines composing the triangle is in BF, and therefore the centre of gravity of the triangle is in BF.

Similarly the centre of gravity of the triangle may be shewn to be in CE, whence we infer that G is the centre of gravity required.

Further, if we join EF,

By similar triangles BGC, FGE;

$$\therefore BG : GF = BC : EF$$
$$= BA : AE \text{ by similar triangles } AEF, ABC$$
$$= 2 : 1;$$
$$\text{i.e. } BG = 2 . GF;$$
$$\therefore BF = 3 . GF;$$
$$\text{i.e. } GF = \tfrac{1}{3} BF, \text{ and } BG = \tfrac{2}{3} BF.$$

In words, if a line be drawn from an angular point to the middle of the opposite side, the centre of gravity of the triangle lies on this line at a distance from the angular point equal to two-thirds of the length of the line.

COR. From this result it is easily seen that the centre of gravity of the triangle coincides in position with that of three equal particles placed at the angular points.

73. *To find the centre of gravity of the perimeter of a triangle—regarding the sides as material lines of uniform thickness.*

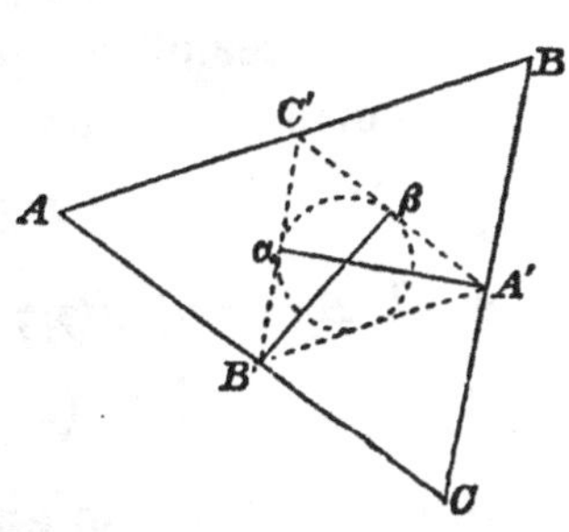

Let A', B', C' be the middle points of the sides of the proposed triangle ABC—then the centre of gravity of the perimeter ABC will be in the same position as that of three particles placed at A', B', C', and whose weights are proportional to BC, CA, AB respectively. Draw

$A'\alpha$, $B'\beta$ bisecting the angles A', B' of the triangle $A'B'C'$, then Euclid VI. 3,

$$B'\alpha : C'\alpha = A'B' : A'C' = AB : AC.$$

Hence α is the centre of gravity of the two sides AB, AC, and therefore the centre of gravity of the whole perimeter lies in the line $A'\alpha$,—similarly it lies in the line $B'\beta$,—the centre of gravity required must therefore be the point of intersection of these two lines—which is the centre of the circle inscribed in the triangle $A'B'C'$.

74. Having shewn that every system of particles has one and only one centre of gravity, we proceed to shew how to find it in any case;

(i) for a series of particles lying in a straight line.
(ii) .... in one plane.
(iii) .... arranged in any manner in space.

I. *To find the centre of gravity of a series of heavy particles lying in a straight line.*

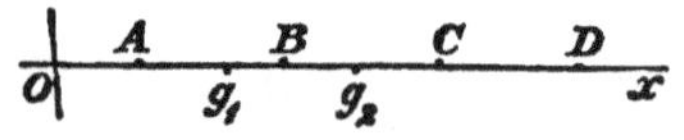

Let A, B, C... be the several particles whose weights are P, Q, R... and lying in the straight line Ox. Let O be a fixed point in the line, and let x_1, x_2, x_3... be the distances of the particles A, B, C...from O; then if g_1 be the centre of gravity of A and B,

$$P : Q = Bg_1 : Ag_1,$$

or $P.Ag_1 = Q.Bg_1$; i.e. $P(Og_1 - x_1) = Q(x_2 - Og_1)$;

i.e. $(P+Q)\ Og_1 = Px_1 + Qx_2$............(i);

a result which we might have obtained at once from the

consideration that since the resultant of the forces P and Q at A and B passes through g_1, the sum of the moments of P and Q about any point O is equal to the moment of their resultant $P+Q$.

Again, considering P and Q as collected at g_1, if g_2 be the centre of gravity of $P+Q$ at g_1 and R at C, we have as before

$$(P+Q+R)\,Og_2=(P+Q)\,Og_1+Rx_3$$
$$=Px_1+Qx_2+Rx_3,\text{ by (i)} \ldots\ldots \text{(ii)}.$$

Similarly $(P+Q+R+S)\,Og_3=(P+Q+R)\,Og_2+Sx_4$
$$=Px_1+Qx_2+Rx_3+Sx_4 \ldots \text{(iii)}.$$

And so on for any number of particles.

Hence if we call $\bar{x}$ the distance of G the centre of gravity of the whole from O,

$$\bar{x}=\frac{Px_1+Qx_2+Rx_3+Sx_4+\ldots}{P+Q+R+\ldots}=\frac{\Sigma(Px)}{\Sigma(P)} \ldots\ldots\ldots\ldots \text{(iv)}.$$

The centre of gravity then is in the same line as the particles, and the distance of it from any assumed point O is given by (iv).

II. *To find the centre of gravity of a series of heavy particles lying in one plane.*

Let $A, B, C\ldots$ be the system of particles whose weights are $P, Q, R\ldots$ and let them be referred to two axes Ox, Oy at right angles to one another in the plane in which the particles are. Join AB, and take g_1 the centre of gravity of P and Q

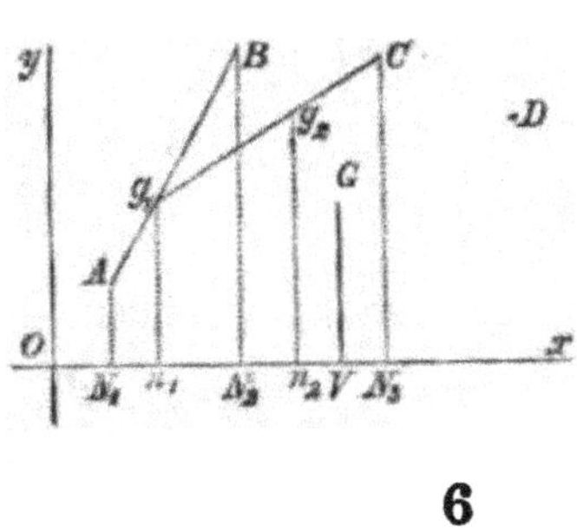

at A and B so that $P : Q = Bg_1 : Ag_1$. Join g_1C, and take g_2 the centre of gravity of $P+Q$ at g_1 and R at C so that

$$P+Q : R = Cg_2 : g_1g_2,$$

and so on till we find G the centre of gravity of the whole, as in Art. 70. Draw AN_1, g_1n_1, BN_2... parallel to Oy, meeting Ox in N_1, n_1, ...

If now we call $\left.\begin{matrix} ON_1 = x_1 \\ AN_1 = y_1 \end{matrix}\right\}$, $\left.\begin{matrix} ON_2 = x_2 \\ BN_2 = y_2 \end{matrix}\right\}$ &c. $\left.\begin{matrix} OV = \bar{x} \\ GV = \bar{y} \end{matrix}\right\}$,

our object is to find $\bar{x}$, $\bar{y}$ which determine the position of G, in terms of x_1y_1... and P, Q...

Now, considering g_1 the centre of gravity of A and B, we have

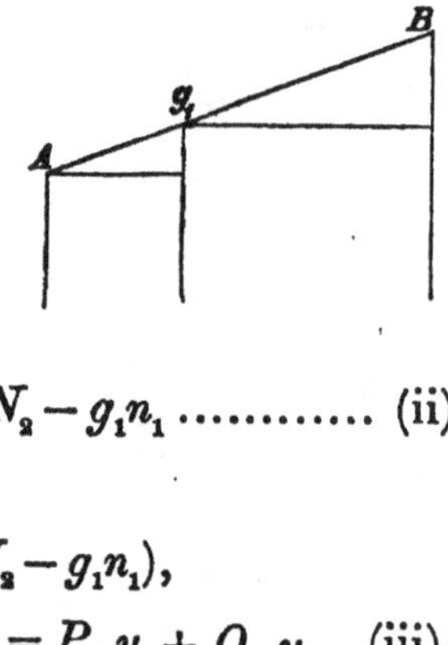

$$P \cdot Ag_1 = Q \cdot Bg_1 \text{............(i)};$$

and if through A and g_1 we draw two lines parallel to N_1N_2 we should have two similar triangles; comparing the sides of which we get

$$Ag_1 : Bg_1 = g_1n_1 - AN_1 : BN_2 - g_1n_1 \text{ .... (ii)},$$

whence from (i) and (ii)

$$P \cdot (g_1n_1 - AN_1) = Q \cdot (BN_2 - g_1n_1),$$

$$\text{or } (P+Q)\, g_1n_1 = P \cdot AN_1 + Q \cdot BN_2 = P \cdot y_1 + Q \cdot y_2 \text{...(iii)};$$

now introducing a third particle C we have similarly

$$(P+Q+R)\, g_2n_2 = (P+Q)\, g_1n_1 + R \cdot CN_3,$$

$$= P \cdot y_1 + Q \cdot y_2 + R \cdot y_3 \text{ .... (iv)},$$

and so on whatever be the number of particles;

$$\text{i.e. } \bar{y} = GV = \frac{P \cdot y_1 + Q \cdot y_2 + \dots}{P+Q+\dots} = \frac{\Sigma(Py)}{\Sigma(P)} \text{ .... (v)}.$$

By a similar mode of proceeding we shall obtain

$$\bar{x} = \frac{\Sigma (Px)}{\Sigma (P)} \text{..........................(vi)}.$$

These two results (v) and (vi) determine the position of the centre of gravity of the system of particles, which lies in the plane of the particles.

III. *To find the centre of gravity of a system of particles arranged in any manner in space.*

Let the system of particles $A, B, C\ldots$ whose weights are $P, Q, R\ldots$ be referred to three lines Ox, Oy, Oz mutually at right angles;

let g_1 be the C.G. of A and B.

g_2 ....A, B, and C, &c.

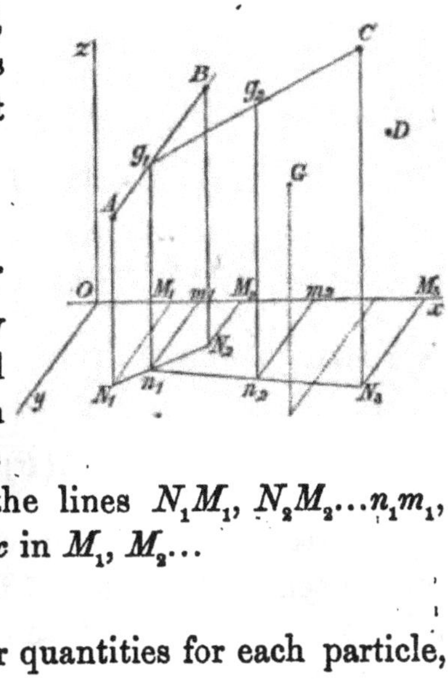

Through $A\ B\ C\ldots g_1 g_2\ldots$ draw AN_1, $BN_2\ldots g_1 n_1$, $g_2 n_2$ parallel to Oz meeting the plane xOy in $N_1, N_2\ldots n_1, n_2\ldots$ and through these points draw in the plane xOy the lines N_1M_1, $N_2M_2\ldots n_1m_1$, $n_2m_2\ldots$ parallel to Oy meeting Ox in $M_1, M_2\ldots$

If now $\left.\begin{aligned} OM_1 &= x_1 \\ M_1N_1 &= y_1 \\ N_1A &= z_1 \end{aligned}\right\}$ and similar quantities for each particle,

and if $\bar{x}\ \bar{y}\ \bar{z}$ be the corresponding quantities for G, the centre of gravity of the system,—we have, considering A and B only at first,

$$P \,.\, Ag_1 = Q \,.\, Bg_1;$$

or if we draw lines through A_1, g_1 parallel to N_1N_2, we have by similar triangles

$$Ag_1 : Bg_1 = g_1n_1 - AN_1 : BN_2 - g_1n_1,$$

whence $P.(g_1n_1 - AN_1) = Q.(BN_2 - g_1n_1)$;

$$\text{i.e.}\quad (P+Q).g_1n_1 = P.AN_1 + Q.BN_2$$
$$= P.z_1 + Q.z_2;$$

similarly introducing another particle C, g_2 being the centre of gravity of A, B, C, and therefore the centre of gravity of $P+Q$ at g_1 and R at C;

$$(P+Q+R)\,g_2n_2 = (P+Q)\,g_1n_1 + R.CN_3$$
$$= P.z_1 + Q.z_2 + R.z_3,$$

and so on for any number of particles—till we get

$$(P+Q+\ldots)\,GV = P.z_1 + Q.z_2 + \ldots$$

$$\text{or } \bar{z} = \frac{P.z_1 + Q.z_2 + \ldots}{P+Q+\ldots} = \frac{\Sigma(Pz)}{\Sigma(P)},$$

we should similarly have

$$\bar{y} = \frac{\Sigma(Py)}{\Sigma(P)} \text{ and } \bar{x} = \frac{\Sigma(Px)}{(\Sigma P)}.$$

These three expressions for $\bar{x}\,\bar{y}\,\bar{z}$ determine the position of the centre of gravity of the system of particles considered. This includes I. and II. as particular cases.

75. *Obs.* In the case III. of the preceding article it will in general be convenient to take the lines Ox, Oy, Oz at right angles, but the student will observe that the course of the proof does not require that the lines Ox, Oy, Oz should be inclined at any particular angles: he may then in any par-

ticular case assume three lines (not in one plane) inclined at any angles which may appear to him most convenient in the case under his consideration;—and a similar remark applies to case II.

DEF. *The moment of a force with respect to a plane* is the product of the *force* into *the distance of its point of application from the plane.* If the points of application of two forces are on opposite sides of a given plane, the moments of the forces with respect to that plane will have opposite signs. This must be carefully distinguished from the moment of a force with respect to a *point* or *an axis*. Art. 31.

COR. 1. We see from the results of Art. 74, that the algebraic sum of the moments of the particles of a system with respect to *any* plane is equal to the moment of the whole (supposed to be collected at the centre of gravity) with respect to the same plane.

From whence follows the conclusion, that if the algebraic sum of the moments of a system taken with respect to any proposed plane be zero, the centre of gravity of the system lies in that plane; and *vice versâ*, if the centre of gravity of a system lie in a given plane, the algebraic sum of the moments of the particles with respect to that plane is zero,—or in other words, the sum of the moments of the particles which are on one side of the plane is equal to the sum of the moments of the particles which are on the other side of the plane.

COR. 2. If we suppose a system to be divided into any number n of particles of equal weights we have the distance of centre of gravity from any plane $=\frac{1}{n}$th the sum of the distances of all the particles from the same plane. Viewed in this manner, the centre of gravity of a body or system is sometimes called the *centre of mean position* of the body or system, or the *centre of figure.*

COR. 3. If a system of particles be projected on any plane, the projection of the centre of gravity of the system on that plane will be the centre of gravity of a system of particles in the plane, equal to the former and coincident with the points of projection of the original system.

This appears at once from the results of Art. (74), for the values of $\bar{x}\,\bar{y}\,\bar{z}$ depend only on the weights of the particles and their distances estimated parallel to Ox, Oy, Oz from the planes yOz, zOx, xOy severally.

76. *Centre of parallel forces.*

If in any of the cases of Art. (74), $A, B, C\ldots$ be the point of application of a system of parallel forces $P, Q, R, \ldots$ the method pursued in that article will lead to formulæ for the co-ordinates of the point of application of the resultant of such a system of parallel forces, viz.

$$\bar{x} = \frac{\Sigma(Px)}{\Sigma(P)}, \quad \bar{y} = \frac{\Sigma(Py)}{\Sigma(P)}, \quad \bar{z} = \frac{\Sigma(Pz)}{\Sigma(P)} \quad \ldots\ldots\ldots \text{(i)},$$

in the most general case.

These results are algebraically true whether the forces act all in the same direction or not—and we may interpret them as stating that the resultant of a system of parallel forces is $= \Sigma(P)$ acting at a point whose co-ordinates are given by equation (i).

If however $\Sigma(P)=0$, and the expressions $\Sigma(Px)$, $\Sigma(Py)$, $\Sigma(Pz)$ do not each $=0$ also, the system will be equivalent to a *couple* which does not admit of being represented by a single resultant force, Art. (30).

77. The position of the centre of gravity of a body or a system of particles depends (as we have seen, Art. 74) only on two things; (i), the form of the body, or, in other words, the arrangement of the particles of the system; and (ii), the relative density of the different parts.

Formulæ have been obtained in Art. 74, by which the centre of gravity of any system of *particles* whose relative weights and position are known, may be found; and we have seen in Cor. 1, Art. 70, that a *body* may be considered as a particle placed at the centre of gravity of the body, so that if the centres of gravity of the several bodies composing a system be known, we are enabled to find the centre of gravity of the system, and the problem assumes a general character.

The determination however of the centre of gravity of a *body* (either a continuous solid body, or a surface regarded as a lamina of matter of indefinitely small thickness) will in general require the aid of the Integral Calculus.

Obs. Cases will not unfrequently arise in which the position of the centre of gravity can be assigned from geometrical considerations such as the following, which are suggested for the consideration of the student.

1°. If in any body or system a plane can be found which divides the body into two parts which are symmetrical with respect to the plane on opposite sides of it, the centre of gravity of the body must lie in that plane.

For since the body is divided symmetrically into two parts, these parts must be equal, and their centres of gravity at equal distances from the plane on opposite sides of it. Hence the centre of gravity of the whole, which is the middle point of the line joining the centre of gravity of the two parts, must lie in the plane under consideration.

2°. Hence it follows readily, that if three planes can be assigned, each of which divides the body or system symmetrically into two parts, the common point of intersection of the planes is the centre of gravity of the body.

3°. Observation 1° applies to all bodies or systems of bodies of uniform density; it is also true if the densities are not uniform, provided the densities of all elements of the body symmetrically situated on opposite sides of the plane are severally the same. The same may be said of curved surfaces. But in the case of plane areas we need only consider lines in its plane which divide the area symmetrically, and we may assert (with a proof similar to that of 1°), that in any plane area if a line can be found which divides it into symmetrical parts, the centre of gravity lies in that line; and further, if two such lines can be found their point of intersection is the centre of gravity of the area.

The same remarks apply in this case as in that of a body, if the density of the area be not uniform.

78. Some conclusions arising from these observations, 1°, 2°, 3°, are the following.

(i) The centre of gravity of a right line is its middle point.

(ii) The centre of gravity of a parallelogram is the intersection of its two diagonals; in other words, the middle point of one of them.

(iii) The centre of gravity of a solid parallelopiped, or of the surface of a parallelopiped, is the intersection of its four diagonals, which is the middle point of any one of them.

(iv) The centre of gravity of a circular area, or of a circular ring, is the centre of the circle.

And that of a solid sphere, or a spherical surface, or spherical shell, is the centre of the sphere.

These results will be of frequent use.

79. *To find the centre of gravity of a pyramid on a triangular base.*

Let ABC be the base of the pyramid, and V its vertex.

Take D the middle point of one of the sides BC, and join AD, VD, in which take E and H such that $AE = \frac{2}{3}AD$ and $VH = \frac{2}{3}VD$, (and HE is therefore parallel to AV); then E, H are the centres of gravity of the triangles ABC, VBC; if now we join VE, AH, they will intersect in some point G, since they both lie in the plane AVD.

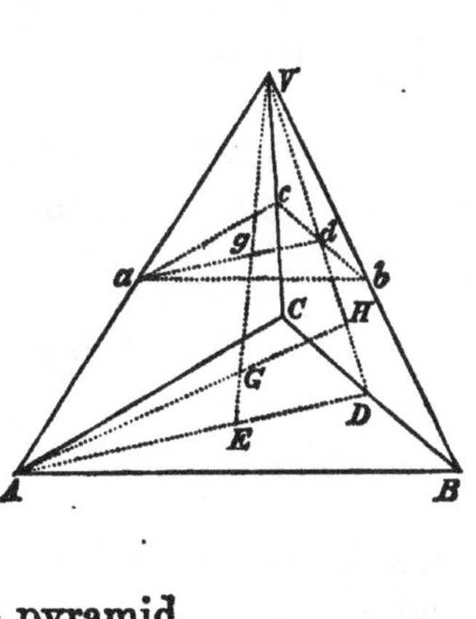

G is the centre of gravity of the pyramid.

For suppose the pyramid to be made up of an indefinite

number of thin triangular plates all parallel and similar to ABC, and let abc be any one of these;

if VD meet bc in d, and VE meet ad in g, we have by similar triangles,

$$ag : AE = Vg : VE = gd : ED;$$

$$\therefore\ ag : gd = AE : ED = 2 : 1.$$

Hence since d is the middle point of bc, g is the centre of gravity of the plate abc.

Similarly it may be shewn that the centres of gravity of all the plates of which the pyramid is composed lie in the line VE.

And in a similar way by supposing the pyramid made up of plates parallel to VBC, the centre of gravity of the whole may be shewn to lie in AH.

Hence G the point of intersection of VE, AH is the centre of gravity of the pyramid.

Further if we join HE which will be parallel to AV, we have by similar triangles AVG, HGE.

$$\frac{VG}{GE} = \frac{AV}{HE} = \frac{AD}{ED} = 3;\ \therefore\ VG = 3 . GE;$$

$$\therefore\ VE = 4GE, \text{ or } EG = \tfrac{1}{4}VE, \text{ and } \therefore\ VG = \tfrac{3}{4}VE;$$

i. e. if the vertex be joined with the centre of gravity of the base, the centre of gravity of the pyramid is a point in this line at a distance of $\frac{3}{4}$ths of it from the vertex, and $\frac{1}{4}$th of it from the base.

COR. 1. *To find the centre of gravity of any pyramid whose base is a plane polygon.*

Join V the vertex with O the centre of gravity of the base, and in this line take a point G at a distance from the base equal to $\frac{1}{4}$th of the length of the line. G shall be the centre of gravity of the pyramid. For it may be shewn as in the present article, by supposing the pyramid to be made up of plates parallel to the base, that the centre of gravity of the pyramid lies in this line.

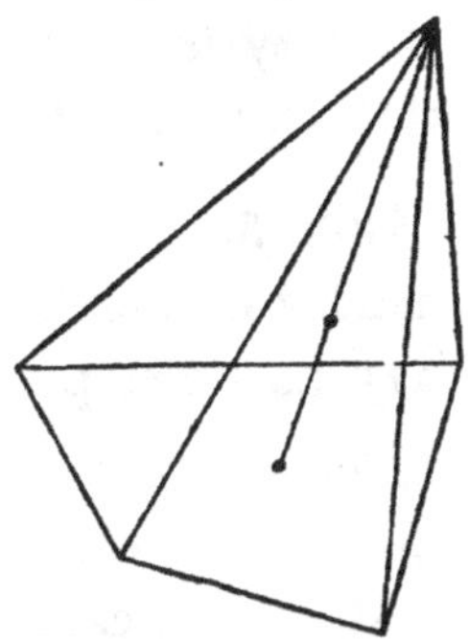

And again, by dividing the base into triangles the pyramid may be divided into a series of triangular pyramids having a common vertex: and if we draw a plane through G parallel to the base, this plane will contain the centres of gravity of all the triangular pyramids, since it would cut the line which joins the vertex with the centre of gravity of the base of any of the triangular pyramids in a point whose distance from the base is $\frac{1}{4}$th of the length of the line.

Since then the centres of gravity of all the triangular pyramids lie in this plane, and it has been shewn to lie in the line VO, G must be the centre of gravity of the pyramid.

COR. 2. Since a curve may be regarded as the limit of a polygon, whose sides are indefinitely increased in number and diminished in magnitude, we may consider a cone on any base as the limit of a pyramid, and its centre of gravity will be in the line joining the vertex with the centre of gravity of the base, at a distance from the vertex equal to $\frac{3}{4}$ths of this line.

If the cone be a right cone on a circular base, the centre of gravity is in the axis of the cone, at a distance from the vertex equal to $\frac{3}{4}$ths of its length.

COR. 3. The centre of gravity of a triangular pyramid coincides in position with the centre of gravity of four equal heavy particles placed at its angular points.

For we easily see by the construction that E is the centre of gravity of three equal particles P placed at A, B, C, and G will be the centre of gravity of $3P$ at E, and P at V, since $GV : EV = 3 : 4$.

COR. 4. We can proceed to find the centre of gravity of any solid bounded by plane faces. For we may divide the solid into a series of pyramids, the centre of gravity of each of which can be found, and if we suppose at each of these points weights to be placed proportional to the several pyramids, the centre of gravity of these weights will coincide with the centre of gravity of the solid.

Similarly with any plane area bounded by straight lines, by dividing it into a series of triangles, and supposing particles placed at the centre of gravity of each triangle proportional to the areas of the triangles, the centre of gravity of these particles will be the centre of gravity of the area.

80. Before concluding this chapter we will give a few general theorems relating to the centre of gravity.

I. *If a body be suspended from a point about which it can swing freely, it will rest with its centre of gravity in the vertical line which passes through the point of suspension.*

Let AC be the body, G its centre of gravity, and S the point of suspension. Draw GV vertical, and SV horizontal to meet GV in V; then the only forces which act on the body are its weight, which acts in the vertical line VG, and the reaction arising from the fixed point S.

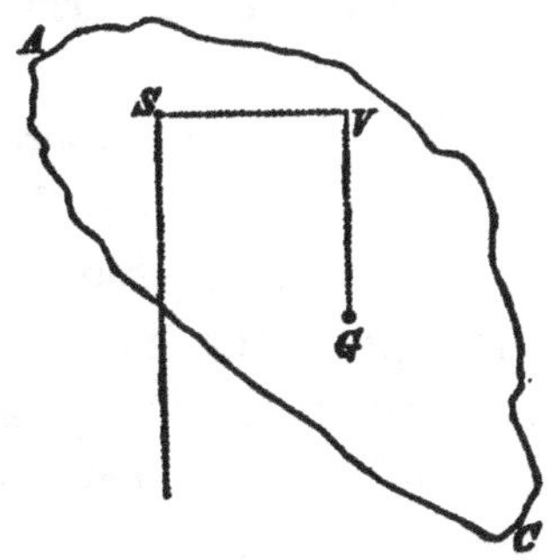

These two forces cannot balance each other (and consequently the body cannot be at rest) unless they act in the same line in opposite directions, i. e. unless VG pass through S.

i.e. the body cannot be at rest unless the vertical line through G pass through S; and when this is the case, the fixed point will exert a force on the body sufficient to balance the weight of the body and therefore equal and opposite to that weight.

Or we might reason thus. When a body is at rest under the action of forces in one plane, the moments of the forces about any point vanish: but in this case, if we take the moments about S, the weight of the body has a moment about S = weight × SV, which is not counterbalanced by any other moment, and this cannot vanish unless $SV = 0$, i. e. unless the line joining S and G is vertical. Whence the same conclusion as before.

COR. This proposition leads to a mode of determining the centre of gravity of a body which may sometimes be practically available, *thus*,—Let the body be suspended freely from any points of its surface in succession, and let the line in the body which is vertical and passes through the point of suspension be noted in each case,—the point of intersection of two such lines is the centre of gravity sought.

81. In the proposition, G may either be directly above or below S when in a position of equilibrium; but the nature of the equilibrium is very different in the two cases. In fig. 2 if the body be slightly displaced by turning it about S through a small angle, it is evident G would be raised, and if the body be then left to the action of gravity, its first tendency would be to return towards its former position of equilibrium.

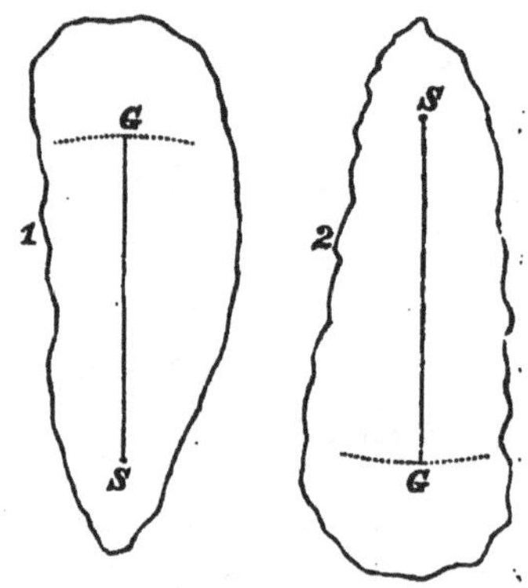

But in figure 1 if the body were slightly displaced by being turned about S through a small angle, the tendency of the body would be to recede further and further from its position of equilibrium.

The above are simple cases of equilibrium, which are called *stable* and *unstable* respectively; the meaning of which the student will understand from the following definition.

Def. When a body is in equilibrium under the action of a system of forces, if the body be slightly displaced the action of the forces on the body in its new position will *in general* tend either to make it return towards or recede from its original position of equilibrium; in the former case the equilibrium is said to be *stable*, or the body to be in a position of *stable* equilibrium; in the latter, the equilibrium is said to be *unstable*, or the body is said to be in a position of *unstable* equilibrium.

We say *in general*, because the above is not always the case, for in certain cases the forces in the new position of the body may still have no tendency to make the body move one way or the other; a position of this kind is called one of *neutral* equilibrium—as in the case of a sphere resting on a horizontal table.

Or again, the forces in the new position may tend to make the body neither return to its former position nor recede from it, but to give it a rocking or rolling motion; as in the case of an ellipsoid resting on a horizontal plane at the extremity of its mean axis.

82. II. *A body placed on a horizontal plane will stand or fall over, according as the vertical line drawn through the centre of gravity of the body falls within or without the base.*

Let $ACBD$ be the base of the body in contact with the plane, GE the vertical line drawn through the centre of gravity of the body and meeting the base in some point E within it.

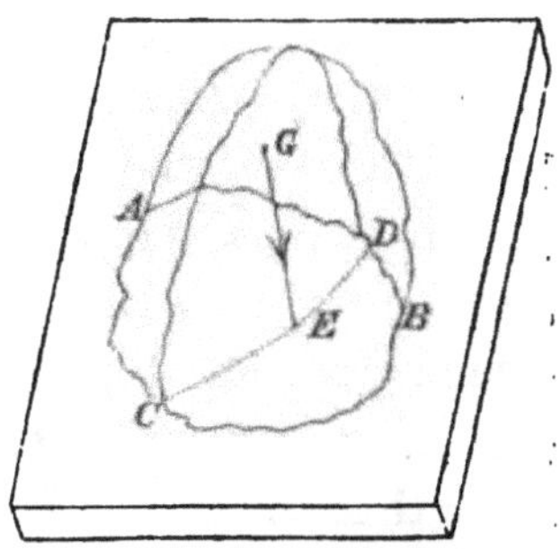

Now the pressure which the weight of the body exercises on the plane is equal to a weight W acting in GE.

And if E lies within the base, the plane will be capable of exercising a vertical pressure passing through E of sufficient magnitude just to balance W; and the body will be in equilibrium.

But if E fall without the base the plane cannot exert a pressure which shall pass through E and balance W: in this case then the body will not be in equilibrium, but will begin to fall over by turning round some tangent line to the perimeter of the base, and this will obviously be about the point of the base which is nearest to E.

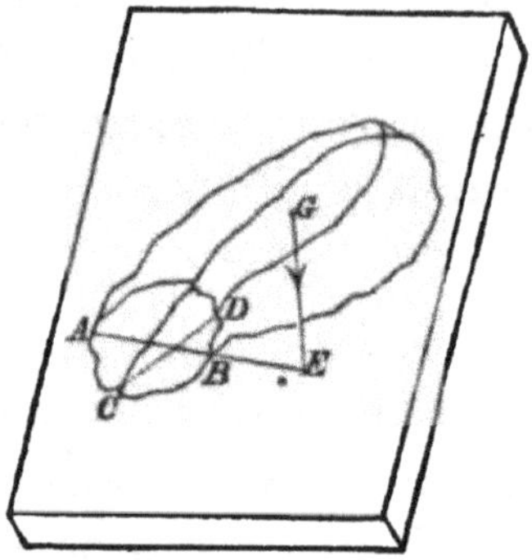

Obs. By the base here is meant the extreme polygon formed by joining all the points of contact of the base—or the area enclosed by a string drawn tightly about the base.

COR. 1. In a similar manner it may be shewn that if a body be placed on an inclined plane and it be prevented from sliding along the plane by friction or otherwise, the body will stand or fall over according as a vertical line drawn through the centre of gravity of the body falls within or without the base.

COR. 2. In figure (1) if an effort were made to make the body turn about some point A in the perimeter of its base, the moment about A of the force employed must be at least equal to the moment of the weight of the body about A; which moment is $= W.AE$. This moment then measures the effort necessary to make the body fall over; and it is clear that the less AE is, the less effort will be required. If $AE = 0$, the moment vanishes, and any the slightest effort would make the body fall over. This accounts for the difficulty of making a body balance about a *point* immediately under the centre of gravity.

Compare with this the remarks on stable and unstable equilibrium, in the previous article.

83. When a rough body BAC rests upon another PAQ fixed—the surfaces near A the point of contact being spherical—the condition of the *stability* or *instability* of the equilibrium may be simply investigated thus.

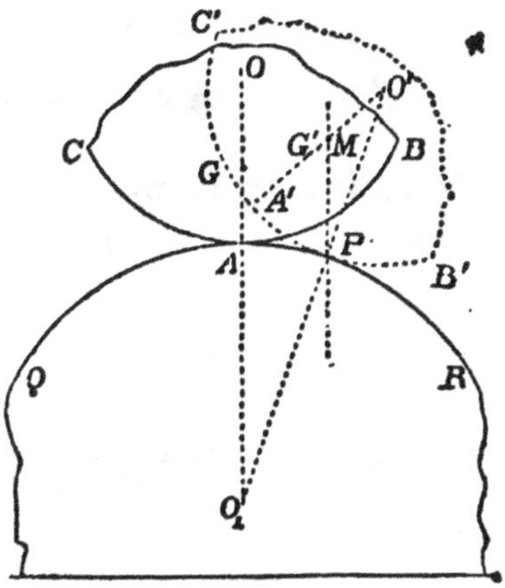

The common normal to the two surfaces at A will be vertical and will pass through O, O_1 the centres of the spherical surfaces of BAC, QAR, and also through G the centre of gravity of BAC. Let BAC be displaced *by rolling through a small angle* so as to come into the position $B'A'C'$—through P the new point of contact draw PM vertical, meeting $A'O'$ in M. Then according as $A'G'$ is $<$ or $>$ $A'M$, the weight of $B'A'C'$ will tend to make it return towards or recede further from its original position of equilibrium by turning about the point of contact P—that is, the equilibrium will be *stable* or *unstable* respectively.

Let $AO = r$, $AO_1 = R$, $AG = h$, $\angle AO_1P = \theta = MPO'$, $A'O'P = \phi$, so that $r\phi = R\theta$ since the arc $AP =$ arc $A'P$.

$$\text{Now } \frac{O'M}{r} = \frac{O'M}{O'P} = \frac{\sin\theta}{\sin(\theta+\phi)} = \frac{\sin\theta}{\sin\left(\frac{R+r}{r}\theta\right)} = \frac{r}{R+r},$$

in the limit when θ is taken very small;

$$\therefore\ O'M = \frac{r^2}{R+r};$$

$$\therefore\ A'M = r - O'M = r - \frac{r^2}{R+r} = \frac{Rr}{R+r},$$

and the equilibrium is stable or unstable according as h is $<$ or $>$ $A'M$, *i. e.* $h <> \frac{Rr}{R+r}$.

Or, as it may be written,

$$\frac{1}{h} >< \frac{1}{r} + \frac{1}{R}.$$

Obs. If G', M coincide—the displacement being *very small*,—in which case $\frac{1}{h} = \frac{1}{r} + \frac{1}{R}$—the equilibrium is said to be *neutral*.

84. *Obs.* (i) If the surface QAR be concave, we may change the sign of R, and we shall have the equilibrium *stable* or *unstable* according as

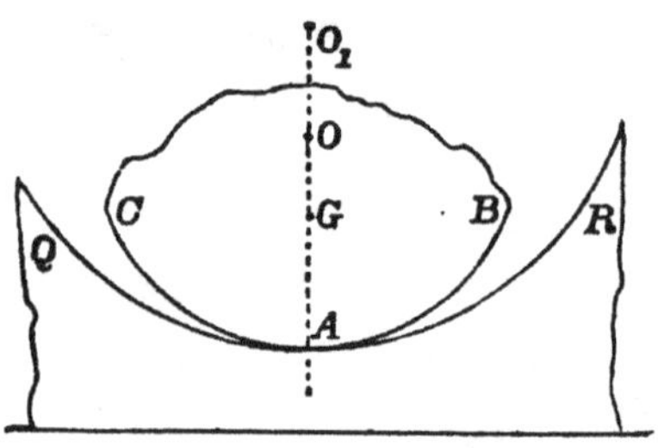

$$\frac{1}{h} > \text{or} < \frac{1}{r} - \frac{1}{R}.$$

(ii) If the surface of BAC be *plane*—as in the case of a solid resting with its plane base upon a curved surface—$r = \infty$, and the equilibrium is *stable* or *unstable* according as

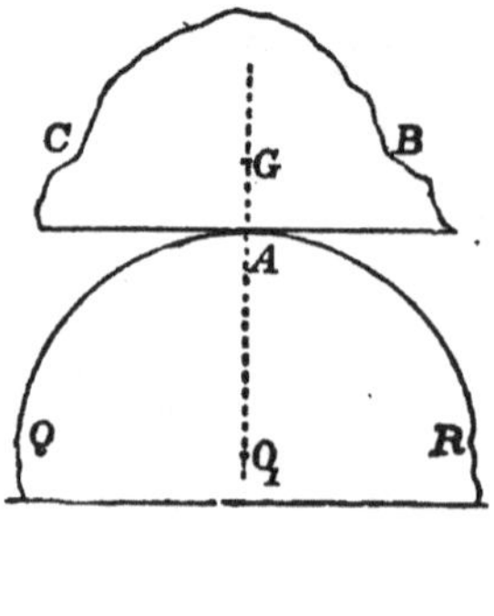

$$h < \text{or} > R.$$

(iii) If the surface of QAR be *plane*—as in the case of a solid resting

with its curved surface upon a horizontal plane—$R=\infty$, and the equilibrium will be *stable* or *unstable* according as

$$h < \text{or} > r.$$

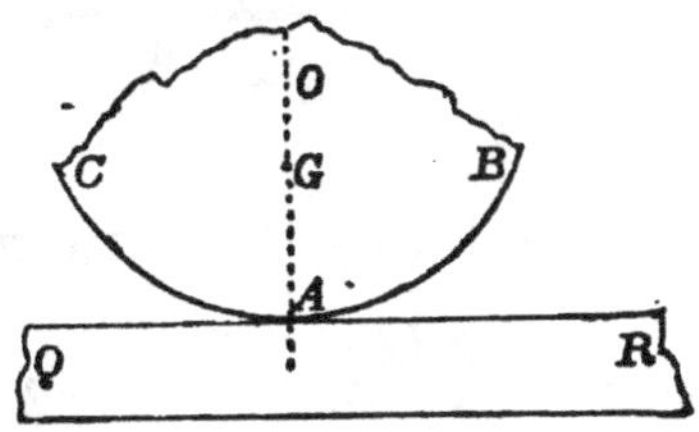

The above particular cases (i), (ii), (iii) of the general one, may be investigated independently by the student.

85. The following is an example of finding the centre of gravity which leads to some useful results.

To find the centre of gravity of n *equal particles arranged at equal intervals along a circular arc.*

Let O be the centre of the circular arc AB, along which the n equal particles $A, P, Q, R, \ldots B$ are arranged;

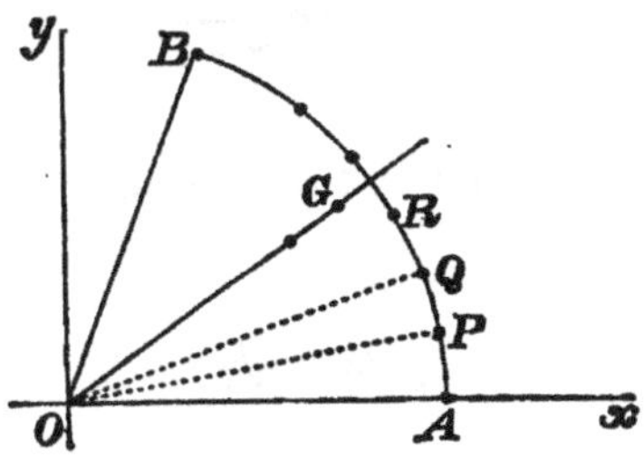

$$\angle AOB = 2\alpha, \quad AO = a,$$

$$\theta = \angle AOP = \angle POQ = \ldots$$

so that $(n-1)\,\theta = 2\alpha$......(i).

Then if $(x_1, y_1)\,(x_2, y_2)\ldots$ be the co-ordinates of the successive particles $A, P, Q\ldots$ referred to Ox, Oy as rectangular axes, we have (Art. 74)

$$\bar{x} = \frac{\Sigma\,(Px)}{\Sigma\,(P)} = \frac{1}{n}\,\{x_1 + x_2 + \ldots + x_n\}$$

$$= \frac{a}{n}\,\{1 + \cos\theta + \cos 2\theta + \ldots + \cos(n-1)\,\theta\}$$

$$= \frac{a}{n}\,\frac{\cos\frac{n-1}{2}\theta\,\sin\frac{n}{2}\theta}{\sin\frac{1}{2}\theta} \qquad \text{(by Trigonometry)}$$

$$=\frac{a}{n}\frac{\cos\alpha\sin\dfrac{n}{n-1}\alpha}{\sin\dfrac{\alpha}{n-1}}\text{..........................(ii)}$$

by substituting for θ in terms of α from (i).

And $\bar{y}=\dfrac{\Sigma(Py)}{\Sigma(P)}=\dfrac{1}{n}\{y_1+y_2+\ldots+y_n\}$

$$=\frac{a}{n}\{\sin\theta+\sin 2\theta+\ldots+\sin(n-1)\theta\}$$

$$=\frac{a}{n}\frac{\sin\dfrac{n-1}{2}\theta\sin\dfrac{n}{2}\theta}{\sin\frac{1}{2}\theta}$$

$$=\frac{a}{n}\frac{\sin\alpha\sin\dfrac{n}{n-1}\alpha}{\sin\dfrac{\alpha}{n-1}}.$$

If G be the centre of gravity,

$$OG=\sqrt{\bar{x}^2+\bar{y}^2}=\frac{a}{n}\frac{\sin\dfrac{n}{n-1}\alpha}{\sin\dfrac{\alpha}{n-1}}\text{...........(iii)},$$

and $$\tan AOG=\frac{\bar{y}}{\bar{x}}=\tan\alpha,$$

i. e. G lies in the line OG which bisects the $\angle AOB$, and (iii) gives its distance from O.

86. Cor. From the preceding investigation we may deduce some useful results.

If the number of particles n be supposed to become indefinitely great,

$$\frac{n\alpha}{n-1} \text{ becomes } = \alpha, \text{ and } n \sin \frac{\alpha}{n-1} \text{ becomes } = \alpha$$

in the limit,

and in this case $$OG = a\frac{\sin\alpha}{\alpha}.$$

I. Since a uniform material circular arc may be regarded as a series of equal particles at small equal intervals,—if AB be a uniform *circular arc* of which O is the centre, and G the centre of gravity, 2α the circular measure of the $\angle AOB$ and $AO = a$;

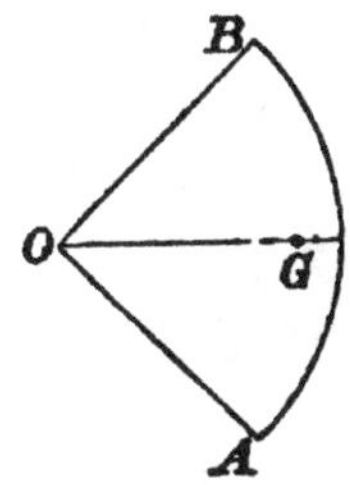

then we infer from the above that OG bisects the $\angle AOB$,

and $$OG = a\frac{\sin\alpha}{\alpha}.$$

II. Again, since we may regard the circular arc AB as the limit of a polygon of a very large number of sides, we may regard the circular sector AOB as made up of a very large number of triangles having a common vertex at O, and the sides of this polygon for their bases,—and if Or be the distance from O of the centre of gravity of any one of these triangles Opq, we shall have (when the $\angle pOq$ is taken very small)

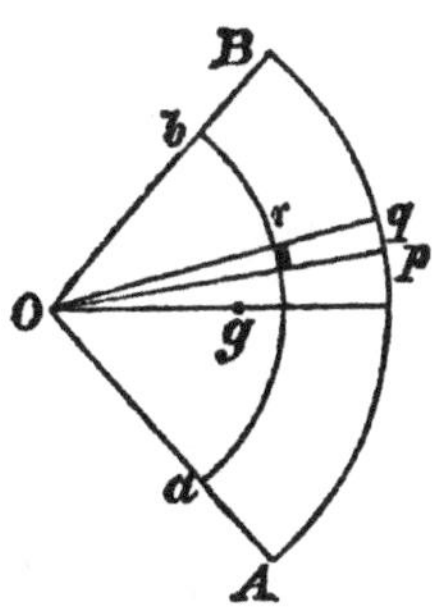

$$Or = \frac{2}{3}\,Op = \frac{2}{3}\,a, \text{ in the limit,}$$

and the centre of gravity g of the *sector* AOB will coincide with the centre of gravity of a uniform circular arc ab whose radius $=\frac{2}{3}\cdot a$.

i.e. Og bisects the $\angle AOB$, and $Og=\frac{2}{3}\cdot a\frac{\sin\alpha}{\alpha}$.

If $\alpha=\frac{\pi}{2}$ the sector becomes a semicircle, and in this case $Og=\frac{4}{3}\frac{a}{\pi}$.

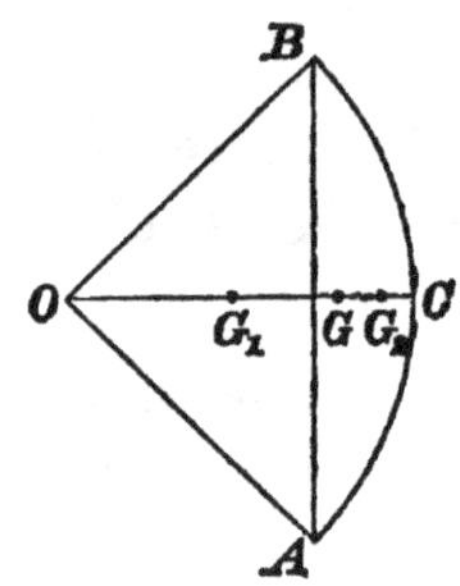

III. The centre of gravity G of the sector AOB being known, as well as G_1 that of the triangle AOB,—we can easily (Art. 71) find G_2 the centre of gravity of the *circular segment* ABC.

For $\Delta AOB=a^2\sin\alpha\cos\alpha$,

sector $AOB=a^2\alpha$,

segment $ABC=a^2(\alpha-\sin\alpha\cos\alpha)$.

Also $OG_1=\frac{2}{3}a\cos\alpha,\quad OG=\frac{2}{3}a\frac{\sin\alpha}{\alpha}$;

$$\therefore\ a^2(\alpha-\sin\alpha\cos\alpha)\,.\,OG_2=a^2\alpha\,.\,\frac{2}{3}a\frac{\sin\alpha}{\alpha}$$

$$-a^2\sin\alpha\cos\alpha\,.\,\frac{2}{3}a\cos\alpha$$

$$=\frac{2}{3}a^3(\sin\alpha-\sin\alpha\cos^2\alpha)$$

$$=\frac{2}{3}a^3\sin^3\alpha;$$

$$\therefore\ OG_2=\frac{2}{3}a\frac{\sin^3\alpha}{\alpha-\sin\alpha\cos\alpha},$$

which determines the C. G. of the *segment*.

IV. The centre of gravity G of a *solid hemisphere* ABC lies in the radius OC which is perpendicular to the base, and $OG = \frac{3}{8}.OC$. Also, the centre of gravity of the *hemispherical surface* ABC *bisects* OC.

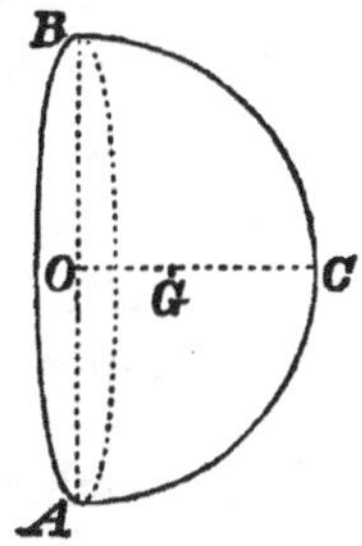

These results may be obtained by processes similar to those employed in this article—but much more easily by employing the Integral Calculus:—we have therefore thought it sufficient to state the results for the information of the student.

87. We will close this chapter with the following elegant theorem—due we believe to Leibnitz.

III. *If a system of forces in equilibrium acting at a point* A *be represented in magnitude and direction by the lines* AP, AQ, AR... *then will the point* A *be the centre of mean position of the points* P, Q, R, ... ; (*in other words*) *the point* A *will be the centre of gravity of a system of equal particles placed at the points* P, Q, R...

Take any line $x'Ax$ passing through A and draw Pp, Qq ... perpendicular to this line; then will Ap, Aq ... represent the projections on $x'Ax$ of the lines AP, AQ... i.e. of the forces P, Q... But since these forces are at equilibrium the algebraic sum of their resolved parts in any assigned direction must be zero by Art. (39).

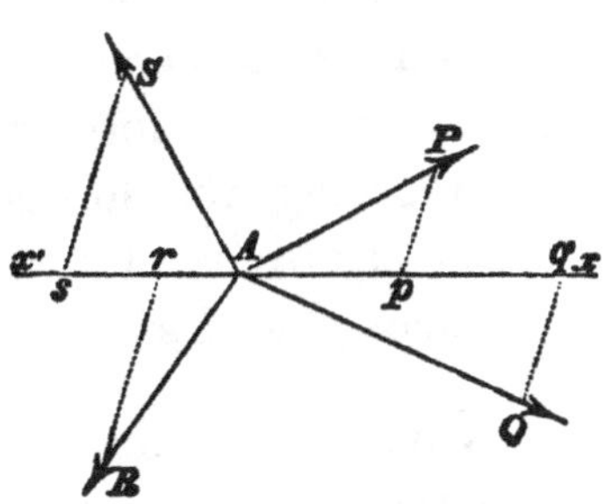

Hence since the algebraic sum of the lines Ap, Aq ... is zero, the centre of gravity of the points P, Q... must be in the plane which passes through A at right angles to $x'Ax$, and since the direction of $x'Ax$ is arbitrary, this centre of gravity must lie in every plane which can be so drawn, and must therefore coincide with the point A, the common point of intersection of these planes.

Hence, when any number of forces acting on a point are in equilibrium, this point is the centre of gravity of a series of equal particles placed at the extremities of lines which represent the forces in magnitude and direction.

And *vice versâ*. If we consider a series of equal particles and we draw lines from each to the centre of gravity of the series, it is clear that a system of forces represented by these lines will be in equilibrium.

For as before draw the lines AP, AQ...; it is clear that A being the centre of gravity, the algebraic sum of the lines Ap, Aq... is *zero;* i.e. the sum of the resolved parts of the forces AP, AQ... taken in *any* direction $x'Ax$ is *zero*, and therefore the forces are in equilibrium.

COR. 1. We see from this theorem that if three forces are in equilibrium about a point, this point is the centre of gravity of the triangle formed by joining the extremities of lines representing the forces in magnitude and direction; for the centre of gravity of a triangle is the same as that of three equal particles placed at its angular points.

Similarly, if four forces are in equilibrium about a point, this point is the centre of gravity of the pyramid whose angular points are the extremities of the straight lines representing the forces: for the centre of gravity of a triangular pyramid is in the same position as that of four equal particles placed at the angular points.

The converse of each of these is also true.

COR. 2. More generally: If all the equal particles of a rigid body of any form are attracted to the same point by forces proportional to their distances from this point they will be in equilibrium if the point be the centre of gravity of the body;—and *conversely*.

CHAPTER VI.

OF THE MECHANICAL POWERS.

88. The simplest machines employed for supporting weights, communicating motion to bodies,—or speaking generally, for making a force which is applied at one point practically available at some other point, are called the *Mechanical Powers;* and by a combination of them all machines, however complicated, are constructed.

They are commonly reckoned as six in number:—the *lever*, the *wheel and axle*, the *pully*, the *inclined plane*, the *wedge*, and the *screw*.

In explaining and discussing these simple machines we shall suppose them to be at rest, so that the force applied at one point is *balanced* by the force or pressure called into action at some other point: we shall also suppose the several parts of them to be without weight and perfectly smooth except when the contrary is expressly stated.

When two forces acting on a machine balance each other, one of them is for convenience called the *power* and the other the *weight*.

89. *The Lever.*

A rigid rod or bar capable of turning about a fixed point of it is called *a lever*. The point about which it can turn is called the *fulcrum*, and the parts into which the rod is divided by the fulcrum are called the *arms* of the lever. When the arms are in a straight line, it is called a *straight lever;* in all other cases it is a *bent lever*.

We have seen in Art. 35, 36, that a body of any form capable of turning about a fixed point O may be considered as a lever, and if two forces P, Q act upon it in a plane passing through O, the lever will be in equilibrium if $P \,.\, Op = Q \,.\, Oq$; i.e. if the moments of P and Q which tend to turn the lever about O be *equal*, and tend in *opposite* directions.

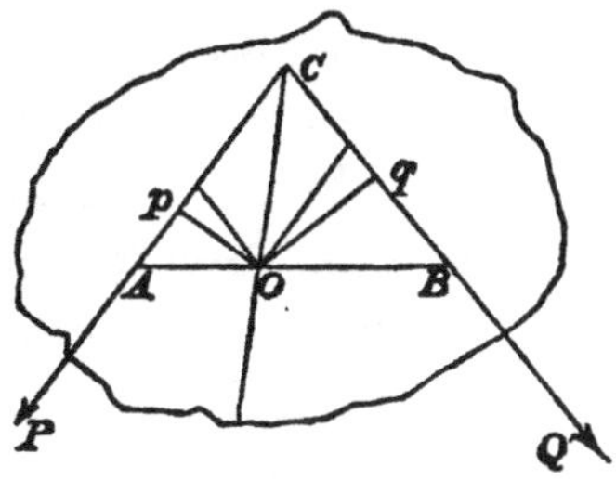

In order however to render our explanation as simple as possible, we will for the present consider the arms of the lever as *straight* and *uniform*, or approximately so.

90. Levers are sometimes divided into *three classes* according to the relative position of the points where the *power* and the *weight* are applied with respect to the fulcrum.

Thus in levers of the *first class*, the power and the weight are applied on *opposite* sides of the fulcrum C, but act in the same direction, as in fig. 1.

Fig. 1.

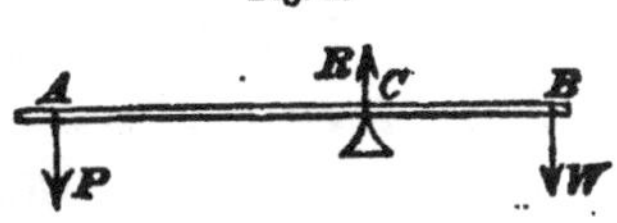

In levers of the *second class*, the power and weight are applied on the *same* side of the fulcrum, but act in opposite directions (as in fig. 2, the power being applied at a greater distance from the fulcrum than the weight is.

Fig. 2.

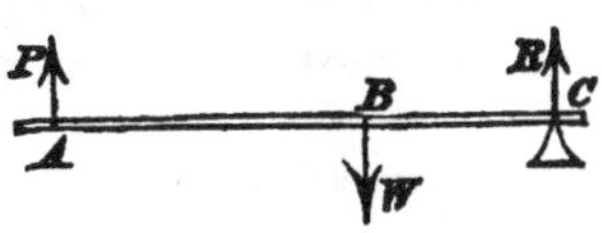

In levers of the *third class* (fig. 3), the power and the weight act on the *same* side of the fulcrum

Fig. 3.

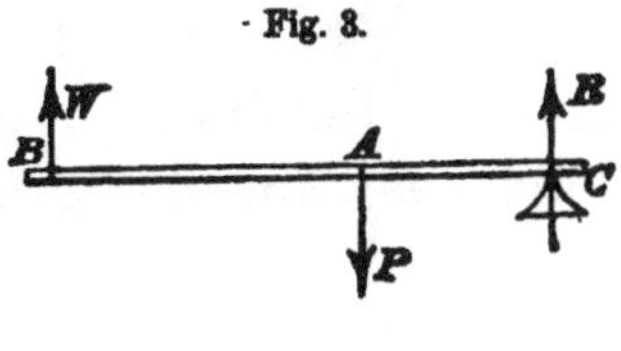

in opposite directions, the power being nearer the fulcrum than the weight is.

The second and third classes it will be observed do not *substantially* differ from each other in their character.

When a lever is employed practically to transmit force applied at one point to some other point,—as, for example, when a crowbar is employed to raise a block of stone—the pressure applied by the hand to one end of the bar corresponds to the power P in the above explanation, and the pressure which the block exerts upon the other end of the crowbar corresponds to the weight W,—the fulcrum being the fixed obstacle against which the crowbar rests, and about which it can turn if P and W do not balance each other.

We have familiar examples of the first species of lever in the *common steelyard*, a *poker*, the *brake* of a pump, the common *claw-hammer*;—a *pair of scissors* and *carpenter's pincers* are double levers of this kind, the joint being the fulcrum.

An *oar*, a *cork-squeezer*, a *pair of nutcrackers* are examples of the second class. In the case of the *oar*, the blade of the oar in the water is the fulcrum.

The *treadle* attached to the axle of the wheel of a lathe, a *pair of shears*,—are instances of the third class of levers, and to this class we may refer the *bones* of the arm and fingers when put in motion by muscular action.

90. *Conditions of equilibrium of a lever.*

(I) *When the lever is a straight one and the power and weight act perpendicularly to the arms, as in any of the three cases represented in figs.* 1, 2, 3 (Art. 90).

Let R be the force (or reaction) which the fulcrum exerts upon the lever, and the lever upon the fulcrum in the opposite direction, then the lever ABC is kept in equilibrium by the three forces P, W, R acting at A, B, C respectively, and these forces must satisfy the conditions of equilibrium of three forces (Art. 45).

Hence, since the directions of P and W are parallel, R must also act in a parallel direction, and in

fig. 1. $R = P + W$,

fig. 2. $R = W - P$,

fig. 3. $R = P - W$.

Also the moments of any two of the forces P, W, R about a point in the line of action of the third must be equal in magnitude and of opposite tendency. Hence taking the moments of P and W about C, we have $P.AC = W.BC$ (i) in each of the three cases.

In levers of the *first class* it is obvious from equation (i) that P will be $>$ or $<$ W according as AC is $<$ or $>$ BC, i. e. according as the fulcrum is nearer to P or to W.

In levers of the *second class*, P is always $< W$.

In levers of the *third class*, P is always $> W$.

(II) *When the lever is of any form, and the power and weight act in any given directions* (fig. Art. 89).

In this case also the three forces P, W, R must act in one plane (Art. 45), and, taking moments about the fulcrum O, we get $$P.\,Op = Q.\,Oq \ldots\ldots\ldots \text{(ii)},$$

Op, Oq being the perpendiculars from the fulcrum upon the lines of action of P and W (Q and W having the same meaning).

The results (i) and (ii) may be stated thus: "the power and the weight which balance each other on a lever must be inversely proportional to the lengths of the perpendiculars drawn from the fulcrum upon their directions," or

$$\frac{P}{W} = \frac{\text{perpendicular upon direction of } W}{\text{perpendicular upon direction of } P}.$$

92. The *magnitude* and *direction* of the pressure R which the fulcrum exerts in case (ii) may be expressed thus,—supposing for simplicity AOB to be a straight line;

put $CAO = \alpha$, $CBO = \beta$, $COB = \theta$, $AO = a$, $BO = b$; then resolving the three forces P, W, R parallel and perpendicular to AB, we get

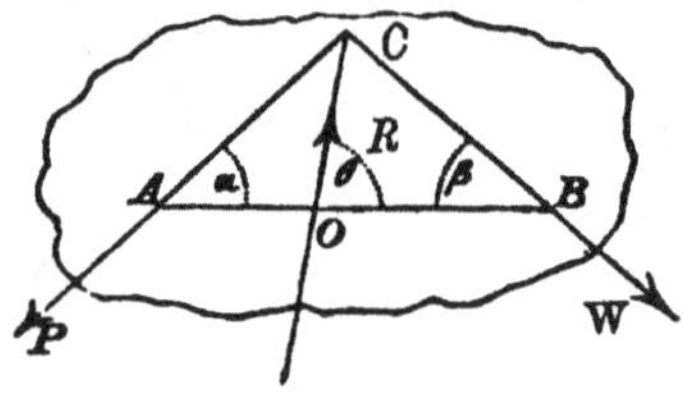

$$R \cos \theta = P \cos \alpha - W \cos \beta,$$
$$R \sin \theta = P \sin \alpha + W \sin \beta;$$

whence, squaring and adding,

$$R = \sqrt{\{P^2 + W^2 - 2PW \cos (\alpha + \beta)\}},$$

also dividing the latter by the former

$$\tan \theta = \frac{P \sin \alpha + W \sin \beta}{P \cos \alpha - W \cos \beta};$$

which two equations express R and θ in terms of known quantities.

Obs. We might, in cases (I) and (II), have obtained other equations of condition by taking moments about some other point; as, for example, about A, in which case we get

$$R . AC = W . AB, \text{ fig. Art. 90,}$$

or, in fig. Art. 92, if Ar, $A\omega$ be perpendiculars drawn from A upon the lines of action of R, W,

$$R . Ar = W . A\omega,$$

which gives R at once independent of P; but conditions so obtained are not independent of those already obtained, but might have been deduced from them, as the student will infer by examining this case in particular, or by referring to the more general case discussed in Art. 45.

93. *If two weights balance each other on a straight lever in any position which is not vertical, they will balance in any other position of the lever.*

Let P, Q be the two weights suspended from the points A, B of the lever whose fulcrum is C and centre of gravity G,

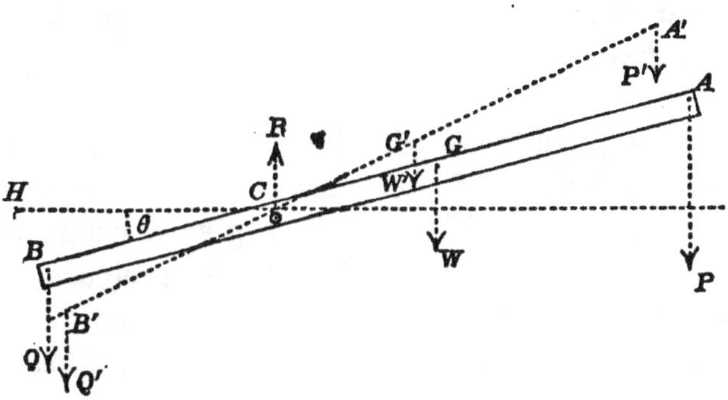

W = weight of the lever, draw HC horizontal in the vertical plane in which the lever can move. Suppose the lever to be in equilibrium when inclined at an $\angle\, \theta$ to the horizon, the points A, G, C, B being in a straight line,—then since P, Q, W act in vertical lines, the reaction R of the fulcrum must also be vertical, and we must have

$$R = P + Q + W \text{ ....(i).}$$

Also taking moments about the fulcrum C, we must have

$$P \,.\, AC \cos\theta + W \,.\, CG \cos\theta = Q \,.\, BC \cos\theta \text{.......(ii),}$$

or since θ is not $= 90^\circ$, and $\therefore \cos\theta$ is not $= 0$, we may divide out $\cos\theta$, and obtain

$$P.AC + W.CG = Q.BC \text{..............(iii)}$$

as the condition of equilibrium—and this is satisfied if the lever assume any other position $A'G'B'$ inclined at any other angle to the horizon. Hence the lever will balance in any other position.

Note. If $\theta = 90^\circ$ then $\cos\theta = 0$, and we should not be justified in deriving equation (iii) from (ii) by dividing out *cos* θ, in fact when the lever is vertical it will balance with *any* weights suspended at A, B.—It is necessary that A, B, G and C—the point where the fulcrum acts on the lever—should be in a straight line.

94. The various kinds of balances which are in use for determining the weight of substances are constructed on the principle of the lever. We will here give a description of the *common* or *Roman steelyard*, the *Danish steelyard*, and of the *common balance;* referring the student for a more complete account to Delaunay's *Cours élémentaire de Mécanique.*

The *common* or *Roman steelyard.*

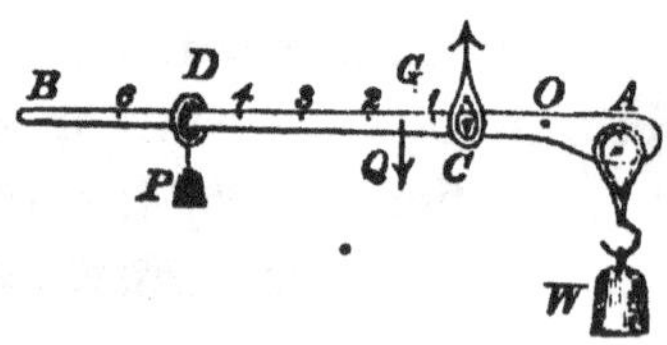

This balance consists of a straight lever AB suspended by the point C, and capable of turning about this point. At a point A on the short arm is attached a hook (or sometimes a scale-pan), from which is suspended the substance whose weight W is required. A ring D, carrying a weight P of constant magnitude, can slide along the graduated arm CB till P and W balance each other about C, when the lever is horizontal. The graduation at which P rests when this is the case indicates the weight of the substance.

In graduating the arm BC account must be taken of the weight of the lever: let Q be the weight of the lever, and G its centre of gravity, D the point from which P is suspended when it balances W at A; then taking moments about C, we have

$$P \,.\, CD + Q \,.\, GC = W \,.\, CA \text{.........}(\alpha).$$

If on the arm CA we take a fixed point O such that $P \,.\, CO = Q \,.\, CG$, the equation (α) becomes

$$P \,.\, CD + P \,.\, CO = W \,.\, CA, \text{ or } P \,.\, OD = W \,.\, CA;$$

$$\therefore OD = \frac{W}{P} \,.\, CA.$$

We may now graduate OB by taking distances from O successively equal to CA, $2CA$, $3CA$, ... and marking them 1, 2, 3, ...—if necessary these distances may be subdivided.

Suppose, for example, that P rests at the fifth graduation, then $OD = 5 \,.\, CA$, and $\therefore W = 5P$, and the weight of P being known that of W is known also.

Obs. By increasing CA, or by diminishing P, the *sensibility* of the steelyard would be increased; i.e. the distance would be increased between the points from which P must be suspended in order successively to balance two weights of given difference.

For suppose D' the point of suspension of P when the weight is W';

$$\text{then } P \,.\, OD' = W' \,.\, CA,$$
$$\text{and } P \,.\, OD = W \,.\, CA;$$

$$\text{therefore } P.DD' = CA.(W' - W),$$

$$\text{or } DD' = \frac{CA}{P}.(W' - W);$$

i. e. $W' - W$ being given, DD' would be increased by an increase of CA or by a diminution of P.

We may regard $\frac{CA}{P}$ as a *measure* of the sensibility of the steelyard, and this being constant in the same steelyard for different positions of D, we infer that the same steelyard is equally *sensible* for all positions of P.

The name of this steelyard has often led to a mistaken idea of its origin—*Romman* is an Eastern word for the pomegranate, and the form of the weight P gave rise to the name.

95. *The Danish Steelyard.*

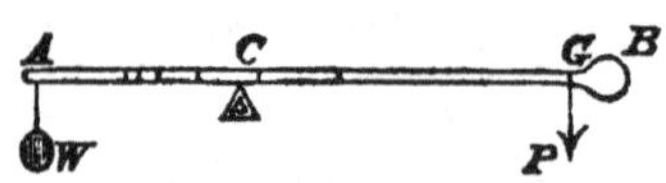

This steelyard consists of a bar AB terminating in a ball B which serves as the *power*, and the substance to be weighed is suspended from the end A; the fulcrum C—which is frequently a loop at the extremity of a string by which the instrument is suspended—is moved backward or forward till P and W balance about it.

To graduate the Danish Steelyard.

Let P be the weight of the bar and ball of the steelyard, which we may suppose to act through its centre of gravity G: and let C be the position of the fulcrum when the substance whose weight is W balances P about the fulcrum. Taking moments about C, we have

$$P.CG = W.AC = P.(AG - AC);$$

$$\therefore AC = \frac{P.AG}{P+W} \text{ ....} (\alpha);$$

by making W successively equal to P, $2P$, $3P$...the successive graduations are determined.

COR. It is obvious from the formula (α) that the distances of successive graduations from A are in harmonic progression.

96. *The common balance.*

This balance consists of a lever AB called the *beam*, suspended from a fulcrum C about which it can turn freely; the point C is a little above the centre of gravity G of the beam, and from the extremities A, B of the arms GA, GB (which ought to be similar and equal) are suspended two scale-pans, in one of which is placed the substance whose weight W is required, and weights of known magnitude are placed in the other till their sum P just balances W; this being the case if the beam be exactly horizontal in a position of rest. In this case if the arms are perfectly equal and similar, and the scale-pans also of equal weight, P will be exactly equal to W. If these weights differ by ever so little,

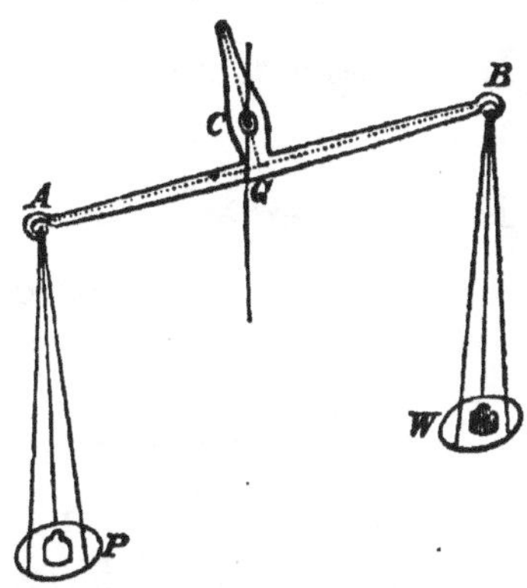

the horizontality of the beam will be disturbed, and after oscillating for a short time, it will rest in a position inclined to the horizon, and the greater this inclination is for a given difference of P and W the greater is the *sensibility* of the balance. A simple way of testing the accuracy of a balance is by interchanging P and W in the scales. The balance ought to retain the same position when this is done.

97. *To determine the position of equilibrium of a balance when loaded with unequal weights.*

Let P and W be the weights in the scales. $AB = 2a$; $h =$ the distance of C the fulcrum from the line joining A, B. W' the weight of the beam and scales, and k the distance from C (measured along the line h) of the point through which the resultant of W' acts—k remains unchanged when the balance is tilted,—θ the angle which the beam makes with the horizon when there is equilibrium.

If we take moments about C, the algebraic sum must be equal to zero.

Now the perpendicular from C

on the direction of $P = a\cos\theta - h\sin\theta$;

.... $W = a\cos\theta + h\sin\theta$;

.... $W' = k\sin\theta$;

we shall have then, taking account of the tendency of the moments of the several forces,

$$P(a\cos\theta - h\sin\theta) - W(a\cos\theta + h\sin\theta) - W'k\sin\theta = 0;$$

$$\therefore \tan\theta = \frac{(P-W)a}{(P+W)h + W'k}.$$

This equation determines the position of equilibrium.

98. *The requisites for a good balance* are

(i) The beam ought to be horizontal when loaded with equal weights in the scales at A and B. This will be the case if the scales are of equal weight, and if the line drawn through C at right angles to AB divides the beam into two similar and equal arms.

(ii) The balance ought to be *sensible;* i. e. the angle θ which the beam makes with the horizon ought to be easily perceptible when the weights P and W suspended at A and B differ by a very small quantity; and the greater $\tan\theta$ is for a given small difference $P - W$, the greater is the *sensibility* of the balance. We may take $\frac{\tan\theta}{P-W}$ as a measure of the sensibility, and hence we see that this requisite will be secured by making $\frac{(P+W)h+W'k}{a}$ as small as possible; thus the smaller h and k are made, the greater will be the sensibility of the balance.

(iii) The balance ought to be *stable;* i. e. if the equilibrium be a little disturbed either way, there ought to be a decided tendency to return to its original position of rest. This tendency, for any position of the beam, will be measured by the moment of the forces tending to restore the beam to its former position of rest. If for example $P=W$, then when the beam is inclined at $\angle\,\theta$ to the horizon the moment of the forces which tend to diminish θ, and therefore to restore the balance to its position of equilibrium, is

$$\{(P+W)h+W'k\}\sin\theta.$$

Hence this ought to be made as large as possible in order to secure the third requisite.

This condition, it will be observed, is to some extent at variance with the condition for sensibility; but they may be reconciled by making $(P+W)h+W'k$ considerable and a large; i.e. by placing the fulcrum at some distance above the centre of gravity of the beam, and by making the arms long.

In a balance of great delicacy the fulcrum should be as thin as possible—it is generally a knife-edge of hardened steel working upon agate plates.

The comparative importance of these qualities of *sensibility* and *stability* in a balance will depend upon the service for which it is intended:—for weighing heavy goods, *stability* is of more importance;—the balance employed in a chemical laboratory must possess great *sensibility*, and such instruments have been constructed to indicate a variation of weight as small as a million-th part of the whole,—and even less.

99. There are various kinds of compound balances formed by combinations of levers in use for weighing heavy articles, as merchandise, baggage, &c.—it will suffice here to give a brief description of the arrangement of the levers in the *Balance of Quintenz* in a simple form.

The figure represents a section of the machine by a plane dividing it into two symmetrical parts.

The platform AB upon which the weight Q is placed is supported at one end upon the knife-edge fulcrum E, and at the other by a piece *DH* which is connected with the upright piece *BC* by a strong brace *CD*.

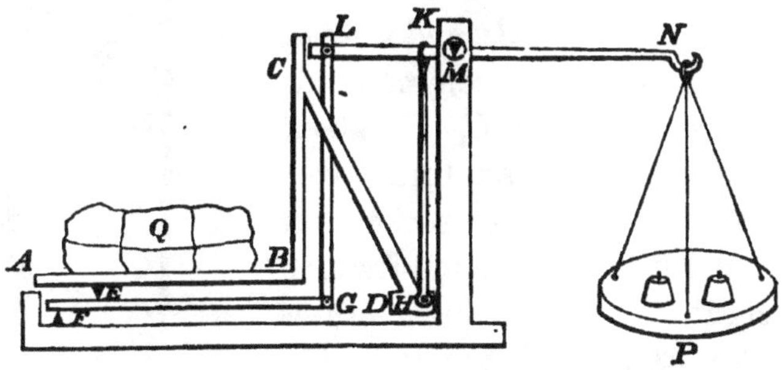

GF is a lever turning about a fulcrum *F* and connected with the horizontal lever *LMN* by a vertical rod *GL*; *HK* is another vertical rod connecting *DH* with the lever *LMN* which turns about the fulcrum *M*, and from the end *N* of this lever the scale-pan *P* is suspended.

The ratio of *FE* : *FG* is by construction the same as the ratio *KM* : *LM*,—usually 1 : 5.

The weight *Q* thus produces pressures at *E* and *H*: the pressure at *E* by means of the lever *FG* and rod *GL* transmits a pressure to the lever *LMN* at *L*, and the pressure at *H* is transmitted to the same lever *LMN* at *K*,—and in consequence of the ratios *FE* : *FG* and *KM* : *LM* being equal, the pressure at *L* produces the same effect on the lever *LMN* as a pressure equal to that at *E* would do if applied at *K*.

Thus the effect on the lever *LMN* is the same as if the whole weight *Q* were suspended at *K*, and equilibrium is produced by placing suitable weights in the scale-pan *P*.

The ratio *KM* : *MN* is commonly 1 : 10,—so that the weight of *Q* is ten times that required to balance it at *P*.

100. *The Wheel and Axle.*

Fig. 1.

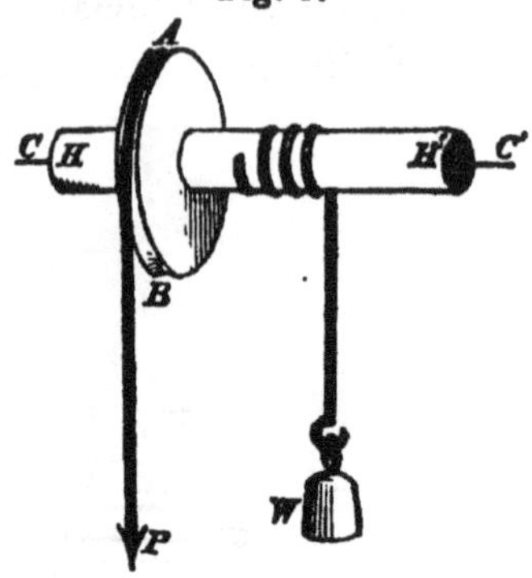

This machine consists of a cylinder HH', called the *axle*, and a *wheel* AB, the two having a common axis terminating in pivots C, C', about which the machine can turn;—the pivots resting in fixed sockets at C, C'. A rope, to one end of which the weight W is attached, passes round the axle, and has its other end fixed to the axle. Another rope passes round the wheel, being attached at one end to the circumference of the wheel, and at the other end the power P is applied. The ropes pass round the *wheel* and the *axle* in opposite directions, and thus tend to turn the machine in opposite directions.

Fig. 2.

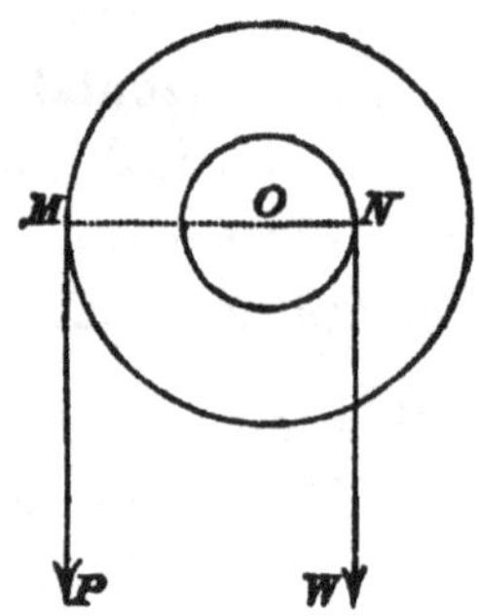

Conditions of equilibrium of the wheel and axle.

The efforts which P or W make to turn the machine about its axis will be the same in whatever plane they act perpendicular to the axis.

Let fig. 2 represent a section of the machine perpendicular to its axis O; M and N the points at which the strings quit the circumferences of the wheel and axle; join OM, ON, which will be perpendicular to MP, NW respectively.

We may regard MON as a lever kept in equilibrium about the fulcrum O by the forces P, W acting at arms

MO, ON, and there will be equilibrium if $P.MO = W.NO$, or $\frac{P}{W} = \frac{NO}{MO}$; i.e. if the power is to the weight as the radius of the axle is to the radius of the wheel.

101. *Obs.* If the thickness of the ropes cannot be neglected, we must suppose the action of P and W to be transmitted along the middle or axis of the ropes, and in this case

$$OM = \text{radius of wheel} + \text{radius of rope},$$
$$ON = \text{radius of axle} + \text{radius of rope}.$$

Instead of the wheel AB (fig. 1), the power P is sometimes applied to a rigid rod fixed into the axle at right angles to it; and in the previous condition of equilibrium we must take OM = length of the arm at which P is applied. The *capstan* is an example of this construction.

COR. 1. In a combination of wheels and axles, in which the string passing round one *axle* also passes round the *wheel* of the next machine, and so on, we should readily obtain

$$\frac{P}{W} = \frac{\text{product of radii of all the axles}}{\text{product of radii of all the wheels}}.$$

Combinations of toothed-wheels are substantially examples of this kind.

COR. 2. If the *power* and *weight* act in parallel directions on the wheel and axle, and on *opposite* sides of the axis, the pressure on the axis $= P + W$; but if they act on the same side of the axis, the pressure on the axis $= P \sim W$. (Art. 91.)

102. *The Pully.*

The *pully* is a small circular disc or wheel having a uniform groove cut on its outer edge, and it can turn about an axis which passes through its centre. This axis rests in sockets within the *block* to which the pully is attached. When the block is *fixed*, the pully is said to be fixed; in other cases it is *moveable*. A cord passes round the pully along the groove, and at its extremities the *power* and *weight* are applied.

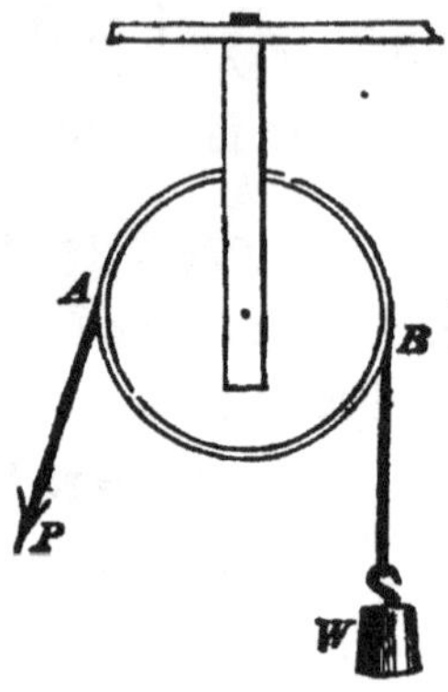

The pully is very useful for changing the direction of the tension of a string; and as we shall here suppose the groove to be perfectly smooth, the tension at all points of the string between the points of application of P and W will be the same. (Art. 43.)

In the following account of some of the more simple combinations of pullies, we shall neglect the weight of the strings, and suppose the radius of any pully to be the distance from the axis to the centre of the chord which passes round it.

103. *Conditions of equilibrium on a single moveable pully.*

(i) *When the strings are parallel.*

Since the tension of the string $PABC$ which passes round the pully is the same throughout, the tension *upwards* of the portions AP, BC are each equal to P; and since there is equilibrium we may suppose the strings AP, BC *attached* to the pully at A and B, the points where they quit the pully; and the weight W, which is suspended from O, the axis of the pully, is supported by the upward tension of the strings AP, BC. Hence, considering AOB as a lever kept in equi-

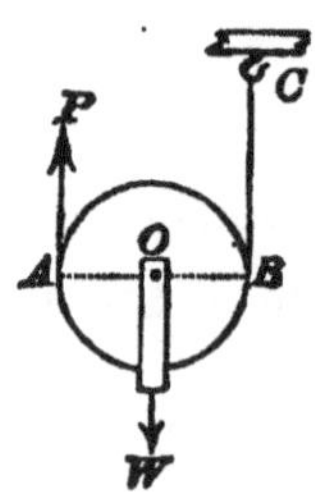

librium about a fulcrum O, we have (Art. 90) $2P = W$ the condition required.

(ii) *When the strings are not parallel.*

Let the string quit the pully at A and B. Then since the tension along AP is equal to that along BC, their resultant will bisect the angle between them, and this resultant must be equal and opposite to the weight W suspended from the axis of the pully, and acting in a vertical direction.

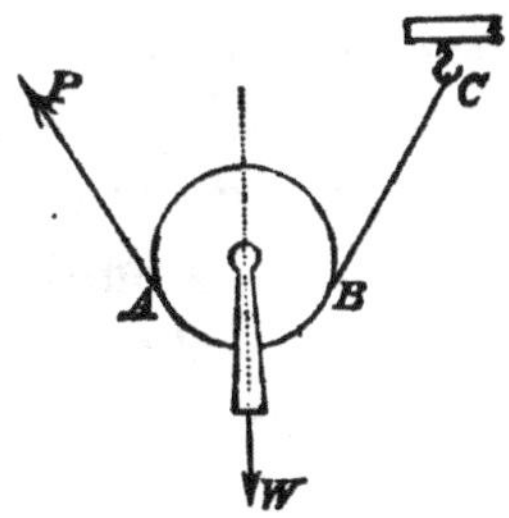

Hence AP, BC must be equally inclined to the vertical; let θ be this inclination, then the resultant of the two tensions, which we may regard as acting at A and B, is $= 2P\cos\theta$, and this must be equal to W; i.e. $2P\cos\theta = W$,—the condition of equilibrium.

Obs. If the weight of the pully be taken into account, let it be w, and we shall obtain $2P\cos\theta = W + w$ for the condition of equilibrium.

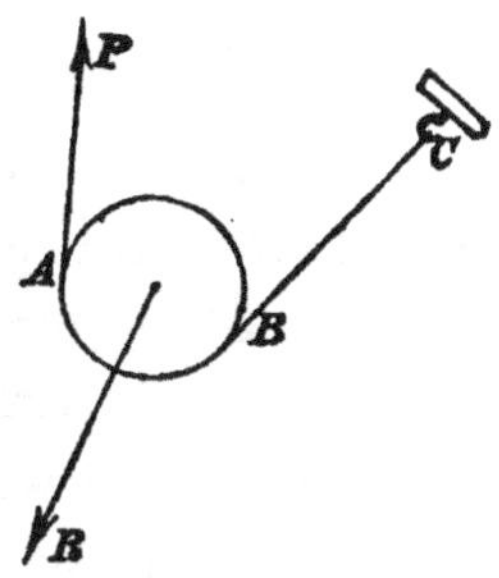

If instead of a weight W hanging vertically, a force R be applied to the pully in direction OR by a string or otherwise, we may shew as before that when there is equilibrium AP, BC must be equally inclined to the direction of R, and we shall have $2P\cos\theta = R$ for the condition of equilibrium, 2θ being the angle which AP makes with BC.

104. *Conditions of equilibrium in a system of pullies.*

I. In a system of pullies in which the string which passes

round any pully has one extremity fixed and the other attached to the pully next above it (as in the figure), the portions not in contact with any pully being all parallel. Let t_1 be the tension of the string which passes round the lowest pully, t_2, t_3,... that of the string passing round the *second*, *third*... pully, and let w_1, w_2, w_3... be the weights of the pullies A_1, A_2, A_3...

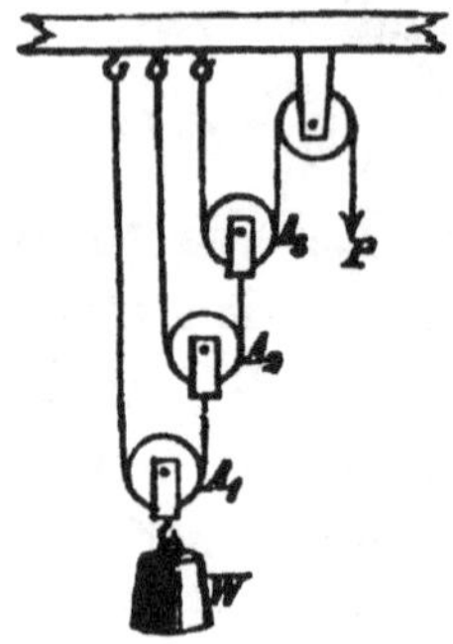

Then for the equilibrium of the pully A_1, we shall have the equation of condition

$$2t_1 = W + w_1 \ldots\ldots\ldots (1) \quad \text{(Art. 91)},$$

and for the equilibrium of A_2, the force upon it downwards is equal to the tension of string $A_2A_1 + w_2$, and the force upwards is $2t_2$, hence we get

$$2t_2 = t_1 + w_2 \ldots\ldots\ldots\ldots (2),$$

$$\text{similarly,} \quad 2t_3 = t_2 + w_3 \ldots\ldots\ldots\ldots (3),$$

and so on for every *moveable* pully; if there be n moveable pullies the last equation will be

$$2t_n = t_{n-1} + w_n \ldots\ldots\ldots (n).$$

Now if we multiply the equations (1), (2), (3) ... (n) by $1 . 2 . 2^2 \ldots 2^{n-1}$ severally, add the corresponding sides together and strike out terms which cancel each other on opposite sides of the resulting equation, we get

$$2^n t_n = W + w_1 + 2w_2 + 2^2 w_3, + \ldots + 2^{n-1} w_n,$$

and it is clear that $t_n = P$, hence the condition of equilibrium becomes

$$2^n P = W + w_1 + 2w_2 + 2^2 w_3 + \ldots + 2^{n-1} w_n \ldots\ldots\ldots (a).$$

COR. 1. If the weight of the pullies be neglected,

$$w_1 = w_2 = \ldots 0,$$

and the condition (α) becomes

$$2^n P = W.$$

COR. 2. If the pullies are all equal and the weight of each $= w$, the condition (α) becomes

$$2^n P = W + (1 + 2 + \ldots + 2^{n-1})\, w,$$

$$\text{or } 2^n P = W + (2^n - 1)\, w,$$

which may be written

$$2^n (P - w) = W - w.$$

105. II. In a system of pullies where there are two blocks, and the *same* string passes round all the pullies (as in the figure), the parts of the string between successive pullies being parallel.

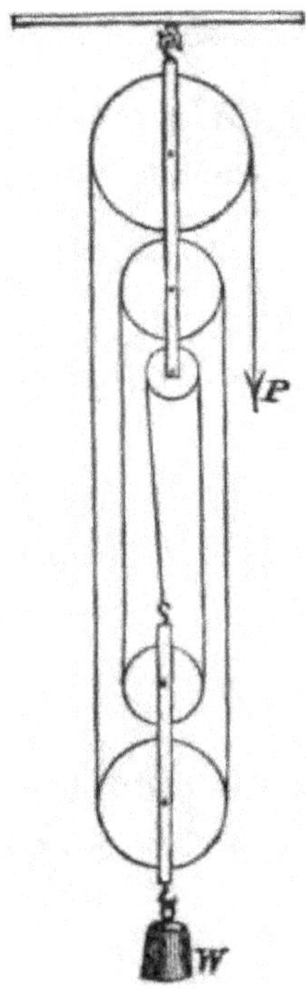

Since the tension of the string is the same throughout, if n be the number of strings at the lower block, nP will be the *resultant* upward tension of the strings upon the lower block, and this must be equal to W when there is equilibrium, that is, $nP = W$ is the condition required; the weight W including the weight of the lower block.

106. III. In a system of pullies where the string which passes round any pully is attached at one end of it to the weight, and at the other end to the next pully (as in the figure), the strings being all parallel.

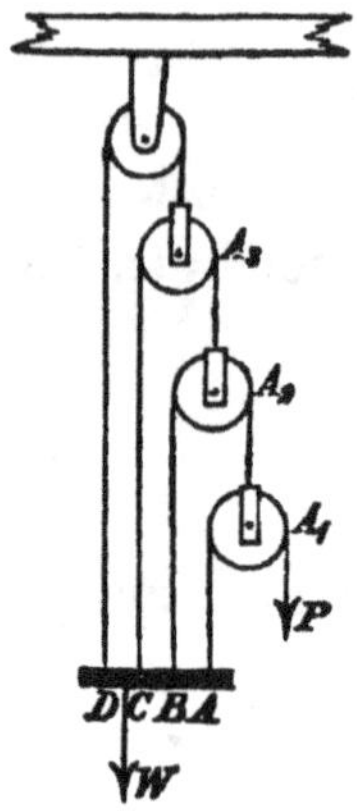

Let $t_1, t_2, t_3 \ldots$ be the tensions of the strings which pass round the successive pullies $A_1, A_2, A_3 \ldots$, and let $w_1, w_2, w_3 \ldots$ be the weights of these pullies severally. Then for the equilibrium of the pullies $A_1, A_2, A_3 \ldots$ in succession, we shall have

$$\left.\begin{aligned} t_1 &= P \\ t_2 &= 2t_1 + w_1 \\ t_3 &= 2t_2 + w_2 \\ .. &= \ldots \\ t_n &= 2t_{n-1} + w_{n-1} \end{aligned}\right\} \ldots\ldots\ldots\ldots\ldots\ldots(\alpha),$$

n being the number of pullies of which $n-1$ only are *moveable*.

Also for the equilibrium of W we shall have $W =$ resultant of the upward tensions of the strings attached to the bar AD;

$$\text{i.e. } t_1 + t_2 + t_3 + \ldots + t_n = W, \ldots\ldots\ldots\ldots\ldots\ldots(\beta).$$

Multiplying the n equations of (α) by $2^n, 2^{n-1}, 2^{n-2} \ldots\ldots 2$ in order, and adding, we get

$$2t_n = 2w_{n-1} + 2^2 w_{n-2} + \ldots + 2^{n-1} w_1 + 2^n P \ldots\ldots\ldots\ldots\ldots\ldots(\gamma).$$

Again, adding equations (α), we get by means of (β)

$$W = P + w_1 + w_2 + \ldots + w_{n-1} + 2(W - t_n);$$

$$\text{i.e. } 2t_n = W + P + w_1 + w_2 + \ldots + w_{n-1} \ldots\ldots\ldots(\delta).$$

Subtracting (δ) from (γ), we get

$$W = (2^n - 1) P + (2^{n-1} - 1) w_1 + (2^{n-2} - 1) w_2 + \ldots$$
$$\ldots + (2^2 - 1) w_{n-2} + w_{n-1},$$

the relation which must hold good between P and W when the system is in equilibrium.

Cor. 1. If the weight of the pullies be neglected,

$$w_1 = w_2 = \ldots = 0,$$

and the relation between P and W requisite for equilibrium becomes

$$W = (2^n - 1) P,$$

a result which the student may investigate independently.

Obs. It is readily seen that the weight of the pullies *assists* the power P in system III., but in the systems I. and II. it increases W.

Cor. 2. If the weight W be suspended from a horizontal bar AD, the point K to which W is attached must be such that the resultant of the tensions at A, B, C... passes through K, otherwise the bar would not remain horizontal.

For example, suppose there are four pullies of equal radius a: then the tension at $A = P$, at $B = 2P$, at $C = 2^2P$, and at $D = 2^3P$, the weights of the pullies being neglected; then, taking moments about A, we must have K such that

$$(P + 2P + 2^2P + 2^3P)\, AK = P.o + 2.P.a + 2^2P.2a + 2^3P.3a;$$

$$\text{i.e. } AK = \frac{2 + 2^2.2 + 2^3.3}{1 + 2 + 2^2 + 2^3}.a = \frac{34}{15}a.$$

107. A very simple and useful combination of pullies is employed in the *Spanish Barton*, the principle of which will be obvious from the annexed figure. C is a fixed pully round which passes a string attached to the two moveable pullies A and B. The weight W is attached to B, and the string which passes round A and B is fixed at one end at D, and the power P acts at the other end.

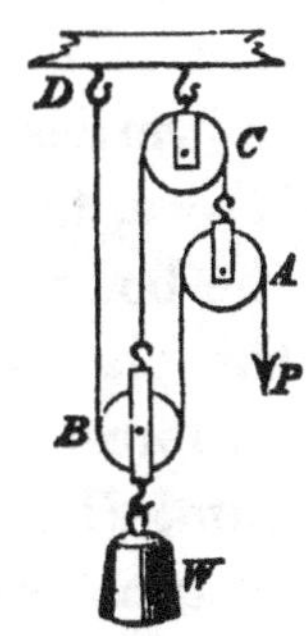

For the conditions of equilibrium we have

from the equilibrium of the pully A, tension of string $ACB = 2P + A = T$ suppose, and the tension of the string $PABD$ being the same throughout and equal to P, we have for the equilibrium of pully B,

$$B + W = 2P + T = \therefore 4P + A;$$
$$\therefore 4P = W + B - A.$$

108. *The Inclined Plane.*

By an inclined plane, as a mechanical power, is meant a plane inclined to the horizon, and the inclination is measured as in Euclid, Book XI., Definition 6. *Or thus:* If a vertical plane be drawn perpendicular to the inclined plane,—which for simplicity of definition we shall call a *principal plane*—the angle between the lines of intersection of this vertical plane with the inclined plane and a horizontal plane is the *inclination* of the proposed plane to the horizon.

Conditions of equilibrium on an inclined plane.

When a body whose weight is W *is supported on an inclined plane by a force* P, *the direction of which makes an angle* ϵ *with the plane*—the plane being smooth.

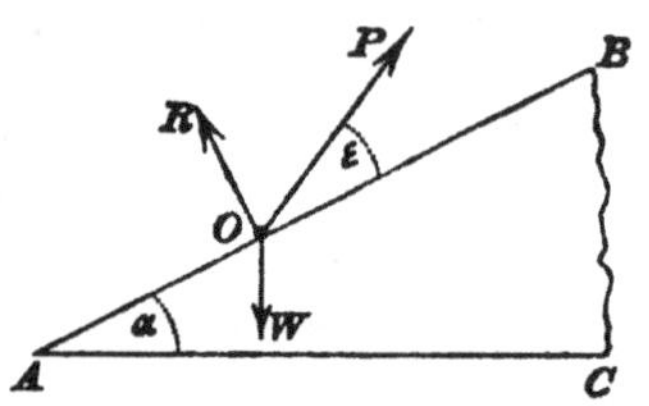

I. Let the figure represent a section of the inclined plane, made by a vertical plane perpendicular to the inclined plane; $BAC = \alpha$, the *inclination* of the plane. Then the forces acting on the body at O are W its weight vertically, R the reaction of the plane acting at right angles to the plane, and P the given force. Hence, in order that the body may be in equilibrium, P must act in the same plane with W and R, i.e. in the vertical plane perpendicular to the inclined plane (represented in the figure).

Let $POB = \epsilon$. Then resolving the forces which act on O, *along* the plane and *at right angles* to it, we get

$$P\cos\epsilon - W\sin\alpha = 0 \text{.........(i)},$$

$$P\sin\epsilon + R - W\cos\alpha = 0 \text{.........(ii)}.$$

Equation (i) gives the relation which must hold between W and P; and the second gives

$$R = W\cos\alpha - P\sin\epsilon = W\left(\cos\alpha - \frac{\sin\alpha\sin\epsilon}{\cos\epsilon}\right) = \frac{W\cos(\epsilon+\alpha)}{\cos\epsilon},$$

which gives the pressure on the plane in terms of W.

109. II. Let the plane be *rough*; and *first*, let P act in the vertical plane which is perpendicular to the inclined plane—i.e. in a *principal plane*—(as in case I.). R, P, W, α, ϵ, the same as in case I.: μ_1 the *coefficient* of the friction actually exerted, *down* the plane suppose, so that $\mu_1 R$ is the friction; then resolving the forces acting on the body, parallel and at right angles to the plane, we get

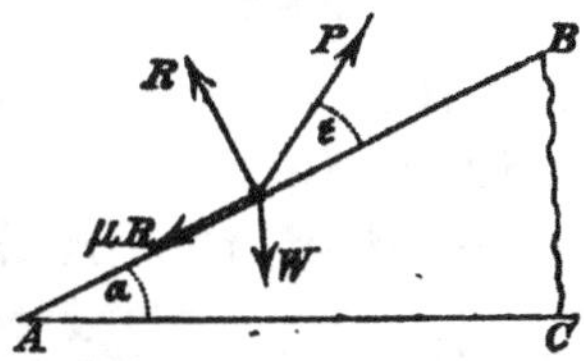

$$P\cos\epsilon - W\sin\alpha - \mu_1 R = 0,$$

$$P\sin\epsilon + R - W\cos\alpha = 0,$$

whence we get

$$P = W\frac{\sin\alpha + \mu_1\cos\alpha}{\cos\epsilon + \mu_1\sin\epsilon} \text{.........(i)},$$

$$R = W\frac{\cos(\alpha+\epsilon)}{\cos\epsilon + \mu_1\sin\epsilon} \text{.........(ii)}.$$

Equation (i) gives the relation between P and W; and (ii) the pressure on the plane.

If the friction acts *up* the plane, we have only to change the sign of μ_1 in the preceding investigation.

Obs. If μ be the coefficient of maximum friction between the substance of which the body is composed and the plane (which is determined by experiment, and generally given in tables of the coefficients of friction), μ_1 cannot be greater than μ numerically, and may be positive or negative so far as equilibrium is concerned.

If the body is *just on the point of moving up* the plane $\mu_1 = \mu$ and $P = W\dfrac{\sin\alpha + \mu\cos\alpha}{\cos\epsilon + \mu\sin\epsilon}$.

If it be *on the point of moving down* the plane $\mu_1 = -\mu$ and $P = W\dfrac{\sin\alpha - \mu\cos\alpha}{\cos\epsilon - \mu\sin\epsilon}$.

If P have any value intermediate to these two, the body will be in equilibrium, and for a given value of P the coefficient of the friction actually in operation will be given by (i); i.e. $\mu_1 = \dfrac{P\cos\epsilon - W\sin\alpha}{W\cos\alpha - P\sin\epsilon}$.

Secondly. If the direction of P does not lie in the vertical plane which is perpendicular to the inclined plane.

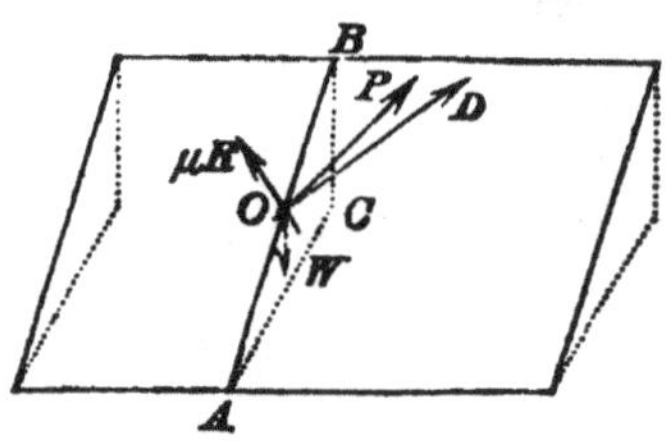

Let OD be the projection of OP on the inclined plane, AB the section of the inclined plane made by the vertical plane through O perpendicular to the inclined plane, $POD = \epsilon$, $BOD = \beta$, $BAC = \alpha$.

Now friction always acts in the direction opposite to that in which the body would begin to move, if the friction were to cease.

The forces acting on O parallel to the plane are $P\cos\epsilon$ along OD, and $W\sin\alpha$ along OA.

Hence μR the friction must be equal and opposite to the resultant of these two forces. Let θ be the angle which this resultant makes with OA.

Then resolving the forces which act on O (i) perpendicular to the plane; (ii) along OA; and (iii) perpendicular to OA along the inclined plane, we get successively

$$P \sin \epsilon + R - W \cos \alpha = 0 \ldots\ldots\ldots \text{(i)},$$

$$P \cos \epsilon \cos \beta + \mu R \cos \theta - W \sin \alpha = 0 \ldots\ldots\ldots \text{(ii)},$$

$$P \cos \epsilon \sin \beta - \mu R \sin \theta = 0 \ldots\ldots\ldots \text{(iii)}.$$

From these three equations we get P, R, and θ; i.e. the force P necessary for equilibrium, the pressure on the plane, and the direction in which friction acts.

If $\beta = 0$, then $\theta = 0$, and the results of this case coincide with the preceding.

110. If $\mu = \tan \phi$, the result of the first case of II. gives

$$P = W \frac{\sin(\alpha + \phi)}{\cos(\epsilon - \phi)},$$

and if we suppose ϵ and P to vary so as to satisfy this relation, we see that P is *least* when $\cos(\epsilon - \phi)$ is greatest; i.e. when $\epsilon = \phi$, and the *least* force which will pull the body *up* the plane is $= W \sin(\alpha + \phi)$.

Also the result $P = W \dfrac{\sin(\alpha \pm \phi)}{\cos(\epsilon \mp \phi)}$ compared with that of case I. shews that the condition of equilibrium on a *rough* plane is the same as that on a *smooth* plane whose inclination to the horizon is increased or diminished by the angle ϕ, the *direction* of P remaining unchanged—*increased* or *diminished* according as the friction acts *down* or *up* the plane.

Cor. If the force P acts horizontally, then $\epsilon = -\alpha$, and the conditions of equilibrium become

in case I. $P = W \tan \alpha$,

in the first instance of case II. $P = W \dfrac{\sin \alpha + \mu \cos \alpha}{\cos \alpha - \mu \sin \alpha}$.

111. *The screw.*

The screw is a spiral thread running along the surface of a circular cylinder, which may be imagined to be generated thus:

Let AG be a rectangle whose base AB is exactly equal to the circumference of the cylinder; make the rectangles BD, CF, EH... equal in every respect, and draw the straight lines AC, DE, FG...; then if the rectangle BH be applied to the surface of the cylinder so that the base AB coincides with the base of the cylinder, the broken lines AC, DE, FG... will form a continuous line on the surface of the cylinder, the point C coinciding with D, E with F, and so on. If we now suppose this *line* to become a protuberant thread, we obtain a *screw*, in which the distance between any point of one thread and the one next below it, measured parallel to the axis of the cylinder, is everywhere the same and equal to BC:—the angle CAB which the thread at any point makes with the base of the cylinder is called the *pitch* of the screw.

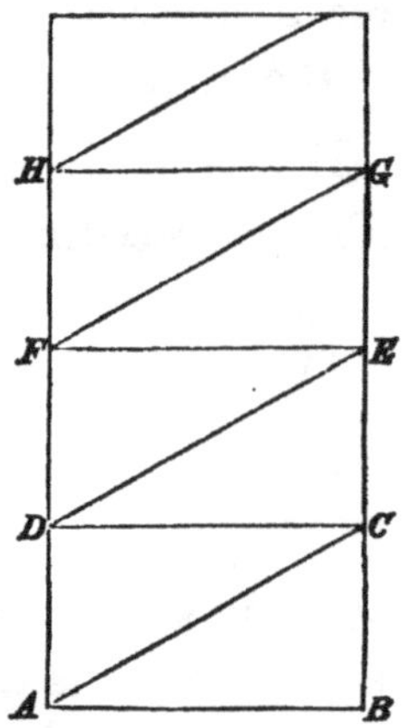

The screw formed on the *solid* cylinder, as above, works in a *hollow* cylinder of equal radius, in which a spiral groove is cut exactly equal and similar to the thread on the solid cylinder, and in which groove the thread of the former can work freely.

A solid and hollow screw related as above are called *companion screws;* and when in action, one of them is fixed and the other is turned by means of a lever fixed into the cylinder at right angles to its axis. By turning the lever a weight is raised, or a pressure produced, at the end of the screw, which pressure acts in direction of the axis of the screw.

When the solid screw is small, it is sometimes called a *nut.*

112. The figure in the margin will convey some idea of one mode of applying a screw to produce pressure, and in all the various applications of the screw we may regard a power P as applied at the extremity of an arm which is at right angles to the axis of the screw so as to produce a pressure *in direction* of the axis, which we shall call the *weight.*

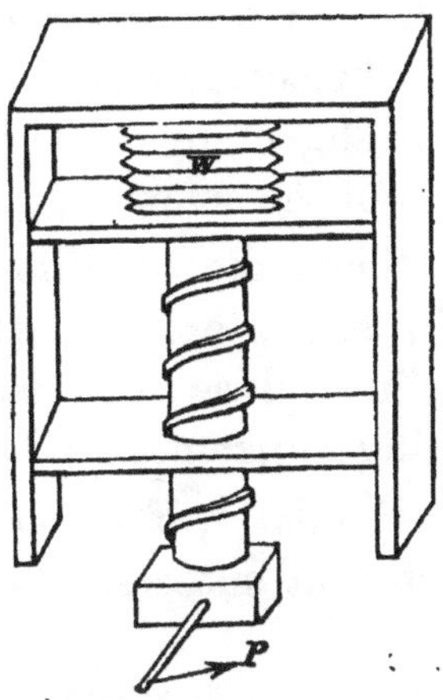

The form of the thread of the screw is not always the same in different screws; we shall suppose a section of it made by a plane through the axis of the screw to be rectangular, so that the surface of the thread will present the same appearance as the under surface of a circular spiral staircase.

113. *Conditions of equilibrium on the screw.*

In investigating the relation between P and W we shall for the sake of simplicity suppose the screw to be vertical, and the pressure which balances P to be a weight W placed on the end of the screw, and which the screw supports.

I. When the screw is *smooth*.

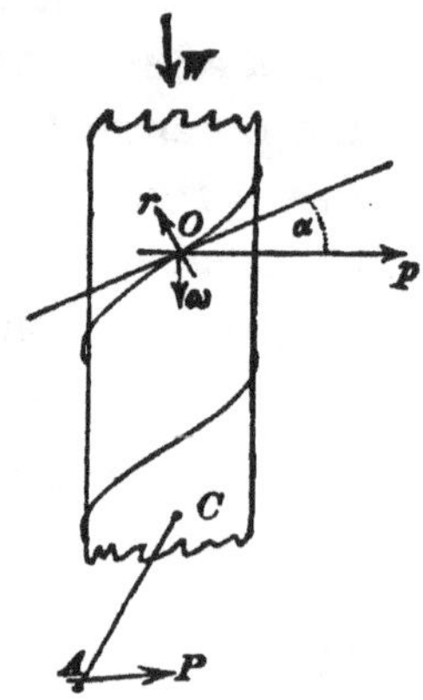

We may suppose the whole weight W to be distributed along the surface of the screw which is in contact with the *companion screw*.

Let w be a portion of W supported at O by the pressure r of the companion screw and by a force p acting horizontally, i. e. perpendicular to the axis of the screw: $\alpha =$ the *pitch* of the screw, i. e. the complement of the angle which the tangent to the thread of the screw at O makes with the axis of the screw.

Then the conditions of equilibrium of w under the action of r and p are the same as those of a body resting on an inclined plane (inclination $= \alpha$) under the action of a force p acting horizontally; hence $p = w \tan \alpha$. (Art. 110, Cor.)

Similarly, if w', w''... be the portions of the weight supported at successive points by the forces p', p''... we should have

$$p' = w' \tan \alpha, \quad p'' = w'' \tan \alpha......$$

$$\text{and } \therefore p + p' + p'' + ... = (w + w' + w'' + ...) \tan \alpha.$$

Now $w + w' + w'' + ...$ must equal W the whole weight, and p, p', p''... acting at the surface of the cylinder perpendicular to its axis produce the same effect to turn the cylinder round its axis as the power P acting at the arm CA.

Hence the *moments* of p, p', p''... about the axis must together be equal to the moment of P about the same; i. e. if

c be the radius of the cylinder, a the length of the arm CA at which P acts, we must have

$$pc + p'c + p''c + \ldots = Pa;$$

$$\text{whence we get } \frac{Pa}{c} = W \tan \alpha;$$

$$\text{or } P = \frac{Wc \tan \alpha}{a} \ldots\ldots\ldots\ldots \text{(i)};$$

the relation between P and W required.

Since $2\pi c \tan \alpha$ = distance between two threads, measured parallel to the axis,

and $2\pi a$ = circumference of the circle described by A,

we may write the condition (i) in the form

$$\frac{P}{W} = \frac{2\pi c \tan \alpha}{2\pi a} = \frac{\text{distance between two threads}}{\text{circumference of circle, radius } CA}.$$

II. *If the screw be rough.*

In this case supposing W distributed, as in case I., the forces which act at O are the weight of w vertically, p horizontally, ρ the normal pressure on the thread of the screw, and $\mu\rho$ the friction *along* the surface of the thread; hence taking the conditions of equilibrium on a rough inclined plane as in (Art. 109), i. e. resolving the forces along the tangent line and perpendicular to it, we get (supposing the friction to act down the screw; i. e. to oppose P,)

$$p \cos \alpha - w \sin \alpha - \mu\rho = 0,$$
$$p \sin \alpha + w \cos \alpha - \rho = 0;$$

whence we obtain

$$p = w \frac{\sin \alpha + \mu \cos \alpha}{\cos \alpha - \mu \sin \alpha}; \quad \rho = \frac{w}{\cos \alpha - \mu \sin \alpha};$$

or if we put $\mu = \tan\phi$, these become

$$p = w \cdot \frac{\sin(\alpha+\phi)}{\cos(\alpha+\phi)}; \quad \rho = \frac{w\cos\phi}{\cos(\alpha+\phi)};$$

whence as before

$$p + p' + p'' + \ldots = (w + w' + w'' + \ldots)\tan(\alpha+\phi),$$

$$\text{and } P\frac{a}{c} = W.\tan(\alpha+\phi); \quad \text{or } P = W\frac{c}{a}\tan(\alpha+\phi),$$

the relation between P and W.

114. *Obs.* If the friction acts up the screw (i.e. assists P), then we must change the sign of μ and therefore of ϕ, and we get in this case

$$P = W\frac{c}{a}\tan(\alpha-\phi).$$

Note. Since the distance between two threads, measured parallel to the axis, is the same at all points of the screw, but the length of one revolution of the screw is greater at greater distances from the axis, it is clear that the *pitch* α is different at points on the surface of the thread which are at different distances from the axis,—being greatest at points nearest the axis. But when the screw is smooth, as in case I., the relation between P and W, viz.

$$\frac{P}{W} = \frac{\text{distance between two threads}}{\text{circumference of the circle, radius } CA},$$

depends only on the distance between the threads and the length CA; hence this result will be true whatever be the *breadth* of the thread.

115. *The wedge.*

The wedge is a solid triangular prism made of hard material such as iron or steel, and is used for separating two bodies, or two parts of the same body, which adhere powerfully to each other. The edge of the wedge is introduced between the parts of the substance, and it is then driven forward by smart blows of a hammer applied at its back, or by some equivalent process. *Hatchets, chisels, nails, carpenters' planes, swords,*—are modifications of the wedge.

The action of the wedge is so essentially *dynamical* that it would serve no useful purpose to discuss its statical condition at any great length; we will only obtain the condition of its equilibrium in a very simple case.

Condition of equilibrium of a wedge.

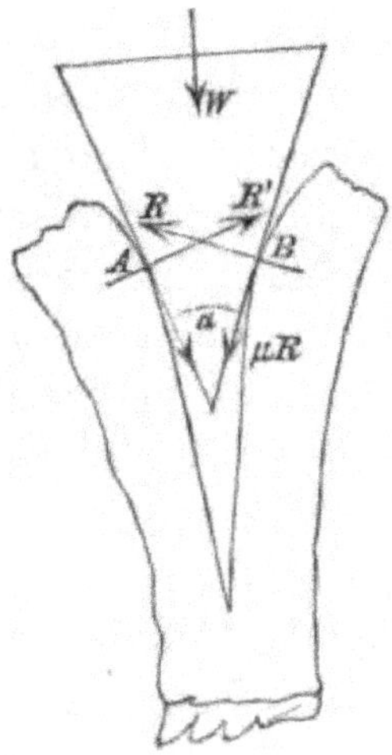

Suppose the wedge isosceles, and let the figure represent the position of the wedge inserted in the obstacle and in contact with it at A and B; R, R' the pressures perpendicular to the faces of the wedge at B, A; μR, $\mu R'$ the friction on the wedge at those points; W the force applied at the middle point of the back of the wedge, and α the angle between the faces of the wedge; then resolving the forces which act on the wedge in direction of W which bisects the angle α, and at right angles to this we get

$$W + \mu(R + R')\cos\frac{\alpha}{2} - (R + R')\sin\frac{\alpha}{2} = 0,$$

$$\mu(R - R')\sin\frac{\alpha}{2} + (R - R')\cos\frac{\alpha}{2} = 0,$$

the latter equation gives $R = R'$, and substituting this in the former, we get

$$W = 2R\left(\sin\frac{\alpha}{2} - \mu\cos\frac{\alpha}{2}\right),$$

μ being the coefficient of friction *actually* in operation.

It may be remarked that in many cases the wedge is kept in its place by friction alone,—in such cases $W = 0$, and

$$\therefore\ \sin\frac{\alpha}{2} - \mu\cos\frac{\alpha}{2} = 0; \quad \text{i.e. } \mu = \tan\frac{\alpha}{2},$$

which gives the coefficient of friction actually required for the equilibrium of the wedge.

116. *Principle of Virtual Velocities.*

Def. If A be the point of application of a force P, and this point receive a *small* displacement so as to come to A', the small space AA' is called the *virtual velocity* of the point A, and if $A'a$ be drawn perpendicular to AP, the small space Aa is called the *virtual velocity* of the force P, and is regarded as *positive* or *negative* according as a lies on the side of A towards which P acts, or the opposite,—in other words, the *virtual velocity* or *displacement* of the point of application resolved in direction of the force is the *virtual velocity* or *displacement* of the force:—the direction of the force $A'P$ in the new position being supposed to remain parallel to AP, or very nearly so.

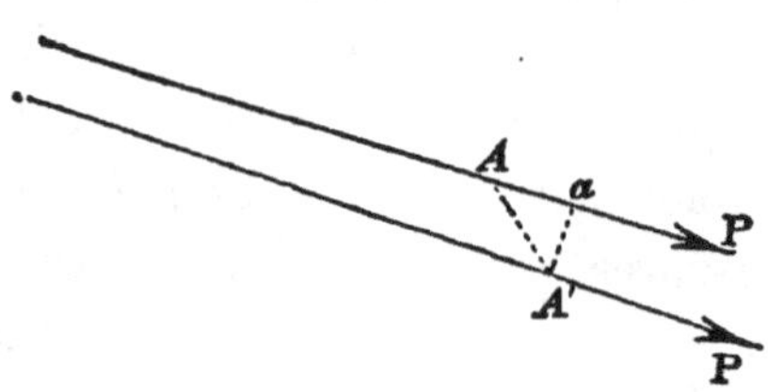

If $A'Aa = \alpha = A'AP$, we have $Aa = AA' . \cos\alpha$; hence the virtual velocity of a force is equal to the virtual velocity of its point of application multiplied by the cosine of the angle, which the direction of the displacement of the point makes with the direction of the force.

The product of any force into its virtual velocity is called the *virtual moment* of the force.

117. When a machine or system of bodies is in equilibrium under the action of several forces, if the point at which any one force is applied be *slightly* displaced without breaking the connexion of any of the parts of the system, the points at which the other forces are applied will, in general, also be displaced to an extent dependent upon the displacement of the first point; and the following singular relation exists among the forces and their several displacements or virtual velocities, viz. *The algebraic sum of each force multiplied by its virtual velocity is equal to zero*, or, in other words, *The algebraic sum of the virtual moments of a system of forces in equilibrium is zero.*

This is sometimes called the equation of virtual velocities.

Since the displacement of the several points would all take place *in the same time*, it is obvious that they would, *if small*, be in the ratio of the *velocities* of the several points; and further, since a system in equilibrium cannot move of itself, the displacements above supposed are *hypothetical* or *virtual* only, and such as would ensue upon the application of some additional force which is supposed to cease as soon as the displacement is effected, and the system to be in equilibrium and at rest in its new position. Hence the term *virtual velocity*.

118. The proof of the principle of virtual velocities in its general form is of too difficult a character to be introduced into an elementary work. We will here shew that the principle holds true in the case of the *lever*, *the wheel and axle*, *the several systems of pullies*, *the screw*, and *the inclined plane;* in other words, when a power and a weight balance each

other on any one of these machines, if the power be slightly displaced, the consequent displacement of the weight is such that P. *displacement of* $P = W$. *displacement of* W,

or P. *virtual velocity of* $P = W$. *virtual velocity of* W...(1).

In each of the following cases, the student will observe that if the displacement of P is in direction of P's action, that of W will be in the direction *opposite* to W's action; i.e. the virtual velocities of P and W are of contrary *algebraic sign*, so that, although for the sake of obtaining more convenient formulæ we shall neglect the algebraic signs of the displacements and regard their actual magnitude alone, the equation (1) would algebraically be written

$$P \,.\, P\text{'s virtual velocity} + W \,.\, W\text{'s virtual velocity} = 0.$$

119. *Case* I. *When P and W balance each other on a bent lever.*

Let ACB be a bent lever whose fulcrum is C; CM, CN the perpendiculars from C on the lines of action of P and W. Let the lever turn about C through a *small* angle $ACA_{,} = \alpha$ so as to come into the position $A_{,}CB_{,}$; then $AA_{,}$, $BB_{,}$ are *small* circular arcs which may approximately be regarded as straight lines, and the angles $CAA_{,}$, $CA_{,}A$, $CBB_{,}$, $CB_{,}B$ as very nearly right angles.

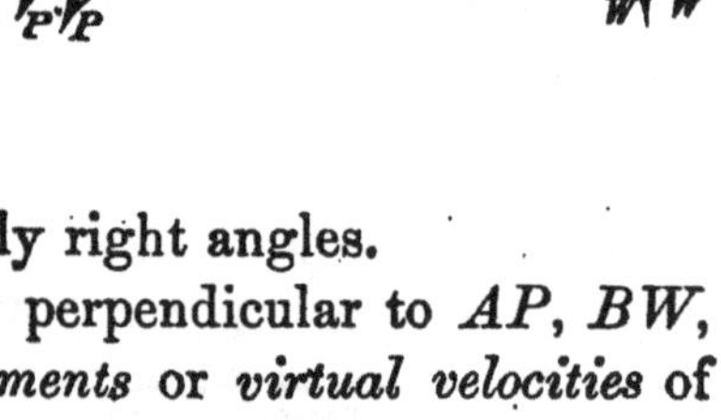

Hence if $A_{,}a$, $B_{,}b$ be drawn perpendicular to AP, BW, then Aa, Bb will be the *displacements* or *virtual velocities* of P and W respectively, and we shall have $AA_{,} = \alpha \,.\, AC$, and

$$Aa = AA_{,} \,.\, \cos A_{,}Aa = AA_{,} \,.\, \sin CAM$$
$$= \alpha \,.\, AC \,.\, \sin CAM = \alpha \,.\, CM.$$

Similarly,

$$Bb = BB_{,} \,.\, \cos B_{,}Bb = BB_{,} \,.\, \sin CBN$$
$$= \alpha \,.\, CB \sin CBN = \alpha \,.\, CN.$$

$$\text{Whence } \frac{Aa}{Bb} = \frac{CM}{CN} = \frac{W}{P} \text{ (Art. 89)};$$

$$\text{and } \therefore P \,.\, Aa = W \,.\, Bb,$$

or $P \,.\, P$'s *virtual velocity* $= W \,.\, W$'s *virtual velocity.*

120. *Case* II. *The wheel and axle.*

Let the machine be turned about its axis through a small angle α, so that the line MON comes into the position mOn; then Mm, Nn will represent the lengths of string which have unwrapped from the wheel and wrapped upon the axle respectively; i.e. Mm, Nn will be equal to the corresponding displacements of P and W.

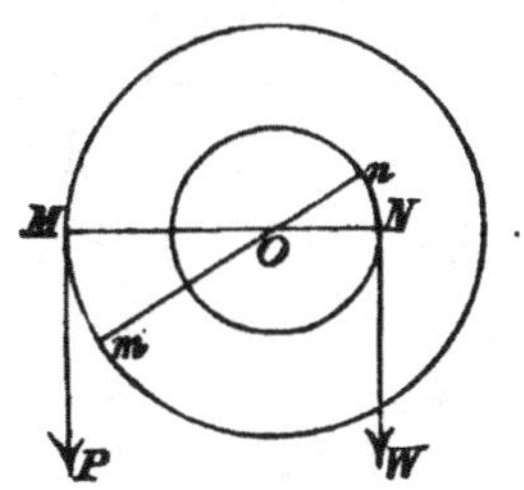

$$\text{And } \frac{Mm}{Nn} = \frac{MO \,.\, \angle\alpha}{NO \,.\, \angle\alpha} = \frac{MO}{NO}$$
$$= \frac{W}{P};$$

$\therefore P \,.\, P$'s *virtual velocity* $= W \,.\, W$'s *virtual velocity.*

121. *Case* III. *The single moveable pully, when the strings are parallel.*

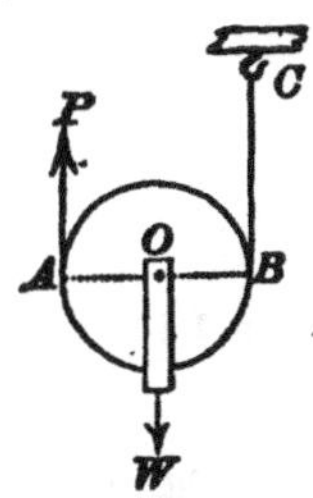

If the weight be raised through any space s, it is clear that the parts of the string on the opposite sides of the pully have to be shortened, each by a length s, in order that the string may become tight; i.e. P must move through a space $2s$;

$$\therefore \frac{P\text{'s virtual velocity}}{W\text{'s virtual velocity}} = \frac{2s}{s} = 2 = \frac{W}{P};$$

$\therefore$ *P.P's virtual velocity* = *W.W's virtual velocity.*

122. *Case* IV. *The single moveable pully when the strings are not parallel.*

Suppose the string fixed at B and to pass round a small peg at A. Let the centre of the pully be raised from O to $O_{,}$ in a vertical direction, and let Q, $Q_{,}$ be the points where the string quits the pully in the two positions; draw $O_{,}Q_{,,}T$ perpendicular to AQ and therefore parallel to OQ. The angle $Q_{,}O_{,}Q_{,,}$ is small and equal to $QAQ_{,}$, and we may regard $Q_{,}Q_{,,}$ as very nearly equal to the small arc of the pully intercepted by $O_{,}Q_{,}$ and $O_{,}Q_{,,}$; therefore since $\angle QOC = \angle Q_{,,}O_{,}C_{,}$, we shall have $QC = Q_{,,}Q_{,}C_{,}$, and $AQ_{,,} = AT$ very nearly.

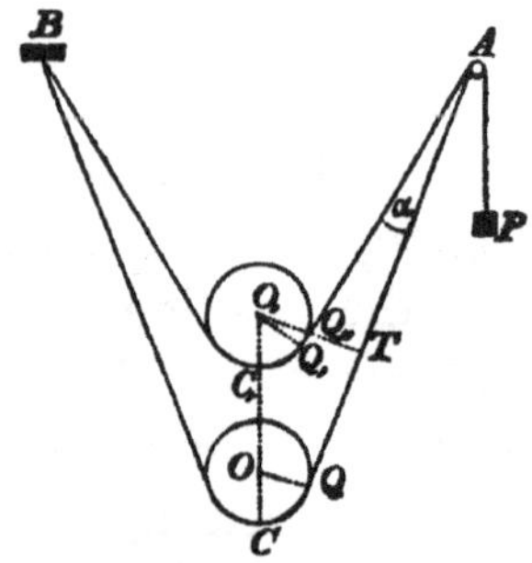

Hence it is clear that TQ will *very nearly* be the difference of lengths of the strings AQC and $AQ_{,}C_{,}$; and by the raising of the pully BC is shortened just as much as AC; i.e. $2TQ$ is the length of string which passes over A,—in other words, $OO_{,}$ and $2TQ$ are the corresponding displacements of W and P;

$$\therefore \frac{P\text{'s virtual velocity}}{W\text{'s virtual velocity}} = \frac{2TQ}{OO_{,}} = 2 \sin TO_{,}O$$
$$= 2\cos\theta,$$

if 2θ be the angle between the strings,

and this is $$= \frac{W}{P};$$

∴ *P. P's virtual velocity* = *W. W's virtual velocity.*

123. *Case* V. *In the system of pullies described* (Art. 104).

If the pully A_1 to which W is fixed be raised through a space s, the next pully A_2 will be raised through $2s$; the next A_3 through $2.2s$, i.e. 2^2s, and so on—so that if n be the number of moveable pullies, P will move through $2^n s$;

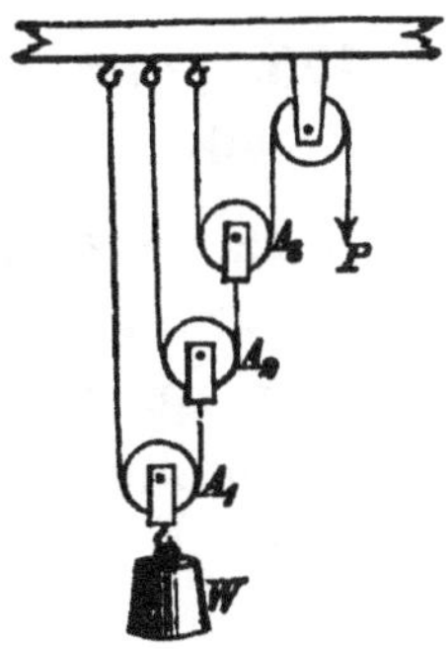

$$\therefore \frac{P\text{'s virtual velocity}}{W\text{'s virtual velocity}} = \frac{2^n s}{s} = 2^n = \frac{W}{P};$$

∴ *P. P's virtual velocity* = *W. W's virtual velocity.*

124. *Case* VI. *In the system of pullies described* (Art. 106).

If the weight be raised through a space s, the pully A_3 will be lowered through s; A_2 will be lowered through $2s$ in consequence of A_3 being lowered through s, and through s besides in consequence of W being raised through s; i.e. A_2 will be lowered through $(2+1)s$; similarly A_1 will be lowered through $2(2+1)s+s$; i.e. through $(2^2+2+1)s$ ... and if there be n pullies P will be lowered through a space

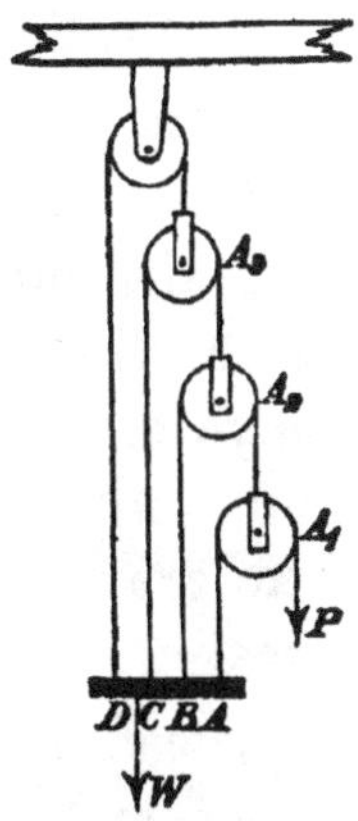

$$(2^{n-1}+2^{n-2}+\ldots+1)s, \text{ or } (2^n-1)s.$$

$$\text{Hence, } \frac{P\text{'s virtual velocity}}{W\text{'s virtual velocity}} = \frac{(2^n-1)s}{s} = 2^n-1 = \frac{W}{P};$$

∴ *P. P's virtual velocity* = *W. W's virtual velocity.*

Note. In the last two cases the weight of the pullies has been neglected,—we leave it as an exercise for the student to prove that when the weight of the pullies is taken account of *virtual moment of* P + *that of* W + *that of each pully* $= 0$.

125. *Case* VII. *In the system of pullies described in* (Art. 105).

If the weight be raised through a space s, each of the strings at the lower block will be shortened by a length s, and consequently P will have to move through ns in order that the string may become tight. Hence

$$\frac{P\text{'s virtual velocity}}{W\text{'s virtual velocity}} = \frac{ns}{s} = n = \frac{W}{P};$$

$\therefore$ *P. P's virtual velocity* = *W. W's virtual velocity.*

COR. In this system of pullies whilst a length s of string passes round the pully A, a length $2s$ will pass round the next pully B, $3s$ round the next pully C, $4s$ round D, and so on.

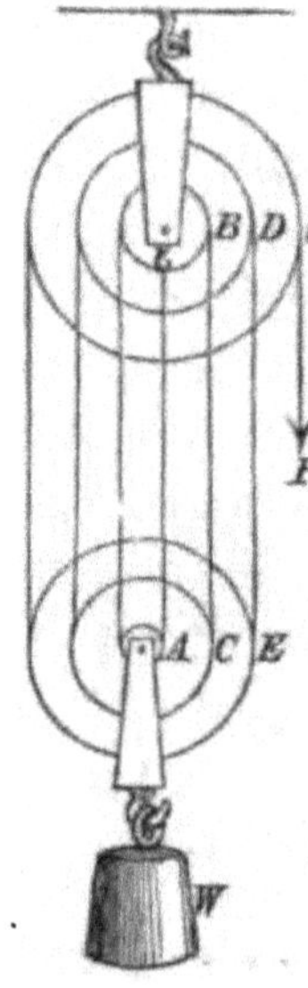

If then the radii of the pullies $A, B, C...$ are in the ratio of consecutive numbers 1, 2, 3, ... the pullies will all revolve *through the same angle*, since the arcs of circles subtending equal angles at the centre are proportional to the radii of the circles.

Instead of supposing the pullies to be distinct and separate, we may suppose circular grooves cut in the upper block (in the figure) with radii in the proportion of the even numbers 2, 4, 6, ... and in the lower block grooves with radii in the proportion of the odd numbers 1, 3, 5, ... and these grooves will answer the purpose of so many distinct pullies; and every point of the circumference of each groove moving just as fast as the part of the string which is in contact with it, there will be no sliding or rubbing of the string over any groove. This is the principle of *White's pully.*

126. *Case* VIII. *The Screw* (Fig. Art. 113).

If the power P make a complete revolution, it is obvious that the weight W will be raised through a space equal to the distance of two threads measured parallel to the axis of the screw, and proportionately for any smaller displacement of P. Hence

$$\frac{P\text{'s virtual velocity}}{W\text{'s virtual velocity}} = \frac{\text{circumference of circle described by } P}{\text{distance between two threads}}$$

$$= \frac{W}{P};$$

$\therefore$ *P. P's virtual velocity* $=$ *W. W's virtual velocity.*

127. *Case* IX. *The inclined plane* supposed smooth.

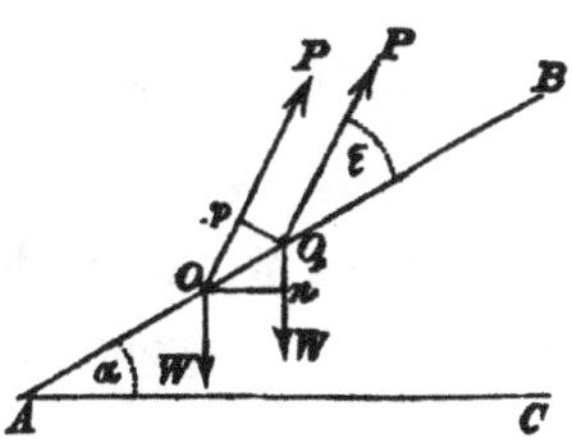

Let the weight be displaced along the plane through a small space OO_1, the direction of P remaining appreciably the same after as before the displacement, draw O_1p perpendicular to OP, and On horizontal; then Op and O_1n are the corresponding displacements of P and W. Hence

$$\frac{P\text{'s virtual velocity}}{W\text{'s virtual velocity}} = \frac{Op}{O_1n} = \frac{OO_1 \cos \epsilon}{OO_1 \sin \alpha} = \frac{\cos \epsilon}{\sin \alpha} = \frac{W}{P};$$

$\therefore$ P. P's *virtual velocity* = W. W's *virtual velocity.*

Note. The student will have little difficulty in proving the *equation of virtual velocities* to hold good in the case of a *rough* inclined plane.

128. *Case* X. *Any combination of Machines.*

We have seen that the *virtual moment* of the *power* P applied to any machine is equal to the *virtual moment* of the *weight* or *force* which balances P in that machine. If now we have any combination of machines $A, B, C\ldots$ the force which balances P on A may be regarded as a power applied to B, and the force which balances this on B may be regarded as a power applied to C, and so on; and from what precedes we infer that the *virtual moments* of each of these forces are equal. If then P be the power applied to the first of a train of machines, and W be the weight or force which balances it on the last machine of the train, we shall have

P. P's *virtual velocity* = W. W's *virtual velocity.*

Conversely, if this equation is satisfied in any combination of machines, we readily infer that P and W balance each other.

129. *Mechanical advantage* and *efficiency.*

Def. The *mechanical advantage* of a simple machine is the *number* expressing the multiple which the *weight* or force produced is of the *power* or force producing it,—in other words, it is the ratio $\frac{W}{P}$; *for instance*, in the case of the system of pullies (Art. 104) the mechanical advantage $=\frac{W}{P}=2^n$.

If for example there be four moveable pullies then the

mechanical advantage is 16, and a power equivalent to 8 lbs. would be able to raise a weight of 16.8 or 128 lbs.

The *advantage* of a combination of machines will be equal to the product of the *advantages* of the several machines in the combination.

130. In the several machines described in this chapter we have supposed the forces just to balance each other, so that no motion would ensue; and we have also in most cases neglected the friction which will in practice exist among the parts of the machine. These suppositions, however, are not quite accurate when any mechanical agent is employed to produce a certain effect by means of a machine; as for instance, when the pressure of the air is employed by means of a windmill to grind corn, or a horse draws a cart along a rough road horizontal or inclined, or a locomotive is propelled along a railroad by steam pressure. In all such cases it is obvious that the pressure applied at first *to put the machine in motion* must *exceed* the resistance to be overcome; and so long as this excess continues, the rate of working of the machine will be increasing: when this rate of working has become sufficiently great, if we suppose the excess of the force over the resistance to cease, the machine will go on working uniformly, and the force or power applied will *just balance* the resistance.

131. The amount of work done by a machine is commonly measured by the product of the pressure exerted at the work and the space through which it is exerted, no regard being had to the rate or speed at which the machine is working.

Def. This is sometimes called the *labouring force* or *work done* or, *efficiency*,—in other words, we may define the *efficiency* of a force to be the product of the number of units of force exerted into the number of units of space through which it acts.

Thus for illustration, if we take as the unit of *efficiency* or the *dynamical unit*, the work performed in raising 1lb. vertically through 1 foot, then the efficiency required to raise a ton through 1 yard would be = 6720.

131. The *standard* of *efficiency* or *work done* assumed by *Watt* and adopted generally by engineers is 33000 *lbs.* raised through 1 *foot per minute*,—the agent working steadily. This is called a *horse-power*, and the efficiency of steam-engines and other machines is commonly expressed in terms of this unit. Thus if a machine of H *horse-power* can raise P *lbs.* through f *feet* in t *minutes*, we shall have these quantities connected by the relation of $Pf = 33000\, H \,.\, t$.

132. We have seen in the case of the simple machines, or any combination of them, that if the system be put in motion, then

$$P \,.\, P\text{'s displacement} = W \,.\, W\text{'s displacement}.$$

This result shews us that however the application of a force be modified or rendered more useful by the intervention of a machine, yet no *efficiency* is gained thereby; and further, the same result put in the form

$$\frac{P\text{'s velocity}}{W\text{'s velocity}} = \frac{W}{P},$$

shews that in whatever proportion the intensity of a force be increased by means of a machine, yet the *space* through which the increased force will operate will be *diminished* in the inverse proportion as compared with the space through which the force applied must operate. Thus for the sake of illustration, suppose a weight of 500lbs. is supported on a machine by a power equivalent to 10 lbs., then in order that the weight might be raised through *one* inch it would be requisite for the power to move through a space of 50 inches in the same time. This diminution of velocity in the inverse proportion of the increase of force is the foundation of the common phrase, applied to machines, that *what is gained in power is lost in velocity;* and we may regard it as another form of stating the principle of virtual velocities in this particular case, or the same as asserting that *no efficiency is gained by the intervention of a machine.*

133. Before closing this chapter we will briefly allude to the principle of the *differential axle* and *Hunter's Screw.*

On the wheel and axle we have seen that (Art. 100)

$$\frac{P}{W} = \frac{\text{radius of axle}}{\text{radius of wheel}}, \quad \text{or } W = P\frac{\text{radius of wheel}}{\text{radius of axle}};$$

from which it would appear that by sufficiently diminishing the *radius of the axle* a given power P might be made to raise a weight W of any magnitude we please. Practically however there is a limit to the thickness of the axle; for if it be made too small, the material of which it is made will not bear the strain upon it, and it will break.

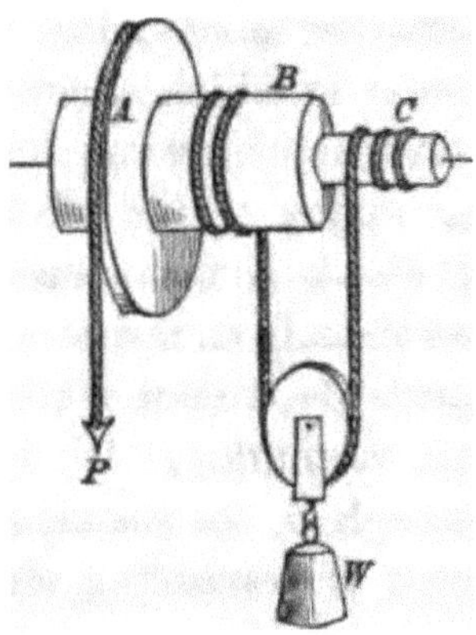

This imperfection is obviated in the *differential axle,* the mode of action of which will be sufficiently clear from the figure,—the string from which W is suspended by a pully passing round the two axles B, C in opposite directions: if T be the tension of this string, a, b, c the radii of A, B, C respectively, we shall have for equilibrium

$$2T = W,$$

$$Pa + Tc = Tb;$$

$$\therefore\ P = \frac{b-c}{a}T = \frac{b-c}{a}\frac{W}{2};$$

and the mechanical advantage $= \frac{W}{P} = \frac{2a}{b-c}$,

which may be increased to any extent by making the axles B and C as nearly equal as we please without unduly reducing the strength of the axle.

134. Again, in the case of the screw, it is obvious from the expression

$$\frac{W}{P} = \frac{\text{circumference of circle described by } P}{\text{distance of two threads}} \text{ (Art. 113)},$$

that by diminishing the distance between two threads sufficiently, we might obtain any *mechanical advantage* we please; but the distance between the threads must not be less than the thickness of the threads, otherwise the companion screws could not work together; and further, if the thickness of the threads be unduly diminished, they will not be able to bear the strain upon them. This difficulty is obviated in *Hunter's Screw*, in which a screw A works within another screw B; thus if c be the radius of the circle described by P,—b, a the distance between two threads in the screws B, A respectively,—then whilst P makes one revolution, W will descend through b, in consequence of the

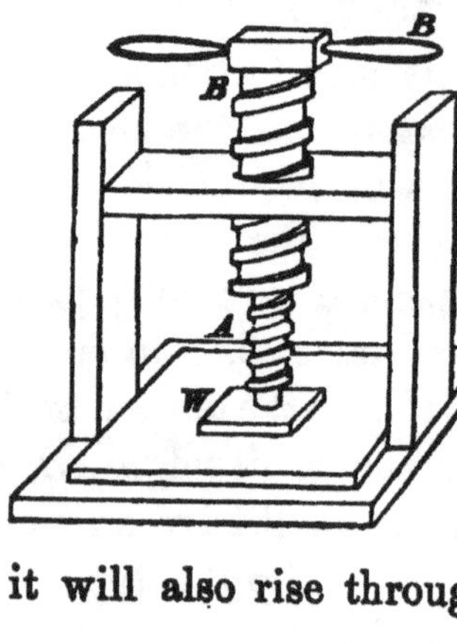

screw B descending through b, but it will also rise through

a in consequence of the screw A making one turn within B; i.e. W will descend through $b-a$.

Whence $P\,.\,P$'s *displacement* $=W\,.\,W$'s *displacement* gives

$$P\,.\,2\pi c=W\,.\,(b-a),$$

$$\text{and}\,\frac{W}{P}=\frac{2\pi c}{b-a};$$

and by making b as nearly equal to a as we please, the *mechanical advantage* may be increased to any extent without unduly weakening the threads of *the screws*.

DYNAMICS.

CHAPTER I.

INTRODUCTION.

1. A MATERIAL particle has been defined to be a portion of matter indefinitely small in all its dimensions. It has therefore no determinate form or volume,—but it has mass, it may be subject to the action of force, and may exert pressure on other particles. This conception of a particle is of course conventional,—a result of arbitrary definition,—so that calculations respecting such a body cannot be *at once* practically applied, since no bodies of which we have any experience correspond to this idea. But a particle having no parts, its motion is one and indivisible, and is therefore of a simpler kind than that of a body of finite size, different points of which might move differently. Hence we are led to consider the motion of a particle preparatory to that of bodies of finite size, and which have a real existence. The motion of such bodies can be reduced to a dependence on that of particles, by the application of *suitable* principles, but in the present treatise we do not propose to consider the motion of anything but particles or bodies regarded as particles; for example, a ball or a body of any kind, whenever it may occur in the following pages, will be considered, so far as its motion is concerned, as a particle coincident in position with the centre of gravity of the ball or body.

2. When the position of a particle relative to certain fixed points is being altered, it is said to be in *motion*,—and its *path* is the line (straight or curved) along which it moves. The tangent to the path at any point is the *direction* of the particle's motion at that point.

Def. *Velocity* is the term employed to express the degree of swiftness or speed with which a body is moving, and this velocity is said to be *uniform* when equal lengths of path are passed over in equal intervals of time, however large or small the intervals be taken; when this is not the case, the velocity is *variable*.

When the velocity of a body is uniform, it is measured by the space passed over in a unit of time,—and is the same at every instant whilst the motion continues uniform.

When the velocity is *not uniform*, it is measured at any instant by the space which the body would describe in a unit of time, if the body retained during that unit the same velocity which it has at the instant when it is under consideration.

3. An illustration may serve to make this mode of measuring variable velocity clearer. The speed of a railway-train is in general continually varying, and considering its motion at any instant we should say that it was travelling at *so many* (say 30) *miles an hour*, without much risk of being misunderstood; we should mean, not that it had travelled 30 miles during the last hour, nor that it would travel 30 miles during the next hour, *but* that if it were to travel for an hour with the speed it possesses at the instant considered, it would pass over exactly 30 miles.

In fact, the velocity of a body at any given instant must be regarded as a *quality* which it then possesses without any reference to its anterior or subsequent state, and without any reference to causes which may have produced or may alter the velocity.

This velocity may and will be influenced *from time to time* by different agents, but the velocity at any instant we regard as a quality which the body then possesses in the same sense that it possesses mass and position.

When then we represent the velocity of a body by a symbol, as v, we mean (certain units of time and of length being understood) that if the velocity continued of the same intensity for a unit of time, the body would in that unit of time pass over v units of length.

And the magnitude of this numerical representative of the velocity (v) will depend upon the magnitudes of the units of time and space, and will vary with them, *viz.* directly as the unit of time, and inversely as the unit of space.

Thus a velocity of 360 feet per minute is equivalent to 120 yards per minute, or to 6 feet per second, or to 2 yards per second.

4. *Formula for uniform motion.*

Let s be the space described in time t by a body moving with uniform velocity v, then since in each successive unit of time the body passes over v units of length, we shall have vt for the whole space passed over in t units of time, i. e. $s = v \,.\, t$,—a formula which holds true whether t be integral or fractional.

5. We proceed next to explain how change of velocity is measured.

When the velocity of a body is continually increasing in such a way that it receives equal increments of velocity in equal successive intervals of time, however large or small these intervals may be, the body is said to be *uniformly accelerated*, or the *acceleration* is said to be *uniform*.

When the velocity changes in any other way, the acceleration is *variable*.

Measure of acceleration.

When the acceleration is uniform, it is measured by the quantity by which the velocity is increased in a unit of time, and is the same at all times during the motion. When the acceleration is variable, it is measured at any instant by *what would be the increase* of velocity in a unit of time, supposing the rate of increase of velocity to be uniform for that unit, and of the same intensity as at the instant considered.

6. When then we express the acceleration of a body by a symbol f, we mean (certain units of time and space being understood) that if the rate of increase of velocity continued of the same intensity for a unit of time, the velocity would be increased by f at the end of that unit.

A second is frequently taken as the unit of time, and a foot of length, but as before in Art. (3), any other units might be chosen instead, and the numerical value of f for given units of time and length being given, its numerical value for any other assigned units of time and length may be found.

Thus, let f feet be the velocity generated in one second, the acceleration being uniform, then $60f$ will be the velocity generated in 60 seconds, i. e. in one minute.

This means that the body at the end of one minute would have acquired a velocity of $60f$ *per second*.

Remembering then that when we use a minute as the unit of time we must measure velocities by the spaces which would be described in one minute, the velocity acquired would be 60 . 60 . f per minute. Hence f feet being the measure of the acceleration when one second is the unit of time, $60^2 . f$ will be the measure of acceleration when a minute is the unit of time.

Thus if the unit of time be altered, the numerical value of the acceleration will vary as the square of the unit of time, and besides—as in the case of velocity, Art. (3)—if the unit of space be altered, the numerical value of f will vary inversely as the unit of length.

Obs. Retardation may in all cases be regarded as a *negative* acceleration.

7. The term *force* has been applied to any cause which tends to move a body or to alter the state of its existing motion. This conception of it renders it unnecessary to consider the manner in which force is produced, whether it be by the agency of living bodies, or the pressure of inanimate substances, or by the intrinsic attraction of matter. We shall regard force simply with reference to its effects, *viz.* the production of *motion* in material bodies; and this points directly to the two particulars to which the student is requested to give his attention in estimating the effects of force,—the *matter* or *mass* moved, and the *velocity* and *change of velocity* produced.

8. We here introduce a new quality, *viz.* that of mass, which is perhaps not familiar to the student. But experience teaches us that *equal* efforts are not required to produce the *same* motion in different bodies. It will probably be admitted without hesitation that equal volumes of the *same* substance would acquire equal velocities by the application to them of equal forces for the same time; but this would not be the

case with *equal* volumes of *different* substances. In fact it will frequently happen that when equal forces are applied for the same time to bodies of different substance and of unequal volume, the velocity acquired by the body of *greater* volume will be *greater* than that of the other, and *vice versâ;* so that the consideration of *volume* is not sufficient for the comparison of bodies under this aspect, and it is necessary to introduce a new idea, *viz.* that of *mass* or *massiveness*, and this must be regarded as a quality of matter *sui generis*, as much so as its *weight*, *form*, *volume*, &c.

9. We give no *definition* of this new species of quantity, which is a fundamental one in Dynamical science; for such definitions as might be given would be as illusory as those which might be given of time, space, and many other species of magnitudes.

But it is necessary clearly to define *equality* between quantities of this new species, so that in estimating the mass of a body it may be referred to the *like quality* of some other body taken as a standard.

We give then the following definition of *equal masses:*

Def. "The *masses* of two particles are said to be *equal* when two equal forces acting on them similarly for the same time generate in them equal velocities."

The notion of equality of mass of two bodies will readily lead to that of bodies whose masses have any assigned ratio. Thus if the masses of two bodies A and B are said to be in the ratio $m : n$, it is meant that A and B might be divided, the former into m equal parts and the latter into n equal parts, any two of which parts are of equal mass and satisfy the above definition.

Def. The mass of a unit of volume of any substance is called its *density*,—so that if m be the mass of a body whose volume is V and density ρ, we have $m = V\rho$.

10. If the notion of mass is not familiar to the student, he will perhaps consider the account of it given above in Arts. (8, 9) vague and unsatisfactory. The same vagueness attaches to any species of quantity or quality till the conception of it is impressed on the mind by continued experience, and this holds more especially with such qualities as are not obvious to the senses. For example, *form* and *volume* being qualities obvious to the eye, the conception of form and volume is much more readily acquired than that of *hardness*, which requires further experience to familiarize the conception of it. So the conception of the *mass* or *massiveness* of matter, not being obvious to the sight or touch requires further experience before it becomes familiar to the mind.

We may regard the *massiveness* of matter as that quality which enables it to act upon other matter isolated from itself: for instance, in the case of bodies at the earth's surface it is that quality which subjects them to the influence of the earth's attraction and causes in them the quality which we call *weight*.

11. The unit of mass may be assumed at our convenience; thus we might take the *mass* of a cubic inch of lead for our unit if it be convenient to do so under any particular circumstances.

And when we express the mass of a body by a symbol m we mean that the body has m times the mass of that body whose mass we have taken for our unit of reference. See Art. (44).

12. *Momentum.*

Def. If m and v be the numerical measures of the mass and velocity of a body, the product mv is called the *momentum* of the body.

The momentum of a particle must be viewed as a quality *sui generis*, and is to be compared only with the same quality of other particles, and apart from any external agency which may have been instrumental in producing it.

Obs. The *velocity* considered in Arts. (2, 3) is sometimes called *absolute* velocity, having been defined and measured with reference to points fixed in space: and this is distinguished from *relative* velocity, which is the term applied to the same quality defined and measured with reference to points which maintain an invariable position with regard to one another, but which are not necessarily fixed in space.

A similar remark applies to *absolute* and *relative* acceleration, and to *absolute* and *relative* momentum.

13. Supposing then a particle's geometrical and dynamical state to be defined at any instant by a knowledge of its mass, position, velocity, acceleration and direction of motion, we proceed to examine and measure the forces to which it is subjected.

It is often convenient to consider the transfer of a body from one position to another without introducing any consideration of the mass of the body, i.e. to treat of the velocity and acceleration exclusively of the mass.

Def. When we regard a force under this aspect, with reference that is to the acceleration it can produce, *or* its power of accelerating a given body, we speak of it as an "accelerating force," and we measure the accelerating force simply by the acceleration of the body, i.e. by the velocity which it can generate in the body in a unit of time, if uniform; or if variable, by the velocity which it would generate in a unit of time, if it acted for a unit of time with the same intensity as at the instant considered.

14. *Obs.* The term *acceleration* or *power of acceleration* would better express that particular effect of a force which is here considered, but the term *accelerating force* has been long sanctioned by usage, and the student is here cautioned that the term is used in the above sense. For example, the phrase "A body subject to an accelerating force f, &c." must be understood to mean "A body subject to a force which can produce an acceleration f in that body, &c."

Thus when we say the accelerating force on a body is f, or a body is subject to an accelerating force f, we mean that f is the acceleration of the body at the instant considered, *or*, that velocity is being generated in the body at that instant at the rate of f units of space per unit of time.

15. *Def.* A force considered as communicating *motion* to *matter*, i.e. regarding both the amount of *mass* moved and the amount of motion which it can communicate to it, is called a *moving force;* and it is measured by the *momentum* which it can generate in a unit of time, the intensity of the force remaining constant for that time.

Thus, if F be the symbol which represents a moving force, and f represents the accelerating force of F on a mass m, i.e. if f represent the velocity which F can generate in m by acting uniformly upon it for a unit of time, we have $F=mf$.

Hence we see that a moving force is expressed by the product of the number of units of mass in the body, and the number of units of acceleration which it can produce in the body.

Obs. This is sometimes given as the definition of moving force, i.e. moving force has sometimes been defined to be the product of the mass into the accelerating force.

16. The definitions above given of mass, momentum, accelerating force, moving force, must be looked upon as arbitrary; but we accept them as convenient terms to employ in expressing the laws of the action of force upon matter and in deducing from them their legitimate consequences. For a knowledge of these laws we must have recourse to experiment, for we can have no *à priori* knowledge of the constitution of matter, or of the principles which regulate and modify its dynamical state or condition.

17. *Impulsive Force.*

The effect of a force to which our attention is to be directed is the motion produced in a given mass; and this effect we regard as produced *gradually* in all cases. In other words, we consider that some *time* is necessary during which a force produces its effect. This *time* may be finite and appreciable, as when a body is pulled along a plane, or when a body falls to the earth under the action of gravity, or when a railway-train gets up its speed from a state of rest by the action of steam-pressure. But cases frequently occur in which the *time* required for the effect of a force to manifest itself is *very small* and, so to speak, *inappreciable;* as for example, when a body is put in motion by a blow, almost instantaneously.

When a force requires a *finite* and *appreciable* time in order to produce an appreciable motion, it is not unfrequently called a *finite* force, as in the cases first mentioned. But when motion is produced by a blow or impulse, as in the latter case, in an indefinitely small time, the force is generally called *impulsive;* but still we regard the effect as produced by the action of a force operating for a very short time.

In such cases the *impulsive force*, or the *force of the blow*, is measured by the *momentum* generated in the body by the impulse.

18. To illustrate this, we may suppose a ball B at rest to be suddenly put in motion by a ball A striking it. The balls will be in contact for a short time (τ suppose), and during this interval A will press B with a force varying in intensity from the beginning to the end of the interval τ. The *moving force* which acts on B will thus be varying, but we may practically consider it to have a *mean* intensity and to remain uniform during the time of contact. If we call this moving force F, and f the acceleration which F can produce in the ball B (the mass of which we will call m), and v the velocity acquired by B at the end of the time τ, we shall have, Arts. (6, 15),

$$v = f\tau, \text{ and } F = mf,$$

consequently $$F\tau = mf\tau = mv.$$

Now v the velocity acquired by B is finite, and therefore the momentum mv is finite, so that although τ is in general so small as to be inappreciable, yet F is so large as to render the product $F\tau$ finite, *and we take this finite product to be the measure of the impulsive force*,—in other words, if P be an impulsive force which produces a velocity v in a mass m, then $P = mv$.

19. Before stating the laws of motion, we proceed to give some explanation of the *geometrical* representation of the

position and motion of a particle; and for the sake of simplicity we will in the following Articles (19—24) suppose the motion to take place in one plane (that of the paper suppose).

If two lines Ox, Oy be drawn in the plane of motion inclined at any given angle, the position of any point P may be simply defined with reference to these lines (as fixed lines of reference), by drawing two lines through P, one of them PN parallel to Ox, the other PM parallel to Oy: if the distances OM, ON corresponding to any point are known, the position of the point is easily determined; for we have simply to draw lines through the points M, N parallel respectively to Oy and Ox, and the point in which these lines intersect is the geometrical position of P.

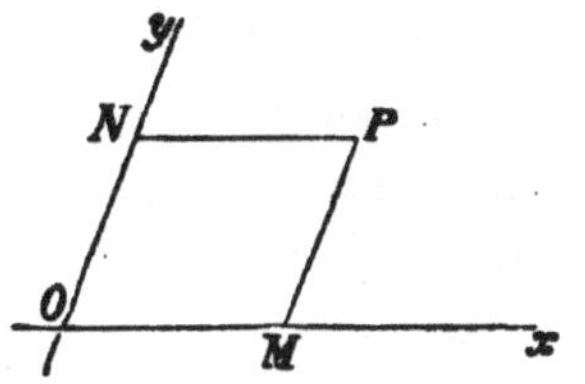

The point M is called the *projection* of the point P on the line Ox, or *the position of P referred to the line Ox*, and similarly N is the *projection* of P on the line Oy, or *the position of P referred to the line Oy*.

Note. The above mode of representing the position of a point will be familiar to the student who is acquainted with co-ordinate geometry as the method of co-ordinates, OM and ON being the *co-ordinates* of P measured along Ox and Oy.

20. *Resolution and composition of velocities.*

Further, if a particle be moving with uniform velocity in a given direction (as PQR), so that P, Q, R are the positions of the particle at given instants, and if we regard those points P, Q, R as determined by

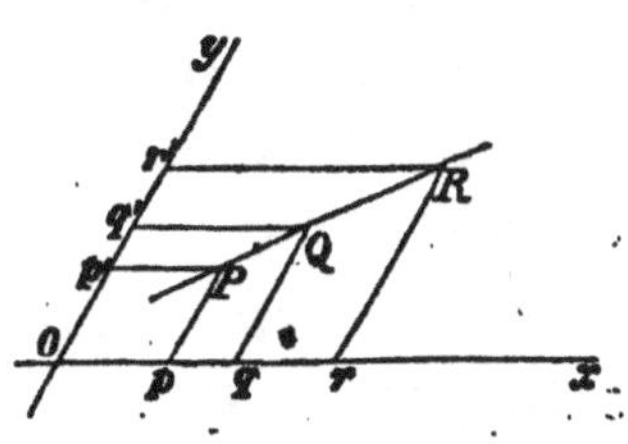

their projections on two fixed lines Ox, Oy, then will p, q, r be the projections of P, Q, R on Ox, and we readily see by simple geometry that the ratio of $pq : pr$ is the same as that of $PQ:PR$, whatever be the intervals of time in which the lengths PQ, PR are described by the particle. That is, if the particle move uniformly, its *projection* on a given line Ox will also move uniformly,—not with the *same* velocity as the particle, but with a velocity which bears to that of the particle a ratio dependent only on the inclination of the direction of motion of the particle to the two lines of reference Ox, Oy. The same is obviously true of the projection of the particle upon the other line of reference Oy.

The velocity of the *projection* of P along Ox is called the *velocity of P resolved along Ox*, or *the velocity of P referred to Ox*; and similarly with respect to the velocity referred to Oy.

21. Now since we regard the velocity of a particle at a given instant as a quality which the particle *then* possesses, without any reference to the *time* during which it retains that velocity, or the *space* through which it moves in consequence of it, and also without reference to any causes which may subsequently modify it,—we may represent the velocity of a particle P by a line PQ drawn in the direction of motion, and proportional to the velocity in magnitude;

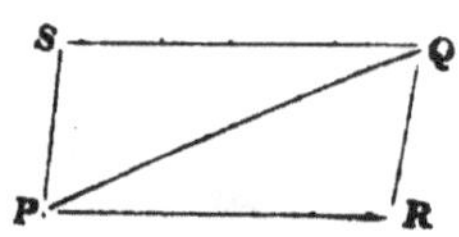

and if a parallelogram be constructed, of which PQ is the diagonal, and the sides of which (viz. PR, PS) are in the direction of known lines of reference, the sides PR, PS will represent the velocity of P *resolved along those lines of reference* severally.

THEOREM. In other words, we have this theorem: "If a straight line PQ which represents the velocity of a particle be made the diagonal of a parallelogram $PQRS$, whose adjacent sides PR, PS are in assigned directions, the resolved velocities in the direction of the sides will be represented by those sides respectively."

And conversely,

"If the *resolved velocities* of a particle in two given directions be represented by two lines PR, PS drawn from a point P, the *actual* velocity of the particle will be represented in magnitude and direction by the diagonal of the parallelogram constructed on those two lines as adjacent sides."

22. In the preceding Article we have represented *velocities* as to magnitude and direction by *lines*, and in a similar manner we may represent *accelerations* by *lines*,—and we may regard an acceleration as *resolved* in given directions in the same way as we supposed a velocity to be resolved in given directions; and with this understanding we shall have the following theorems respecting acceleration analogous to the preceding ones respecting velocity, viz.

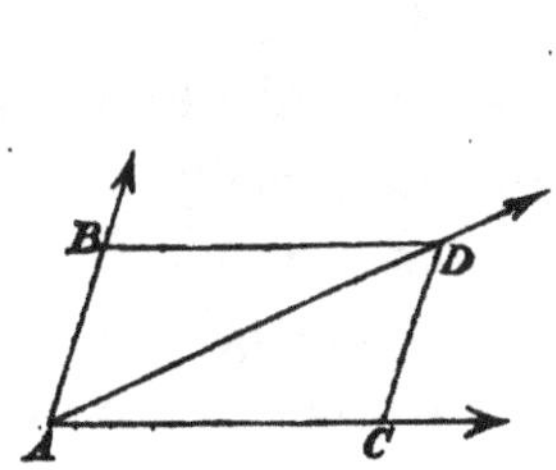

THEOREM. "If a line AD, which represents the acceleration of a particle, be made the diagonal of a parallelogram $ACDB$, whose adjacent sides AC, AB are in assigned directions, the resolved accelerations in the directions of the sides will be represented by those sides respectively."

And conversely,

"If the *resolved accelerations* of a particle in two given directions be represented by two lines AC, AB drawn from a point A, the *actual* acceleration of the particle will be represented in magnitude and direction by the diagonal of the parallelogram constructed on those two lines as adjacent sides."

23. The theorems of the two preceding Articles may be called the *Parallelogram of Velocities*, and the *Parallelogram of Accelerations*. They are analogous to the *Parallelogram of Forces* in Statics, and admit of the same extension as the latter theorem, so far as *composition* and *resolution* are concerned; but the student must bear in mind that these two theorems respecting velocity and acceleration form part of a purely conventional mode of *representing geometrically* the position and motion of a particle; and he must be careful not to confound the meaning of *lines* which in one problem may be employed to represent velocity, with the meaning of *other lines*, which in the same or other problems may be taken to represent acceleration, and *vice versâ*.

24. The results of the parallelogram of velocities may be stated as follows, with algebraic symbols—results which may easily be obtained by trigonometry. A velocity V, in a direction inclined at angles α, β to the lines Ox, Oy is equivalent to the velocities

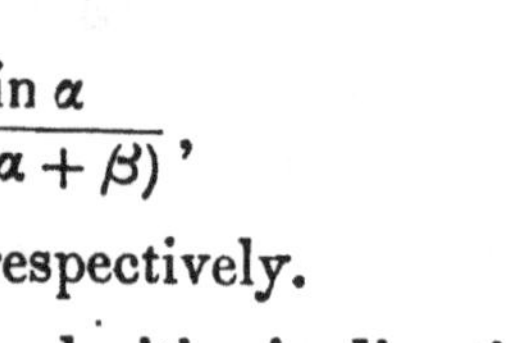

$$V\frac{\sin\beta}{\sin(\alpha+\beta)} \text{ and } V\frac{\sin\alpha}{\sin(\alpha+\beta)},$$

resolved in the direction of Ox and Oy respectively.

And conversely, if these component velocities in direction of Ox, Oy be represented by X and Y, the actual velocity V and its direction will be determined from the equations

$$X = V\frac{\sin\beta}{\sin(\alpha+\beta)}, \quad Y = V\frac{\sin\alpha}{\sin(\alpha+\beta)},$$

which give
$$\left.\begin{aligned} V^2 &= X^2 + Y^2 + 2XY\cos(\alpha+\beta) \\ \tan\alpha &= \frac{Y\sin(\alpha+\beta)}{X+Y\cos(\alpha+\beta)} \end{aligned}\right\},$$

which two equations determine the magnitude and direction of the actual velocity,—the angle $(\alpha+\beta)$ between the fixed lines Ox, Oy being a known angle.

The same formulæ, substituting *acceleration* for *velocity*, will hold good for the resolution and composition of acceleration.

25. The advantage of the mode of geometrical representation explained in Articles (19—24) will become obvious to the student when he has become acquainted with the laws of motion, and the application of them to determine the position and motion of a particle when acted on by known forces.

Obs. We have supposed, as was before mentioned (19), that the motion is entirely in one plane; when this is not the case, the method must be extended by taking *three* lines of reference in space analogous to the method of co-ordinates in geometry of three dimensions; but in the present treatise we shall have occasion to consider but few cases of motion which may not be regarded as taking place in one plane.

26. Having explained the mode of representing the motion of a particle geometrically, we proceed to enunciate and illustrate certain principles deduced from observation and experiment which are commonly called *laws of motion*, and according to which the motion of a body considered as a particle are calculated.

FIRST LAW OF MOTION.

27. *A particle if at rest will continue at rest, and if in motion will move in a straight line with uniform velocity unless it is acted on by an extraneous force.*

This law is sometimes referred to as the *law of Inertia* or the *principle of Inertia.* It expresses the fact that a particle of matter has no power within itself of altering or influencing its own state of rest or motion.

Of this principle no direct proof can be given, but it may be rendered probable by such experiments as the following. If a ball be projected along a smooth pavement it will continue in motion for a considerable time, and its path will be more nearly a straight line the smoother the pavement is; but the friction will gradually reduce it to rest: if it be projected along a sheet of ice, it will continue longer in motion, and will move more uniformly. Such experiments may *suggest* the inference that if all extraneous force could be removed, the ball would go on for ever with uniform velocity.

28. Having established the principle that a particle cannot put itself in motion, nor alter in any manner the nature of its own motion when it is in motion, we next require some principle which will enable us to calculate the effects of forces on a particle in motion. The experiments and researches of philosophers have led to the following, which may be called

THE SECOND LAW OF MOTION.

29. *When a particle is in motion under the action of any force, the acceleration of the particle estimated in any assigned*

direction is wholly due to the force resolved in that direction,—and is the same in intensity as if that resolved force alone acted on the particle at rest.

Thus for example, if the particle P be moving with any velocity v in the direction PV, and if X, Y be the forces acting upon P at that instant resolved in directions parallel to two fixed lines Ox, Oy,—this second law asserts that (at the instant under consideration) the *accelerations* of P *estimated in directions parallel to* Ox *and* Oy are the same as would arise from the separate and independent action of X, Y upon P at rest, in direction of Ox and Oy.

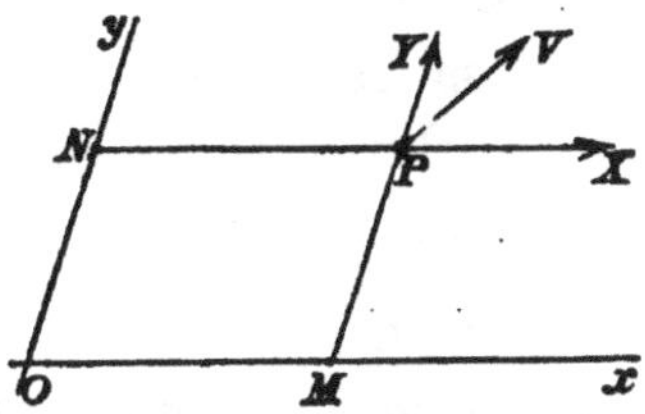

By the acceleration due to a force is meant of course the acceleration which that force is capable of producing in the particle. And if several forces act simultaneously on the particle, the force mentioned in the enunciation of the *second law* must be taken to mean the *resultant* of the several forces which act upon the particle: this resultant being determined in the same way as the resultant of statical forces is determined.

The enunciation of this second law further implies the fact, that the *accelerating power* of a given force upon a particle (or what we have before called the *accelerating force*) estimated in the direction of its action, is of the same intensity whatever be the dynamical state of the particle, i.e. whatever be the velocity and direction of the particle's motion,—or, the same as it would be if the particle *were for an instant at rest.*

30. The principle stated in the second law of motion will be sufficient (theoretically speaking) when the accelerating

forces acting upon a particle are given, to enable us *to determine the motion of the particle*, i.e. to determine its position and velocity at any time; for we should only have to calculate its position and velocity referred to two fixed lines as Ox and Oy (Art. 19, &c.) (or referred to three lines fixed in space if the motion be not in one plane), and when its motion referred to these lines is known, its *actual* position and velocity are known.

It will however frequently be the case in nature that the forces on a particle will vary with the position of the particle, and thus its motion will indirectly affect the forces which act upon it. To determine the motion of a particle generally will require the processes of the *Integral Calculus*, but in the present treatise we do not propose to consider any motions which require for their calculation anything beyond ordinary algebra; such for example as arise from the action of uniform forces or from impulsive action, or these combined.

31. *Illustrations of the second law of motion.*

Experiments such as the following may be mentioned as illustrating and confirming the second law of motion.

If a ship be moving uniformly, a ball when thrown with the same force will go to equal distances from the ship, whether it be thrown towards the bow or the stern, or at right angles to the direction in which the ship is moving. A ball let drop from the top of the mast will strike the deck at the foot of the mast, and will fall in the same time, whether the ship be at anchor or moving uniformly. A ball let drop from the top of a railway-carriage in uniform motion, will strike the floor of the carriage at the point directly beneath the point from which it started. A pendulum will vibrate in the same time from east to west, as from north to south, or in any other direction; thus shewing that whilst it is carried uniformly in one definite direction by the earth's rotation, its motion relatively to bodies on the earth's surface which have the same motion as the pendulum arising from the earth's rotation, is uninfluenced by the motion thence arising.

32. Experiments such as these, of course, do not *prove* the law. Strictly speaking it could only be proved by shewing it to be true for every individual case that can occur, which is manifestly impracticable. But when the results of numerous and intricate calculations based upon it are invariably found to agree with observation, we arrive at a *moral conviction* of its truth. And the principle itself having been obtained by *induction* from a considerable number of facts and observations, we employ it with confidence in *deducing* other consequences from it.

33. The mode of obtaining the magnitude of the acceleration which a given force is capable of producing in a given particle will be explained presently (see *third law of motion*); and assuming the principle which has been stated in the second law of motion, and illustrated in the preceding articles, we shall know how to obtain the magnitude of the acceleration of the particle, *estimated in any proposed direction*, when we know the forces which are acting upon it. Now the effect of an acceleration on a particle is to create or modify velocity in the particle, and we may regard the velocity with which a particle is at any instant animated, as the *accumulation* of the effects of the accelerating forces which have acted upon it during the successive portions of the interval of time during which it has been in motion. This consideration will

readily lead us to the following conclusion as a necessary consequence of the second law of motion stated in Article 29, viz. the velocity of a particle estimated in a given direction is wholly due to the acceleration which has operated on it in that direction.

34. In order to obtain *actually* the velocity acquired by a particle by the action of given forces, we shall in general require (as before remarked) the integral calculus: but we will here give the solution of a particular problem of frequent occurrence, which can be readily inferred from the second law of motion.

35. *If there be simultaneously impressed on a particle two velocities which would separately be represented by the lines AB, AC, the actual velocity will be represented by the line AD, which is the diagonal of the parallelogram of which AB, AC are adjacent sides.*

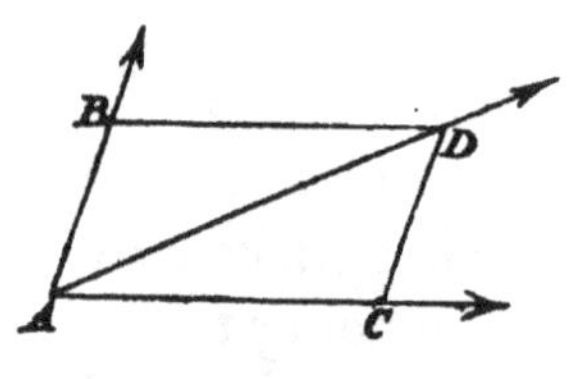

Let the motion of the particle be referred to the directions *AB*, *AC*, then we may suppose the particle at rest at *A* to receive simultaneously two blows in directions *AB*, *AC* respectively, which would (if they operated independently of each other) generate velocities represented by *AB*, *AC*. Complete the parallelogram *ABDC*. Then since the instant after the blows are communicated to the particle it is subject to no force, it must move with uniform velocity in some straight line (by first law of motion), and this straight line must be such that the velocity along it when referred to the lines *AB*, *AC* will be represented by the lines *AB*, *AC* (by the second law). The resultant velocity then must be represented by AD the diagonal of the parallelogram $ABDC$.

36. In the problem of the previous article instead of supposing *two* blows to be given to the particle simultaneously, we may suppose *one* blow given to the particle already in motion; for example, if the particle be moving in direction AC with a velocity represented by AC, and at the instant the particle is at A let a blow be given to it in direction AB, capable of producing on the particle at rest a velocity represented by AB: the actual velocity as regards direction and magnitude (by the same reasoning as the above) will be represented by AD.

Hence it appears that velocities (regarded as the effects of impulses) may be compounded in the same way that statical forces are compounded by the *polygon of forces*, and the same theorem *mutatis mutandis* will hold good for velocities as for statical forces.

37. The theorem stated and proved in Article (35), may for convenience be referred to as the *dynamical parallelogram of velocities*;—it is a consequence of the second law of motion, and exhibits the application of that law to find the effect of one or more impulsive forces—those effects being expressed in accordance with the geometrical mode of defining and estimating motion previously explained (Art. 19—25). The student will be careful to distinguish it from the *geometrical parallelogram of velocities* explained in Art. (20), which is simply a geometrical convention.

In a similar manner from observing the analogy between the statical parallelogram of force and the second law of motion, we may regard the second law as the *dynamical parallelogram of accelerations*; carefully distinguishing it from the *geometrical parallelogram of accelerations* stated in Art. (22).

38. We may, if we please, regard any velocity with which a particle is animated as remaining permanently impressed upon it, and when force acts on the body, the velocity arising from the action of that force may be regarded as *superadded* (so to speak) to the existing velocity—so that the actual velocity of the particle at any time in a given direction will be the *algebraic sum* of the velocities which have been impressed upon it in that direction.

39. The following experimental illustration may be given of the dynamical parallelogram of velocities.

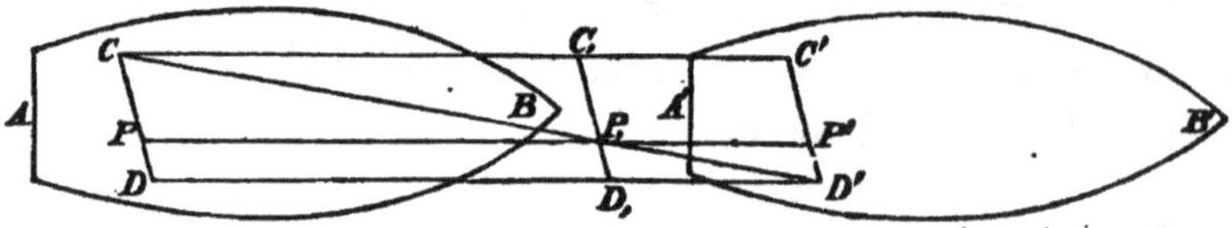

Let AB represent the deck of a ship which is moving uniformly parallel to itself from left to right, and let a body on the deck have a velocity communicated to it, which if the ship were at rest would make it move uniformly from C to D along the line CD in the same time that the ship moves from AB to the position $A'B'$.

It is found by experience that the body moves on the deck relatively to it in exactly the same way as if the ship were at rest, i.e. (drawing the parallelograms as in the figure) if in any time τ the line CD would have been brought to $C_{,}D_{,}$ by the motion of the ship, and CP be the space which the body would have moved through in the same time τ if the ship had been at rest, then it is found that $P_{,}$ is the position of the body ($C_{,}P_{,}=CP$) at the end of the time τ, whatever be the magnitude of τ.

Thus, in reality, the velocity of the ship has been compounded with that of the body, and the body has described *in space* the line CD' *uniformly* and *in the same time* that the point C on deck has moved to C'.

This confirms the dynamical parallelogram of velocities, and by inference the second law of motion also, so far as one experiment can do so.

40. Thus we see that if a body be moving along with a space which moves uniformly, and if any velocity be impressed on the body, the motion of the body *relatively to that space* will be the same as if the body and the space had been originally at rest; and more generally (if the second law of motion be true) we infer that if several bodies be in uniform motion, but be at rest *relatively to each other;* and if any force acts on one of them, the motion of this one *relatively* to the others is the same as if they had been all originally at rest.—Or we may state this principle as follows: "If all the points of a system have uniform and equal velocities and move in parallel directions, and if one of these points or particles be acted on by any force, its motion relative to the other particles will be the same as if the common motion of the system did not exist, and the particle in question were acted on by the same force acting in the same direction."

And from hence also it is obvious that we may (when we find it convenient to do so) impress *any the same* uniform velocity on each of the bodies composing a system, without affecting the motion of these several bodies relative to each other.

41. When the acceleration of a body for all successive instants is known, the motion of the body can be calculated as has been stated before. Now experience shews that the accelerations produced in *different* bodies by *equal* forces are not the same. We require then some principle based upon experiment which will enable us to determine the acceleration of a body of given mass when acted on by a given force or pressure. The principle required for this purpose is called the *third law* of motion, and may be stated thus.

THIRD LAW OF MOTION.

42. *When a force or pressure acts on a particle, the moving force on the particle is proportional to the force or pressure acting upon it.*

That is, if P, P' be two forces measured statically (viz. by the weights they would respectively support) acting on two particles whose masses are m, m', and if f, f' be the consequent accelerations of the two particles, then

$$P : P' :: mf : m'f',$$

$$\text{or } P \propto mf.$$

Since our units of force, mass, and acceleration are arbitrary, we may for convenience make $P' = 1$, $f' = 1$, $m' = 1$, and we shall then obtain $P = mf$. In other words, if we take our unit of mass to be such that a unit of force acting upon it would produce in it a unit of acceleration, then *referred to these units* the number expressing the force will be equal to the product of the numbers which express the mass and acceleration.

43. If W be the weight of a body whose mass is m, and g the accelerating force of gravity at the surface of the earth (i.e. the acceleration which the attraction of the earth, acting

freely on the body *in vacuo*, would produce in the body), we shall have by the previous article $W = mg = V\rho g$. (Art. 9.)

The numerical value of g must of course be determined by experiment, and the observations made upon pendulums are those which give the most trustworthy results. They are however of too refined a character to be introduced here; and it may be sufficient for the present purpose of the student to state, that if a *foot* and a *second* be taken for the units of space and time, the numerical value of g, in the latitude of London, is 32·19 or 32·2 nearly.

The value of g is found by experiment to be slightly different at different places on the earth's surface, but the variation is so small, that we may for all ordinary purposes assume the value of g to be that just given.

Or we may state the above result respecting the value of g thus:

A body falling freely from rest *in vacuo* under the action of gravity will, in one second from the beginning of its motion, have acquired a velocity of 32·2 feet per second.

44. If we call the *moving force* the *dynamical* measure of a force, the third law of motion establishes a connexion between the statical and dynamical measures of force, and asserts that the statical measure is proportional to the dynamical measure.

Considering the equations

$$m = V\rho, \quad W = mg = V\rho g;$$

we see from the former that *the unit of mass* would be the *mass of a body of a unit of volume and a unit of density;* and from the latter, since $g = 32·2$ when a foot and a second are taken for the units of space and time respectively, the *unit of weight* is the *weight of* a body of the *unit of density and of volume equal to the* $32 \cdot 2^{th}$ *part of the unit of volume.*

The density of distilled water is generally taken as the unit of density, and a cubic foot as the unit of volume.

The weight of a cubic foot of distilled water is 1000 *oz.* avoirdupois, nearly.

45. The equation $P = mf$ must be always understood in accordance with the explanation given in Article (42). As a further illustration, we will apply it to the following problem.

A body weighing 24 lbs. is moved by a constant force, which generates in a second a velocity of 3 feet per 1"; find what weight the force would statically support.

If we take m to represent the mass of the body and P for the number of lbs. the force would support, g the accelerating force of gravity, we have

$$24 = mg,$$
$$P = mf,$$

m being the same in both equations. And by the question, f the acceleration produced by P in the mass m is represented by 3, a foot and a second being the units of space and time,—and with the same units, g the accelerating force of gravity is $= 32 \cdot 2$.

Whence $P = \frac{f}{g} 24 = \frac{3}{32 \cdot 2} 24 = 2 \cdot 236$ lbs. nearly; that is, the force which acts on the body would support in equilibrium a weight equal to 2·236 lbs.

46. *Action and Reaction.*

If two bodies A and B are in contact and *at rest*, we know from statical principles that the pressure which A exerts upon B is *equal* in magnitude, and *opposite* in direction to that which B exerts upon A; and again, if two bodies A and B at rest are connected by a fine thread, the strain which the thread exerts upon one of the bodies is equal in magnitude and opposite in direction to that which it exerts upon the other. The question will arise, "Is this the case when the bodies are in motion? or, if the mutual pressures which they exert on each other are not equal, what relation subsists between them?" And to these questions (which must arise in all problems where there is any mutual action between the different parts of a system of bodies), the principles which we have already stated afford no satisfactory answer. *It is assumed*, however, that when one particle acts on another particle, *in motion* as well as *at rest*, the second exerts on the first a force equal in magnitude and opposite in direction to that which the first exerts on the second. If the force which the first exerts on the second be called "*action*," that which the second exerts on the first may be called "*reaction*," and the principle just stated may in other words be expressed thus: "Whenever one body A acts on another B, the latter reacts on the former, and this action and reaction are equal in magnitude and opposite in direction."

47. The action here spoken of may be of any kind whatever; as for example, when two bodies *in motion or at rest* press against each other, their mutual pressures are equal and opposite; or in other words, the action and reaction are equal in magnitude and opposite in direction. Or again, when two particles move in any manner connected by a string, the force which the string exerts on one is equal and opposite to the force it exerts on the other. Or again, if two particles attract or repel each other, the dynamical measure of the force which one of them A exerts upon the other B, is equal to that which

B exerts upon *A*. This principle is frequently embodied in the brief statement that "*Action and Reaction are equal and opposite.*"

48. For some illustration of the third law of motion, we may refer to the observations made with Atwood's machine (Arts. 80—82); but the motions of the heavenly bodies afford the most interesting as well as the most searching test of the truth of the dynamical principles which are employed in investigating them.

It has been before remarked, that the laws of motion are enunciated and asserted to be true only with respect to *particles*,—and of course, as we have no practical experience of particles, in the mathematical sense of the word, the student must not expect to find them *proved* with that degree of strictness which attaches to geometrical demonstration. He is recommended for the present to accept them as conclusions which have been arrived at by philosophers after much painful inquiry and observation, and not to trouble himself much with the particular experiments which may be said to suggest these laws, or with the calculations of more complex phenomena which are based upon them, till he has grasped their meaning, and applied them to a variety of problems. He will then be able more fully to appreciate the bearing of particular experiments on the principles which they are intended to illustrate and confirm. But as no individual experiment will involve *one* law of motion to the exclusion of *the others*, the laws of motion must be taken as a whole,—and when we find the observations of numerous and complex phenomena agreeing with calculations based upon these principles and involving them in every variety of combination, we arrive at a moral conviction of their truth.

CHAPTER II.

OF UNIFORM MOTION AND COLLISION.

49. WHEN a body, regarded as a particle, is subject to no extraneous force it moves with uniform velocity in a straight line (first law of motion). If then v represent this uniform velocity, and s be the length of path described or passed over in any interval of time t, we shall have $s = vt$; which is the formula for uniform motion.

The equation $s = vt$ which connects the three quantities s, v, t will still be true if the path of the body be curvilinear, provided the velocity be uniform: but when the path is not a straight line there must be some force acting on the body which deflects it from a rectilinear path; and if the velocity be uniform, this force must always act perpendicularly to the direction of the body's motion at any time, and the magnitude of this force will depend upon the curvature of the path. This kind of motion however we do not propose to discuss.

50. *The position, velocities, and direction of motion, of two particles at any time being given, to find after what interval they will be at an assigned distance from each other, and to determine their position at that time: the motion being in one plane.*

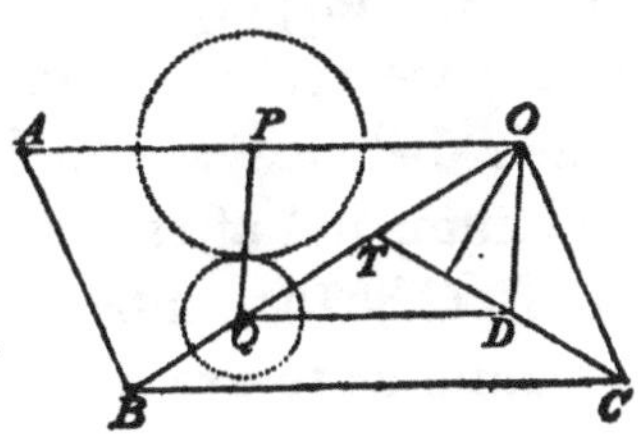

Let A, B be the position of the particles at first, and AO, BO the directions of their motion. Take AO to represent the velocity of A, and BT, on the same scale, to represent that of B. Complete the parallelogram AC and join CT. Let a circle with centre O and radius equal to the proposed distance, cut CT in D: join OD and complete the parallelogram PD. Then will P, Q be contemporary positions of the particles originally at A, B, and the time of moving from A to P : that from A to O :: $CD : CT$.

For by the construction

$$PO : QT = QD : QT = BC : BT = AO : BT;$$

$$\therefore AO - PO : BT - QT = AO : BT;$$

$$\text{i.e. } AP : BQ = AO : BT;$$

that is, AP, BQ are in the proportion of the velocities of the particles, and therefore they are simultaneously at P, Q, and the distance PQ is equal to OD, the distance proposed; and further, time of moving from A to P : time from A to O

$$= AP : AO = BQ : BT$$

$$= CD : CT \text{ by similar triangles.}$$

Cor. 1. Since the circle with centre O and radius OD will in general cut CT in two points, there will in general be two periods at which the particles are at a distance from each other equal to OD; we leave it as an exercise for the student to form the construction for the other position.

Cor. 2. Since OD cannot be less than a certain distance, viz. the perpendicular from O to CT (unless T and O coincide) we see that the particles will approach each other till their distance is equal to this perpendicular, and is then a minimum, and afterwards they will recede from each other.

If P, Q be the centres of two spherical balls, the proposition will enable us to examine the circumstances of their approach to each other &c.;—if the distance PQ = sum of the radii of the balls, we find when and where they will come into contact—if the sum of their radii be $<$ the perpendicular from O to CT, we can find when and where they are nearest to each other.

51. *An analytical solution of the above problem may be given as follows.*

Let a, b be the co-ordinates of one particle A, and a', b' of the other B, at first; u, v the velocities of A estimated in direction of the axes of x, y; u', v' the corresponding velocities of the other B; then after an interval of time t the co-ordinates of

$$A \text{ will be } a+ut,\ \ b+vt, \text{ and of}$$
$$B \ldots\ldots\ldots a'+u't,\ \ b'+v't,$$

and if δ be their distance at this time we must have

$$\delta^2 = \{a-a'+(u-u')\,.\,t\}^2 + \{b-b'+(v-v')\,.\,t\}^2,$$

an equation for determining t, the time when the distance between the particles is δ. This equation has two roots, from which we may draw the same conclusion as in Cor. 1, Art. 50.

We may arrange the equation in the form

$$\delta^2 = E - 2Dt + Ct^2,$$

in which E, D, C do not involve t, but only the known quantities a, a', b, b', u, u', v, v',

$$\text{or } \delta^2 = \frac{EC-D^2+(Ct-D)^2}{C};$$

from which we see that as $EC-D^2$ is essentially positive, δ will be least when $Ct-D=0$, which corresponds to the case of Cor. 2.

52. We proceed to discuss the problem of the collision of two bodies.

All bodies with which we are acquainted are capable of being compressed more or less, and have a tendency in different degrees to recover their original forms when the compressing force is removed. This property we call their *elasticity:* and the internal force which any body exerts to recover its original form is called the *force of restitution.*

The ratio which the force of restitution bears to the force of compression is found by experiment to be the same for the same substance, whatever be the amount of the compressing force, but to be different for different substances. This ratio, which is generally represented by the symbol e, is taken as the measure of the elasticity of any substance, and is frequently called the *modulus of elasticity.*

This modulus can in no case be greater than unity; those substances for which it is equal to *unity* are said to be *perfectly elastic,* all others are *imperfectly elastic;* and the greater the numerical value of this modulus, the greater do we regard the elasticity of the substances we are comparing.

Probably no substances are perfectly elastic; in steel balls the value of the modulus e is about $\frac{5}{9}$, in glass about $\frac{15}{16}$.

For the results of experiments on the elasticity of bodies see *Reports of the British Association for the Advancement of Science,* Vol. III.

53. In considering the effects of collision we shall suppose the bodies to be spheres, perfectly smooth, and of uniform density,—so that their centres of gravity coincide with their geometrical centres.

Def. The line joining the centres of the spheres at the instant of impact is called *the line of impact;* when the centres are moving in the line of impact, the impact is said to be *direct,*—and in all other cases *oblique.*

When a ball A impinges directly on a ball B, the effect of the mutual pressure between them will be to accelerate B and retard A; and this will continue till their velocities become equal. When the velocities are equal the mutual pressure between them will cease, if the balls are inelastic, and the balls will move on together uniformly with the velocity which they then possess.

The intensity of this mutual pressure will vary during the short time the balls *press* against each other; but so far as its effect in producing momentum is concerned we may regard it as retaining some mean uniform value (see Art. 18), and we may measure the effect of the collision by the momentum X gained by B and lost by A: these effects on A and B being equal in magnitude and opposite in direction (Art. 46).

54. If the balls are *elastic*, the mutual pressure between them will continue after their velocities have become equal, in consequence of the efforts they make to recover their original forms; and the momentum gained by one and lost by the other after that time (which we may call X') will bear to the momentum generated during the first part of the collision a ratio ($e : 1$) depending upon the elasticity of the substances: so that $X' = eX$, and the *whole momentum* gained by B and lost by A will be expressed by $X + X'$ or $(1 + e) X$.

The time during which this entire action is performed is too small to be appreciated, but the illustration we have given may serve to render the nature of it more intelligible, and convey an idea of what is meant when it is said that *Impact is a pressure of short duration.*

55. *Two inelastic balls moving with given velocities impinge directly upon each other; to find the velocity of each after impact.*

Let u, v be the velocities of the two balls A and B respectively, before impact; and let the direction of the arrows indicate the direction of motion. Since they are inelastic, they will move on together in the same direction after the impact with some common velocity, which we may call u',—let X be the momentum lost by A and gained by B during the impact;

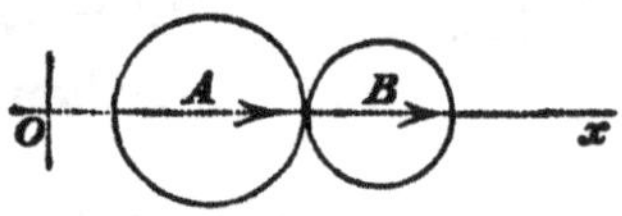

then Au' = momentum of A after the impact,

= momentum before impact $- X$,

$$= Au - X \qquad \text{(i)},$$

$$Bu' = Bv + X \text{ by similar reasoning} \qquad \text{(ii)};$$

$$\therefore \text{ adding } (A+B)\,u' = Au + Bv \qquad \text{(iii)},$$

$$\text{or } u' = \frac{Au + Bv}{A+B} \qquad \text{(iv)},$$

and substituting this in (i),

$$X = Au - Au' = A\,(u - u')$$

$$= A\left(u - \frac{Au + Bv}{A+B}\right) = \frac{AB\,(u-v)}{A+B} \;\ldots\; \text{(v)}.$$

Equation (iv) gives the common velocity of each ball after the impact, and (v) gives the momentum gained by B and lost by A.

COR. 1. We see from (iii) that the *whole* momentum of the two balls is the same after impact as before it,—a result we might have anticipated from the principle of Art. 46.

COR. 2. We may put the results in the following form:

$$\text{velocity lost by } A = u - u' = \frac{X}{A} = \frac{B(u-v)}{A+B},$$

$$\text{velocity gained by } B = u' - v = \frac{X}{B} = \frac{A(u-v)}{A+B};$$

in which shape they are sometimes useful.

Obs. If B be moving in a direction opposite to that of A before impact, we have only to change the sign of v in the above investigation: in other words, we may regard u, v as representing the velocities of A, B *algebraically*,—the proper *signs* being given to them in any particular example in accordance with the *actual* directions of motion.

The same remark applies to the subsequent propositions of this chapter.

COR. 3. If A impinges on B *at rest*, we have simply to put $v=0$ in the above results.

56. *Two imperfectly elastic balls moving with given velocities impinge directly upon each other; to find the velocity of each after impact.* (See fig. Art. 55.)

Let u, u' be the velocity of A before and after the impact;

v, v' the same with respect to B;

and let A, B represent the masses of the balls, the direction of their motion being indicated by the arrows in the figure.

Let A impinge upon B, and let X be the momentum lost by the former and gained by the latter during the first part of the impact, i.e. before their velocities become equal, generated by the force of compression; and X' the momentum generated by the force of restitution, after the velocities have become equal, and which causes the balls to separate.

Then if e be the modulus of elasticity $X' = eX$, and $X + X'$ or $(1+e)X$ is the whole momentum lost by A and gained by B,

$$\text{whence } \left.\begin{aligned} Au' &= Au - (1+e)X \\ Bv' &= Bv + (1+e)X \end{aligned}\right\} \text{............ (i).}$$

Now X, being the momentum generated by the mutual pressure of the balls before their elasticity comes into play, is the same in magnitude as if the balls were inelastic, and therefore, by the previous proposition $X = \dfrac{AB(u-v)}{A+B}$.

Hence, substituting in (i),

$$\left.\begin{aligned} u' &= u - (1+e)\frac{X}{A} = u - (1+e)\frac{B(u-v)}{A+B} \\ v' &= v + (1+e)\frac{X}{B} = v + (1+e)\frac{A(u-v)}{A+B} \end{aligned}\right\} \text{......(ii).}$$

These two equations give the velocities of A and B after impact.

COR. 1. By adding equations (i) we get $Au' + Bv' = Au + Bv$; that is, the whole momentum is unchanged by the impact.

COR. 2. We may put the results expressed by (ii) in the form

$$\left.\begin{aligned} \text{velocity lost by } A = u - u' &= (1+e)\frac{B(u-v)}{A+B} \\ \text{velocity gained by } B = v' - v &= (1+e)\frac{A(u-v)}{A+B} \end{aligned}\right\} \text{...(iii).}$$

Also from (ii) we get by subtraction

$$v' - u' = v - u + (1+e)(u-v) = e\,.\,(u-v) \text{...... (iv);}$$

i.e. the *relative* velocity of A and B *after* impact: their *relative* velocity *before* impact $= v' - u' : u - v = e : 1$.

COR. 3. If A impinges upon B *at rest*, we have simply to put $v = 0$ in the above results.

57. The problem of direct collision of two balls (Art. 56), is sometimes solved by assuming (i) that the total momentum after impact is the same as before impact,—this would follow from the principle that action and reaction are equal and opposite;—and (ii) that the *relative* velocity of the two balls after impact bears a constant ratio to their relative velocity before impact, say the ratio $e : 1$;—this result being the statement of an experimental fact, and e being then *defined* to be the *modulus of elasticity*.

On these two assumptions we should have, with the notation of the preceding article,

$$\left.\begin{array}{r} Au' + Bv' = Au + Bv \\ \text{and } v' - u' = e(u - v) \end{array}\right\},$$

from which we readily obtain the results marked (ii) in Art. (56), or we may obtain u' v' in the equivalent forms

$$\left.\begin{array}{l} u' = \dfrac{Au + Bv}{A + B} - e \cdot \dfrac{B(u - v)}{A + B} \\[2ex] v' = \dfrac{Au + Bv}{A + B} + e \cdot \dfrac{A(u - v)}{A + B} \end{array}\right\}.$$

Obs. We prefer the mode of treating the problem given in Art. (56), as it is more strictly referred to the simple laws of motion than the method of this article.

58. *Two smooth imperfectly elastic balls, moving in one plane with given velocities in given directions, impinge obliquely on each other,—to determine the motion of each after impact.*

Let Ox be the line passing through the centres of the balls at the instant of impact, and let the arrows indicate the direction of motion of the balls before and after impact.

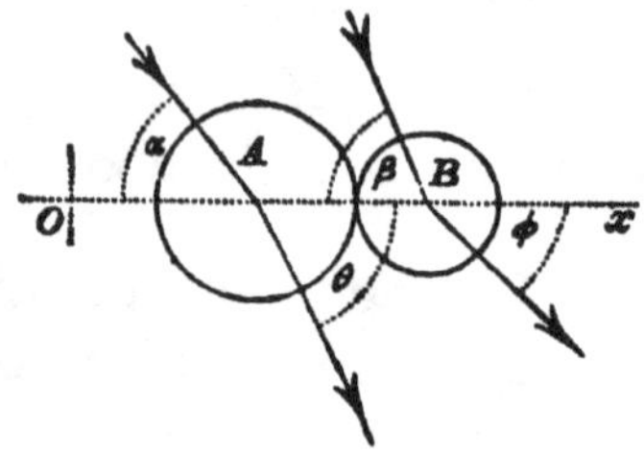

Let u, u' be the velocities of A before and after impact in directions making angles α, θ with Ox,

v, v', β, ϕ similar quantities with respect to B.

Now, since the balls are *smooth* the mutual action between them will take place *entirely* in the direction Ox, and hence it will be convenient to estimate the velocities of the balls in direction of Ox (Art. 20), and at right angles to Ox; and these motions may, by the second law of motion, be treated separately. Since no force acts on either ball perpendicular to Ox their velocities resolved at right angles to Ox will remain unchanged by the impact, whence we get

$$\left.\begin{array}{l} u' \sin\theta = u \sin\alpha \\ v' \sin\phi = v \sin\beta \end{array}\right\} \begin{array}{r} \ldots\ldots\ldots\ldots\ldots\ldots\ldots \text{(i)}, \\ \ldots\ldots\ldots\ldots\ldots\ldots\ldots \text{(ii)}, \end{array}$$

and further, the resolved velocities in direction Ox are affected by the impact just to the same extent as if these resolved velocities alone existed.

Now, $\left.\begin{array}{r} u\cos\alpha \\ u'\cos\theta \end{array}\right\}$, $\left.\begin{array}{r} v\cos\beta \\ v'\cos\phi \end{array}\right\}$ being the velocities of A, B resolved along Ox, $\left.\begin{array}{c} \text{before} \\ \text{after} \end{array}\right\}$ the impact,—if X be the momentum gained by B and lost by A during the impact, we should get as in Art. (56),

$$X = \frac{(1+e)\,AB\,(u\cos\alpha - v\cos\beta)}{A+B},$$

and we get

$$\left.\begin{aligned} u' \cos\theta &= u\cos\alpha - (1+e)\frac{B}{A+B}(u\cos\alpha - v\cos\beta) \quad \ldots \text{(iii)},\\ v' \cos\phi &= v\cos\beta + (1+e)\frac{A}{A+B}(u\cos\alpha - v\cos\beta) \quad \ldots \text{(iv)}. \end{aligned}\right\}$$

The equations (i), (iii) suffice to determine u' and θ, and (ii), (iv) to determine v' and ϕ:—and these four quantities define the magnitude and direction of the velocities of the two balls.

Obs. The above expresses in general terms the solution of the problem of the collision of two balls moving in one plane; any particular cases can of course be deduced from it, by assigning to the symbols involved their proper values, and this the student can readily do for himself. We will only notice the following interesting case.

Cor. If a ball A impinge obliquely upon a *very large* ball B *at rest*, we have

$$v=0; \quad \frac{A}{A+B}=0; \quad \text{and } \frac{B}{A+B}=1, \text{ very nearly,}$$

so that we get

$$\left.\begin{aligned} u' \sin\theta &= u\sin\alpha \\ u' \cos\theta &= -eu\cos\alpha \end{aligned}\right\}, \text{ which give } u' \text{ and } \theta,$$

and $v'=0$, very nearly.

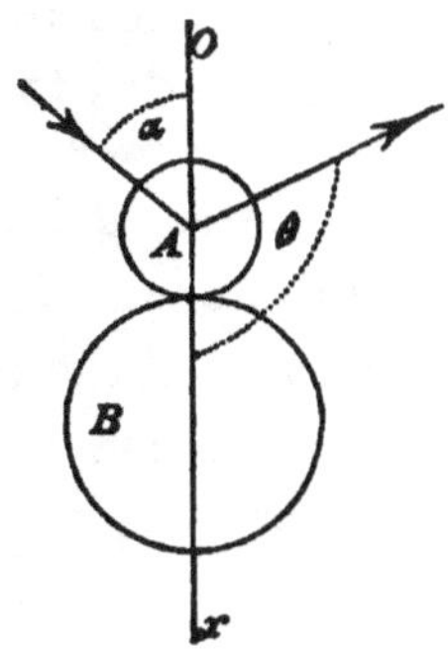

This shews that the motion which is communicated to B is inappreciable; and since $\cot\theta = -e\cot\alpha$ we must have $\theta > 90°$, and therefore A is reflected:—a ball striking a *fixed* plane is a case of this kind; or again, when a ball strikes the earth, the mass of the earth is so great compared with that of the ball that the motion communicated to it is insensible.

59. When two balls impinge upon one another and their motion does not take place in one plane, in order to determine the subsequent motion of the balls we must employ the same principles as those we have used in Art. (58), viz. resolve the velocities of the balls *in the direction* of impact and *at right angles to it:* the latter will be unaffected by the impact, and the former will be altered in the same manner as if they alone existed. The formulæ which express the general solution of the problem require a knowledge of *Geometry of three dimensions*, and are too complicated to be given here.

60. *A ball impinges obliquely upon a fixed smooth plane; to find the motion of the ball after impact.*

Let PQ be the normal to the plane at the point where the ball is in contact at the instant of impact: let the plane of the paper contain this normal, as well as the line of A's motion before impact, and intersect the fixed plane in the line CPD; then the line of A's motion after impact will lie in this same plane, since no force acts on the ball during the impact at right angles to this plane.

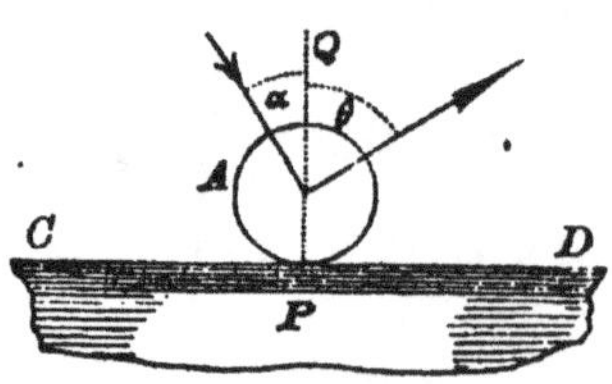

Let α, θ be the inclination to PQ of A's velocities before and after the impact; u, u' the velocity of A before and after impact, X the momentum destroyed by the force of compression. Then the velocity parallel to CD being unaffected by the impact, we have

$$u' \sin\theta = u \sin\alpha \,.........(\text{i});$$

and since the momentum of A resolved along the normal QP is entirely destroyed by the plane

$$X = Au \cos \alpha,$$

and eX is the additional momentum generated in the opposite direction by the elasticity, or force of restitution;

$$\therefore\ eX = Au' \cos \theta,$$

$$\text{whence,}\quad u' \cos \theta = eu \cos \alpha \ldots\ldots\ldots\ldots\ldots \text{(ii)}.$$

From (i) and (ii) we get

$$\left.\begin{aligned} \cot \theta &= e \cot \alpha \\ u' &= u \sqrt{(\sin^2 \alpha + e^2 \cos^2 \alpha)} \end{aligned}\right\} \ldots\ldots\ldots \text{(iii)}.$$

These equations (iii) determine the velocity and direction of motion of A after impact.

Obs. The student may compare this solution with the solution of what is substantially the same problem, deduced in Art. (58), Cor.

COR. 1. If the ball be inelastic, $e = 0$; whence $\theta = 90°$, and $u' = u \sin \alpha$; i.e. when an inelastic ball impinges obliquely on a fixed plane, after impact it will move along the plane with a velocity equal to $u \sin \alpha$.

COR. 2. The impulse sustained by the plane will be

$$= A(u \cos \alpha + u' \cos \theta) = (1 + e) Au \cos \alpha.$$

61. *To find the velocity of the centre of gravity of two balls moving uniformly in one plane.*

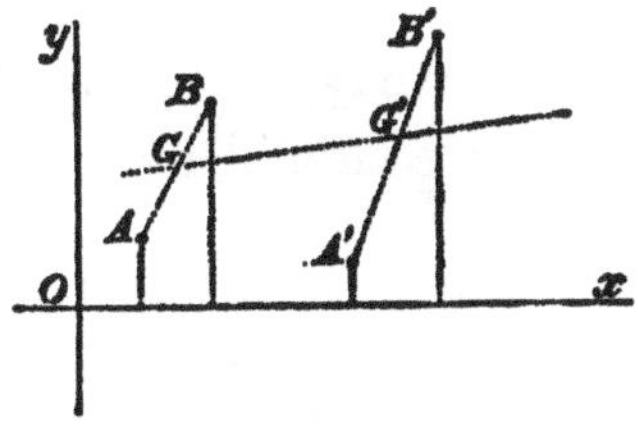

Let the position and motion of the two balls be referred to the two rectangular axes Ox, Oy in the plane in which they move, which we may suppose to be the plane of the paper.

Let A, B be the centres of the balls at first,

A', B' .... after an interval t,

a, b co-ordinates of A, B measured along Ox,

x, x' .... A', B' ....

u, u' the velocities of A and B resolved parallel to Ox, which will be uniform, since the balls are supposed to move uniformly (Art. 20),

$$\text{then } \left.\begin{aligned} x &= a + ut \\ x' &= b + u't \end{aligned}\right\} \quad \text{(i)}.$$

and if $\bar{x}$, $\bar{x}'$ be the co-ordinates of G the centre of gravity of A and B in the first and second positions of A and B, measured along Ox,—we have by *Statics*, Art. 74,

$$\left.\begin{aligned} (A+B)\,\bar{x} &= Aa + Bb \\ (A+B)\,\bar{x}' &= Ax + Bx' \end{aligned}\right\} \quad \text{(ii)};$$

$$\begin{aligned} \therefore\ (A+B)\,(\bar{x}' - \bar{x}) &= A\,(x-a) + B\,(x'-b) \\ &= (Au + Bu')\,t; \end{aligned}$$

$$\therefore\ \bar{x}' - \bar{x} = \frac{Au + Bu'}{A+B} \cdot t \quad \text{(iii)}.$$

Now this represents the space passed over by G, measured parallel to Ox,—and it $\propto t$ the time—consequently the velocity of G parallel to Ox is uniform and

$$= \frac{Au + Bu'}{A+B} = \bar{u} \text{ suppose.}$$

Similarly, if v, v', $\bar{v}$ be the velocities of A, B, G parallel to Oy we should have

$$\bar{v} = \frac{Av + Bv'}{A+B};$$

whence $\bar{u}$, $\bar{v}$ being known, the motion of G is known.

COR. 1. If there were three or more balls, by a similar process we should obtain

$$\bar{u} = \frac{Au + Bu' + Cu'' + \ldots}{A + B + C + \ldots} = \frac{\Sigma(Au)}{\Sigma(A)},$$

$$\bar{v} = \frac{Av + Bv' + Cv'' + \ldots}{A + B + C + \ldots} = \frac{\Sigma(Av)}{\Sigma(A)};$$

and if the motions of the balls were not confined to one plane, and we introduced a third co-ordinate axis at right angles to Ox and Oy, and represented the velocities parallel to this axis by $\bar{w}$, w, w'... we should have

$$\bar{w} = \frac{Aw + Bw' + Cw'' + \ldots}{A + B + C + \ldots} = \frac{\Sigma(Aw)}{\Sigma(A)}.$$

These formulæ are analogous to those for the position of the centre of gravity of a system of bodies (*Statics*, Art. 74). They may be expressed generally thus: *The velocity of the centre of gravity of a system of bodies estimated in a given direction is equal to the sum of the momenta of the several bodies estimated in the same direction, divided by the mass of the system. Or, if each body of a system be moving uniformly, the centre of gravity of the system also moves uniformly with a velocity such that the whole momentum of the system estimated in any given direction is equal to that of a single body* (*equal in mass to that of the system*) *coincident with the centre of gravity, and moving with the same velocity as the centre of gravity.*

N.B. The *acceleration* of the centre of gravity would be obtained by formulæ exactly similar to those obtained above for the *velocity*—the *accelerations* of the several bodies being written in the formulæ instead of their *velocities*.

COR. 2. Since it appears by Art. 40 that if we impress any the same velocity upon each body of a system, the *relative* motions of the parts of the system are not affected thereby,—suppose we wish to reduce the centre of gravity of two balls to rest by impressing velocities equal to $-\bar{u}$, $-\bar{v}$... on each ball, we see that the *momentum* to be communicated to A, B for this purpose would be

$$-A\bar{u},\ -B\bar{u}\ldots \text{ or } -A\,.\,\frac{Au+Bu'}{A+B},\quad -B\,.\,\frac{Au+Bu'}{A+B}.$$

parallel to Ox; and $-A\bar{v}$, $-B\bar{v}$ parallel to Oy.

62. *When two smooth balls impinge upon one another the motion of the centre of gravity is unaltered by the impact.*

First, let the balls be moving in the line of impact Ox, i.e. let the impact be direct (fig. Art. 55),

$$\left.\begin{matrix} u,\ u' \\ v,\ v' \end{matrix}\right\} \text{velocities of } \left.\begin{matrix} A \\ B \end{matrix}\right\} \text{ before and after impact,}$$

$\bar{u}$, $\bar{u}'$ velocity of the centre of gravity before and after impact;

$$\text{then } \bar{u} = \frac{Au+Bv}{A+B},\quad \bar{u}' = \frac{Au'+Bv'}{A+B};$$

and (Art. 56, Cor. 1) the whole momentum is the same after impact as before, therefore $Au+Bv = Au'+Bv'$; whence we get $\bar{u} = \bar{u}'$, which proves the proposition.

Secondly, let the impact be oblique.

Resolve the velocity of each ball *in direction of* impact and *at right angles* to it; by the first case the velocity of the centre of gravity in direction of impact will be unaltered; and since the velocity of each ball resolved at right angles to the direction of impact is unaffected by the impact, the velocity of the centre of gravity in this direction will not be changed by the impact,—consequently the velocity and direction of motion of the centre of gravity of the balls are the same after impact as before.

COR. We can without much difficulty extend the theorem of this article to the case of several balls, and shew that "the motion of the centre of gravity of any number of smooth balls is not changed by the impact *inter se* of two or more balls of the system."

Examples and Problems.

63. (I) A ball of 4 lbs. weight moving from left to right, with a velocity of 8 yards per second, impinges directly upon a ball of 10 lbs. weight moving in the same direction with a velocity of 2 yards per second; determine their motion after the impact.

(i) When the balls are inelastic. (Art. 55.)

Since the weights of the balls are in the ratio of their masses, we may take 4 and 10 to represent their masses, and we shall have

$$\text{their common velocity after impact} = \frac{Au + Bv}{A + B}$$

$$= \frac{4 \cdot 8 + 10 \cdot 2}{4 + 10} = \frac{52}{14} = 3\tfrac{5}{7} \text{ yards per second;}$$

$$\text{and } X = \frac{AB(u - v)}{A + B} = \frac{4 \cdot 10 \cdot (8 - 2)}{4 + 10} = \frac{240}{14} = 17\tfrac{1}{7},$$

i.e. the mutual pressure between the balls is capable of generating a velocity of $17\frac{1}{7}$ yards per second in a mass whose weight is 1 lb.

(ii) If the balls are elastic, then using the same notation as in Art. (56), velocity of A after impact $= 8 - \dfrac{(1+e)\,10\,(8-2)}{4+10} = \dfrac{26}{7} - \dfrac{30}{7}e,$

$\ldots\ldots\ldots\ldots B \ldots\ldots\ldots\ldots\ldots = 2 + \dfrac{(1+e)\,4\,(8-2)}{4+10} = \dfrac{26}{7} + \dfrac{12}{7}e,$

$$\text{and } X = 17\tfrac{1}{7}(1+e).$$

If $e = \dfrac{13}{15}$, the ball A will be at rest after the impact; and according as $e <$ or $> \dfrac{13}{15}$, A will follow B with a less velocity or be reflected back and move in the opposite direction.

64. (II) A ball A moving with a given velocity impinges directly upon a ball B at rest, and B afterwards impinges directly upon a ball C at rest; find the velocity communicated to C.

If u be the original velocity of A, we have by Art. (56),

velocity of B after first impact $= \dfrac{(1+e)\,A}{A+B}u = v$ suppose,

velocity of C after impact $= \dfrac{(1+e)\,B}{B+C}v = \dfrac{(1+e)^2AB}{(A+B)(B+C)}u.$

Cor. 1. The velocity communicated to C by the intervention of B will vary with the magnitude of B, and will be the greatest possible when $\dfrac{B}{(A+B)(B+C)}$ is greatest;

$$\text{i.e. when } \frac{(A+B)(B+C)}{B} \text{ is least,}$$

and since this may be written in the form

$$\left\{\sqrt{(B)} - \sqrt{\left(\frac{AC}{B}\right)}\right\}^2 + \{\sqrt{(A)} + \sqrt{(C)}\}^2,$$

this will be the case when $B=\sqrt{(AC)}$;—in other words, the velocity of C will be greatest when B is a mean proportional between A and C.

65. (III) A particle is to be projected from a given point P so as to pass through another given point Q, after being reflected at a given fixed plane AB; to find the direction of projection.

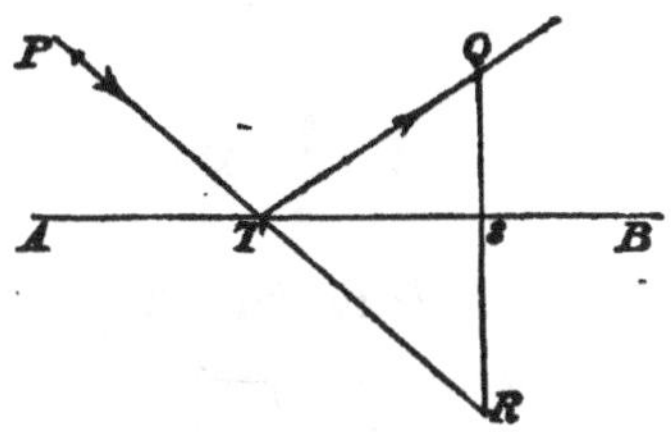

Suppose T to be the point where the particle must strike the plane, then the plane PTQ must be perpendicular to the fixed plane, and will cut it in a straight line AB.

Now the particle impinging on the plane in direction PT and being reflected in direction TQ, we must have

$$\tan QTS = e \cdot \tan PTA \text{......(i) Art. (60).}$$

If QS be drawn perpendicular to AB, and PT produced to meet QS in R, we shall have

$$\tan QTS = e \tan RTS,$$

and therefore $QS = e \cdot SR$.

This suggests the following simple construction for determining T. Draw QS perpendicular to AB and produce it to R, making $SR = \frac{1}{e} \cdot QS$; join PR cutting AB in T. Then the condition (i) is satisfied, and PT is the direction in which the particle must be projected.

Cor. If the particle is to pass through Q after reflexion at two planes TV, US in succession, we have the following construction. Draw QSR perpendicular to the latter plane, making

$$SR = \frac{1}{e} . QS.$$

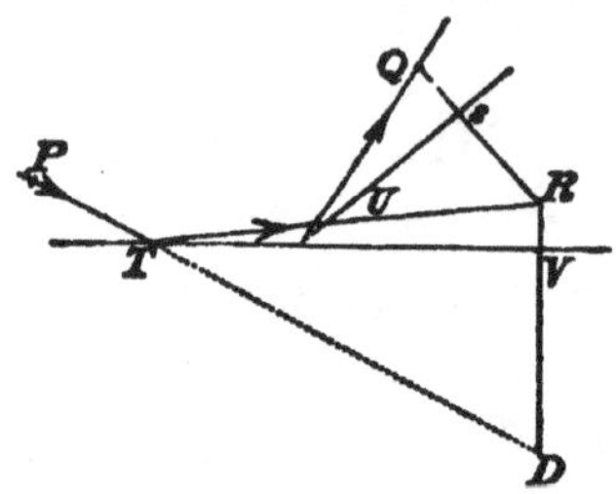

Draw RVD perpendicular to the first plane, making

$$VD = \frac{1}{e} . RV;$$

join PD cutting the first plane in T,—join TR cutting the second plane in U,—then if the particle be projected in direction PT it will be reflected along TU and again reflected at U in direction UQ, and so pass through the point Q.

66. (IV) A heavy particle impinges upon a fixed rough plane; to find its motion after impact.

Let the plane of the paper represent the plane of impact, i.e. the plane which contains the direction of motion of the particle before impact, and the normal to the fixed plane at the point of contact.

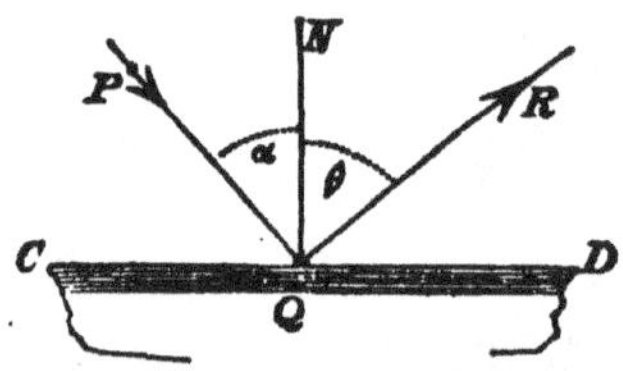

Let u, u' be the velocities of the particle (mass A) before and after impact.

α, θ the angles its direction of motion makes with the normal QN before and after impact.

X, F the momentum generated by the fixed plane in the particle, in directions QN and QC,—the latter arising from the roughness of the plane.

Then resolving the motion in direction QN and CD, we have, as in Art. (60),

$$u' \cos \theta = eu \cos \alpha \quad \text{(i)},$$

the complete value of $X = (1 + e)\, Au \cos \alpha$ .... (ii),

and $Au' \sin \theta = Au \sin \alpha - F$ .... (iii).

Now we may take $F = \mu X$ (iv), where μ depends upon the roughness of the plane, and is a numerical quantity to be determined by experiment, it is sometimes called the *coefficient of dynamical friction;* from these four equations we get

$$\left.\begin{aligned} u' \cos \theta &= eu \cos \alpha \\ u' \sin \theta &= u \sin \alpha - \mu (1 + e)\, u \cos \alpha \end{aligned}\right\},$$

which two equations determine u' and θ, i.e. the velocity and direction of motion after impact.

CHAPTER III.

OF UNIFORMLY ACCELERATED MOTION.

67. THE accelerating force upon a particle is said to be uniform when equal increments of velocity are added in equal increments of time, however large or small these increments of time may be.

Hence, in accordance with the definitions and conventions of Arts. 5, 13, if v be the velocity of a particle at the end of a time t, during which it has been subject to a uniform accelerating force f, and if u were its velocity to begin with, we shall have $f \,.\, t$ to represent the increment of velocity, and

$$v = u + ft \ldots\ldots\ldots\ldots\ldots(\text{i}).$$

If the particle started from rest $u = 0$ and $v = ft$.

Obs. The formula (i) is algebraically true in any case where the force is really a *retarding* force (Art. 6, *Obs.*), or where the velocity u at the beginning of the time t exists in a direction opposite to that in which v is measured: in any case it is necessary simply to assign the proper algebraic sign to u and f, and the result (i) will be available.

68. *If s be the space described from rest in time t by a particle under the action of a uniform accelerating force f, then will $s = \frac{1}{2} ft^2$.*

Let the time t be subdivided into n intervals, each equal to τ, so that $n\tau = t$; then the velocities at the beginning of the

	1st	2nd	3rd	nth of these intervals of τ
will be	0	$f\tau$	$2f\tau\ldots$	$(n-1)f\tau$;

and at the *end* of the same intervals will be

$$f\tau, \quad 2f\tau, \quad 3f\tau \ldots nf\tau.$$

Now if the particle were to move during each successive interval of τ, with the velocity which has at the beginning of that interval, the space described would be

$$= 0 \,.\, \tau + f\tau \,.\, \tau + 2f\tau \,.\, \tau + \ldots + (n-1) f\tau \,.\, \tau,$$

which is

$$= f\tau^2 \{1 + 2 + \ldots + (n-1)\}$$

$$= \frac{n(n-1)}{1 \,.\, 2} f\tau^2 = \frac{1}{2} ft^2 \left(1 - \frac{1}{n}\right), \text{ since } n\tau = t.$$

And again, if the particle were to move during each successive interval, with the velocity which it has at the end of that interval, the space described would be

$$= f\tau \,.\, \tau + 2f\tau \,.\, \tau + 3f\tau \,.\, \tau + \ldots + nf\tau \,.\, \tau,$$

which is

$$= f\tau^2 (1 + 2 + \ldots + n) = n\frac{(n+1)}{2} f\tau^2 = \frac{1}{2} ft^2 \left(1 + \frac{1}{n}\right).$$

Since the velocity is continually increasing during the time t, the space *actually* described by the particle will be intermediate to the spaces described under these two hypotheses, i.e.

$$s \text{ lies between } \frac{1}{2} ft^2 \left(1 - \frac{1}{n}\right) \text{ and } \frac{1}{2} ft^2 \left(1 + \frac{1}{n}\right)$$

however large n be taken; but when n is taken indefinitely large, these two limits each become $\frac{1}{2} ft^2$, and therefore s which always lies between them must coincide with them in the limit, that is $s = \frac{1}{2} ft^2$; and if v be the velocity at time t we have $v = ft$ and thence $v^2 = 2fs$.

69. The same result ($s = \frac{1}{2}ft^2$) may be arrived at very simply by the following geometrical process.

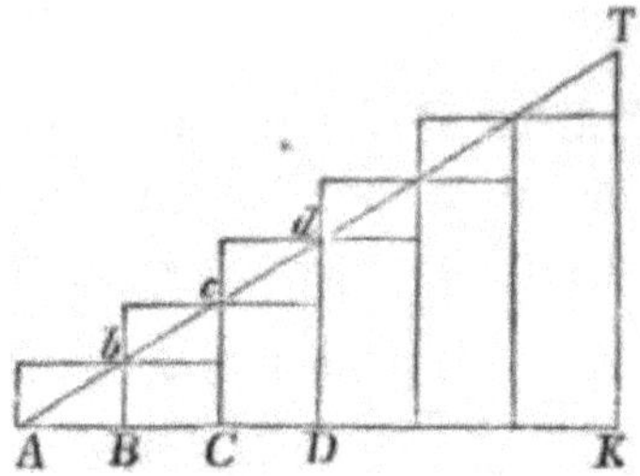

Let the straight line AK represent the time (s) of motion from rest, and let this be divided into n equal parts AB, BC, CD... let the lines Bb, Cc,...KT drawn at right angles to AK represent the velocities acquired at the end of the successive intervals; the points b, c ... T will lie in a straight line, since the velocity varies as the time from rest. Complete the inner and outer series of parallelograms, as in the figure.

Now if the particle be supposed to move uniformly during any interval (as CD) with the velocity Cc which it has at the beginning of that interval, the *number of units of area* in the parallelogram cD will represent the *number of units of length* passed over by the particle during that interval. With this understanding, the sum of the *inner* or *outer* series of parallelograms will represent the space passed over by the particle, supposing it to move during each interval with the velocity which it has at the *beginning* or *end* of that interval respectively; and the actual space described lies between the spaces described on these two several suppositions. But when the number of intervals is increased, and their magnitude diminished indefinitely, each series of parallelograms approximates to the triangular area AKT, which will represent the actual space described by the particle; and since

$$AK = t, \text{ and } KT = ft = \text{velocity at time } t,$$

$$\therefore\ s = \tfrac{1}{2}AK \,.\, KT = \tfrac{1}{2}t \,.\, ft = \tfrac{1}{2}ft^2.$$

Obs. The student will remark that the above is substantially a geometrical illustration of the proof of the proposition given in Art. 68.

70. *A particle is projected with velocity u, and acted upon by an accelerating force f in the direction of motion. To find the relation between the space (s) passed over, the time (t) of motion and velocity (v) acquired.*

The particle at any time is moving with a certain velocity, and so far as the subsequent motion is concerned it is immaterial how we suppose that velocity to have been acquired. Let then the force f generate a velocity u by acting for a time t' and through a space s', then we have $u = ft'$; and if the particle continues subject to the action of the same force, and passes over a space s in time t, we have $s + s'$ described *from rest* in time $t + t'$;

$$\therefore\ s + s' = \tfrac{1}{2}f(t + t')^2 \text{ and } s' = \tfrac{1}{2}ft'^2;$$

$$\therefore\ s = \tfrac{1}{2}f(t^2 + 2tt') = ut + \tfrac{1}{2}ft^2 \ldots\ldots\ldots\ldots \text{(i)};$$

$$\text{also } v = f(t' + t) = u + ft \ldots\ldots\ldots\ldots \text{(ii)};$$

whence also

$$v^2 = (u + ft)^2 = u^2 + 2f(ut + \tfrac{1}{2}ft^2) = u^2 + 2fs \ldots \text{(iii)}.$$

Equations (i), (ii) express the relations required.

Obs. If the force act in a direction opposite to that in which s, u, and v are estimated *positive*, we must change the sign of f in (i), (ii), (iii), and we get

$$s = ut - \tfrac{1}{2}ft^2,\ \ v = u - ft,\ \ v^2 = u^2 - 2fs \ldots\ldots \text{(iv)}.$$

The student will have little difficulty in obtaining any of the results of (i), (ii), (iii), (iv), of this article, by a geometrical proof similar to that in Art. 69.

71. We may arrive at the same results thus by an application of the principle stated in Art. 40.

Let the particle be projected from A in direction AP with the velocity u;—the *relative* motion of A and P will be the same if we impress upon *both* a velocity equal to u in the opposite direction; this reduces P to initial rest, and if P, A' be simultaneous positions of the particle and of A, v their relative velocity at that time t, and $A'P = s$, we have

$$AP = \tfrac{1}{2}ft^2 \quad AA' = ut \ldots\ldots \text{(i)};$$

$$\therefore\ s = ut + \tfrac{1}{2}ft^2 \ldots\ldots\ldots \text{(ii)},$$

$$\text{and } v = u + ft;$$

the same results as before.

72. *Note.* The same results might have been arrived at by a process similar to those employed in Art. 69. These we leave as an exercise for the student.

We would here caution him likewise against a loose and incorrect application of the second law of motion to this problem which we have noticed in some works on dynamics. They state that the space described in consequence of the initial velocity is $= ut$, and the space that would be described in the same time by the action of the accelerating force f is $= \frac{1}{2}ft^2$, and *therefore by the second law of motion*, the whole space described is the sum of these two, or $s = ut + \frac{1}{2}ft^2$. The *result* arrived at is true, but the principle assumed is unsound, for the second law of motion states the theory of the action of forces at a *particular instant*, and asserts nothing *directly* as to the quantitative effects accruing in any *finite* time.

73. When a particle starts from rest (Art. 68)

$$v = ft \text{ and } s = \tfrac{1}{2}ft^2;$$

and from these two equations a relation can be obtained between *any three* of the quantities v, s, f, t.

Thus

$$\left.\begin{aligned} v &= ft = \frac{2s}{t} = \sqrt{(2fs)} \\ s &= \tfrac{1}{2}ft^2 = \tfrac{1}{2}vt = \frac{v^2}{2f} \\ t &= \frac{v}{f} = \frac{2s}{v} = \sqrt{\left(\frac{2s}{f}\right)} \\ f &= \frac{v}{t} = \frac{v^2}{2s} = \frac{2s}{t^2} \end{aligned}\right\}.$$

And again, if the particle start with the velocity u

$$v = u + ft,$$

$$s = ut + \tfrac{1}{2}ft^2 = \frac{v+u}{2}t,$$

$$v^2 = u^2 + 2fs;$$

forms which it is desirable the student should remember.

Cor. The space described in t'' from rest $= \frac{1}{2}ft^2$,

..........................$(t-1)''$ ...... $= \frac{1}{2}f(t-1)^2$;

$\therefore$ space described *during* the tth second $= \frac{1}{2}f(2t-1)$.

Hence the spaces described during the 1st, 2nd, 3rd,... seconds are $\frac{1}{2}f.1$, $\frac{1}{2}f.3$, $\frac{1}{2}f.5$, ... &c., and are in the ratio of the consecutive odd numbers, 1, 3, 5...

The result $s = \dfrac{v+u}{2}t$ shews that the space described in any time is the same as if the particle had moved *uniformly* during the whole time with the *mean velocity*.

74. One of the simple cases of a uniform force is that of gravity, the accelerating effect of which is uniform. (Art. 43.) We give an example of the application of the preceding results to this case.

Ex. *A particle is projected vertically upwards with a velocity of* 100 *feet per second, to find* (i) *its height at the end of* 3″, *and* (ii) *the time when it is at a height of* 140 *feet above the point of projection.*

When a *foot* and a *second* are taken as the units of space and time the numerical value of $g = 32.2$, (Art. 43), and if u be the velocity of projection, and s the height at time t after projection, we have $s = ut - \frac{1}{2}gt^2$, (Art. 70).

For the first part of the example $t = 3$, $u = 100$;

$\therefore\ s = 3.100 - \frac{1}{2}\, 32.2\,.\,(3)^2 = 155.1$ feet

= height of the particle at the end of 3 seconds.

For the second part of the example $s = 140$, $u = 100$; and we have to find t from the quadratic equation

$$s = ut - \tfrac{1}{2}gt^2.$$

Solving the equation we get

$$t = \frac{u \pm \sqrt{(u^2 - 2gs)}}{g}.$$

Substituting the numerical values of u, g, s, we get after reduction,

$$t = \frac{100 \pm 31.36}{32.2} = 2''.13 \text{ or } 4''.08,$$

a double result, which is to be explained thus,—at the end of 2″.13 the particle is at a height 140 feet in its *ascent*, and at the end of 4″.08 it is again at the same height of 140 feet on its *descent*, after having reached its highest point and then descending.

75. We subjoin a few interesting problems which can be solved by the principles already explained.

PROB. *Two bodies P, Q are connected by an inextensible string which passes over a smooth fixed pully; to determine the motion of each body, and the tension of the string.*

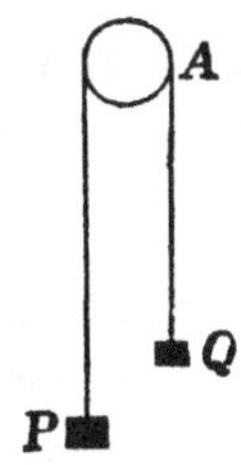

Let P, Q represent the *masses* of the bodies; T the tension of the string, the mass of which we will neglect, and suppose $P > Q$.

Now *moving force* on P downwards $= Pg - T$,

.... Q upwards $= T - Qg$;

$$\left.\begin{array}{l} \therefore \textit{ accelerating force} \text{ on } P \text{ downwards} = \dfrac{Pg - T}{P} \\ \ldots\ldots\ldots\ldots\ldots\ldots\ldots\ldots\ Q \text{ upwards} = \dfrac{T - Qg}{Q} \end{array}\right\} \ldots\ldots\ldots \text{(i)}.$$

Now the string being always stretched and inextensible, the velocity of P downwards and of Q upwards will be *always* equal, and therefore the rate of change of their velocities, i.e. the acceleration of the two bodies must be equal;

$$\therefore \frac{Pg - T}{P} = \frac{T - Qg}{Q},$$

$$\text{whence } T = \frac{2PQ}{P + Q} g \ldots\ldots\ldots\ldots\ldots\ldots \text{(ii)},$$

which gives the tension of the string,—and further substituting this value of T in either of the expressions (i), we get the acceleration on P downwards and on Q upwards

$$= g - \frac{T}{P} = g - \frac{2Q}{P + Q} g = \frac{P - Q}{P + Q} g.$$

Also velocity of P and Q after time t *from rest* $= \dfrac{P - Q}{P + Q} gt$.

...... space described .... $s = \dfrac{1}{2} \dfrac{P - Q}{P + Q} gt^2$.

COR. 1. By taking $P-Q$ as small as we please we may make the motion as slow as we please, and so capable of being measured,—by which means the value of g might be obtained from observation. This is substantially the principle of Atwood's machine, which will be described hereafter, (Art. 82).

COR. 2. If at any instant a *part* (R) of one of the bodies (Q for instance) were suddenly detached, there would be no *instantaneous* change of the velocity of either body, but the *acceleration* would become $\frac{P-Q+R}{P+Q-R}g$, and the tension of the string would become $\frac{2P(Q-R)}{P+Q-R}\cdot g$.

76. PROB. *Two bodies P, Q are in motion, connected by a string which passes over a smooth fixed pully; another body R is suddenly attached to Q;—find the change of velocity and the impulsive strain on the string.*

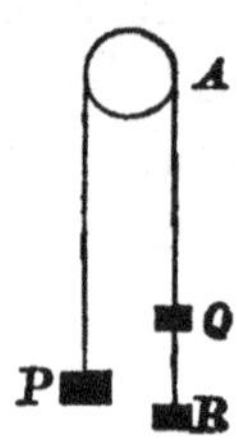

Let P, Q, R be the masses of the bodies, and suppose R to become attached to Q by a string connecting them suddenly becoming tight. Let V be the velocity of P and Q at the instant before this takes place, and V' the common velocity of the three the instant after, X_1, X_2 the impulsive strain on the strings PAQ, QR, respectively; then for the motion of the three bodies we have (Art. 46)

$$PV' = PV - X_1,$$
$$QV' = QV + X_1 - X_2,$$
$$RV' = X_2;$$

whence by adding $(P+Q+R)\,V' = (P+Q)\,V$,

$$\text{or } V' = \frac{P+Q}{P+Q+R}\,V \quad \text{.............. (i)},$$

$$\text{and } X_1 = P(V - V') = \frac{PR}{P+Q+R} V \text{.........} \quad \text{(ii)},$$

$$X_2 = \frac{(P+Q)R}{P+Q+R} V \text{ ....} \quad \text{(iii)}.$$

Equations (i), (ii), (iii) determine the three quantities required to determine the change of motion completely.

MOTION ON AN INCLINED PLANE.

77. PROB. *A heavy body Q is drawn up a smooth inclined plane by another body P, which descends vertically; P being connected with Q by an inextensible string passing over the vertex of the plane.*

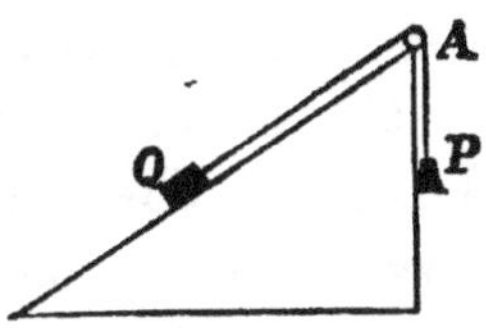

Let P, Q be the masses of the bodies, T the tension of the string, and α the inclination of the plane to the horizon, R the pressure of Q on the plane.

Then resolving the motion of Q parallel to the plane and perpendicular to it, the weight of Q is equivalent to a force $Qg \sin \alpha$ down the plane,

$Qg \cos \alpha$ perpendicular to the plane,

the latter force is balanced by R, the pressure of the plane,

$$\text{whence } R = Qg \cos \alpha \text{..........................} \quad \text{(i)},$$

$$\text{and acceleration of } Q \textit{ up} \text{ the plane} = \frac{T - Qg \sin \alpha}{Q},$$

$$\text{................}P \text{ downwards } = \frac{Pg - T}{P}.$$

And since the string continues stretched, the velocities of

14—2

P and Q in these two directions are always equal and therefore the accelerations upon them are equal, that is,

$$\frac{Pg-T}{P}=\frac{T-Qg\sin\alpha}{Q},$$

$$\text{whence } T=\frac{PQ(1+\sin\alpha)\,g}{P+Q} \quad\ldots\ldots\ldots\ldots\ldots\ldots \text{(ii)},$$

and acceleration on P *downwards* and on Q *up* the plane

$$=\frac{Pg-T}{P}=\frac{P-Q\sin\alpha}{P+Q}\cdot g \quad\ldots\ldots\ldots\ldots\ldots\ldots \text{(iii)},$$

equation (ii) gives the tension of the string, and (iii) gives the acceleration from which the velocity acquired and space passed over in any time may readily be obtained.

COR. The preceding problem may be varied by supposing Q to move on a smooth horizontal table. The student may either investigate the motion in this case independently, or deduce the results from the present Art. by making $\alpha=0$.

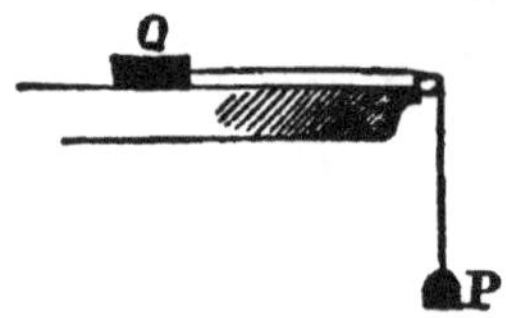

78. *A heavy body descends freely down a smooth inclined plane;—to find the time of motion and the velocity acquired.*

Let P be the mass of the body moving down the plane BA, the inclination of which to the horizon is α, R the pressure on the plane.

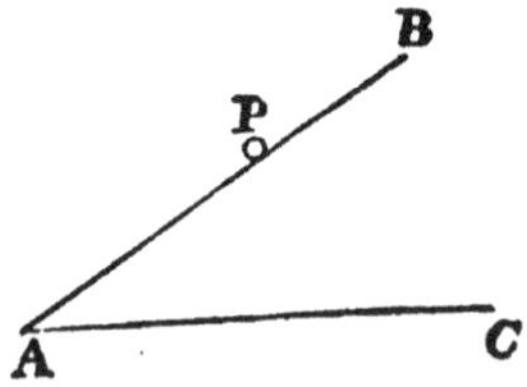

Then resolving the forces on P parallel to the plane and perpendicular to it, we have moving force down the plane $= Pg \sin \alpha$,

.... perpendicular to the plane $= Pg \cos \alpha$,

and this latter force is counteracted by R, since there is no *motion* perpendicular to the plane;

$$\therefore\ R = Pg \cos \alpha, \text{ which determines } R,$$

and accelerating force down the plane $= g \sin \alpha$;

if t be the time of moving over BA from rest, and v the velocity acquired,

$$AB = \tfrac{1}{2} g \sin \alpha \,.\, t^2, \quad v = g \sin \alpha \,.\, t.$$

$$\text{Whence } t = \sqrt{\left(\frac{2AB}{g \sin \alpha}\right)}, \text{ and } v = \sqrt{(2g \,.\, \sin \alpha \,.\, AB)}$$

$$= \sqrt{(2g \,.\, BC)}.$$

The latter result shews that the velocity at A is the same as that of a body falling freely through a vertical height equal to BC,—that of the plane.

Cor. If the body start at B with a velocity u, and v be its velocity after describing any length BA, and h be the *vertical* depth of A below B, we shall readily obtain

$$v^2 = u^2 + 2gh.$$

79. *A heavy particle is projected with given velocity up an inclined plane—to find its velocity at any point of its course.*

We suppose the motion to take place in a *vertical* plane BAC which is *perpendicular* to the inclined plane.

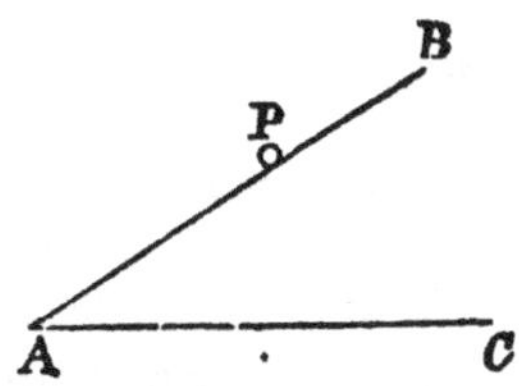

Let the particle P be projected from A with velocity u up the plane, v the velocity after a time t when it has described the space $AP = s$, z the vertical height of P above the horizon AC, α the inclination of the plane, so that $z = s \,.\, \sin\alpha$: the resolved force of gravity down the plane tending to retard P is $= g\sin\alpha$.

Hence (Art. 70) $$v = u - g\sin\alpha \,.\, t \text{..................(i)},$$
$$s = ut - \tfrac{1}{2}g\sin\alpha \,.\, t^2 \text{..............(ii)},$$
two equations connecting the three quantities v, s, t, so that any one of them being given, the other two may be found: these results are algebraically true if v and s be one or both *negative*.

If we eliminate t we obtain
$$v^2 = u^2 - 2g\sin\alpha \,.\, s = u^2 - 2gz \text{.........(iii)},$$
a result which shews that the change of velocity can be expressed in terms of the *vertical* height through which the particle has ascended—and is the same in amount as if the particle had been moving freely in a vertical line upwards—the *time* of motion however would not be the same in the two cases.

From (ii) we can derive the value of t corresponding to any value of s, viz.
$$t = \frac{u \pm \sqrt{u^2 - 2gs \,.\, \sin\alpha}}{g\sin\alpha} = \frac{u \pm \sqrt{u^2 - 2gz}}{g\sin\alpha} \text{.........(iv)},$$
a double result, indicating the times at which the particle will pass through the position P—($AP = s$)—on its way *up* and *down* the plane.

The maximum value of s is $= \dfrac{u^2}{2g\sin\alpha}$ and of z is $= \dfrac{u^2}{2g}$, as may be seen from equations (iii) or (iv).

Obs. The results of this article will be applicable to the case of a particle projected freely *vertically upwards*, if we write $\alpha = 90°$, and $\therefore \sin\alpha = 1$.

80. We may apply the results of the previous article to the following problem.

The time of descent of a particle down any chord of a vertical circle beginning at the highest point of the circle is the same.

Let AB be the vertical diameter of the circle, AP any chord drawn from A. Then the accelerating force on the particle down $AP = g \cos PAB = g \sin PBA$,

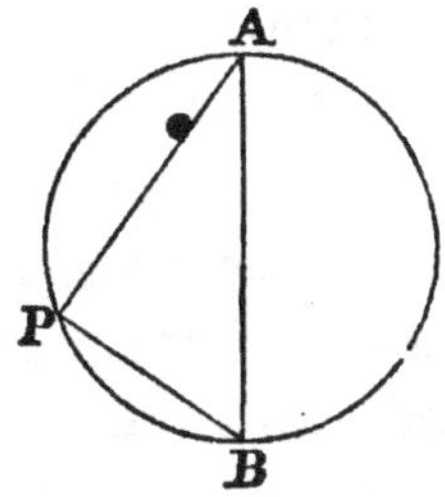

and time down $AP = \sqrt{\left(\dfrac{2AP}{g \sin PBA}\right)}$

$= \sqrt{\left(\dfrac{2 \cdot AB}{g}\right)}$, since $AP = AB \sin PBA$;

and since this result is independent of the direction of AP, the time down all chords drawn from A will be equal.

COR. Similarly, it may be shewn that the times down all chords terminating in B are equal.

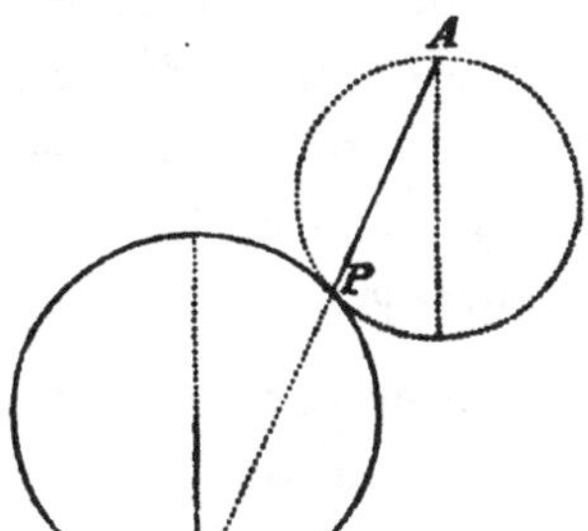

The above result leads to the solution of several curious problems of lines of quickest descent. We give one such problem.

To find the line of quickest descent from a given point A to a given circle.

Construct a circle of which A shall be the highest point, and which shall touch the given circle in some point P, then will AP be the line of quickest descent required. For if we join A with any other point of the given circle, the joining line will be longer than the part of it intercepted by the second circle, and therefore the time down the joining line would be longer than the time down the corresponding chord of the second circle, i.e. greater than the time of descent down AP; consequently AP is the line of quickest descent from A to any point of the given circle.

If the circle be drawn it can easily be shewn that AP produced will pass through the *lowest* point of the given circle,—whence we have the simple rule: Join A with the lowest point of the given circle, and the part of this line without the circle is the line required.

81. An accurate knowledge of the numerical value of g the accelerating force of gravity is of great importance, and various methods have been employed to determine it. If a body were sliding down a smooth inclined plane of elevation α, the acceleration upon it would be $g \sin \alpha$; so that by diminishing α sufficiently, the force acting upon the body might be reduced so as to admit of the motion being observed, without the *law* of the motion being affected. This method of determining g was suggested by Galileo,—but since no surface can be obtained sufficiently smooth, the method does not practically admit of great accuracy.

A machine invented by Atwood for the purpose of making observations on the laws of falling bodies, leads to results much more trustworthy than the preceding.

We will here give a short description of the machine.

82. Two equal weights P, Q are attached to the extremities of a fine thread which passes round a pully C. The axis of C rests in a horizontal position on four wheels, of which two only are represented in the figure; the object of these wheels being to diminish the friction on the axis of C, which they do very considerably, since the friction of

rolling is much less than that of *rubbing*. Hence they are called *friction wheels*.

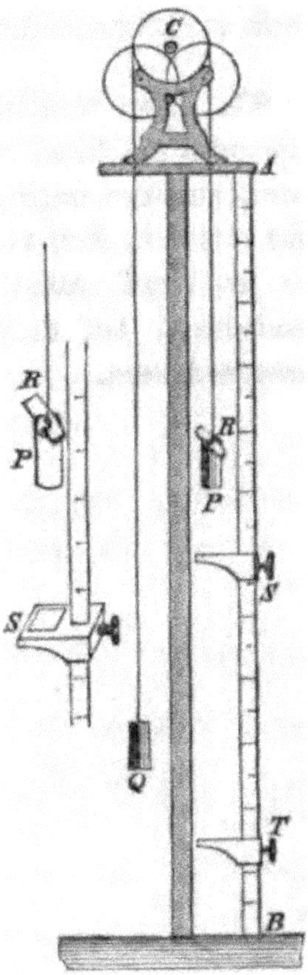

Now P and Q being equal would be in equilibrium, but if a weight R be placed upon P, it would begin to descend subject to an acceleration $\frac{R}{P+Q+R} \cdot g$, (see Art. 75), if the motion of the pully C were neglected. It is found that the *rotation* of the heavy pully C has the effect of adding something to the weights moved (viz. $P+Q+R$), without altering the force which produces motion, (viz. the weight of R). Atwood determines by experiment what this is,—call it W,—then the acceleration upon P becomes $\frac{R}{P+Q+R+W} g$, $(=f)$ suppose, and by diminishing R sufficiently, this may be reduced to as small a quantity as we please.

AB is a vertical graduated bar, and S, T are two platforms capable of motion backward and forward along the bar, and of being fixed in any position by screws. The platform S is pierced so that P can pass freely through it, but not R.

If now the system be allowed to start from rest with P at a given position (say A), P will move through the space AS

subject to the uniform acceleration f,—and R being caught off at S, P will move on through ST uniformly with the velocity acquired. The times occupied in moving through AS and ST are observed with considerable accuracy by a contrivance of clock-work attached to the machine.

83. The results of numerous experiments made with Atwood's machine, lead to the conclusions that gravity has a uniform accelerating effect, and that its numerical value is that stated in Art. 43. The most trustworthy results however are (as there stated) to be obtained from experiments on pendulums, but they are of too refined a character to be discussed here.

CHAPTER IV.

OF THE MOTION OF PROJECTILES.

84. In the present Chapter we shall consider:

(i) The projectile as a single heavy particle, (ii) that the accelerating force of gravity is uniform, and acts in the same direction at all points of the path of the projectile; (iii) that the effect of the rotation of the earth is neglected, and (iv) that the motion takes place *in vacuo*—no account being taken of the resistance of the air. See Art. 94.

85. *A body projected in any direction which is not vertical, and acted on by the force of gravity only, will describe a parabola.*

Let the body be projected from the point A in direction AT with velocity v. Draw AV vertical and downwards, and let P be the position of the body at any time t after the instant of projection.

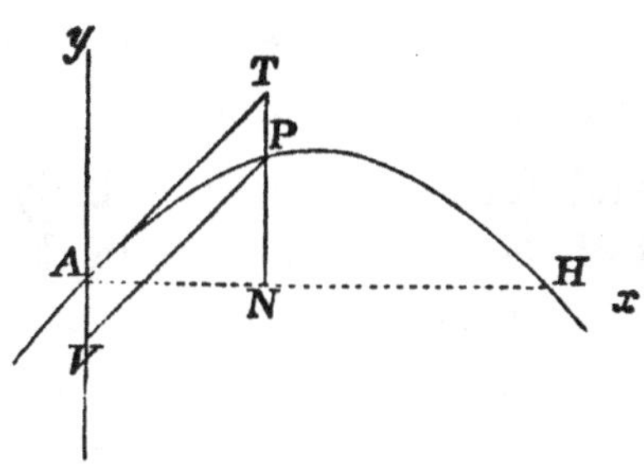

Let the motion of the body be referred to the directions AT, AV (Art. 19), and draw PT, PV parallel to AV, AT;—now the motion being at any and every instant referred to the directions AT, AV—the force of gravity will have a *uniform accelerating effect* (g) in direction AV and there will be *no acceleration* in direction AT, we shall have therefore

$$PV = AT = vt \quad \text{(Art. 49)},$$

$$AV = \tfrac{1}{2}gt^2 \quad \text{(Art. 68)},$$

$$\text{whence } PV^2 = v^2t^2 = \frac{2v^2}{g} \,.\, AV.$$

This relation between PV and AV shews that the path AP is a parabola whose axis is vertical, and directrix consequently horizontal; AV being a *diameter*, and AT the tangent at A, the *parameter* at A being $= \dfrac{2v^2}{g}$.

COR. 1. If h be the space due to the velocity of projection v, (i. e. the space through which a body must fall freely from rest under the action of gravity, in order to acquire the velocity v,) $v^2 = 2gh$; wherefore $PV^2 = 4h \,.\, AV$. Hence $4h$ is the parameter at A, and therefore h is equal to the vertical distance of A below the directrix.

COR. 2. The result of Cor. 1 may be thus interpreted: "The velocity of projection of a projectile is the same as would be acquired by a body falling freely from the directrix to the point of projection."

And further, since the body after passing through any point of its path will move in the same way as if it had been *projected* from that point with the *velocity* it then has, and in the *direction* in which it is then moving,—hence, "the velocity of a projectile at any point P of its path is equal to that due under the action of gravity to the *vertical* distance of that point from the directrix."

Obs. Let the horizontal plane which passes through the point of projection A meet the parabola again in H, and let T be the time of passing from A to H, $AH = R$,—then

R, T are called the *range*, and *time of flight* of the projectile on the horizontal plane; and if α be the angle which the direction of projection makes with the horizon, the angle α is called the *elevation* of the projectile.

86. If the motion of the body be estimated vertically and horizontally—along Ay and Ax,—the velocity of projection vertically is $v \sin \alpha$, and horizontally is $v \cos \alpha$;—the horizontal velocity will remain uniformly equal to $v \cos \alpha$ during the motion, since there is no *force* in direction Ax; the vertical velocity will gradually be reduced to zero by the action of gravity, and the body is then at its greatest height z above the horizontal plane AH, but the continued action of gravity will generate velocity *downwards*, and bring the body to the plane at H after a time equal to that in which it moved from A to the highest point. We shall have the following results,

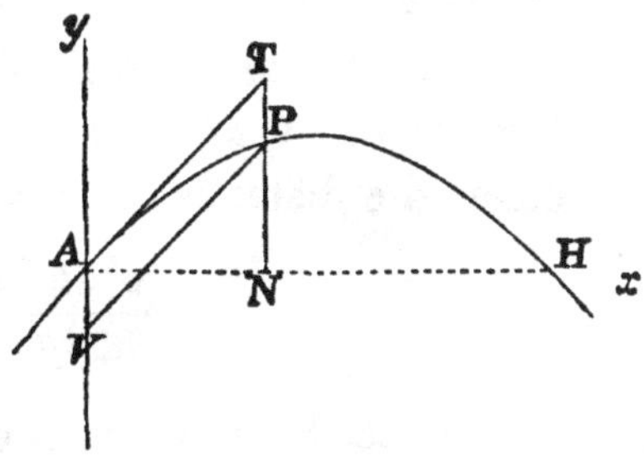

if τ be the time of moving from A to the highest point

= time in which the initial vertical velocity $v \sin \alpha$ is destroyed by force of gravity g,

$$\tau = \frac{v \sin \alpha}{g}, \quad \text{and } z = \frac{(v \sin \alpha)^2}{2g} \;\ldots\ldots\ldots\ldots \text{(i)}.$$

$$\text{Hence } T = \frac{2v \sin \alpha}{g} \;\ldots\ldots\ldots\ldots\ldots\ldots \text{(ii)},$$

and the horizontal velocity is uniform and equal to $v \cos \alpha$;

$$\therefore R = T \,.\, v \cos \alpha = \frac{2v^2 \sin \alpha \cos \alpha}{g} = \frac{v^2 \sin 2\alpha}{g} \;\ldots\ldots \text{(iii)}.$$

This result is the same if $\frac{\pi}{2} - \alpha$ be put for α; shewing that there are two directions in which a body may be projected with a given velocity, so as to have the same horizontal range.

For a given velocity of projection v, the horizontal range R will be greatest when $\sin 2\alpha = 1$; i.e. when $\alpha = 45°$.

Again, the *latus rectum* of the parabola is the *parameter* at the highest point, and the velocity at the highest point being $= v \cos \alpha$, the distance of that point from the directrix is

$$= \frac{v^2 \cos^2 \alpha}{2g} \text{ (Cor. 2)},$$

$$\text{hence the latus rectum} = \frac{2v^2 \cos^2 \alpha}{g} = 4h \cos^2 \alpha.$$

87. *To find the range* (R) *and time of flight* (T) *of a projectile on an inclined plane.*

Let i be the inclination of the plane to the horizon,

α the *elevation* of projection; then initial velocity perpendicular to the plane $AP = v \sin (\alpha - i)$, initial velocity parallel to the plane $AP = v \cos (\alpha - i)$; accelerating force of gravity perpendicular to the plane $= g \cos i$, accelerating force of gravity parallel to the plane $= g \sin i$;

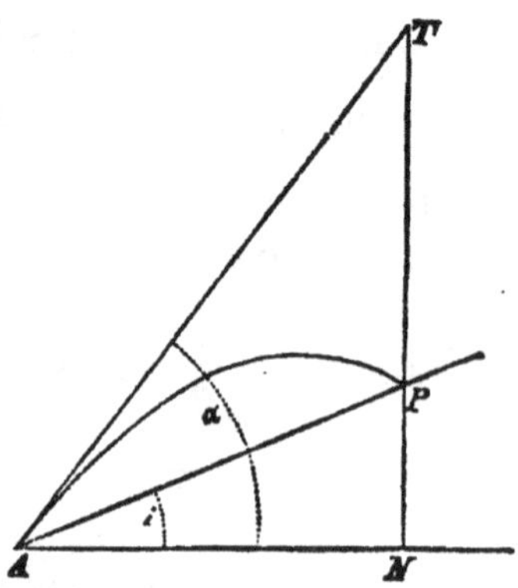

and these two resolved parts of gravity are constant.

Hence if T be twice the time in which the velocity

$v \sin(\alpha - i)$ would be generated or destroyed by the force $g \cos i$; we have

$$T = \frac{2v \sin(\alpha - i)}{g \cos i} \quad \text{..................... (i);}$$

$$\therefore R = v \cos(\alpha - i) \,.\, T - \tfrac{1}{2} g \sin i \,.\, T^2 \quad \text{(Art. 70),}$$

$$= \frac{2v^2 \cos\alpha \sin(\alpha - i)}{g \cos^2 i} \quad \text{....................... (ii),}$$

by substituting for T, and reducing;

or we might obtain R, thus

$$R = AP = \frac{AN}{\cos i} = \frac{v \cos\alpha \,.\, T}{\cos i}$$

(since the horizontal velocity $v \cos\alpha$ is uniform)

$$= \frac{2v^2 \cos\alpha \sin(\alpha - i)}{g \cos^2 i} \quad \text{...............(iii).}$$

COR. The greatest perpendicular distance of the particle from the plane will be when the velocity is entirely parallel to the plane,

i.e. after a time $\dfrac{v \sin(\alpha - i)}{g \cos i}$;

and this perpendicular distance $= \dfrac{v^2 \sin^2(\alpha - i)}{2g \cos i}$.

Further, by putting (iii) in the form

$$R = \frac{v^2 \{\sin(2\alpha - i) - \sin i\}}{g \cos^2 i},$$

we see that for a given velocity of projection the range is greatest when $\sin(2\alpha - i) = 1$,

i.e. $2\alpha - i = \dfrac{\pi}{2}$, or $\alpha = \dfrac{\pi}{4} + \dfrac{i}{2}$,

in other words, when the direction of projection bisects the angle between the plane and the vertical.

88. *To find the equation to the path of a projectile referred to horizontal and vertical co-ordinate axes.*

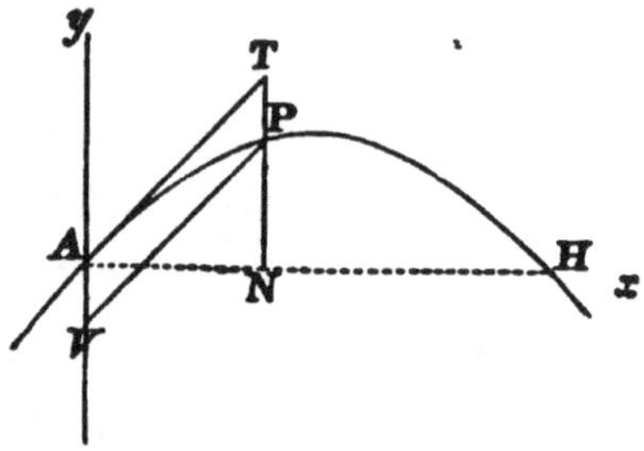

Let A be the point of projection, Ay vertical, and Ax horizontal in the plane in which the projectile moves.

$AN=x$, $NP=y$, the horizontal and vertical co-ordinates of the particle at time t after projection, v the velocity and α the elevation of projection. Let NP be produced to meet in T the line AT which represents the direction of projection.

Then the horizontal velocity $=v\cos\alpha$, which remains uniform, and the *initial* vertical velocity $=v\sin\alpha$.

And we have

$$x=AN=v\cos\alpha\,.\,t. \qquad \text{(i).}$$

And NP represents the space passed over parallel to Ay in time t by a particle projected with a velocity $v\sin\alpha$, and retarded by a force g—hence by Art. (70)

$$y=NP=v\sin\alpha\,.\,t-\tfrac{1}{2}gt^2 \qquad \text{(ii).}$$

Eliminating t between (i), (ii), we get

$$y=x\tan\alpha-\frac{gx^2}{2v^2\cos^2\alpha} \qquad \text{(iii),}$$

which is the equation to the path required, and represents a parabola.

If h be the height due to the velocity of projection $v^2=2gh$, and equation (iii) may be written

$$y=x\tan\alpha-\frac{x^2}{4h\cos^2\alpha} \qquad \text{(iv).}$$

From equation (iii) or (iv) the elements of the parabolic path may easily be deduced.

COR. 1. The equation $y = x \tan \alpha - \dfrac{x^2}{4h \cos^2 \alpha}$ may by a little reduction be put in the form

$$(x - 2h \sin \alpha \cos \alpha)^2 = 4h \cos^2 \alpha \, (h \sin^2 \alpha - y),$$

from which we may readily infer that the co-ordinates (x_0, y_0) of the vertex of the parabola are

$$x_0 = 2h \sin \alpha \cos \alpha, \;\; y_0 = h \sin^2 \alpha;$$

and the latus rectum $= 4h \cos^2 \alpha$.

COR. 2. If we make $y = 0$ in equation (iv), we get

$$0 = x \tan \alpha - \frac{x^2}{4h \cos^2 \alpha};$$

$$\text{i.e. } x = 0, \text{ or } x = 4h \sin \alpha \cos \alpha;$$

the former value of x indicates the point of projection, the latter gives the *range* on the horizontal plane Ax, and accords with the result obtained in Art. (86).

COR. 3. If ϕ be the angle which the direction of motion of the projectile at a time t after projection makes with the horizon, its *altitude* above the point of projection being y and its velocity v'—we shall have

$$\text{vertical velocity} = v' \sin \phi = v \sin \alpha - gt,$$

$$\text{horizontal velocity} = v' \cos \phi = v \cos \alpha,$$

whence we get

$$\tan \phi = \frac{v \sin \alpha - gt}{v \cos \alpha},$$

and

$$v'^2 = (v \sin \alpha - gt)^2 + (v \cos \alpha)^2$$
$$= v^2 - 2g\,(v \sin \alpha \,.\, t - \tfrac{1}{2}gt^2)$$
$$= v^2 - 2gy.$$

89. *Motion of a projectile on a smooth fixed inclined plane under the action of gravity.*

With the diagram of Art. 88, let Ax, Ay be rectangular axes on the inclined plane (elevation $= i$), Ax being drawn *horizontal* and Ay *up* the plane—Ay will be a line of *greatest slope* on the inclined plane.

If the projectile start from A with a velocity v in direction AT along the plane ($TAx = \alpha$) the acceleration of P will be *zero* parallel to Ax,—$g \sin i$ parallel to Ay—and $g \cos i$ perpendicular to the plane, the equation to the path will be as in Art. 88,

$$y = x \tan \alpha - \frac{g \sin i \,.\, x^2}{2v^2 \cos^2 \alpha},$$

a parabola, the elements of which can be obtained as in the previous article.

If v' be the velocity at any point $P\,(x, y)$ of the path, ϕ the angle which the tangent at P makes with Ax, t the time of motion from A to P, z the *vertical* altitude of P above A, so that $z = y \sin i$, we shall have

$$v' \cos \phi = v \cos \alpha \text{ .... (i)},$$
$$v' \sin \phi = v \sin \alpha - g \sin i \,.\, t \text{ .... (ii)},$$
$$y = v \sin \alpha \,.\, t - \tfrac{1}{2}g \sin i \,.\, t^2 \text{......... (iii)},$$
$$x = v \cos \alpha \,.\, t \text{....................... (iv)};$$

from (i), (ii), (iii), we get

$$v'^2 = v^2 - 2g \sin i \,.\, y = v^2 - 2gz,$$

a result which shews that the change of *velocity* is the same as if the projectile had moved *freely* under gravity, through the same *vertical* height.

90. PROB. *A body is projected with a given velocity v from a given point, to find the direction of projection that it may strike another given point.*

Employing the notation of Art. (88),

Let A be the point of projection, P the point through which the body is to pass, h the height due to the velocity of projection, and α the required elevation of projection.

Then the equation of the path is

$$y = x \tan \alpha - \frac{x^2}{4h \cos^2 \alpha};$$

if (a, b) be the co-ordinates of P, we have the equation

$$b = a \tan \alpha - \frac{a^2}{4h \cos^2 \alpha},$$

$$\text{or } b = a \tan \alpha - \frac{a^2}{4h} (1 + \tan^2 \alpha),$$

from which to determine α.

This equation is a quadratic in $\tan \alpha$:—when the two roots are real and unequal, there are two directions of projection which will satisfy the problem;—when the two roots are real and equal, these two directions coincide,—and when the roots are unreal the problem is impossible, i.e. there is no direction in which the body could be projected with the proposed velocity so as to pass through the given point.

This problem admits of a simple geometrical construction. From the point of projection A draw AH vertical and $= h$, through H draw HL horizontal, then HL will be the directrix of the parabolic path Art. (85), Cor. The problem then resolves itself into this—to construct a parabola which shall pass through each of the points A, P and shall have HL for its directrix. With A and P as centres describe circles touching the line HL, and let S be one of the points in which these circles intersect.

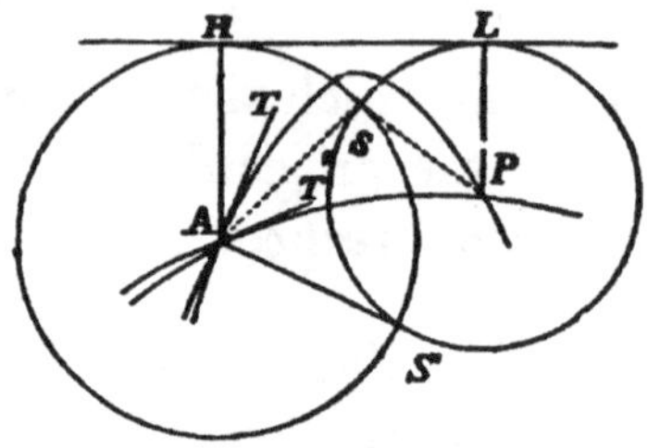

Then since $SA = AH$ and $SP = PL$, A, P are points in a parabola whose focus is S and HL the directrix, and if AT bisect the angle HAS it is a tangent to the parabola at A, and consequently indicates the direction of projection.

If S' be the other point in which the circles intersect, and AT' bisect the angle HAS, then AT' indicates another direction of projection which will equally satisfy the problem. If the circles touch each other, then S, S' coincide, and there is but one parabola and one direction of projection. If the circles do not meet there exists no direction of projection which will satisfy the problem.

The student will have little difficulty in reconciling the results of the above analytical and geometrical solutions of this problem.

Cor. The locus of points P to any one of which there is but *one* parabolic path for the particle projected from A with given velocity, is a parabola having A for its focus, and H its vertex.

91. We have seen in Art. (89) that when a particle moves on a smooth inclined plane the change of velocity in passing from one position to another is the same as if the particle moved *freely under the action of gravity through the same vertical space.* We shall see in the next chapter that the same conclusion is true, if the particle be moving on a smooth curve.

If then a particle moving on a smooth plane or curve quit it and subsequently describe a parabolic trajectory under the action of gravity—and if $v=\sqrt{2gh}$ be the velocity at any point A of the path on the surface, h will be the *vertical* altitude above A of the directrix of the parabola:—so that we may find the position of this directrix without necessarily determining where the particle quits the surface.

We will make use of the above result in the following problem.

92. *An inclined plane is fixed on a table, and from the foot of it a body is projected upwards along the plane with the velocity due to the height h; after passing over the top of the plane the body strikes the table at distance z from the foot of the plane;—shew that if the length of the plane be l, and α its inclination to the horizon be $<\frac{\pi}{4}$, the greatest value of z for given values of h and α is $\frac{h}{\sin\alpha\cos\alpha}$, and corresponds to the value $l=2h\frac{\cot 2\alpha}{\cos\alpha}$.*

Let $AB\,(=l)$ be the inclined plane, AP the table. Draw $AD=h$ vertical, DT horizontal, produce AB to meet DT in T and draw TP at right angles to AT meeting the table in P.

Now the particle projected from A with velocity $=\sqrt{2gh}$ after quitting the plane at B will describe a parabola to which BT is a tangent and of which DT is the directrix.

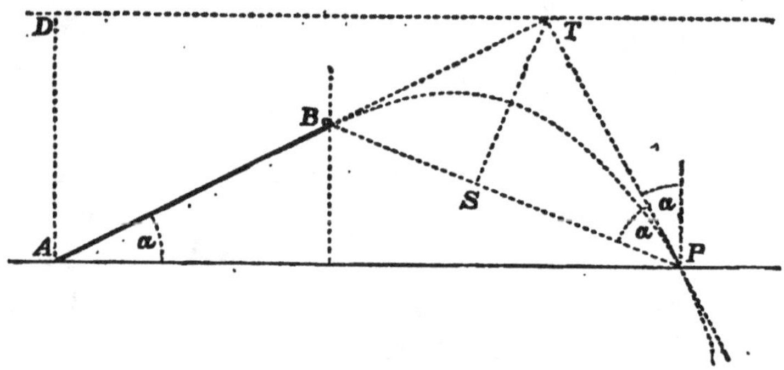

Also since tangents to a parabola which meet in the directrix are at right angles to one another, therefore TP touches the parabola somewhere:—since then the body cannot pass beyond the line TP, the range on the plane AP will evidently be greatest when it touches at P, and we have

$$z = AP = AT \cdot \sec\alpha = \frac{h}{\sin\alpha\cos\alpha} = \frac{2h}{\sin 2\alpha}.$$

Also BP will pass through the focus S, TS will be perpendicular to BP, and the angles which TP makes with PB and the vertical are each $=\alpha$,

whence $$\frac{l}{z} = \frac{AB}{AP} = \frac{\cos 2\alpha}{\cos\alpha};$$

$$\therefore l = \frac{2h\cot 2\alpha}{\cos\alpha}.$$

Further, BP would not meet the table to the right of A

if 2α be $> \frac{\pi}{2}$, hence in order that the problem may be possible α must be $< \frac{\pi}{4}$.

Senate-House Prob. Jan. 18, 1854.

93. PROB. *A particle (whose elasticity is e) is projected with velocity v at an elevation α from a point in a horizontal plane; to find the time in which the vertical velocity will be destroyed by successive rebounds and the total horizontal range described in that time.*

The particle will describe a series of parabolic curves in one plane; the initial vertical velocity being $v \sin \alpha$, and the vertical velocities at the successive rebounds being $ev \sin \alpha$, $e^2 v \sin \alpha$, $e^3 v \sin \alpha$, &c.

Now the time of describing *any one* of these parabolic curves in which the initial vertical velocity is u, is $= \frac{2u}{g}$, Art. (86). Hence the whole time which elapses before the initial vertical velocity $v \sin \alpha$ is destroyed by successive rebounds is

$$= 2\frac{v \sin \alpha}{g}(1 + e + e^2 + e^3 + \dots) = \frac{2v \sin \alpha}{g(1-e)}.$$

And since the horizontal velocity continues uniform and $= v \cos \alpha$, the whole horizontal range described in this time will be

$$= \frac{2v \sin \alpha}{g(1-e)} \cdot v \cos \alpha = \frac{v^2 \sin 2\alpha}{g(1-e)}.$$

The particle will afterwards move along the horizontal plane (supposed smooth) with the uniform velocity $v \cos \alpha$.

COR. The vertical velocity at the beginning of the nth curve will be $= e^{n-1} . v \sin \alpha$, and if α_n be the *elevation* at that time, we shall have, since $v \cos \alpha$ is the horizontal velocity,

$$\tan \alpha_n = \frac{\text{vertical velocity}}{\text{horizontal velocity}} = e^{n-1} . \tan \alpha.$$

Also the time of describing the first n parabolas

$$= \frac{2v \sin \alpha}{g} (1 + e + e^2 + \ldots + e^{n-1}) = \frac{2v \sin \alpha}{g} . \frac{1 - e^n}{1 - e};$$

and the sum of the ranges of these n parabolas

$$= \frac{2v \sin \alpha}{g} . \frac{1 - e^n}{1 - e} . v \cos \alpha = \frac{v^2 \sin 2\alpha}{g} . \frac{1 - e^n}{1 - e};$$

94. The theory of the motion of projectiles given in this Chapter depends upon the suppositions stated in Art. 84, which are all inaccurate. The force of gravity without the Earth's surface varies inversely as the square of the distance from the centre of the Earth; but the height to which a body can be projected from the surface is so small, that the variation of the force arising from the change of the distance from the centre may be safely neglected. The direction of the force is everywhere perpendicular to the horizon,—but if perpendiculars were drawn to the horizon at points on the Earth's surface five miles apart, the angle between them would not exceed 1′, so that any error arising from the non-parallelism of the force of gravity may be neglected; and the same may be said of the very small errors arising from the rotation of the Earth about her axis, and her motion of translation in space about the Sun. The principal cause of error is the

resistance of the air, and this is so considerable as to render the conclusions drawn from the theory almost entirely inapplicable in practice. From experiments made to determine the motion of cannon-balls, it appears that when the initial velocity is considerable, the resistance of the air is 20 or 30 times as great as the weight of the ball; and the horizontal range is often a small fraction of that which the preceding theory gives. Such experiments have been made with great care, and shew how little the parabolic theory is to be depended upon in determining the motions of military projectiles.

From a long series of experiments made at Woolwich, Dr Hutton arrived at the conclusion that the velocity v of a cannon-ball on quitting the gun could be nearly expressed by the formula $v = 1600\sqrt{\frac{2P}{W}}$, P being the weight of the charge of powder and W that of the ball.

And further, if the projectile be of finite size, and have a *rotatory* as well as a *progressive* motion, the resistance of the air, which acts along the surface of the body (or tangentially), will in general change its direction, or the plane of its motion, or both. For this resistance increases with the velocity and the density of the air, and will consequently be greater on that side of the body where the rotatory and progressive motions conspire, than on the other side where they oppose each other: and the density of the air immediately in front of the body is greater than behind it.

Another cause of irregularity will also exist if the ball be not homogeneous—as for example if it contain air-bubbles within, from imperfection in the casting—so that its centre of gravity does not coincide with its centre of figure.

The non-symmetrical action of these causes on the body will make it deviate from its plane of motion, except in the single case when the *axis of rotation* coincides with the direction of *progressive* motion. On this principle has been explained the irregular motion of a tennis-ball and the deviation of a bullet from the vertical plane. It is in a great measure remedied in the case of a rifle ball, since the rifling of the barrel communicates to the ball a rotation about an axis in the direction in which the ball is projected.

(See Robins' *Gunnery*; Hutton's *Tracts*; Art. *Gunnery* in the *Encyclopædia Britannica.*)

CHAPTER V.

MOTION ON A CURVE.

95. WHEN a body moves along a smooth curve the curve exerts a pressure or reaction upon the body at every point, but since this reaction is always perpendicular to the curve, it has no tendency to accelerate or retard the body. In order to determine the velocity of the body in any position we must resolve the forces upon the body in direction of the motion at successive instants, and examine the effect of these resolved forces.

96. *An inelastic particle descends down a smooth curve in a vertical plane under the action of gravity, to find the velocity of the particle in any position.*

We may regard the curve as the limit of a polygon whose sides are equally inclined to one another, by supposing the number of sides to be indefinitely increased, and the angle between consecutive ones to become evanescent.

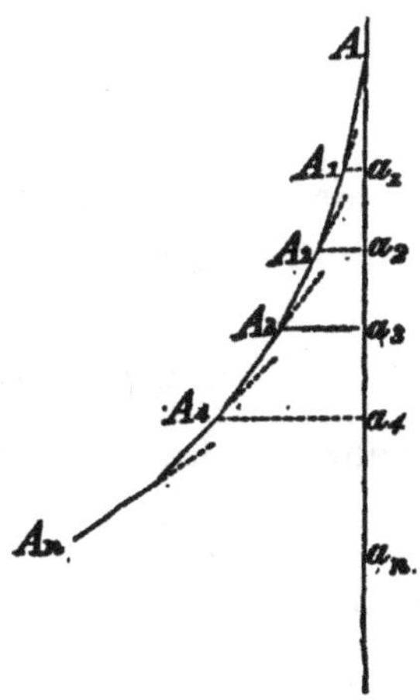

Let $AA_1 \ldots A_n$ be such a polygon; draw A_1a_1, A_2a_2, $A_3a_3 \ldots$ perpendiculars on the vertical line through A.

Let θ be the angle between successive sides of the polygon which are not necessarily of equal length,

u the velocity at A in direction AA_1,

v_1 .... A_1 .... AA_1,

v_2 .... A_2 .... A_1A_2,

....

v_n .... A_n .... $A_{n-1}A_n$.

Then we shall have (Art. 89)

$$\left.\begin{aligned} v_1^2 &= u^2 + 2g\,.\,Aa_1 \\ \text{similarly, } v_2^2 &= v_1^2\cos^2\theta + 2g\,.\,a_1a_2 \\ v_3^2 &= v_2^2\cos^2\theta + 2g\,.\,a_2a_3 \\ &= \ldots\ldots\ldots\ldots\ldots \\ v_n^2 &= v_{n-1}^2\cos^2\theta + 2g\,.\,a_{n-1}a_n \end{aligned}\right\}$$

when the particle comes to A_1 it is deflected in direction A_1A_2 and starts along A_1A_2 with velocity $v_1\cos\theta$;

adding and transposing we get

$$v_n^2 + (v_1^2 + v_2^2 + \ldots + v_{n-1}^2)\sin^2\theta = u^2 + 2g\,.\,Aa_n \ldots\ldots \text{(i)}.$$

Now if α be the angle between the directions of motion at A and A_n, and v' the greatest of the velocities $v_1, v_2 \ldots$

$$\text{and } Aa_n = h, \qquad \text{we have } \alpha = (n-1)\,\theta,$$

$$\text{and } (v_1^2 + v_2^2 + \ldots + v_{n-1}^2)\sin^2\theta < (n-1)\,v'^2\sin^2\theta;$$

$$\therefore\ < \alpha\theta v'^2\,.\left(\frac{\sin\theta}{\theta}\right)^2,$$

and this vanishes in the limit when n is indefinitely increased, α remaining finite, (in which case the polygon becomes the curve);

$$\therefore\ \grave{a}\ fortiori\ (v_1^2 + v_2^2 + \ldots + v_{n-1}^2)\sin^2\theta$$

vanishes in the limit, in comparison with v_n^2.

Hence in the limit when the polygon becomes the curve, the equation (i) becomes

$$v_n^2 = u^2 + 2gh,$$

which expresses the velocity at any point on the curve in terms of the initial velocity, and the *vertical* height through which the particle has fallen; or suppressing the suffix,

$$v^2 = u^2 + 2gh.$$

97. *Obs.* In the above investigation we have supposed the particle inelastic and moving on the concave side of the curve, *towards* which the force of gravity pulls the particle; these suppositions being made in order that the particle may remain in contact with the curve. We shall see hereafter that a particle moving on a curve will, under certain conditions, quit the curve; but the necessity of the supposition here referred to would be obviated by supposing the polygon $AA_1A_2 \ldots$ to be a polygonal tube (becoming a curvilinear one in the limit) of small bore, just sufficient to allow the free passage of the particle. The result arrived at for the velocity at any point would hold good in this case, and will be equally true for a particle moving either on the *concave* or *convex* side of a curve, *so long as it remains in contact with the curve.*

Cor. 1. If the particle start from rest at A, then $u=0$, and $v^2 = 2gh$; i.e. the velocity, acquired from rest, down a smooth curve is equal to that which would be acquired by a body falling freely through the same vertical height. More generally we may interpret the equation $v^2 = u^2 + 2gh$ thus: *the square of the velocity at any point A_n, is equal to the square of the velocity at any other point A, increased by the square of the velocity which the force of gravity would generate in the body in drawing it from rest through the same vertical space.*

This result it will be observed is independent of any particular form of the curve.

Cor. 2. If a body be projected up a curve, the vertical

height to which it will rise is equal to that through which it must fall in order to acquire the velocity of projection; for the body in its ascent will be retarded by the same degrees that it would be accelerated in its descent.

If u be the velocity at any point of a particle moving up a curve, v its velocity after describing a *vertical* height h, we shall have $v^2 = u^2 - 2gh$.

Hence if BAB' be a curve in a vertical plane, the lowest point of which is A, and the parts AB, AB' are similar and equal, a body in falling down BA will acquire a velocity which will carry it up to B'; and the velocities at all equal altitudes in the ascent and descent being equal, the whole time of ascent will be equal to the whole time of descent.

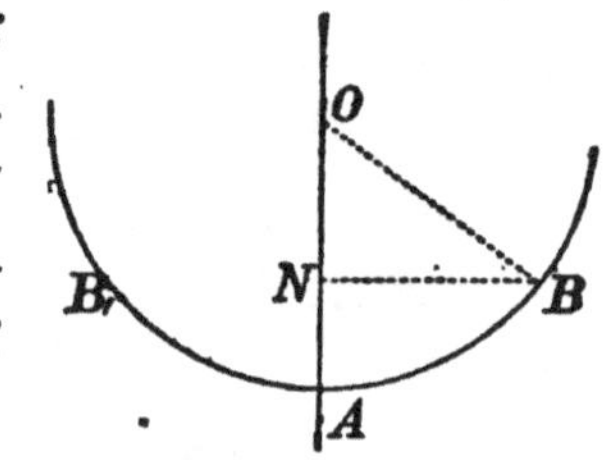

It is moreover obvious that when the particle has arrived at B' it will descend again to A and rise to B, and so on continually; i.e. the motion will be a reciprocating or oscillatory one, and the time of passing from B to B' through the lowest point A is called the *time of oscillation*.

COR. 3. Let BAB' be a circle (radius a) of which A is the lowest point, AO the vertical radius, and BN drawn perpendicular to AO; v the velocity acquired by a particle in descending from rest at B to the lowest point A; then we shall have

$$v^2 = 2g \cdot AN = 2g \cdot \frac{(\text{chord } AB)^2}{2a} = \frac{g}{a} \cdot (\text{chord } AB)^2;$$

$$\therefore v = \sqrt{\left(\frac{g}{a}\right)} \cdot \text{chord } AB \propto \text{chord } AB;$$

i.e. *the velocity at the lowest point varies as the chord of the arc of descent.*

The result will be the same if instead of the curve BAB' we suppose the particle attached to an inextensible string of length OA, and fixed at O.

98. *Obs.* The time in which a particle will fall from rest from a point B to the lowest point A will not, in most cases, be the same for different positions of B. But if the curve be a *cycloid* the time of falling to the lowest point will be the same, whatever be the point from which the body starts; in other words, the time of oscillation in a cycloid (whose axis is vertical and vertex downwards) is the same whatever be the arc of oscillation. For this reason the cycloid is called an *isochronous* curve.

This property of the cycloid is of great importance in the theory and construction of pendulums.

We proceed to give a proof of it: but for the convenience of the student we will first give a proof (in the following three articles) of the properties of the cycloid which it will be necessary for him to be acquainted with.

99. *Def.* If a circle as TPS roll in one plane upon a straight line CBD, any point P fixed on the circle will trace out a curve $CPAD$ called *a cycloid*.

Let $CPAD$ be the complete curve formed in one revolution of the circle, C, D the points where the tracing point P quits and returns to the line CD, SPT the position of the circle when the tracing point is at P, BQA its position when the tracing point P is furthest from the line CD; then it is evident that the parts of the curve AC, AD will be equal and similar,—AB which bisects CD at right angles is called the *axis*, CD the *base*, and A the *vertex* of the cycloid.

Draw PQN perpendicular to AB, join PS, PT.

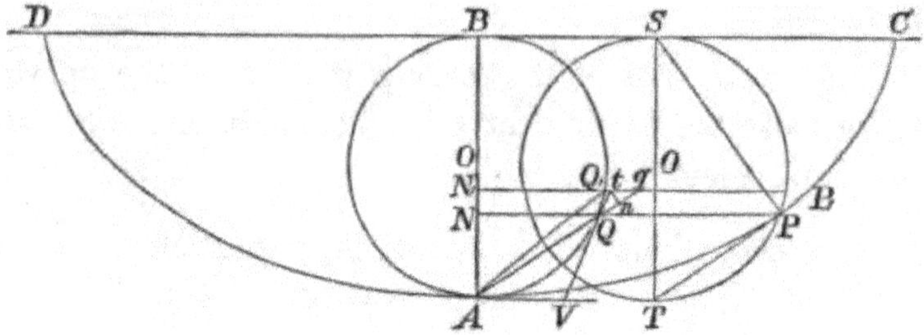

Since P starts from C, and every point of the arc SP has been in contact with the line CS,—the arc $SP = SC$; and since the line CB is equal to the semicircle BQA, which is $=$ semicircle SPT, therefore arc $PT = BS = PQ$, since BQ is parallel and equal to PS.

Hence if we suppose the circle to begin rolling from the position BQA with the tracing point at A, when it arrives at any position P, the arc $AQ = BS = PQ$.

(i) PT is a tangent to the cycloid at P.

For when the tracing point is at P, the generating circle is in contact with the line CD at S, and this point S of the circle is at rest for an instant, or the circle is turning about S,—consequently P is moving perpendicularly to SP, i.e. PS is a normal to the cycloid at P, and PT (which is at right angles to SP) is the tangent at P.

(ii) The length of any arc AP starting from the vertex is twice the chord AQ of the circular arc AQ cut off by the ordinate PQN.

Let $P_{,}Q_{,}N_{,}$ be an ordinate very near to PQN; draw AV, VQt tangents to the circle at A, Q; then AV is parallel to the base (and also to $P_{,}Q_{,}N_{,}$)—let VQ, AQ produced meet $P_{,}Q_{,}N_{,}$ in t, q; and draw tn perpendicular to Qq.

Now AV, VQ being tangents to the same circle $\angle VAQ = \angle VQA$, and $\angle VQA =$ opposite $\angle tQq$, and $\angle tqQ =$ alternate $\angle VAQ$.

Hence $\angle tQq = \angle tqQ$, and $\therefore tq = tQ$; consequently $Qq = 2 . Qn$.

Further, the smaller $QQ_{\prime}$ is taken, the more nearly does the arc $QQ_{\prime}$ coincide with its tangent Qt, and is ultimately equal to it (Newton, Lemma VII). Hence tn is ultimately a small arc of a circle, whose centre is A and radius $AQ_{\prime}$—i.e. AQ,—and Qn ultimately measures the increment of the chord AQ.

Also Qq is parallel to the tangent to the cycloid at P, and is therefore ultimately equal to the arc $PP_{\prime}$.

Hence the increment $PP_{\prime}$ of the arc of the cycloid is ultimately twice the corresponding increment of the chord AQ,—and the arc AP and chord AQ begin together at A,—therefore *arc* $AP = 2$. *chord* $AQ = 2$ *chord* TP.

COR. 1. Since $AQ^2 = AN . AB$, $\therefore AP = 2\sqrt{(AB . AN)}$.

COR. 2. The *arc* $AC = 2 . AB$.

100. (iii) *To make a pendulum oscillate in a given cycloid.*

Let AB be the axis and DC the base of the given cycloid, and let EC be a semicycloid exactly equal to DA placed with its vertex at C and base EF parallel to BC;—ED another semicycloid equal to CA placed with its vertex at D and base parallel to DB.

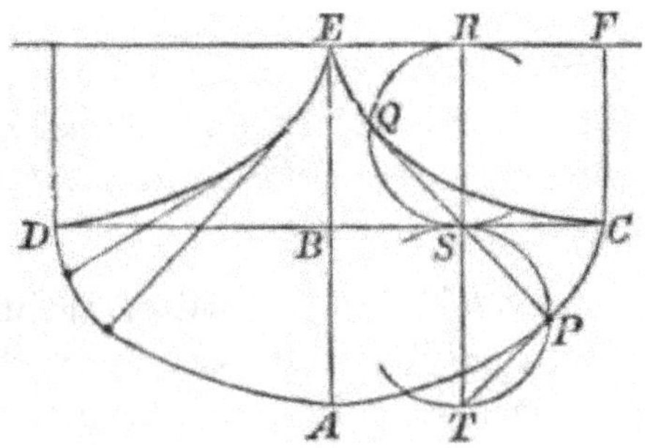

Let RQS, SPT be any positions of the generating circles of the cycloids touching each other at S; Q, P the positions of the tracing points,—join QS, SP.

Then arc $PS = SC = RF =$ arc SQ; hence since the circles are equal, the angles PSC, QSB are equal, and therefore PSQ is a straight line.

But QS is a tangent at Q to the cycloid EQC, and PS is normal at P to the cycloid CPA.

Also the arc $CQ = 2 \,.\, \text{chord } SQ = PQ$.

Hence if we suppose a string of length = length of semicycloid EQC to be fastened at E and applied to the cycloid EQC, and if it be then unwrapped, being kept always stretched, it will always be a tangent to the cycloid EQC, and its extremity will trace out the cycloid CA.

We have then this practical way of making a pendulum vibrate in a cycloid.

Let two equal material semicycloids EQC, ED, be placed so as to have a common vertical tangent at E, and let a fine string of length equal to the semicycloid EQC be fastened at E, and have a heavy particle attached to its other end P. The particle will oscillate in the cycloid CAD, the string unwrapping from EC as P describes CA and then wrapping itself on ED, whilst P describes AD,—and *vice versâ*, continually.

101. (iv) The radius of curvature at any point P of the cycloid $= PQ = 2 \,.\, PS = 2 \,.\,$ *normal*; as is evident from the preceding article, *or* we may arrive at this result independently thus with the fig. Art. 99.

Join BQ', BQ—the latter cutting AQ' in o, let PS, $P'S'$ the normals at P, P' intersect in O' the centre of curvature at P, then since PO', $P'O'$ are parallel to BQ, BQ' respectively, and $PP' = 2 \,.\, Q'o$ ultimately,

$$\therefore PO' = 2 \,.\, Bo = 2 \,.\, BQ = 2 \,.\, PS \text{ ultimately,}$$

i.e. *rad. curv.* $= 2 \,.\,$ *normal.*

102. *To find the time in which a particle will fall down any arc of an inverted cycloid.*

Let V be the point from which the particle starts from rest; VH horizontal meeting the axis of the cycloid AB in H.

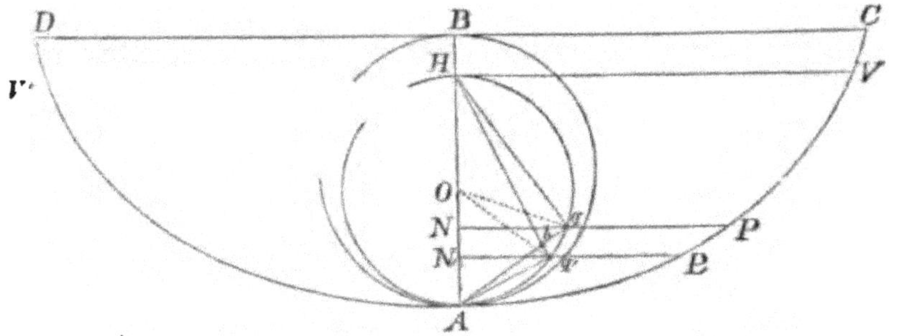

On AH describe a circle, and let the ordinates PN, $P'N'$ of two contiguous points meet this circle in q, q'; join Hq, Hq', and Aq cutting Hq' in b.

Now

$$\text{arc } AP = 2\sqrt{(AB \,.\, AN)} = 2\sqrt{\left(AB \,.\, \frac{Aq^2}{AH}\right)} = 2Aq \,.\, \sqrt{\left(\frac{AB}{AH}\right)},$$

$$\text{similarly arc } AP' = 2Aq' \sqrt{\left(\frac{AB}{AH}\right)};$$

$$\therefore\ PP' = 2\,(Aq \sim Aq')\sqrt{\left(\frac{AB}{AH}\right)}.$$

Again, since the particle starts from rest at V, the velocity at $P =$ velocity acquired in falling freely through the vertical height HN

$$= \sqrt{(2g \,.\, HN)} = \sqrt{\left(2g \,.\, \frac{Hq^2}{AH}\right)} = Hq \,.\, \sqrt{\left(\frac{2g}{AH}\right)};$$

and since PP' is very small the velocity of the particle whilst describing PP' will be very nearly uniform and equal to its velocity at P, and the smaller PP' is taken the more nearly will this supposition be true; also, on the same supposition $Aq - Aq'$ may be ultimately taken to be $= bq$,—since $Aq'b$ being $= 90°$, $Ab = Aq'$ ultimately, and $\therefore$ $Aq - Aq' = bq$.

Hence time of describing $PP' = \dfrac{\text{arc } PP'}{\text{velocity at } P}$ ultimately,

$$= 2\,(Aq - Aq')\sqrt{\left(\frac{AB}{AH}\right)} \div Hq\sqrt{\left(\frac{2g}{AH}\right)}$$

$$= 2\,\frac{bq}{Hq}\cdot\sqrt{\left(\frac{AB}{2g}\right)} = 2\,\angle\, qHq'\cdot\sqrt{\left(\frac{AB}{2g}\right)};$$

$$\left(\text{since } \frac{bq}{Hq} = \text{circular measure of } \angle\, qHq', \text{ ultimately}\right);$$

i.e. the time of describing any *small* arc PP' varies as the circular measure of the *corresponding* angle qHq'.

If then we take the sum of successive small intervals starting from V, we get the time of describing VP,—and the sum of the corresponding small angles is $= \angle\, VHq$,

$$\text{whence time of describing } VP = \angle\, VHq\cdot\sqrt{\left(\frac{2AB}{g}\right)}.$$

COR. 1. When P comes to A the $\angle\, VHq$ becomes $VHA = \dfrac{\pi}{2}$;

$$\therefore \text{ time from } V \text{ to } A = \frac{\pi}{2}\sqrt{\left(\frac{2AB}{g}\right)}.$$

The body after coming to A will ascend the opposite semicycloid AD to a point V' such that $AV' = AV$; and the time of ascending AV' will be equal to the time of descending VA. Hence the time of a complete oscillation from V to V' is

$$= \pi\sqrt{\left(\frac{2AB}{g}\right)}.$$

COR. 2. Since the time of oscillation in a cycloid does not depend upon the particular point from which the body starts from rest, the time is the same whatever be the arc of oscillation,—in other words, *the curve is isochronous.*

COR. 3. If two equal semicycloids EC, ED (fig. Art. 100) be placed in contact at E with their common tangent vertical, and a string of length equal to either of them be fastened at E, and have a heavy particle attached to the other end,—this particle will oscillate in the cycloid CAD in exactly the same way as a free particle moving on a material cycloid CAD.

If l be the length of the string, i.e. of the pendulum, $l = AE = 2AB$; and the time of an oscillation from *rest* to *rest* will be

$$= \pi \sqrt{\frac{l}{g}}.$$

Hence at the same place on the Earth's surface *the time of oscillation* $\propto \sqrt{}$ *(length of the pendulum).*

COR. 4. The cycloid for a short distance from A will very nearly coincide with its circle of curvature at A, which is the circle whose centre is E and radius AE.

If then a pendulum of length l oscillate in a circular arc of *very small* amplitude, the time of oscillation $= \pi \sqrt{\dfrac{l}{g}}$.

COR. 5. If l be the length of the *seconds* pendulum, i.e. of the pendulum which oscillates from *rest* to *rest* in a second,

l' the length of the pendulum which oscillates once in n seconds, —we have

$$1 = \pi \sqrt{\frac{l}{g}}, \quad n = \pi \sqrt{\frac{l'}{g}};$$

$$\therefore \; l' = n^2 . l.$$

103. The length of the *seconds* pendulum in the latitude of London has been found by experiment to be 39·1386 inches:—from this value of l we can find g the accelerating force of gravity, for we have $1 = \pi\sqrt{\frac{l}{g}}$;

$$\therefore g = \pi^2 . l = 386{\cdot}28 \text{ inches} = 32{\cdot}19 \text{ feet}.$$

COR. If g, g' be the force of gravity at two places A, B where the same pendulum beats n, n' times respectively in the same given time, we can easily compare g, g' in terms of n, n'.

For if T be the given interval, we have

$$\frac{T}{n} = \pi\sqrt{\frac{l}{g}}, \quad \frac{T}{n'} = \pi\sqrt{\frac{l}{g'}};$$

$$\therefore \left(\frac{n'}{n}\right)^2 = \frac{g'}{g};$$

$$\therefore \frac{g'-g}{g} = \frac{n'^2}{n^2} - 1 = \frac{n'^2 - n^2}{n^2}$$

$$= \frac{n'-n}{n} . \frac{n'+n}{n} = 2\,\frac{n'-n}{n} \text{ nearly},$$

if $n' \sim n$ be small compared with n.

104. *A seconds pendulum is taken to the top of a mountain of height h; to find the number of beats it will lose in a day.*

Suppose the force of gravity to vary inversely as the square of the distance from the centre of the Earth.

Let r be the Earth's radius, h = the height of the mountain, g, g' the force of gravity at the foot and top of the mountain,

$$\text{then } g' = g\,\frac{r^2}{(r+h)^2};$$

if t, t' be the time of an oscillation at the foot and top of the mountain,

$$t = \pi\sqrt{\frac{l}{g}},\ t' = \pi\sqrt{\frac{l}{g'}},$$

and if n, n' be the number of beats in the same time at the foot and top respectively,

$$nt = n't';$$

$$\therefore\ \frac{n}{n'} = \frac{t'}{t} = \sqrt{\frac{g}{g'}} = \frac{r+h}{r} = 1 + \frac{h}{r},$$

$$\frac{n-n'}{n} = 1 - \frac{1}{1+\frac{h}{r}} = \frac{h}{r} \text{ nearly};$$

if h be 1 mile, $r = 4000$; $n = 24.60.60$,

$$n - n' = \frac{24.60.60}{4000} = 21\cdot 6;$$

that is, a seconds pendulum would in this case lose about 21·6 beats in 24 hours.

N. B. For points outside the Earth, the force of gravity varies inversely as the square of the distance from the centre of the Earth:—for points within the Earth the force of gravity varies as the distance from the centre.

105. *When a particle moves on a plane curve under the action of any force, to find an expression for the acceleration at any point of its path in the direction of the normal.*

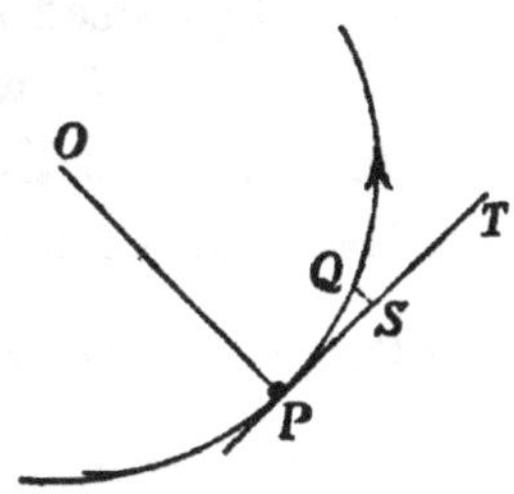

Let v be the velocity of the particle at any point P of its path, PO the normal, PT the tangent at P. Take PQ any small arc described in time t, and draw QS perpendicular to PT, and therefore parallel to PO. As the particle moves from P to Q the velocity and acceleration will in general vary.

Let v', v'' be the greatest and least velocity estimated parallel to PT, as the particle moves from P to Q; f', f'' the greatest and least acceleration estimated parallel to PO; then QS being the space through which the particle is drawn *in direction* PO in the time t by a force always intermediate to f', f'', we shall have

$$QS > \tfrac{1}{2}f''t^2 < \tfrac{1}{2}f't^2,$$

$$\text{and } PS > v''t < v't;$$

$$\text{therefore } \frac{PS^2}{2 \cdot QS} > \frac{v''^2}{f'} < \frac{v'^2}{f''}.$$

Now when the arc PQ is taken continually smaller and smaller, each of the expressions $\frac{v''^2}{f'}$, $\frac{v'^2}{f''}$ becomes $\frac{v^2}{f}$ in the limit, and $\frac{PS^2}{2 \cdot QS}$ in the same limit becomes the radius of curvature at P ($=\rho$ suppose). (See Evans's Newton, p. 15.)

Hence $\frac{v^2}{f} = \rho$, or $f = \frac{v^2}{\rho}$, the expression for the normal acceleration required.

106. By the first law of motion we know that if the force acting upon a particle were to cease at any instant it would proceed to move with the velocity it then has and in the direction in which it is then moving, i.e. in the tangent to the curve at the point where it was at the instant the force ceased. If then the particle continues to pursue a curvilinear path, the value of the expression $\frac{v^2}{\rho}$ at any point measures the acceleration in direction of the normal, which must operate upon the particle in order to deflect it from the tangent and

retain it in its curvilinear path. This accelerating force in direction of the normal has been frequently called the *centrifugal force* of the particle,—vaguely conveying an impression as it were that the particle *of itself* resisted curvilinear motion and exerted a force *per se* to move in a rectilinear path, which innate tendency was only overcome by the action of some external force; whereas the dynamical principles now universally accepted, teach us that a particle of matter exerts no force upon itself, but submits passively to the action of any external force; retaining whatever motion has been impressed upon it till it is modified by the action of some new force. We would recommend the student to avoid this vague use of the term *centrifugal force*, or if he uses it at all, to use it simply as an equivalent for the force in direction of the normal, viz. $\frac{v^2}{\rho}$ or $\frac{mv^2}{\rho}$, according as he is estimating the *accelerating* or *moving* force in that direction (m being the mass of the particle).

107. *A particle moves on a cycloid whose axis is vertical under the action of gravity; to find the pressure on the curve.* (Fig. Art. 100.)

Let m be the mass of the particle moving on the concave side of the curve, R the reaction or pressure which the material curve exerts on the particle *towards the concavity*, which is consequently equal to the pressure which the particle exerts on the curve in the opposite direction, then $\frac{R}{m}$ will be the accelerating force of this pressure; also let ϕ be the angle which the normal PQ makes with the vertical; then since gravity acts *downwards*, $g \cos\phi$ will be the resolved part of the accelerating force of gravity estimated in direction

QP, and $\frac{R}{m} - g \cos \phi$ will be the whole actual acceleration in direction of the normal.

But $\frac{v^2}{\rho}$ measures the acceleration necessary to make the particle move on the curve as it actually does (Art. 105). These two expressions then must be equivalent, and we shall have

$$\frac{v^2}{\rho} = \frac{R}{m} - g \cos \phi;$$

$$\therefore R = m\left(\frac{v^2}{\rho} + g \cos \phi\right),$$

the required expression for the pressure.

COR. 1. If the particle describe a cycloid by being attached to a string, as in Art. (102, Cor. 3), the tension of the string on the particle must be the same as the pressure of the curve in the previous Article, i.e. tension of the string in any position $EQP = m\left(\frac{v^2}{\rho} + g \cos \phi\right)$.

COR. 2. If a particle move on *any* curve under the action of any force, and S be the resolved accelerating force in direction of the normal, estimated *positive* towards the concavity, we should get by the same reasoning as in the present Article, $R = m\left(\frac{v^2}{\rho} - S\right)$.

COR. 3. Since the curve can only exercise a pushing force upon the particle, if the expression for R becomes negative in any case (which indicates that the curve ought to exercise a pulling force) the particle will *quit* the curve,—and moreover will quit it at the point where R is $= 0$, provided that as the particle passes through that point the expression for R changes sign from positive to negative.

If the particle be moving in a tube of very small bore, instead of on a curve simply, the direction of the pressure which the tube exerts upon the particle will change its direction at such a point as is here contemplated, i.e. if when the particle is on one side of the point the pressure acts towards the concave side of the curve, when the particle is on the other side of the point the pressure will act towards the convex side of the curve, and *vice versâ*.

108. We will illustrate the principles of this chapter by the following problems.

PROB. *A particle descends down the arc of a smooth vertical circle, starting from rest at the vertex; to find where the particle will quit the circle.*

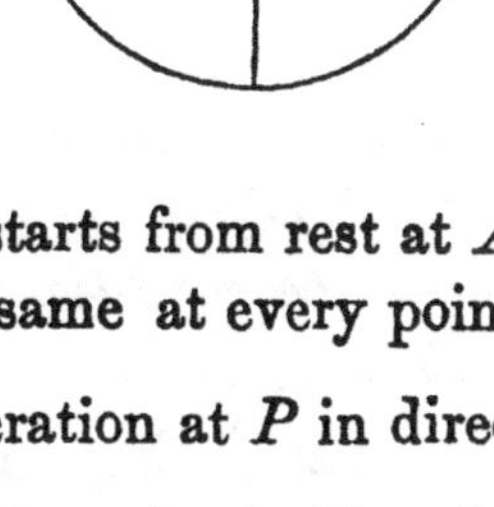

Let v be the velocity of the particle in any position P in its course down the circle.

AO the vertical diameter, O the centre of the circle whose radius $= a$.

PN horizontal, $POA = \theta$, R the pressure of the circle on the particle *outwards* from O.

Then $v^2 = 2g \,.\, AN$ since the particle starts from rest at A, and since the radius of curvature is the same at every point, and $= a$, therefore $\dfrac{v^2}{a}$ measures the acceleration at P in direction PO: but $g \cos \theta$ is the resolved part of gravity in direction PO, and therefore $g \cos \theta - \dfrac{R}{m}$ is the whole actual acceleration on the particle in direction PO;

$$\therefore \frac{v^2}{a} = g \cos\theta - \frac{R}{m};$$

$$\therefore R = m\left(g\cos\theta - \frac{v^2}{a}\right),$$

$$\text{and } v^2 = 2gAN = 2ga(1 - \cos\theta);$$

$$\therefore R = mg(3\cos\theta - 2).$$

This gives the pressure at any point P, and so long as $\cos\theta$ is $> \frac{2}{3}$, R is positive and the particle remains in contact with the curve; but when θ becomes so large that $\cos\theta < \frac{2}{3}$, then R becomes negative, and it would require the curve to exert a pulling force in order to retain the particle in contact with it. Hence at the point where $\cos\theta = \frac{2}{3}$, R changes sign from positive to negative, and the particle quits the curve.

At the point where $\cos\theta = \frac{2}{3}$, $AN = \frac{1}{3}AO$.

After quitting the curve the particle proceeds to describe a parabola.

109. PROB. *A particle is whirled round in a vertical plane, being attached to one end of an inelastic string, the other end of which is fixed,—to find the tension of the string in any position, and the conditions that the particle may describe a complete circle.*

Let O (Fig. p. 251) be the fixed end of the string whose length is $= a$, P the position of the particle when the string PO makes any angle θ with the vertical OA, draw PN horizontal, then

$$AN = a(1 - \cos\theta).$$

Let T be the tension of the string when the particle is at P; u, v the velocity when it is at A, P respectively; then

$$v^2 = u^2 + 2g \,.\, AN = u^2 + 2ga\,(1 - \cos\theta).$$

Also $\dfrac{T}{m}$ = accelerating force of the tension of the string in direction PO,

$g\cos\theta$ = resolved part of gravity in direction PO;

$$\therefore\ \frac{T}{m} + g\cos\theta = \text{whole acceleration in } PO,$$

$$= \frac{v^2}{a}, \text{ by Art. (107)},$$

$$= \frac{u^2}{a} + 2g\,(1 - \cos\theta);$$

$$\therefore\ T = m\left\{\frac{u^2}{a} + g\,(2 - 3\cos\theta)\right\}.$$

This gives the tension of the string in any position.

T is least when $\cos\theta = 1$; i.e. when $\theta = 0$ or P is at A, and increases continually as θ increases, till when $\theta = \pi$ (or the particle is at the lowest point), T is greatest.

In order that the particle may describe a *complete* circle, the tension must never be negative, otherwise the string would become slack.

If we make the least value of T zero, i.e. put $T = 0$ when $\theta = 0$, we get

$$\frac{u^2}{a} + g\,(2 - 3) = 0, \text{ or } u^2 = ga, \text{ or } u = \sqrt{(ga)};$$

which expresses the least velocity the particle may have at the highest point in order to describe a complete circle.

The greatest velocity is at the lowest point, and if

$$u = \sqrt{(ga)},$$

$$\text{the greatest velocity} = \sqrt{(5ga)}.$$

The expression for the tension in this case becomes

$$T = 3mg\,(1 - \cos\theta),$$

the maximum value of which is when $\cos\theta = -1$, or when the particle is at the lowest point; the tension is then equal to $6mg = 6$. *weight of the particle.*

The conditions necessary to be fulfilled in order that a complete circle may be described are

(i) the velocity at the lowest point must not be $< \sqrt{(5ga)}$.

(ii) the string must be capable of sustaining a strain equal to at least six times the weight of the particle.

110. We will conclude this chapter with a short account of the method employed by Newton to determine the elasticity of different substances.

Let A, B be two balls suspended from fixed points C, D by parallel strings, so that they may be in contact at the extremities of horizontal diameters. If the balls be drawn aside through given arcs, the velocities with which they strike each other can be found (Art. 97, Cor. 3), and by a proper arrangement of these arcs they can be made to impinge upon each other when they are in their lowest position. By observing the arcs through which they rebound, the velocities with which they separate after the impact can be obtained, and thence the coefficient of elasticity.

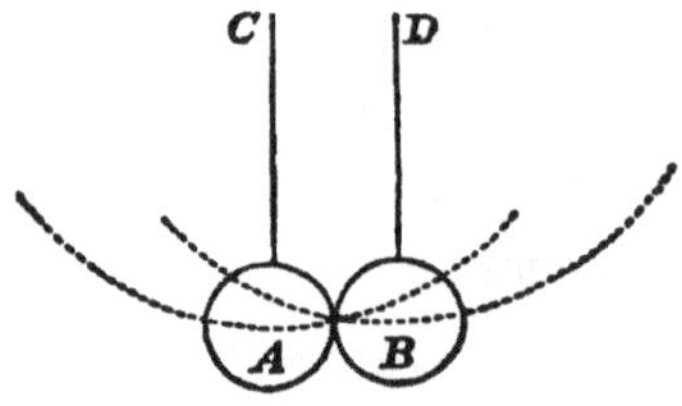

By experiments of this kind Newton determined the coefficient (e) of elasticity of balls of worsted to be about $\frac{5}{9}$,—of balls of steel it was nearly the same,—of cork a little less,—of ivory $e = \frac{8}{9}$,—and of glass $e = \frac{15}{16}$. See *Principia*, Bk. I. *Scholium to the Laws of Motion;* where Newton further shews how allowance may be made for errors arising from the resistance of the air.

Again, if B be drawn aside and allowed to impinge upon A at rest, the velocities of each after impact will be found to be the same as result from the principles assumed in the chapter on collision.

Or again, suppose the balls to be of wood, and let one of them B have a small steel point projecting from it which would cause it to stick to A after the impact,—by properly adjusting the arcs through which the balls are displaced their velocities at impact can be made to be inversely proportional to their masses, and by loading one of them with lead their masses can be made to bear any proportion,—it will be found that they remain at rest after the impact, shewing that equal momenta in opposite directions destroy each other.

PROBLEMS AND EXAMPLES.

EXAMPLES NOT INVOLVING FRICTION. CHAPTERS I. II.

1. Two given forces act at a point; if the angle between their directions be increased, the magnitude of their resultant will be diminished, and *vice versâ*.

2. Three given forces cannot be made to balance each other by any arrangement of their directions, if the sum of any two be less than the third.

3. Two equal forces applied at a given point have a resultant given in magnitude and direction,—find the locus of the extremity of the straight line which represents either force.

4. If O be a point within a triangle ABC, and D, E, F the middle points of the sides,—the system of forces represented by OA, OB, OC will be equivalent to those represented by OD, OE, OF.

5. A circular hoop is supported in a horizontal position, and three weights P, Q, R are suspended over its circumference by three strings meeting in the centre; what must be their positions so that they may balance each other?

The angle between the directions of any two strings will be given by the formulæ of Art. 23.

6. The angles A, B, C of a triangle are 30°, 60°, 90° respectively. The point C is acted on by forces in directions

CA, CB inversely proportional to CA, CB. Find the magnitude and direction of their resultant.

Result. The resultant makes an angle 60° with CA and its magnitude : force in CA :: $AB : CB$.

7. If a point be acted on by three forces parallel and proportional to the three sides AB, BC, DC of a quadrilateral, shew that the resultant of the forces is represented in magnitude and direction by ECE', E being the middle point of AD, and CE' being equal to EC.

8. If two forces P and Q act at such an angle that $R=P$, shew that if P be doubled, the new resultant will be at right angles to Q.

9. The resultant of two forces P and Q acting on a particle is the same when their directions are inclined at an $\angle\, \theta$ as when they are inclined at an $\angle\, \frac{\pi}{4} - \theta$ to each other:—shew that $\tan\theta = \sqrt{2} - 1$.

10. A uniform sphere moveable about a fixed point in its surface, rests against an inclined plane; find the pressure on the fixed point.

Result. If α be the inclination of the plane and β the angle which the radius to the fixed point makes with the vertical,

$$\text{pressure} = \frac{\sin\alpha}{\sin(\alpha+\beta)} \cdot \textit{weight of sphere}.$$

11. Two equal weights P, Q are connected by a string which passes over two smooth pegs A, B situated in a horizontal line, and supports a weight W which hangs from a smooth ring, through which the string passes. Find the position of equilibrium.

Result. The depth of the ring below the line AB

$$= \frac{W}{2\sqrt{4P^2 - W^2}} \cdot \text{length } AB.$$

12. The resultant of two forces P, Q acting at an angle θ is equal to $(2m+1)\sqrt{(P^2+Q^2)}$; when they act at an angle $\frac{\pi}{2}-\theta$, it is equal to $(2m-1)\sqrt{(P^2+Q^2)}$; shew that

$$\tan\theta=\frac{m-1}{m+1}.$$

13. Six forces in one plane represented in magnitude and direction by the lines OA, OB, OC, $O'A$, $O'B$, $O'C$, when applied at a point, balance each other. Prove that the algebraical sum of the triangles OBC, $O'BC$ (considered of different signs when O, O' are on opposite sides of BC) is equal to two-thirds of the triangle ABC.

* * * * * * *

14. A rod 5 feet long has a string 7 feet long attached to its ends, and by this it is hung over a small smooth fixed peg, so that the parts of the string are as 4 : 3. Find the position of the centre of gravity of the rod and the pressure on the peg.

Result. Depth of centre of gravity of the rod below the peg $=\frac{12\sqrt{2}}{7}$, inclination of the rod to the vertical $=\sin^{-1}\frac{7}{5\sqrt{2}}$, pressure on peg = weight of rod.

15. A smooth circular ring is fixed in a horizontal position, and a small ring sliding upon it is in equilibrium when acted on by two strings in the direction of the chords PA, PB; shew that if PC be a diameter of the circle the tensions of the strings are in the ratio of BC to AC.

16. Three forces P, Q, R acting upon a point and keeping it at rest, are represented by lines drawn from that point. If P be given in magnitude and direction, and Q in magni-

tude only, find the locus of the extremity of the line which represents the third force R.

17. At any number of points of a parabola forces are applied, represented by the tangents and normals at those points,—shew that the parabola will remain at rest if the focus is fixed.

18. A circular disc is kept at rest by three forces acting perpendicularly to the circumference at three given points therein; shew that the forces are as the sides of the circumscribing triangle that pass through those points.

19. R being the resultant of P and Q, let R be equal to $\sqrt{3}\,.\,Q$, and make an angle of 30° with P;—find P in terms of Q.

Result. $P=Q$ or $P=2Q$.

20. AB is a uniform rod,—of weight W,—moveable in a vertical plane about a hinge A; a given weight P sustains the rod by means of a string BCP passing over a smooth pin C, situated in the vertical through A and at a distance $AC=AB$. In the oblique position of equilibrium of the rod,

$$\angle ACB = \cos^{-1}\frac{P}{W}.$$

21. Two rods similar in every respect—(the weight of each being W)—are capable of motion in a vertical plane round a common fixed pivot at one extremity of each, and they are kept in equilibrium in a position inclined at $\angle\,\theta$ to the horizon by a string placed over the other ends and kept stretched by two equal weights (P, P) at its extremities. Shew that

$$\tan\theta = \frac{2P+W}{2P}.$$

* * * * * * * *

22. $ABDC$ is a quadrilateral, and is acted on by forces which act in the direction of, and are proportional to, AB, AC, DB, DC respectively; shew that their resultant is parallel and proportional to the line joining the middle points of the diagonals.

23. A lever without weight in the form of the arc 2α of a circle subtending an $\angle\, 2\alpha$ at its centre, having two weights P and Q suspended from its extremities, rests with its convexity downwards upon a horizontal plane; determine the position of equilibrium.

Result. The chord PQ is inclined to the horizon at an angle

$$\tan^{-1}\left(\frac{P-Q}{P+Q}\tan\alpha\right).$$

24. The ends of a uniform heavy rod are connected, by inextensible strings without weight, with the ends of another uniform rod which is moveable about its middle point. Prove that, when the system is in equilibrium, either the rods or the strings are parallel.

25. If a uniform heavy rod be supported by a string fastened at its ends, and passing over a smooth peg; prove that it can only rest in a horizontal or vertical position.

26. Two equal circles intersect in A and B: any line PQN perpendicular to AB meets the circles in P and Q and AB in N. Prove that the resultant of four forces represented by PA, PB, QA, QB is of constant magnitude.

* * * * * * *

27. Explain how a vessel is enabled to sail in a direction nearly opposite to that of the wind.

28. Explain how the force of the current may be taken advantage of to urge a ferry-boat across a river; the centre of

the boat being attached, by means of a long rope, to a mooring in the middle of the stream.

29. The whole length of each oar of a boat is 10 feet, and from the hand to the rowlock the distance is 2 ft. 6 in.; each of eight men sitting in the boat pulls his oar with a force of 54 lbs. Supposing the blades of the oars not to move through the water, find the resultant force propelling the boat.

Result. Propelling force = 144 lbs.

30. At what height from the base of a pillar must the end of a rope of given length be fixed, so that a given power acting at the other end may be most effectually exerted to overturn the pillar?

Result. $\frac{1}{\sqrt{2}}$. length of rope.

31. A uniform beam of length $2a$ rests against a vertical plane and over a peg at a distance h from the plane; shew that the inclination of the beam to the vertical is $= \sin^{-1} \sqrt[3]{\left(\frac{h}{a}\right)}$.

32. A uniform rod whose weight is W is supported by two fine strings (one attached at either end), which passing over small fixed smooth pullies carry weights w_1, w_2 respectively. Shew that the inclination of the rod to the horizon is

$$\sin^{-1} \frac{w_1^2 \sim w_2^2}{W\sqrt{2(w_1^2 + w_2^2) - W^2}}.$$

33. Two equal uniform heavy straight rods are connected at one extremity by a string, and rest upon two smooth pegs in the same horizontal line, one rod upon one peg, and the other upon the other:—the distance between the pegs being equal to the length of each rod, and the

length of the string being half the same: shew that the rods rest at an angle θ to the horizon, such that

$$2\cos^3\theta = 1.$$

34. A string is knotted so as to form an equilateral triangle, and is placed symmetrically within another equilateral triangle nine times as great, each knot being connected with the two nearest angles of this triangle by strings solicited with a tension P. If T be the tension of the triangular string, then will $P = T\sqrt{21}$.

35. Two straight lines AB, AC make an $\angle\, 2\alpha$ with each other: when a certain force R is resolved into two forces parallel and perpendicular to AB, P is the component parallel to AB; similarly, when R is resolved into two forces parallel and perpendicular to AC, Q is the component parallel to AC,—shew that

$$R = \tfrac{1}{2}\{(P+Q)^2\sec^2\alpha + (P-Q)^2\operatorname{cosec}^2\alpha)^{\frac{1}{2}},$$

and that the direction of R makes an angle

$$\tan^{-1}\left(\frac{P-Q}{P+Q}\cot\alpha\right)$$

with the straight line bisecting the $\angle\, BAC$.

36. Two equal weights (P, P) are attached at the extremities of a string which passes over three small pullies forming an equilateral triangle; a small heavy ring (W) is slipped over the uppermost pully and descends by its own weight; find the position of equilibrium.

Result. The portions of the string which are not vertical are inclined to the vertical at an angle $2\sin^{-1}\left(\frac{1}{2}\sqrt{\frac{W}{P}}\right)$.

37. A uniform heavy rod of given length is to be supported in a given position, with its upper end resting at a

given point against a smooth vertical wall, by means of a fine thread attached to the lower end of the rod and to a point in the wall. Find by a geometrical construction the point in the wall to which the string must be attached.

38. A flat semicircular board with its plane vertical, and curved edge upwards, rests on a smooth horizontal plane, and is pressed at two given points (P, Q) of its circumference by two beams which slide in smooth vertical tubes; find the ratio of the weights of the beams that the board may be in equilibrium.

Result. If α, β be the angles which the radii at P, Q make with the horizon—then the weight of the beam at P : that at $Q = \tan\alpha : \tan\beta$.

39. Three equal heavy cylinders,—(weight of each $= W$),—each of which touches the other two, are bound together by a string and laid upon a horizontal plane; the tension (T) of the string being given, find the pressures between the cylinders.

Result. Pressure between the upper and either of the lower cylinders $= T + \frac{W}{\sqrt{3}}$—between two lower cylinders $= T - \frac{W}{2\sqrt{3}}$.

40. Three straight tobacco-pipes rest upon a table, with their bowls mouth-downwards in the angles of an equilateral triangle, the tubes being supported in the air by crossing symmetrically, each under one and over the other, so as to form another equilateral triangle; shew that the mutual pressure of the tubes varies inversely as the side of the latter triangle.

41. If ABC be a right-angled triangle, and $ABDE$, $ACFG$ be the squares on the sides constructed as in Euclid I. 47, prove that the resultant of forces represented by CD, BF is parallel to a diagonal of the rectangle whose sides are AE, AG.

42. An elliptic lamina is acted on at the extremities of pairs of conjugate diameters by forces in its own plane tending outwards and normal to its edge: there will be equilibrium if the force at the end of every diameter be proportional to the conjugate.

43. Three equal rods are jointed by smooth compass-joints at the extremities so as to form an equilateral triangle. Find the direction of the pressures on the lower joints when the triangle is suspended from one angle.

Result. They are inclined to the horizon at an angle $\tan^{-1}\frac{\sqrt{3}}{2}$.

44. One corner of a square lamina is fixed, and equal forces (P, P) act in order of direction along the two sides which do not pass through that corner. If a single force applied at the centre of the lamina keeps it at rest, determine this force, and the pressure on the fixed point.

Result. A single force $R=2\sqrt{2}P$ acting perpendicular to the diagonal passing through the fixed point: and pressure on fixed point $=\sqrt{2}P$ acting parallel and opposite to R.

45. A cylindrical shell, without a bottom, stands on a horizontal plane, and two smooth spheres are placed within it, whose diameters are each less whilst their sum is greater than that of the interior surface of the shell; shew that the cylinder will not upset if the ratio of its weight to the weight of the upper sphere be greater than $2c-a-b : c$,—where a, b, c are the radii of the spheres and cylinder.

46. Two forces in the ratio $1+n:1$ where n is small, act upon a point in directions inclined at an angle α; shew that the sine of the angle which the direction of the resultant makes with that of the larger force $=\left(1-\frac{n}{2}\right)\sin\frac{\alpha}{2}$ nearly.

47. An endless string supports a system of equal heavy pullies, the highest one of which is fixed, the string passing round every pully and crossing itself between each. If α, β, γ, &c. be the inclinations to the vertical of the successive rectilinear portions of string, prove that $\cos\alpha$, $\cos\beta$, $\cos\gamma$, &c. are in arithmetic progression.

48. A heavy rod—(weight W, length $2a$)—can turn freely about a hinge at one extremity A; and it carries a heavy ring (P) which is attached to a fixed point C in the same horizontal plane with the hinge, by means of a string of length (c) equal to the distance between the point and the hinge. The $\angle\,\theta$ which the rod makes with the horizon in the position of equilibrium is defined by the equation

$$\cos 2\theta + \frac{Wa}{2Pc}\cos\theta = 0.$$

49. A sphere of weight W is moveable about a point in its circumference, at which a string is attached which passes over the sphere and supports a weight P; shew that the diameter of the sphere which passes through the point of suspension is inclined to the vertical at an angle

$$= \sin^{-1}\left(\frac{P}{P+W}\right).$$

50. In a triangular lamina ABC, AD, BE, CF are the perpendiculars on the sides, and forces represented by the lines BD, CD, CE, AE, AF, BF, are applied to the lamina; prove that their resultant will pass through the centre of the circle described about the triangle.

51. Two uniform rods AB, BC of similar material are connected by a smooth hinge at B, and have smooth rings at their other extremities, which slide upon a fixed horizontal

wire: shew that the only positions of equilibrium are those in which the lesser rod is vertical.

52. Two small rings without weight slide on the arc of a smooth vertical circle,—a string passes through both rings, and has three equal weights attached to it, one at each end and one between the rings;—in the position of equilibrium the distance between the rings is equal to the radius of the circle.

53. A ring whose weight is P, is moveable along a smooth rod inclined to the horizon at an angle α, another ring of weight P' is moveable along another rod in the same vertical plane as the former, and inclined at an angle α' to the horizon; a string which connects these rings passes through a third ring of weight $2W$ which hangs freely; shew that the system cannot be in equilibrium unless

$$P \tan \alpha - P' \tan \alpha' + W(\tan \alpha - \tan \alpha') = 0.$$

54. A square rests with its plane perpendicular to a smooth wall, one corner being attached to a point in the wall by a string whose length is equal to a side of the square; shew that the distances of three of its angular points from the wall are as 1 : 3 : 4.

55. A uniform square board is capable of motion in a vertical plane about a hinge A at one of its angular points; a string attached to C one of the nearest angular points and passing over a pully vertically above the hinge, at a distance from it equal to a side of the square, supports a weight whose ratio to the weight of the board is $1 : \sqrt{(2)}$. Find the positions of equilibrium.

Result. AC makes with the vertical an $\angle 30^\circ$ or $\angle 90^\circ$.

56. One end of a beam whose weight is W, is placed on a smooth horizontal plane; the other end, to which a string is

fastened, rests against another smooth plane inclined at an angle α to the horizon; the string passing over a pully at the top of the inclined plane hangs vertically, supporting a weight P. Shew that the beam will rest in all positions if

$$2P = W \sin \alpha.$$

57. Two equal circular discs—of radius r—with smooth edges are placed on their flat sides in the corner between two smooth vertical planes inclined at $\angle 2\alpha$, and touch each other in the line bisecting the angle; the radius of the least disc which may be pressed between them without causing them to separate

$$= r \cdot \frac{1 - \cos \alpha}{\cos \alpha}.$$

58. One end of a string is fixed to the extremity of a smooth uniform rod, and the other to a ring without weight which passes over the rod, and the string is hung over a smooth peg. Determine the least length of the string for which equilibrium is possible, and shew that the inclination of the rod to the vertical cannot be less than 45°.

59. Two similar and equal smooth rods AB, BC, have a compass-joint at B; a ring without weight slides on BC, being attached to A by a string, so that the rods can rest with their ends on a smooth horizontal plane. Shew that the mutual pressure at B is perpendicular to BC.

60. Shew that the moment of a force represented by AB about any line passing through a point P will be represented by double the projection of the triangle PAB on a plane perpendicular to the line.

Prove by this method of projection—or otherwise—that the sum of the moments of two forces (whose lines of action intersect) about any line is equal to the moment of their resultant about the same line.

* * * * * * *

61. The sides of a rhombus $ABCD$ are hinged together at the angles; at A, C are two pulling forces (P, P) acting in the diagonal AC; and at B, D there are two other pulling forces (Q, Q) acting in BD; shew that

$$\angle DAB = \cos^{-1}\left(\frac{P^2 - Q^2}{P^2 + Q^2}\right).$$

62. If the parallelogram of forces be true for any two forces making a given angle with each other, prove that it will be also true for any two forces making any other angle with each other.

63. A particle P is placed in a smooth horizontal tube AB, and is acted on by two forces tending to two fixed points C, D, and proportional to the distances CP, PD; find the force necessary to keep P at rest in a given position.

64. Two equal heavy beams AB, CD are connected diagonally by similar and equal elastic strings AD, BC,—determine the position of equilibrium when AB is held horizontal: and shew that if the natural length of each string equals AB, and the elasticity be such that the weight of AB would stretch the string to 3 times its natural length, then

$$\frac{1}{AB} = \frac{1}{BC} + \frac{1}{AC}.$$

65. A small smooth ring is capable of sliding on a fine elliptic wire, whose transverse axis is vertical; two strings attached to the ring pass through small smooth rings at the foci and sustain given weights: shew that if the ring be in

equilibrium at any point, besides the highest and lowest points of the wire, it will be in equilibrium in every position.

66. Two equal rods AB, AC without weight are connected by a hinge at A and are placed in a vertical plane resting on a smooth sphere so that the point A is vertically over the centre O. A heavy ring slides on a string attached to the two ends B and C, the length of the string being twice that of either rod. If BD be the perpendicular drawn from B on AO produced, prove that in the position of equilibrium $AO \cdot AD = 2BD^2$:—supposing the sphere to be so small that the string is clear of it.

67. A small ring (weight W_1) is moveable on a rod whose inclination to the horizon is α_1; another ring (weight W_2) is moveable on another rod in the same vertical plane, whose inclination is α_2; a slender thread connecting the rings carries a ring (weight W). Shew that

$$\frac{\tan \alpha_1}{\tan \alpha_2} = \frac{W + 2W_2}{W + 2W_1}.$$

68. Forces are applied at the middle points of the sides of a rigid plane polygon, perpendicular to the sides, and proportional to them in magnitude, all the forces tending inwards *or* all outwards; shew that the system of forces is in equilibrium.

69. Two rods of equal uniform thickness have their ends joined by a compass-joint and rest in a circle whose plane is vertical; prove that if the rods are at right angles they are equally inclined to the horizon.

70. A smooth heavy rod AB—weight W—moveable in a vertical plane about a hinge at A, leans against a heavy

prop CD—weight P—also moveable in the same plane about a hinge at C. Find the position of equilibrium.

Result. If $AB=2a$, $CD=2b$, $CA=c$, $\angle BAC=\theta$, $\angle DCA=\phi$, we shall have $c\sin\theta=2b\sin(\theta+\phi)$ and $aW\sin 2\theta\cos(\theta+\phi)+Pb\sin 2\phi=0$.

71. A cylinder—(length $=h$, rad. base $=a$, weight $=W$)—rests with its base on a smooth inclined plane—(inclination $=\alpha$);—a string attached to its highest point, passing over a pully at the top of the inclined plane, hangs vertically and supports a weight P; the portion of the string between the cylinder and pully is horizontal: determine completely the conditions of equilibrium.

Result. We must have $P=W\tan\alpha$, with the condition that $\tan\alpha$ is not $>\frac{2a}{h}$.

72. A cylinder with its base resting against a smooth vertical plane is held up by a string fastened to it at a point of its curved surface whose distance from the vertical plane is h. Shew that h must be $> b-2a\tan\theta$ and $< b$; where $2b$ is the altitude of the cylinder, a the radius of the base, and θ the angle which the string makes with the vertical,

73. Four rods jointed at their extremities form a quadrilateral which may be inscribed in a circle; if they be kept in equilibrium by two strings joining the opposite angular points, shew that the tension of each string is inversely proportional to its length.

74. A regular hexagon composed of six equal heavy rods, moveable about their angular points, is suspended from one angle, which is connected by threads with each of the opposite angles. The tensions of the threads are as $\sqrt{3}:2$.

75. A string 9 feet long has one end attached to the extremity of a smooth uniform heavy rod two feet in length,

and at the other end carries a ring which slides upon the rod. The rod is suspended by means of the string from a smooth peg; prove that if θ be the angle which the rod makes with the horizon, then $\tan\theta = 3^{-\frac{1}{3}} - 3^{-\frac{2}{3}}$.

76. If two forces acting along chords of a circle are inversely proportional to the lengths of the chords, their resultant will pass through one or other of the points of intersection of lines drawn through the extremities of the chords.

77. A thread passing over a vertical hoop is held to the hoop by two equal rings P_1, P_2, and a third equal ring P_3 hangs on the thread between the two; prove that if Q be the point in which a tangent to the hoop parallel to P_1P_3 meets the vertical through P_3, then P_3 is situated at the centre of gravity of the triangle P_1QP_2.

78. If lines be drawn from any point whatever to four fixed points in the same plane with it, and these lines represent forces all acting *from* or all *towards* the point; shew that their resultant will pass through a certain fixed point and will be proportional to the distance of the first fixed point from it.

79. Three uniform beams AB, BC, CD, of the same thickness and of lengths l, $2l$, l respectively, are connected by hinges at B and C, and rest on a perfectly smooth sphere, the radius of which $= 2l$, so that the middle point of BC and the extremities of A, D are in contact with the sphere; shew that the pressure at the middle point of $BC = \frac{91}{100}$ of the weight of the beams.

80. Three forces act in equilibrium at the angles of a triangle, one bisecting the angle at which it acts, and the other two making equal angles with the side opposite to that angle; shew that the forces are as the sides opposite to their points of application, and that they will balance if turned through any equal angles in the same direction.

81. A quadrilateral is formed by four rigid rods jointed at the ends; shew that two of its sides must be parallel, in order that it may preserve its form when the middle points of either pair of opposite sides are joined together by a string in a state of tension.

82. A cube whose weight is W rests upon a horizontal table, and is cut by three planes passing through a diagonal of the upper face and the several corners of the lower face. If the parts cut off be placed together again, their faces being supposed perfectly smooth, and be kept in equilibrium by a horizontal string tied round the cube,—prove that the tension of the string is $\frac{1}{6}W$.

83. A uniform beam PQ of given weight (W) and length rests in contact with a fixed vertical circle, whose vertical diameter is AB, in such a manner that strings AP, BQ attached to the rod and circle are tangents to the circle at the points A and B. Find the tensions of the strings, and shew that the conditions of the problem require that the inclination of the beam to the vertical must be

$$< \sin^{-1}\left\{\frac{\sqrt{5}-1}{2}\right\}.$$

Result. If α = inclination of beam to the vertical, the tensions of the strings are $\frac{1}{2}W(\cot\alpha \pm \sec\alpha)$.

84. A particle is placed on a smooth square table at distances c_1, c_2, c_3, c_4 from the corners, and to it are attached

strings passing over smooth pullies at the corners, and supporting weights P_1, P_2, P_3, P_4; shew that if there is equilibrium,

$$\left(\frac{P_1}{c_1}+\frac{P_2}{c_2}+\frac{P_3}{c_3}+\frac{P_4}{c_4}\right)\frac{c_1^2-c_3^2}{a^2}=2\left(\frac{P_3}{c_3}-\frac{P_1}{c_1}\right),$$

a being a side of the table.

85. A cone of given weight W is placed with its base on a smooth inclined plane (α), and supported by a weight W' which hangs by a string fastened to the vertex of the cone, and passing over a pully in the inclined plane at the same height as the vertex. Find the angle (2β) of the cone when the ratio of the weights is such that a small increase of W' would cause the cone to turn about the highest point of the base, as well as slide.

Result. $\tan\beta=\frac{3}{8}\sin 2\alpha$.

86. A cone, the vertical angle of which is $2\tan^{-1}\frac{3}{8}$, rests with its vertex against a smooth vertical wall, a point in its base being attached to a point in the wall by a string to which the axis of the cone is parallel when it is in equilibrium; shew that the tension of the string is $W\sqrt{2}$, and that the distance of the vertex of the cone from the fixed point in the wall is $\frac{3h\sqrt{2}}{8}$:—where W is the weight of the cone, and h the length of its axis.

87. A bowl is formed from a hollow sphere of radius a: it is so placed that the radius of the sphere drawn to each point in the rim makes an $\angle\alpha$ with the vertical, and the radius drawn to a point A of the bowl makes an $\angle\beta$ with the vertical;—if a smooth uniform rod remains at rest

when placed with one extremity at A, and with a point in its length on the rim of the bowl, shew that the length of the rod is $=4a\sin\beta\sec\frac{\alpha-\beta}{2}$.

FRICTION. CHAP. III.

1. Two parallel vertical walls—at a distance c—are one smooth and the other rough, and between them is supported a hemisphere—radius a and weight W—with its curved surface in contact with the smooth wall, and a point in its rim in contact with the rough wall; the pressure on each wall $=\frac{1}{\mu}W$, and the least coefficient of friction consistent with equilibrium $=\frac{\sqrt{2ac-c^2}}{c-a+\frac{3}{8}\sqrt{2ac-c^2}}$.

2. Two rough bodies rest on an inclined plane in a *principal plane*, and are connected by a string which is parallel to the plane; if the coefficient of friction be not the same for both, find the greatest inclination (α) of the plane which is consistent with equilibrium.

Result. If W, W' be the weights, μ, μ' their coefficients of friction, the value of $\alpha=\tan^{-1}\frac{\mu W+\mu' W'}{W+W'}$.

3. A uniform ladder 10 ft. long rests with one end against a smooth vertical wall and the other on the ground, the coefficient of friction being $=\frac{1}{2}$; find how high a man (whose weight is 4 times that of the ladder) may rise before it begins to slip, the foot of the ladder being 6 feet from the wall.

Result. $\frac{85}{12}$ feet, along the ladder.

4. A uniform and straight plank—length $2a$—rests with its middle point upon a rough horizontal cylinder—radius c—which is fixed, their directions being perpendicular to each other. Find the greatest weight that can be put upon one end of the plank without its sliding off the cylinder.

Result. $P = \frac{c \tan^{-1}\mu}{a - c \tan^{-1}\mu}$. weight of plank.

5. At what angle of inclination should the traces be attached to a sledge, that it may be drawn up a given hill with the least exertion?

Result. The inclination of the traces to the hill $= \tan^{-1}\mu$.

6. A string fixed to a point in a rough vertical wall is wrapped round a ball, which is then allowed to hang in contact with the wall; determine the limiting positions of equilibrium. Find the coefficient of friction so that it may be possible for the position of the string not in contact with the ball to be horizontal.

Result. The angle the string makes with the wall $= \sin^{-1}\frac{1}{\mu}$. For the latter part of the question $\mu = 1$.

7. Two uniform rods of equal weight AB, BC are in a vertical plane and connected by a free joint at B; the point A is fixed and C can move on a rough horizontal plane passing through A: if λ be the $\angle$ of friction and θ, ϕ the angles which the rods make with the vertical when on the point of sliding,

$$\cot\theta - 3\cot\phi = 2\cot\lambda.$$

8. P, Q are two pegs, G the centre of gravity of a slender rod passing over the nearer peg P and under the farther peg Q, and just kept from sliding in direction of its length by the friction between it and the pegs. Find the ratio of PG to PQ

in terms of μ, the coefficient of friction between the rod and pegs, and of α the inclination of the rod to the vertical.

Result. $PG : PQ = \cot\alpha - \mu : 2\mu$.

9. A ladder rests against a vertical wall, and is prevented from sliding by the friction of the ground and wall; shew that when the ladder is on the point of sliding down in a vertical plane,

$$\text{tangent of inclination to horizon} = \frac{a - \mu\mu' b}{\mu(a+b)},$$

where μ, μ' are the coefficients of friction of the ground and wall, and a, b the distances of the foot and top of the ladder from its centre of gravity.

Will the extreme angle of inclination be increased or diminished if a man stand on the ladder?

10. A heavy hoop—weight W—which has a string coiled round its circumference and a weight P attached to the free extremity of the string, is hung on a rough horizontal peg; determine the positions in which it will rest.

Result. If θ be the angle which the radius drawn through the peg makes with the vertical, then $\frac{\sin\theta}{1-\sin\theta} = \frac{P}{W}$ and $\tan\theta = \mu =$ coefficient of friction actually in operation.

11. The axis of a rough parabola is vertical, shew that the distance of the extreme points at which a particle will rest under the action of gravity is $= \mu$. *latus rectum.*

12. A heavy body is kept at rest on a given inclined plane by a force making a given angle with the plane; shew that the reaction of the plane, when it is smooth, is a harmonic mean between the normal components of the greatest and least reaction, when it is rough.

13. A right cone, the height of which is h, rests with its base on an inclined plane; when the cone is on the point of sliding the coefficient of friction between the plane and the base of the cone is μ. Shew that the resultant action of the plane on the cone then acts at a point distant $\frac{\mu h}{4}$ from the centre of its base.

* * * * * * *

14. A square lamina has a string, of length equal to a side, attached to one of the angular points; the string is also attached to a point in a rough vertical wall, against which the lamina rests; shew that, the coefficient of friction being unity, the angle which the string makes with the wall lies between $\frac{\pi}{4}$ and $\frac{1}{2}\tan^{-1}\frac{1}{2}$.

15. One end A of a heavy rod ABC rests against a rough vertical plane, and a point B of the rod is connected with a point in the plane by a string, the length of which is equal to $AB = c$; determine the position of equilibrium of the rod, and shew how the direction in which the friction acts depends upon the position of B.

Result. The angle θ which the rod makes with the vertical *upwards*

$$= \tan^{-1}\frac{2c-a}{\mu a},$$

and the friction acts up or down according as $c >$ or $< \frac{a}{2}$.

16. A cylinder, with its axis horizontal, is held at rest on an inclined plane (α) by a string coiled round its middle, and then fastened on the plane; find the conditions of equilibrium, friction being considered.

If θ be the angle the string makes with the plane obtain the equation

$$\cos(\theta \sim \alpha) = \frac{\sin\alpha}{\mu} - \cos\alpha,$$

and discuss it.

17. A cylinder with its axis horizontal, is supported on a rough inclined plane, by a string coiled round it, which after passing over a smooth fixed pully supports a weight n times the weight of the cylinder. Prove that $\sin\alpha$ is $< 2n$, and that $\mu\{\cos\alpha + \sqrt{2n\sin\alpha - \sin^2\alpha}\}$ is $> n$, where α is the inclination of the plane, and μ the coefficient of friction. Determine the sign of the radical.

18. A sphere of radius a is supported on a rough inclined plane—(friction $= \mu$)—by a string of length $\frac{a}{\mu}$, attached to it and to a point in the plane. Prove that the greatest possible elevation of the plane in order that the sphere may rest when the string is a tangent is $2\tan^{-1}\mu$, and find the tension of the string and the pressure on the plane in this case.

19. An elastic string has its ends attached to two points on the circumference of a vertical circular wire, the line joining them being horizontal and equal to the string's natural length and their distance 120°. The string passes through a small ring which slides on the wire. Find the oblique positions of equilibrium, and shew that there are none if the coefficient of elasticity be not $> \frac{2}{\sqrt{3}}$ of the ring's weight.

20. OA, OB are radii of a circular arc AB, the former horizontal and the latter inclined at 60° to OA; find the coefficient of friction according as a weight Q at B is on the point of moving up or down the arc, a weight P being attached to Q by a string PAQ and hanging freely.

Result. In the latter case $\mu = \frac{Q - \sqrt{3}P}{\sqrt{3}Q - P}$, in the former $\mu = \frac{\sqrt{3}P - Q}{\sqrt{3}Q - P}$.

21. A heavy hemisphere rests with its convex surface on a rough inclined plane. Find the greatest possible inclination (α) of the plane.

Result. $\alpha = \tan^{-1}\frac{3}{8}$.

22. A board moveable about a horizontal line in its own plane is supported by resting on a rough sphere which lies on a horizontal table; find the greatest inclination θ at which the board can rest.

Result. If μ = coefficient of friction between the board and sphere,

$$\tan\frac{\theta}{2} = \mu.$$

23. A cylinder is supported on a rough inclined plane, with its axis horizontal, by means of a string which is coiled round it, and is attached to a point in the plane, so that the part uncoiled is horizontal. If α be the angle of the plane and the cylinder be only just supported—shew that the coefficient of friction $= \tan\frac{\alpha}{2}$, and the resistance of the plane = weight of the cylinder.

24. A heavy circular tube hangs over a rough peg, and a rough particle of $\frac{1}{n}$th the weight of the tube rests within it; find the highest position of equilibrium of the particle.

If $\tan\phi$ be the coefficient of friction between the particle and the tube, shew that the tube will be on the point of slipping over the peg, provided the coefficient of friction between the tube and peg be $= \dfrac{\sin\phi}{\sqrt{(n+1)^2 - \sin^2\phi}}$.

25. Two weights P, Q of similar material, rest on a double rough inclined plane, and are connected by a fine

string passing over the common vertex: Q is on the point of motion down the plane—shew that the weight which may be added to P without producing motion is

$$P\frac{\sin 2\phi \sin (\alpha+\beta)}{\sin (\beta-\phi) \sin (\alpha-\phi)},$$

α, β being the angles of inclination of the planes, and $\tan\phi$ the coefficient of friction.

26. A uniform rod rests with one extremity against a rough vertical wall $\left(\mu=\frac{7}{3}\right)$, the other extremity being supported by a string three times the length of the rod, attached to a point in the wall; shew that the angle the string makes with the wall in the limiting position of equilibrium is

$$\tan^{-1}\frac{5}{27} \text{ or } \tan^{-1}\frac{1}{3}.$$

* * * * * * *

27. Two equal rough balls lie in contact on a rough horizontal table, and another equal ball is placed upon them so that the centres of the three are in a vertical plane; find the coefficient of friction between the upper and lower balls μ, and between the lower balls and the table μ', when the system is on the point of motion.

Result. $\mu=3\mu'=2-\sqrt{3}.$

28. A rectangular table stands on a rough inclined plane, and has two sides horizontal; if the coefficient of friction of the lowest feet be μ, and that of the two others be μ', find the inclination (α) of the plane when the table is on the point of sliding.

Result. If the centre of gravity of the table be at a distance c from the plane, and $2a$ be the distance between the upper and lower feet, then

$$\tan\alpha=\frac{(\mu'+\mu)a}{2a+(\mu'-\mu)c}.$$

29. A straight uniform beam is placed upon two rough planes, whose inclinations to the horizon are α and α', and the coefficients of friction $\tan\lambda$ and $\tan\lambda'$; shew that if θ be the limiting value of the angle of inclination of the beam to the horizon at which it will rest, W its weight, and R, R' the pressures upon the planes,

$$2\tan\theta = \cot(\alpha'+\lambda') - \cot(\alpha-\lambda),$$

and $$\frac{R}{\cos\lambda\sin(\alpha'+\lambda')} = \frac{R'}{\cos\lambda'\sin(\alpha-\lambda)} = \frac{W}{\sin(\alpha-\lambda+\alpha'+\lambda')}.$$

30. One end of a beam can turn in every direction about a fixed point. The other rests upon the upper surface of a rough plane (coefficient of friction μ), which is inclined to the horizon at an angle α. If β be the angle which the beam makes with the plane, prove that the beam will rest in any position if $\tan\alpha$ be not $> \dfrac{\mu}{\sqrt{(1+\mu^2\tan^2\beta)}}$.

31. Find the minimum eccentricity (e) of an ellipse capable of resting in equilibrium on a perfectly rough inclined plane.

Result. If α = inclination of plane, we must have

$$e^2 \text{ not } < 2\tan\alpha(\sec\alpha - \tan\alpha).$$

32. A rod of uniform thickness is placed within a rough hollow sphere, in a vertical plane passing through the centre; shew that if θ be the inclination of the rod to the horizon, when bordering upon motion, 2α the angle subtended by it at the centre of the sphere, and $\tan\beta$ the coefficient of friction, then

$$\tan\theta = \frac{\sin\beta\cos\beta}{\cos(\alpha+\beta)\cos(\alpha-\beta)}.$$

33. A smooth sphere BCD rests against a smooth vertical plane CE, and is propped up by a beam AB whose

extremity A rests on the rough horizontal plane EA, the weights of the sphere and beam being equal. Shew that if A be on the point of sliding, the angle which the beam makes with the horizon is $\tan^{-1}\left(\frac{3}{4\mu}\right)$, μ being the coefficient of friction between the beam and plane.

34. Two bodies of the same weight rest upon two equally rough inclined planes, being connected by a string passing over the common vertex of the planes, the vertical plane which contains the two bodies being at right angles to each inclined plane:—if they be bordering on motion, shew that the coefficient of friction is equal to the tangent of half the difference of the angles of inclination of the planes to the horizon.

35. A smooth sphere of radius a rests upon two parallel rods, which themselves are supported upon two fixed horizontal rods also parallel, and at right angles to the former. If $\tan\lambda$ be the coefficient of friction, and the weight of one of the moveable rods be $= \frac{1}{2}\sec 2\lambda$. *weight of sphere*, then the distance between the two moveable rods in the position of rest

$$= 2a \sin 2\lambda.$$

36. A rough elliptical ring hangs across a horizontal rod: shew that it will balance on it with any point in contact if $\mu > \frac{e^2}{2\sqrt{1-e^2}}$.

37. A uniform rod passes over one rough peg and under another—(friction $= \mu$). The pegs are distant b feet apart and the line joining them makes an $\angle\, \beta$ with the horizon. Shew that equilibrium is not possible unless the length of the rod be $> b\left\{1 + \frac{\tan\beta}{\mu}\right\}$ *feet.*

38. A rod of length a turns freely about a point O which is at a vertical distance c above a rough inclined plane; the lower end of the rod rests upon the plane: shew that if in its position of equilibrium the vertical plane through the rod cuts the inclined plane in a horizontal line, then

$$\mu = \tan\alpha \,.\, \sqrt{\frac{a^2 - c^2\cos^2\alpha}{a^2 - c^2}}.$$

39. A rod rests in a state bordering on motion, with one end fixed at a hinge and the other resting against a rough vertical wall. Prove that the pressure on the hinge is to the weight of the rod as

$$\sqrt{1 + \mu^2 + 4\cot^2\alpha} \,:\, 2\sqrt{\mu^2 + \cot^2\alpha},$$

μ being the coefficient of friction, and α the angle between the rod and the wall.

FORCES NOT IN ONE PLANE. CHAPTER IV.

1. If a uniform heavy triangle is suspended from a fixed point by strings attached to the angles, the tension of each string is proportional to its length.

2. If forces act along the sides AB, AC, BC of a triangle, respectively proportional to those sides—find the line of action of their resultant.

3. The line joining the hinges of a gate whose weight is W is inclined at an angle α to the vertical; shew that the moment of the couple which will hold the gate in a position inclined at an $\angle\,\beta$ to its position of equilibrium is proportional to $\sin\alpha \sin\beta$.

4. A straight rod without weight is placed between two pegs and forces P and Q act at its extremities in parallel directions, inclined to the rod; required the conditions under which the rod will be at rest and the pressures on the pegs.

5. $ABCD$ is a square, and forces P, $2P$ act along AB, BC respectively, forces $4P$, $2P$ along AD and DC,—find the locus of the points, any one of which being fixed equilibrium would exist, and the pressure on such a point.

6. A string fastened at a point A supports a weight P by passing under a rough handle of any form, the loose end being held so that the parts on each side of the handle are parallel; find the least force which will prevent the weight from falling, and the greatest which will not draw it up.

7. A heavy uniform beam has its extremities attached to a string which passes round the arc of a rough vertical circle; if in the limiting position of equilibrium the beam be inclined at an $\angle 60^\circ$ to the vertical, and the portion of string in contact with the circle cover an arc of 270°, shew that the coefficient of friction is $= \frac{1}{3\pi} \log_e 3$.

8. A heavy particle is attached to an endless string which passes round a rough circular cylinder in a vertical plane perpendicular to its axis. If in the limiting position of equilibrium the string in contact with the cylinder covers an arc of 270°, shew that the inclination to the horizon of the two portions of the string adjacent to the particle are

$$\tan^{-1} \epsilon^{\frac{3\mu\pi}{2}} \text{ and } \tan^{-1} \epsilon^{-\frac{3\mu\pi}{2}}.$$

9. An unstretched elastic string just surrounds a fixed square, two of whose sides are vertical, an equal square being

introduced in the same plane as the former, and between it and the lower portion of the string, just rests without touching it. The lower square is now turned about a vertical axis through an $\angle\, \pi$, so that the string crosses between the squares; shew that the acute $\angle\, \theta$ included in the position of equilibrium by the two portions of the string between the squares is given by the equation

$$\sin\left(\frac{\pi}{8}+\frac{\theta}{4}\right)=2^{-\frac{3}{4}}.$$

10. The ends of an elastic string without weight are fastened to two points A, B, which are in the same horizontal line, at a distance equal to the unstretched length of the string. A weight equal to the modulus of elasticity is attached to any point C of the string. If AD, BD be drawn at right angles to AC, BC, prove that

$$\frac{AC}{AB+AD}+\frac{BC}{BA+BD}=1.$$

11. A number of unequal weights are attached to an endless string which is slung over a rough horizontal cylinder so that all the weights hang free from the cylinder. Shew that in the limiting positions of equilibrium the vertical through the centre of gravity of the weights divides the line joining the points where the string leaves the cylinder in the ratio $1 : e^{\mu a}$, where a is the circular measure of the part of the cylinder free from the string.

If the cylinder be smooth the centre of gravity of the weights is vertically below the centre of the cylinder.

12. An elastic string whose natural length $= c$ passes round three rough pegs A, B, C, which form an equilateral triangle whose side $= a$. The natural length of the part AB of

the string $= c - a$, and it is on the point of slipping both at A and B; shew that the coefficient of friction

$$\mu = \frac{3}{2\pi} \log_e \left(\frac{2a - c}{c - a}\right).$$

13. A string passes over a rough pully (rad. $= a$) having a concentric circular hole of radius b supported by a rough axle. If the equilibrium be *limiting* for both, shew that

$$e^{\mu a} + e^{-\mu a} = 2 \frac{(1 + \mu^2) a^2 - \mu^2 b^2 \cos a}{(1 + \mu^2) a^2 - \mu^2 b^2},$$

where a is the angle of contact.

14. Three equal smooth spheres each weighing W, rest within a hollow sphere of n times their radius: shew that the pressure between any two of the small spheres

$$= \frac{2W}{\sqrt{3(3n^2 - 6n - 1)}}.$$

15. An elastic band whose unstretched length is $2a$ is placed round four rough pegs A, B, C, D, which constitute the angular points of a square whose side is a: if it be taken hold of at a point P between A and B and pulled in direction AB, shew that it will begin to slip round A and B at the same time, if $AP = \dfrac{a}{1 + e^{\frac{\mu\pi}{2}}}$, μ being the coefficient of friction.

CENTRE OF GRAVITY. CHAPTER V.

1. $ABCD$ is any plane quadrilateral figure, and a, b, c, d are respectively the centres of gravity of the triangles BCD, CDA, DAB, ABC; shew that the quadrilateral $abcd$ is similar to $ABCD$.

2. A triangular lamina, of which the sides are a, b, c cannot rest on its side c on a horizontal plane if c be

$$<\sqrt{\frac{a^2 \sim b^2}{3}}.$$

3. At each of $n-1$ of the angular points of a regular polygon of n sides a particle is placed, the particles being equal. Shew that the distance of their centre of gravity from the centre of the circle circumscribing the polygon is $\frac{r}{n-1}$, r being the radius of the circle.

4. From an isosceles triangular lamina ABC, of which the sides AB, BC are equal, an isosceles portion APC is cut away, AP, PC being equal; (i) find G the centre of gravity of the remainder. Also (ii) find the condition that it may rest in neutral equilibrium when supported at the point P.

Result. Draw BPD perpendicular to AC, then G is in this line, and (i) $BG = \frac{1}{3}(BP + BD)$—(ii) $BD = 2 \,.\, BP$.

5. Find the locus of the centres of gravity of all triangles inscribed in a circle, the vertex being fixed, and the base of a given length.

Result. A circle.

6. A triangular lamina ABC having a right angle at C is suspended from the angle A, and the side AC makes an $\angle\, \alpha$ with the horizon; it is then suspended from B, and the side BC makes an $\angle\, \beta$ with the horizon; shew that

$$BC^2 \,.\, \tan\alpha = AC^2 \,.\, \tan\beta.$$

7. If the sides of a triangle be taken, two and two, to represent forces, acting in each case from the angle made by

the sides,—prove that there is one point about which each of the three pairs will balance, and find the point.

Result. The point is the centre of gravity of the triangle.

8. If the centre of gravity of a triangular pyramid be the common vertex of four pyramids whose bases are the faces of the original pyramid severally, shew that these four pyramids are of equal volume.

9. A square is divided into four equal triangles by drawing its diagonals which intersect in O; if one triangle be removed, find the centre of gravity G of the figure formed by the three remaining triangles.

Result. $OG = \frac{1}{9}$. side of square.

10. Five pieces of a uniform chain are hung at equidistant points along a rigid rod without weight, and their lower ends are in a straight line passing through one end (O) of the rod; find the centre of gravity of the system.

Also, shew that if the system balance about a point of the rod in one position it will balance about it in any position.

Result. If OC be drawn to C the middle point of the longest piece of chain, G the centre of gravity is in OC and $OG = \frac{11}{15} \cdot OC$,—the distance from O to the first piece of chain being the same as the distance between any two adjacent pieces.

11. AB, BC are two rods freely jointed at B, A is fixed; find at what point in BC a prop must be placed so as to support them in a horizontal position.

12. A triangle rests in a fixed hemispherical bowl, shew that the pressures at its three angular points are all equal.

13. A straight uniform wire ABC is bent at B so that the $\angle ABC = \alpha$, and it is then suspended by a string from the point A: shew that it will rest with BC horizontal, if

$$BC^2 = (AB^2 + 2\,AB\,.\,BC)\cos\alpha.$$

14. Explain why in ascending a hill, we appear to lean forwards; in descending, to lean backwards.

15. Why does a person rising from a chair bend his body forward and his leg backward?

16. What is the use of a rope-dancer's pole?

17. A cone whose height is equal to four times the radius of its base is hung from a point in the circumference of its base; find the position in which it will rest.

Result. The base and axis are equally inclined to the vertical.

18. Of what dimensions must a right cone be, in order that, when the greatest sphere possible has been cut out of it, the centre of gravity of the remainder may coincide with that of the cone?

Result. The diameter of the base : altitude of cone $= 1 : \sqrt{2}$.

19. A smooth body in the form of a sphere is divided into hemispheres, and placed with the plane of division vertical upon a smooth horizontal plane: a string loaded at its extremities with two equal weights hangs upon the sphere, passing over its highest point and cutting the plane of division at right angles; find the least weight P which will preserve the equilibrium.

Result. $P = \frac{3}{16}$ weight of sphere.

20. A weight of given magnitude moves along the circumference of a circle in which are fixed also two other

weights; prove that the locus of the centre of gravity of the three weights is a circle.

If the immovable weights be varied in magnitude, their sum being constant, prove that the corresponding circular loci intercept equal portions of the chord joining the immovable weights.

21. The three corners of a triangle are kept on a circle by three rings capable of sliding along the circle, and the circle is inclined to the horizon at a given angle; find the positions of equilibrium.

22. If the lengths of the sides of a polygon be inversely proportional to the perpendiculars let fall upon them from a point O, within the polygon,—and if G, G' be the centres of gravity, respectively, of the polygon, and of a series of equal heavy particles placed at its angular points, prove that OGG' will be a straight line, and that $OG = 2 . GG'$.

23. A thin uniform wire is bent into the form of a triangle ABC, and heavy particles of weights P, Q, R are placed at the angular points; prove that if the centre of gravity of the weights coincide with that of the wire

$$P : Q : R :: AB + AC : BC + BA : CA + CB.$$

24. If α, β, γ be the feet of the perpendiculars from A, B, C upon the opposite sides of the triangle ABC; p, q, r the distances of the centre of gravity of triangle $\alpha\beta\gamma$ from the sides a, b, c of ABC, shew that

$$\frac{p}{a^2 \cos (B - C)} = \frac{q}{b^2 \cos (C - A)} = \frac{r}{c^2 \cos (A - B)}.$$

25. The portion of a right cone cut off by a plane will only just balance on a horizontal plane with the shortest side

VA in contact: prove that the vertical through *A* in that position divides the opposite side *VB* in the ratio 3 : 2.

26. Three uniform rods connected by smooth hinges form a triangle *ABC*:—the weights of the rods being proportional to their lengths. If the rod *AB* be held in a horizontal position with the plane of the triangle vertical, shew that the direction of the strain on the hinge at *C* is inclined to *AB* at an angle θ given by

$$\tan\left(\theta - \frac{A-B}{2}\right) = \frac{\sin(A-B)}{1+\cos(A+B)}.$$

27. If x_1, x_2, x_3 be the co-ordinates of the angular points of a triangle referred to any axis, the co-ordinate of the centre of gravity of the triangle is $= \frac{1}{3}(x_1 + x_2 + x_3)$.

And if x_1, x_2, x_3, x_4 be the co-ordinates of the angular points of a tetrahedron, the co-ordinate of its centre of gravity is $= \frac{1}{4}(x_1 + x_2 + x_3 + x_4)$.

* * * * * * *

28. *A, B, C, D, E, F* are six equal particles at the angles of *any* plane hexagon, and *a, b, c, d, e, f* are the centres of gravity respectively of *ABC, BCD, CDE, DEF, EFA*, and *FAB*. Shew that the opposite sides and angles of the hexagon *abcdef* are equal, and that the lines joining opposite angles pass through one point which is the centre of gravity of the particles *A, B, C, D, E, F*.

29. The line which joins the middle points of any two opposite edges of a triangular pyramid is bisected by the centre of gravity of the pyramid.

30. From the fact that a system of heavy particles has *one* centre of gravity *only*, shew that the lines joining the

middle points of opposite sides of any plane quadrilateral bisect each other.

31. If the centre of gravity of a four-sided figure coincide with one of its angular points, shew that the distances of this point and of the opposite angular point from the line joining the other two angular points are as 1 : 2.

32. A cone whose semivertical angle is $\tan^{-1}\frac{1}{\sqrt{(2)}}$ is enclosed in the circumscribing spherical surface; shew that it will rest in any position.

33. Give a geometrical construction for finding the centre of gravity of a plane quadrilateral area.

34. If G be the centre of gravity of a triangle ABC, shew that

$$3(AG^2 + BG^2 + CG^2) = AB^2 + BC^2 + CA^2.$$

35. Two sides AB, CD of a quadrilateral are parallel, and their middle points O, T are joined by a line OT of length c; if $AB = a$, $CD = b$, and G be the centre of gravity of the figure, shew that

$$OG = \frac{c}{3} \cdot \frac{a + 2b}{a + b}.$$

36. A pack of cards is laid on a table, and each projects in direction of the length of the pack beyond the one below it; if each projects as far as possible, prove that the distances between the extremities of successive cards will form a harmonic progression.

37. Prove the following geometrical construction for the centre of gravity of any quadrilateral. Let E be the intersection of the diagonals, and F the middle point of the line

which joins their middle points; draw the line EF and produce it to G, making FG equal to one-third of EF; then G shall be the centre of gravity required.

38. A right cone whose axis is a, and vertical angle $2\sin^{-1}\sqrt{\left(\frac{3}{7}\right)}$, is placed with its base in contact with a smooth vertical wall, and its curved surface on a smooth horizontal rod parallel to the wall; shew that it will remain at rest if the distance of the rod from the wall be not $> a$ nor $< \frac{a}{7}$.

39. The weights of three particles A, B, C at the angular points of the triangle ABC are respectively proportional to the opposite sides of the triangle; the centre of gravity of the three particles coincides with the centre of the circle inscribed in the triangle.

40. A piece of uniform wire is bent into three sides of a square $ABCD$ of which the side AD is wanting; shew that if it be hung up by the two points A and B successively, the angle between the two positions of BC is $\tan^{-1} 18$.

41. A frustum is cut from a right cone by a plane bisecting the axis and parallel to the base. Shew that it will rest with its slant side on a horizontal table if the height of the cone bear to the diameter of the base a greater ratio than

$$\sqrt{7} : \sqrt{17}.$$

42. A weight W is placed at O on a triangular table ABC, supported in a horizontal position by three props at the angular points; shew that the portions of the weight sustained by the props at A, B, C are proportional to the areas of the triangles BOC, AOC, AOB.

43. A right-angled triangle is suspended successively from its acute angles, and when at rest, the side opposite the point of suspension in each case makes angles θ, ϕ with the vertical,—shew that $\tan\theta\tan\phi = 4$.

44. Through the angles of a triangular board lines are drawn to the opposite sides, each dividing the triangle into two equal parts. Shew that the area of the figure formed by joining the centres of gravity of these parts is $\frac{1}{8}$ of the area of the triangle.

45. A heavy square board of uniform thickness is suspended freely by one corner: and at each end of the diagonal which does not pass through that corner a weight is suspended,—shew that the inclination of that diagonal to the horizon is $= \tan^{-1}\left(\frac{P \sim Q}{P+Q+W}\right)$,—where P, Q are the weights and W the weight of the board.

46. Parallel forces act at the angles A, B, C of a triangle, and are respectively proportional to the sides a, b, c,—shew that their resultant acts at the centre of the inscribed circle.

47. Prove the following rule for finding the centre of gravity of any quadrilateral lamina $ABCD$. a, c are the perpendicular distances of A and C from BD. Take F in AC such that $FA : FC :: c : a$. Join F with E the middle point of BD and take $GE = \frac{1}{3}EF$. G is the centre of gravity required.

* * * * * * *

48. If the vertical angle of a right cone of circular base be $> \sin^{-1}\frac{1}{4}$, the upper frustum cut off by any plane will be supported with its base on a horizontal plane.

If the vertical angle be $< \sin^{-1}\frac{1}{3}$, determine the limits for the inclination of the cutting plane to the axis that the frustum may stand.

49. A heavy right cone rests with its base on a fixed rough sphere of given radius, determine the greatest height of the cone compatible with stability.

50. Find the centre of gravity of an isosceles triangle, out of which an inscribed square has been cut.

Result. If $B=C$ in the triangle ABC and AD be drawn from A perpendicular to the base, G the centre of gravity required lies in AD, and if $\angle A=2\alpha$

$$AG=\frac{2}{3}\frac{1+6\tan^2\alpha+8\tan^3\alpha}{(1+2\tan\alpha)(1+4\tan^2\alpha)}.AD.$$

51. A triangular prism, each side of whose base $=a$, rests symmetrically between two smooth parallel horizontal bars at a distance $=2c$ from each other; if the prism be divided into two equal parts by a vertical plane which bisects the lowest angle of the prism, the parts will remain in equilibrium, provided c be $<\frac{5}{12}a$ and $>\frac{1}{24}a$.

52. A cube has two equal portions cut off by planes passing through a diagonal of one of its faces and two corners of the opposite face. If it be suspended freely from one of the extremities of the diagonal, shew that its two remaining edges will be inclined at $\tan^{-1}\frac{4\sqrt{2}}{5}$ to the vertical.

53. Two pieces of flexible chain of different weights but of equal lengths are fastened together so as to have a common extremity. They are then laid over a smooth vertical circle resting wholly in contact with it. Find the position of equilibrium.

54. A piece of uniform heavy wire is formed into a triangle ABC, and the middle points of the sides are joined by pieces of wire of the same thickness. If the framework so formed be hung up from the $\angle A$, shew that AB, AC make with the vertical angles θ, ϕ such that

$$\frac{\sin\theta}{\sin\phi} = \frac{5c(a+c)+2bc}{5b(a+b)+2bc}.$$

55. The centres of gravity of the area and perimeter of a polygon circumscribed about a circle, lie on a diameter; and their distances from the centre are as 2 : 3.

56. If ABC be an isosceles triangle having a right angle at C, and D, E be the middle points of AC, AB respectively, prove that a perpendicular from E upon BD will pass through the centre of gravity of the triangle BDC.

57. From a given rectangle $ABCD$ cut off a triangle CDO (the point O being in AD) so that when the figure $ABCO$ is suspended from O the sides AO, BC may be horizontal.

Result. $AO : AD = \sqrt{3} - 1 : 2$.

58. A uniform beam of thickness $2b$ rests symmetrically on a perfectly rough horizontal cylinder of radius a;—shew that the equilibrium of the beam will be stable or unstable according as b is less or greater than a.

59. A uniform wire is bent into the form of three sides AB, BC, CD of an equilateral polygon, and its centre of gravity is at the intersection of AC, BD; shew that the polygon must be a regular hexagon.

60. A pyramid, the base of which is a square, and the other faces equal isosceles triangles, is placed in the circumscribing spherical surface; prove that it will rest in any

position, if the cosine of the vertical angle of each of the triangular faces be $= \frac{2}{3}$.

61. Two equal heavy particles are situated at the extremities of the latus-rectum of a parabolic arc without weight, which is placed with its vertex in contact with that of an equal parabola whose axis is vertical and concavity downwards; prove that the parabolic arc may be turned through any angle without disturbing its equilibrium, provided no sliding be possible between the curves.

62. Find the centre of gravity of the volume included between two *similar* parallelopipeds which have a common angle. Also determine the limiting position of the centre of gravity when the parallelopipeds approach equality.

63. The centres of two circles which touch each other internally are made to approach indefinitely near to each other,—find the ultimate position of the centre of gravity of the area included between the circumferences of the circles.

Also find according to what power of the distance from a fixed point in the circumference the density of a circular wire must vary, that its centre of gravity may coincide with that of the above figure.

64. The centres of gravity of the area and perimeter of a plane triangle lie in a line which passes through the centre of the inscribed circle, at distances from it which are as 2 : 3.

65. If n lines drawn from a point represent in magnitude and direction a system of forces acting at that point, shew that the resultant of the system of forces will be represented in magnitude and direction by n times the line drawn from that point to the centre of gravity of n equal particles placed at the extremities of the lines.

66. The centre of the circumscribing circle of any triangle is the centre of gravity of four equal particles placed at the centres of the inscribed and escribed circles.

67. If a portion of a parabola bounded by the latus rectum (L) be placed with its vertex on that of a given cycloid, the convexities of the two curves being turned in opposite directions, the equilibrium will be neutral if $3L = 28a$, where a equals diameter of generating circle of the cycloid.

68. An elliptic cylinder, whose semiaxes are a, b, rests between two smooth inclined planes at right angles to one another, prove that there will be *three* positions of equilibrium if the inclinations of the planes to the horizon be $> \tan^{-1}\dfrac{b}{a}$.

69. A plane quadrilateral $ABCD$ is bisected by the diagonal AC, and the other diagonal divides AC into two parts in the ratio $p : q$; shew that the centre of gravity of the quadrilateral lies in AC and divides it into two parts in the ratio $2p+q : p+2q$.

70. If a right-angled triangular lamina ABC be suspended from a point D in its hypotenuse AB,—prove that in the position of equilibrium, AB will be horizontal if

$$AD : DB :: AB^2 + AC^2 : AB^2 + BC^2.$$

71. If G be the centre of gravity of a system of particles,—D, Δ the distances of any one of them m from G, and O (any other point),—shew that

$$\Sigma\,(mD^2) = \Sigma\,(m\Delta^2) - \Sigma\,(m)\;GO^2.$$

72. AB, BC are rods having a joint at B, A being a fixed hinge; find the position in which the system will rest

when a string from A is attached to a ring sliding on BC, supposed smooth. Find also the tension of the string.

73. In a triangular pyramid $ABCD$ if a, b, c be the sides of the triangle ABC, and α, β, γ the edges meeting in D, shew that if G be the centre of gravity of the pyramid

$$DG = \tfrac{1}{4}\{3(\alpha^2+\beta^2+\gamma^2)-(a^2+b^2+c^2)\}^{\frac{1}{2}}.$$

74. If each particle of a system be multiplied by the square of its distance from an assumed point O, the sum of these products will be least when O coincides with the centre of gravity of the system of particles.

MACHINES. CHAPTER VI.

1. The arms of a balance are equal in length, but one scale is loaded; find the true weight of the body in terms of its apparent weights when suspended at each end in succession.

Result. The true weight = semi-sum of the apparent weights.

2. Two men A, B of the same height bear a weight hung on a pole which rests on their shoulders; where must the weight be placed in order that A may support n times as much as B?

Result. The distance of the weight from B must $= n$. *times* its distance from A.

3. A uniform steel rod AB having a constant weight P, and a scale-pan of weight kP, suspended at B and A respectively, is used as a balance by moving the rod back-

wards and forwards upon the fulcrum C on which the whole rests. Shew that the beam must be graduated by the formula

$$AC = \frac{1 + \frac{k'}{2}}{n + k + k' + 1} \cdot AB;$$

the weight of the rod being $k'P$, and n being each of the natural numbers 1 . 2 . 3... taken in succession.

4. If the *pitch* of a screw be $\frac{\pi}{4}$, $\tan \phi$ the coefficient of friction, P the least force which will prevent the weight from descending, P' the greatest which can be applied without its rising, then

$$\frac{P' - P}{P' + P} = \sin 2\phi.$$

5. Weights of 3 oz. and $\frac{1}{2}$ lb. balance on a straight lever of which the longer arm is 2 feet; find the length of the shorter arm.

Result. 9 inches.

6. In any system of pullies in which a separate string passes over each pully and the strings are parallel, prove that, if the tensions of the strings increase in geometric progression, so do the weights of the pullies.

7. Two weights P, Q are connected by a string PAQ passing over a pully A,—P hangs vertically and Q rests on a rough inclined plane (α) and λ is the angle of friction :—if the greatest and least angles which AQ can make with the plane be ϵ, λ, shew that

$$\tan^2 \frac{\epsilon + \lambda}{2} = \tan \lambda \cdot \cot \alpha.$$

8. If P support W on a rough inclined plane (α), P acting in a *principal plane* and at an angle ϵ with the plane, and if P may have any magnitude intermediate to P', P'' without producing motion and the plane be but slightly rough, shew that $\mu = \frac{P' \sim P''}{P' + P''} \cdot \frac{\sin \alpha \cos \epsilon}{\sin (\alpha + \epsilon)}$, *nearly.*

In what case will this be the exact value of μ?

9. The length of the shorter arm of a common steelyard $= 4$ *inches:* the removal of P through $\frac{1}{8}$ *inch* indicates an increase of 2 *oz.* in the weight W:—and the notch corresponding to a weight of 4 *lbs.* is 3 *inches* from the fulcrum:—determine the moment of the beam.

10. If the same body be weighed successively at the two ends of a false balance whose arms are of unequal length, its true weight is the square root of the product of the apparent weights.

* * * * * * *

11. If a man sitting in one scale of a weighing-machine press with a stick against any point of the beam between the point from which the scale is suspended and the fulcrum, he will appear to weigh more than before.

12. Explain how a man by walking slowly up the surface of a large rough sphere may make it roll up an inclined plane or along a horizontal plane in any direction.

13. If a tradesman's balance have unequal arms, a, b, and he weighs goods alternately from one scale and the other, does he gain or lose by his balance not being true? and how much?

Result. His loss : *apparent* weight which he dispenses :: $(a-b)^2 : 2ab$.

14. The sensibility of a Danish steelyard at any point varies as the square of the distance of the point from the end where W is suspended.

15. If a uniform wire be bent into the form of a triangle, and at the middle points of the sides there be placed three beads whose weights are proportional to the sides on which they are; prove that when the beads are moved with equal velocities in the same direction along the sides there will be no change in the position of the centre of gravity of the whole system.

16. If two weights support each other on inclined planes by means of a string passing over the common vertex of the planes, and the system is set in motion, the centre of gravity of the weights moves in a horizontal line.

17. When P supports W on a rough inclined plane, and R is the pressure on the plane, explain the result when

$$\epsilon + \phi \text{ is } > 90^\circ. \quad \text{(Art. 110.)}$$

18. In the system of pullies where each string is attached to the weight, if one of the strings be nailed to the block through which it passes, shew that the power may be increased up to a certain limit without producing motion. If there be three pullies, and the action of the middle one be checked in the manner described, find the tension of each string for given values of P and W.

19. In a wheel and axle, if the axis about which the machine turns coincide with that of the axle but not with the axis of the wheel, find the greatest and least ratios of the power and weight necessary for equilibrium, neglecting the weight of the machine.

20. Why is it easier to move a heavy body when placed upon rollers than to draw it upon a rough horizontal plane? Compare the rates of motion of the body and of the centres of the rollers.

21. In the system of pullies of *Article* 106—if the weight of the lowest pully be equal to the power P, of the second $3P$, and so on, that of the highest movable pully being $3^{n-2}P$—the ratio of P to W will be $2 : 3^n - 1$.

22. In the Danish Steelyard, if a_n be the distance of the fulcrum from that end of the steelyard at which the weight is suspended, the weight being n lbs. prove that

$$\frac{1}{a_{n+2}} - \frac{2}{a_{n+1}} + \frac{1}{a_n} = 0.$$

* * * * * * *

23. In each of the three systems of pullies, if P and W receive any displacement their centre of gravity remains unchanged in position.

24. If three forces P, Q, R are in equilibrium when acting on a particle, and the particle be slightly displaced so that p, q, r are the virtual velocities of P, Q, R respectively, shew that $Pp + Qq + Rr = 0$.

Prove the principle of virtual velocities in the case of the Spanish Barton. (Art. 107.)

25. In the system of pullies where each hangs by a separate string, determine the relation between the radii of the pullies in order that, if their centres be at any time in a straight line, they may always continue to be so.

26. If a common steelyard be constructed with a given rod, whose weight is inconsiderable compared with that of

the sliding weight, shew that the sensibility varies inversely as the sum of the sliding weight and the greatest weight which can be weighed.

27. A heavy insect of weight w crawls on the lower circumference of the wheel of a *wheel and axle*, and so just raises a weight $5w$, the ratio of the radii of the wheel and axle being $10 : 1$,—find the inclination to the vertical of the radius of the wheel which passes through the position of the insect:—shew that the insect is in a position of stable equilibrium, but that if it were on the upper surface of the wheel and at a point vertically above its present position, its equilibrium would be unstable.

28. If a wheel and axle be similar coaxial regular prisms so placed that every plane bisecting an angle of one bisects a side of the other, shew that the ratio of the least to the greatest power which will support a given weight is $\cos^2\frac{\pi}{n} : 1$, where n is the number of faces of the prism.

29. If a power P balance a weight W in a combination of n movable pullies, each of weight ω, shew that

$$W = (P + \omega)(2^{n+1} - 1) - (n + 1)\,\omega,$$

the cords being parallel and each attached to the weight.

Also if the weights of the movable pullies be P, $2P$, $3P$,... the pully whose weight is P being furthest from the weight, shew that

$$W = P\left\{n2^{n+1} - \frac{n(n+1)}{2} + 1\right\}.$$

30. Apply the principle of Virtual Velocities to determine the ratio of the power to the weight, when the weight slides along a smooth vertical rod, and is attached by an

inextensible string to a point in the rod, while the power acts horizontally at the middle point of the string.

31. A heavy particle rests on a rough inclined plane (α), being attached to a point in the plane by a string which makes an angle θ with the line of greatest slope down the plane;—find the tension of the string, and shew that θ must not be $> \sin^{-1}(\mu \cot \alpha)$: where $\mu =$ coefficient of friction. Explain this result if $\mu > \tan \alpha$.

32. A rod AB, whose weight (p) and centre of gravity G are given, is to be used as a Danish balance, the substance to be weighed being suspended from B; A_1, A_2,...A_n the points where the fulcrum is to be placed to weigh 1, 2,...n pounds respectively, are marked by pins (each of a given weight ω) being driven in; find a formula for the graduation.

Result. If A_0 be the position of the fulcrum when there is no weight at B, $BA_0 = z$, $A_0A_1 = x_1$, $A_1A_2 = x_2 \ldots A_{r-1}A_r = x_r \ldots$ we shall have n equations of the type

$$x_r = \frac{rz}{r + p + n\omega} - x_1 - x_2 - \ldots - x_{r-1}$$

by giving r successive integral values 1.2.3...n, which together with the equation

$$p(BG - z) = \omega\{x_n + 2x_{n-1} + \ldots (n - r + 1)x_r + \ldots + nx_1\}$$

are sufficient to determine the $n + 1$ quantities z, x_1, $x_2 \ldots x_n$.

33. A person suspended in a balance of which the arms are equal, thrusts his centre of gravity out of the vertical by means of a rod fixed to the furthest extremity of the beam of the balance, the direction of the rod passing through his centre of gravity; given that the rod and the line from the nearer end of the beam of the balance to his centre of gravity make angles α, β with the vertical, shew that his apparent and true weights are in the ratio

$$\sin(\alpha + \beta) : \sin(\alpha - \beta).$$

MISCELLANEOUS EXAMPLES IN STATICS.

1. A body consisting of a cone and hemisphere having the same base, is placed upon a rough horizontal table; determine the greatest height of the cone that the equilibrium may be stable.

Result. Altitude of cone $= \sqrt{3}$. radius of the hemisphere.

2. A solid is composed of a cylinder and hemisphere of equal radius, fixed base to base; find the ratio of the height to the radius of the cylinder, that the equilibrium may be neutral when the spherical surface rests on a horizontal plane.

Result. Altitude of cylinder $= \frac{1}{\sqrt{2}}$ radius.

3. When a man stands on a hill, how is he inclined to the horizon and to the hill?

4. Two forces F and F' acting in the diagonals of a parallelogram, keep it at rest in such a position that one of its edges is horizontal; shew that

$$F \sec \alpha' = F' \sec \alpha = W \operatorname{cosec} (\alpha + \alpha'),$$

where W is the weight of the parallelogram, α and α' the angles between its diagonals and the horizontal side.

5. A cylinder rests with the centre of its base in contact with the highest point of a fixed sphere, and four times the altitude of the cylinder is equal to a great circle of the sphere; supposing the surfaces in contact to be rough enough to prevent sliding in all cases, shew that the cylinder may be made to rock through an angle of 90°, but not more, without falling off the sphere. The base of the cylinder being supposed to be sufficiently large.

6. If three parallel forces acting at the angular points A, B, C of a triangle are respectively proportional to the opposite sides a, b, c; prove that the distance of the centre of parallel forces from A

$$= \frac{2bc}{a+b+c} \cos \frac{A}{2}.$$

7. Two equal spheres placed in a paraboloid with its axis vertical touch one another at the focus. If W be the weight of a sphere, R, R' the pressures upon it, prove that

$$W^2 : R \, . \, R' :: 3 : 2.$$

8. Three equal cylindrical rods are placed symmetrically round a fourth one of the same radius, and the bundle is then surrounded by two equal elastic bands at equal distances from the two ends; if each band when unstretched would just pass round one rod, and a weight of 1 lb. would just stretch one to twice its natural length, shew that it would require a force of 9 lbs. to extract the middle rod, the coefficient of friction being equal to $\frac{\pi}{6}$.

9. $ABCD$... is a string without weight suspended from two points A, F in a horizontal line; and given weights W_1, W_2, W_3... are hung from the knots B, C, D...; determine the proportion of these weights when the string hangs in a given form. (N.B. This is called a *funicular polygon*.)

If the weights be all equal, shew that the co-tangents of the angles which successive portions of the string make with the vertical are in arithmetic progression.

10. Two strings of the same length have each of their ends fixed at each of two points in the same horizontal plane. A smooth sphere of radius r and weight W is supported upon

20—2

them at the same distance from each of the given points. If the plane in which either string lies makes an angle α with the horizon, prove that the tension of each is $= \frac{Wa}{8r} \operatorname{cosec} \alpha$; a being the distance between the points.

11. Strings are fixed to any number of points $A, B, C\ldots$ in space, and are pulled towards a point P with forces proportional to PA, PB, PC; shew that wherever the point P be situated the resultant of these forces will always pass through a fixed point.

12. Two equal weights P, P are attached to the ends of two strings which pass over the same smooth peg, and have their other extremities attached to the ends of a beam AB (weight W) which rests thus suspended; shew that the inclination of the beam to the horizon is

$$= \tan^{-1}\left(\frac{a-b}{a+b} \tan \alpha\right):$$

a, b being the distances of the centre of gravity of the beam from its ends, and $\sin \alpha = \frac{W}{2P}$.

13. A particle is placed in the middle point of a horizontal, equilateral, and triangular board, and is kept in equilibrium by three equal weights, which act by means of strings passing through the angular points. When the particle is moved in direction of one of the angular points, find the force tending to restore it to its position.

If the force be half of the weight, the inclination of the strings will be $= \cos^{-1}\left(-\frac{3}{4}\right)$.

14. A cylinder—length b, diameter c—open at the top, stands on a horizontal plane, and a uniform rod—length $2a$—rests partly within the cylinder, and in contact with it at its upper and lower edges; supposing the weight of the cylinder to be n times that of the rod, find the length of the rod when the cylinder is on the point of falling over.

Result. $2a = (n+2)\sqrt{b^2+c^2}$.

15. A uniform bent lever whose arms are at right angles to each other, is capable of being enclosed in the interior of a smooth spherical surface,—determine the position of equilibrium.

Result. The arms of the lever will be equally inclined to the vertical.

16. If c be the length of the axis of a frustum of a pyramid,—a, b homologous sides of its larger and smaller ends, the distance of the centre of gravity from the end a—measured along c—is

$$=\frac{c}{4}\cdot\frac{a^2+2ab+3b^2}{a^2+ab+b^2}.$$

What does this become (i) when $a=b$, (ii) when $b=0$?

17. If a triangle be supported in a horizontal position by vertical threads fastened to its angular points, each of which can just bear an additional tension of 1 lb., determine within what portion of the area a weight less than 3 lbs. may be placed without destroying the equilibrium.

18. A square—whose side $=2a$—is placed with its plane vertical between two smooth pegs which are in the same horizontal line at a distance c; shew that it will be in equilibrium when the inclination of one of its edges to the horizon

$$=\tfrac{1}{2}\sin^{-1}\frac{a^2-c^2}{c^2}, \text{ or } =\frac{\pi}{4}.$$

19. A sphere rests upon a string fastened at its extremities to two fixed points; shew that if the arc of contact of the string and sphere be not $< 2\tan^{-1}\frac{48}{55}$, the sphere may be divided into two equal portions by means of a vertical plane without disturbing the equilibrium.

N.B. The centre of gravity of a half sphere, is at a distance from the centre of the spherical surface equal to $\frac{3}{8}$ of the radius.

20. A polygon of an even number of sides is formed by a number of rods which are connected by free joints at their extremities, and is kept in equilibrium by forces applied perpendicularly to the rods at their middle points—shew that the sums of the alternate angles are equal.

If the polygon be of an odd number $(2n+1)$ of sides, and $\alpha_1, \alpha_2 \ldots \alpha_{2n+1}$ be the angles,—shew that the direction of the strain at α_1 on the side adjacent to α_1, α_{2n+1} is inclined to that side at an angle whose complement is $\dfrac{\Sigma_0^n \alpha_{2r+1} - \Sigma_1^n \alpha_{2r}}{2}$, the forces being all supposed to tend inwards.

21. An endless elastic string (without weight) when unstretched, just passes round two pegs in a horizontal plane: two weights W, W' are hung upon it in such a manner that the string forms two festoons, the angles in these being 2θ, 2ϕ respectively: shew that if λ be the modulus of elasticity, then

$$\operatorname{cosec}\theta + \operatorname{cosec}\phi - 2 = \frac{W}{\lambda}\sec\theta = \frac{W'}{\lambda}\sec\phi.$$

22. Three equal rods connected by two free joints are attached by similar joints to two points in the same horizontal plane. If the rod next to one of these joints makes an $\angle\,\alpha$ with the horizon—and the reaction on the joint at its lower end an $\angle\,\theta$,—then $\tan\theta = \frac{1}{2}\tan\alpha$.

23. A heavy equilateral triangle hung up on a smooth peg by a string, the ends of which are attached to two of its angular points, rests with one of its sides vertical—shew that the length of the string is double the altitude of the triangle.

24. A fine string $ACBP$ tied to the end A of a uniform rod AB of weight W, passes through a fixed ring at C, and also through a ring at the end B of the rod, the free end of the string supporting a weight P: if the system be in equilibrium, prove that $AC : BC :: 2P + W : W$.

25. A vertical cylinder is cut into parts by a plane inclined at an $\angle\, \alpha$ to the axis, and the parts are held together by a string passing in a horizontal plane round the cylinder, find the tension of the string, and shew how it varies for different positions of the string:—the common surface of the two parts being smooth.

26. AB, BC are two equal uniform beams united by a free joint at B, and hanging freely from a peg at A to which is attached a string passing to C;—prove that the *action* at the joint is to the weight of each beam as

$$\sqrt{4 - 3\cos^2 C} : 2\sqrt{4 - 3\sin^2 C}.$$

27. A picture frame is supported by one cord, which passes over a smooth peg and through two smooth rings, symmetrically situated at the back of the frame: the cord is weightless and elastic, and when unstretched, it just reaches through the rings:—e being the modulus of elasticity, and w the weight of the frame. Shew that the vertical $\angle\, (2\alpha)$ of the triangle formed by the string is determined by the equation $e(1 - \sin\alpha) = w\tan\alpha$.

28. Two small smooth rings of equal weight slide on a smooth elliptical wire of which the axis major is vertical, and are connected by a string passing over a smooth peg at the upper focus:—prove that the rings will rest in whatever position they may be placed.

29. A right cone is held with its base against a rough vertical wall by means of a string attached to its vertex, and to a point of the wall vertically above the highest point of its base:—find the greatest length of the string for which equilibrium in such a position is possible.

30. A rectangular board whose sides are a, b, and weight W, is supported in a horizontal position by vertical strings at three of its angular points,—a weight $5W$ being placed on the board the tensions of the strings become W, $2W$, $3W$; find all the positions of the weight.

Compare Prob. 42, p. 293.

31. Two weights support each other on two smooth inclined planes, which have a common vertex, by means of a string which passes over a smooth pully at a given height vertically above the vertex; find the position of equilibrium, and, if the planes themselves be capable of motion along a smooth horizontal plane, determine the horizontal force necessary to keep them at rest.

32. Any number of forces act upon a rigid body in one plane,—one point being supposed fixed, whose co-ordinates $\bar{x}$, $\bar{y}$ are given by the equations

$$\bar{x}\Sigma X + \bar{y}\Sigma Y = \Sigma(xX + yY);$$
$$\bar{x}\Sigma Y - \bar{y}\Sigma X = \Sigma(xY - yX);$$

prove that the forces will keep the body at rest; and will also keep it at rest if their directions be also turned through any given angle.

33. A number n of particles of equal weight w are fastened to an endless inelastic thread of given length c, at equal distances from each, and the necklace so formed is placed on a smooth cone (2α) with its axis vertical and vertex upwards; find the tension t of the portions of thread, and the distance x of each particle from the vertex of the cone.

Deduce the tension T of a heavy string W placed in the same manner on the cone.

Result.
$$t = \frac{w}{2}\cos\alpha\,\mathrm{cosec}\left(\frac{\pi\sin\alpha}{n}\right),$$
$$x = \frac{c}{2n}\,\mathrm{cosec}\left(\frac{\pi\sin\alpha}{n}\right),\quad T = W\frac{\cot\alpha}{2\pi}.$$

34. A thin rod rests in a horizontal position between two rough planes equally inclined to the horizon and whose inclination to each other is 2α; if μ be the coefficient of friction, shew that the greatest possible inclination of the line of intersection of the planes to the horizon is $\tan^{-1}.\dfrac{\mu}{\sin\alpha}$.

35. The line of intersection of two smooth planes A, B is horizontal; a rod CD rests first with its extremity C in contact with the plane A, and secondly with the extremity D in contact with the same plane. If θ, ϕ be the inclinations of the rod to the horizon in these two positions of equilibrium, prove that $\tan\theta + \tan\phi$ is invariable, whatever be the length of the rod, or the position of its centre of gravity.

36. Three rods OA, OB, OC are jointed together at O in such a manner that they can be fixed in any position in

which the angles they make with one another are not less than right angles. The system is then placed successively on each of its three points A, B, C with the lower rod vertical, the angle between the upper two being the greatest possible. If α, β, γ be the values of this angle in the three cases (α the least of them) prove that

$$\cos\alpha + \cos\beta\cos\gamma = 0.$$

37. Two smooth rings are connected with a third by inextensible strings without weight. The three rings slide on a smooth wire bent into the form of a vertical circle. Find the position of equilibrium: and prove that, if the mass of each ring be multiplied by its distance from the vertical diameter of the wire, the algebraical sum of the products (considered of different signs when the rings are on opposite sides of the diameter) will be zero.

38. A rod AB is placed in a fixed smooth hemispherical bowl of radius c, so as to lean against the edge of the bowl at P, with one end A within it. Find the position of equilibrium.

Result. If ϕ be the inclination of the rod to the horizon, it is determined by the equation

$$\cos 2\phi = \frac{a}{2c}\cos\phi.$$

39. Three equal right cones stand on a rough horizontal plane with the rims of their bases in contact with each other and a heavy smooth sphere is placed between them. If the vertical angle of each cone be 60°, and the coefficient of friction for the surface in contact be cot 60°, shew that the greatest weight of the sphere consistent with equilibrium is two-thirds of the weight of each cone: and find the magnitude

and position of the sphere if the cones are on the point of falling over.

40. A weight P being placed upon a triangular table, place another given weight Q upon the table in such a position that the pressure on the three props at the angles may be equal. Within what limits is the problem possible?

Employ Prob. 42, p. 293.

41. If an even number of uniform beams of equal length and weight rest in equilibrium in the form of an arch, and α_1, $\alpha_2 \ldots \alpha_n$ be the respective angles of inclination of the first, second...n^{th} beams to the horizon, counting from the top, prove that

$$\tan \alpha_{n+1} = \frac{2n+1}{2n-1} \cdot \tan \alpha_n.$$

42. $ABGC$, DEF are two horizontal levers without weight, B, F their fulcrums; the end D of one lever rests upon the end C of the other; HK is a rod without weight suspended by two equal parallel strings from the points E, G. Prove that a weight P at A will balance a weight W placed any where on the rod HK, provided

$$\frac{EF}{DF} = \frac{BG}{BC}, \text{ and } \frac{P}{W} = \frac{BG}{AB}.$$

43. Two equal particles (w, w) are connected by two given strings ($2c$, $2c'$) without weight, which are placed like a necklace on a smooth cone (2α) with its axis vertical and vertex upwards; find the tensions of the strings.

Result. The tensions t, t' are given by the equations

$$\frac{t}{\cos\phi'} = \frac{t'}{\cos\phi} = \frac{w\cos\alpha}{\sin(\pi\sin\alpha)},$$

and $$\tan\phi = \frac{c\sin(\pi\sin\alpha)}{c'+c\cos(\pi\sin\alpha)}, \quad \tan\phi' = \frac{c'\sin(\pi\sin\alpha)}{c+c'\cos(\pi\sin\alpha)}.$$

44. Two particles are joined to a string, and the system is in equilibrium on the convex surface of a cycloid whose axis is vertical, and convexity upwards; shew that the distances along the cycloid from the highest point are inversely proportional to the weights.

45. A sphere of given weight rests upon three planes whose equations are $lx + my + nz = 0$; $l_1x + m_1y + n_1z = 0$; $l_2x + m_2y + n_2z = 0$; the axis of z being vertical; shew that the pressures upon them are respectively proportional to $l_2m_1 - m_2l_1$, $m_2l - l_2m$ and $ml_1 - m_1l$,—and find each pressure.

46. If through the centre of gravity of each of the faces of any polyhedron there act a force, in direction perpendicular to the face and in magnitude proportional to its area, the system will be in equilibrium, supposing all the forces to act inwards or all to act outwards.

47. A frame formed of four uniform rods of the length (a) connected by smooth hinges is hung over two smooth pegs in the same horizontal line at a distance $\frac{a}{\sqrt{2}}$, the two pegs being in contact with different rods. Shew that in the position of equilibrium each angle $= 90°$.

Is the equilibrium stable or unstable?

48. A heavy triangle ABC is suspended from a point by three strings, mutually at right angles, attached to the angular points of the triangle; if θ be the inclination of the triangle to the horizon in its position of equilibrium, then

$$\cos\theta = \frac{3}{\sqrt{(1 + \sec A \sec B \sec C)}}.$$

49. From a right cone, the diameter of whose base is equal to its altitude, is cut a right cylinder the diameter of

whose base is equal to its altitude,—their axes being in the same line, and the base of the cylinder lying in the base of the cone; from the remaining cone a similar cylinder is cut, and so on, indefinitely; shew that the distance of the centre of gravity of the remaining portion from the base of the cone is $\frac{17}{80}$ altitude of cone.

50. A uniform rod of length l is cut into three pieces a, b, c, and these are formed into a triangle; when the triangle is placed in unstable equilibrium, resting with its plane vertical and one of its angular points upon a smooth horizontal plane, find the angle which the uppermost side makes with the horizon;—and shew that if α, β, γ be the three angles corresponding to the several cases of a, b, c being the uppermost side, then

$$(l+a)\tan\alpha + (l+b)\tan\beta + (l+c)\tan\gamma = 0.$$

51. A string of equal spherical beads is placed upon a smooth cone (2α) having its axis vertical, the beads being just in contact with each other, so that there is no pressure between them. Find the tension t of the string; and deduce the limiting value T, when the number of beads is indefinitely great.

Result. If W = sum of the weights of the beads

$$t = \frac{W\cot\alpha}{2n\sin\frac{\pi}{n}}, \quad T = \frac{W\cot\alpha}{2\pi}.$$

52. A weight is supported on a rough inclined plane (α) by a force exactly equal to it. Shew that the direction of the force may be changed through an angle $4\tan^{-1}\mu$ without disturbing the equilibrium of the weight,—provided that

$$\tan^{-1}\mu \text{ is not } < \frac{\alpha}{2} \text{ nor } > \frac{\pi}{2} - \alpha.$$

53. An even number of equal and uniform spherical balls are slung in contact with each other on a fixed smooth cylinder, whose axis is horizontal, by means of a string which passes through smooth grooves pierced from the points of contact of adjacent balls to the centres of the respective balls. If the balls entirely surround the cylinder, and the tension of the string be such that there is *no pressure* between the fixed cylinder and the lowest ball which touches the cylinder at its lowest point, shew that the pressure between the cylinder and the highest ball is *four times the weight of each ball.*

54. Three particles are connected by strings so as to form a triangle and they are mutually repulsive: shew that if one particle be suddenly annihilated the tension of the string connecting the other two will remain unaltered.

55. The particles of two circular discs repel each other with a force varying as the distance. An endless elastic string passes round their circumferences crossing between them. If the discs were held in contact, the string would be unstretched, and the resultant repulsion would be equal to the modulus of elasticity. Shew that for equilibrium

$$\sin\theta(\sin\theta - \theta\cos\theta) = \frac{\pi}{2},$$

where 2θ is the $\angle$ between the radii of either disc at the points where the string leaves it.

56. Two uniform beams whose lengths are a and c are capable of moving about hinges at their extremities placed in the same horizontal plane. Another beam b is hinged to their other extremities so that the system is above the horizontal plane. If there be equilibrium the difference between

the lengths of the beam will be proportional to the difference between the tangents of the angles which they make with the horizon.

57. Two equal beams AB, AC, connected by a hinge at A, are placed in a vertical plane with their extremities B, C, resting on a horizontal plane; they are kept from falling by strings connecting B and C with the middle points of the opposite sides; shew that the ratio of the tension of either string to the weight of either beam $= \frac{1}{8}\sqrt{(8\cot^2\theta + \operatorname{cosec}^2\theta)}$, θ being the inclination of either beam to the horizon.

58. A uniform beam is supported upon the circumference of a circle of radius r in a vertical plane, by means of a string of given length c, fastened at one end to the highest point of the circumference, at the other end to one extremity of the beam; find the length of the beam that the string may be horizontal.

Result. Length of beam $=2c\left(\frac{r^2+c^2}{r^2-c^2}\right)^2$.

59. If the sector of a circle balance about the chord of the arc, prove that, 2α being the angle of the sector,

$$2\tan\alpha = 3\alpha.$$

60. Two spheres of densities ρ, σ and radii a, b rest in a paraboloid whose axis is vertical, and touch each other at the focus,—shew that $\rho^3 a^{10} = \sigma^3 b^{10}$. Also if W, W' be their weights, and R, R' the pressures on the paraboloid at the points of contact,

$$\frac{R}{W} - \frac{R'}{W'} = \frac{1}{2}\left(\frac{R}{W'} - \frac{R'}{W}\right).$$

61. Two weights of different material are laid on an inclined plane, connected by a string extended to its full

length, inclined at an $\angle\,\theta$ to the line of intersection of the inclined plane with the horizon; if the lower weight be on the point of motion, find the magnitude and direction of the force of friction on the upper weight.

62. An endless string hangs at rest over two pegs in the same horizontal plane, with a heavy pully in each festoon of the string;—if the weight of one pully be double that of the other, shew that the angle between the portions of the upper festoon must be $> 120°$.

63. Two uniform beams loosely jointed at one extremity are placed upon the smooth arc of a parabola, whose axis is vertical and vertex upwards. If l be the semi-latus-rectum of the parabola, and a, b the lengths of the beams, shew that they will rest in equilibrium at right angles to each other, if $l\,(a+b)\,(a^4+b^4)^{\frac{3}{2}} = a^4b^4$,—and find the position of equilibrium.

64. A heavy ring hangs loose upon a fixed horizontal cylinder, and is pulled by a string at its lowest point parallel to the axis of the cylinder: find the limiting position of rest when the coefficient of friction is given;—and shew that if the coefficient of friction exceed a certain value, no force so applied can make the ring slide.

65. A rod of length a is placed horizontally between two pegs whose distances from opposite ends are respectively $\frac{1}{8}a$ and $\frac{1}{4}a$; if weights w and $3w$ be suspended from the ends of the rod, find the tendency to break at any point of the rod, and shew at what point it is the greatest.

66. A uniform rod (of length c) has smooth rings at each extremity, one of which slides on a fixed vertical rod, and through the other passes a fine string which is fixed at

two points A, B in the same horizontal line, the length of the string being $= 2 . AB$; prove that the $\angle$ which the rod makes with the horizon in a position of equilibrium $= \cos^{-1} \frac{h}{c-a}$; h being the distance of the fixed rod from the middle point of AB and $AB = 2a$.

67. Five equal rigid heavy rods (each of weight W) hinged together so as to form a regular pentagon $ABCDE$, are set in a vertical plane with one of them CD resting on a horizontal table, and the form of the regular figure is preserved by help of an inextensible string connecting the hinges B and E. Shew that the tension of the string

$$= \tfrac{1}{2} W (\tan 54^\circ + 3 \tan 18^\circ).$$

68. A string of length l is laid over two smooth pegs which are in the same horizontal line and at a distance a from each other. Two unequal heavy particles, which attract each other with forces varying as the distance, are attached, one to each end of the string: shew that the inclination (θ) of either portion of the string to the horizon is given by the equation

$$a \tan \theta - b = (l - a) \sin \theta;$$

where $2b =$ (the sum of the weights) $\div$ (the attraction of the particles at the unit of distance).

69. Four equal particles are mutually repulsive, the law of force being that of the inverse distance. If they be joined together by four inextensible strings of given length so as to form a quadrilateral,—prove that when there is equilibrium, the four particles lie in a circle.

70. A particle is at rest on a smooth vertical circle under the action of gravity, and a force varying as the dis-

tance from the extremity of a horizontal diameter,—the absolute force being such that the attraction on a particle placed at the centre equals gravity:—shew that the particle will rest half-way between the centre of force and the lowest point of the circle,—and find the pressure on the curve.

71. A uniform bar is bent so as to form a triangle, and the system rests on a smooth horizontal cylinder, whose radius is nearly equal to that of the inscribed circle,—shew that there will be no pressure on the greatest side a, and that its inclination to the vertical will be

$$\tan^{-1}\frac{r(3a-2s)}{(b\sim c)(2a-s)},$$

r being the radius of the cylinder, a, b, c the sides of the triangle and $2s=a+b+c$.

72. A heavy rod is placed in any manner resting on two points of a rough horizontal curve, and a string attached to the middle point C of the chord is pulled in any direction, so that the rod is on the point of motion. Prove that the locus of the intersection of the string with the directions of the frictions at the points of support is an arc of a circle and a part of a straight line.

Find also how the force must be applied that its intersections with the frictions may trace out the remainder of the circle.

Routh and Watson's Senate-House Problems for 1860, p. 26.

73. $ABCD$ is a quadrilateral, O the intersection of the diagonals; P, Q points in BD, AC such that $QA=OC$ and $PB=OD$. Prove that the centre of gravity of the quadrilateral coincides with that of the triangle OPQ.

This simple and elegant construction for the centre of gravity of a plane quadrilateral is given in the *Quarterly Journal of Mathematics*, Vol. VI. p. 127.

DYNAMICS.

INTRODUCTION. CHAPTER I.

1. A railway train travels over 150 miles in 5 *h.* 40 *m.* What is its average velocity in feet per second?

Result. 38·8 nearly.

2. What is the velocity of a particle which describes 4·38 miles in 31′ 50″:—a foot and a second being the respective units of space and time?

3. If f, F be the numerical values of any the same acceleration referred to units of time and space t, s; τ, σ respectively, shew that $F = \frac{s}{\sigma}\left(\frac{\tau}{t}\right)^2 f$.

What would be the numerical value of the accelerating force of gravity, if a mile and an hour were the units of space and time?

4. If v, v' be two component velocities of a particle, and α the angle between their directions, the resulting velocity is $= \sqrt{(v^2 + v'^2 + 2vv' \cos \alpha)}$.

5. If the unit of pressure (or statical force) be 1 lb. and the unit of accelerating force be the force which in a second generates a velocity of one foot per second, what is the unit of mass?

Result. The mass of a weight of 32·2 lbs.

6. If the area of a field of ten acres be represented by 100, and the acceleration of a heavy falling particle by $58\frac{2}{3}$, find the unit of time.

7. In the equation $w=mg$, what must be the relation between the units of time and space, in order that the unit of mass may be the mass of a unit of weight?

8. Shew from the second law of motion that if a system of particles subject to gravity be projected simultaneously from a point in directions which all lie in one plane, the locus of the particles at any subsequent instant will be a parallel plane.

9. If the unit of weight be 1 oz., and one cubic foot of the substance of standard density weigh 162 lbs., what must be the unit of linear measure, that the formula $W=V\rho g$ may be true, g being equal to 32 feet?

Result. 4 inches.

10. In the equation of relation $P=mf$ (Art. 42) supposing the unit of force to be 5 lbs. and the unit of acceleration, referred to a foot and a second as units, to be 3,—find the unit of mass.

Result. The unit of mass is the mass of $53\frac{2}{3}$ lbs. *nearly.*

11. The radius of the earth at the equator is 3962·8 miles, and it makes a complete revolution about its axis in 23 *h.* 56 *m.*; find the velocity of a point at the equator in feet per second.

Result. 1526 nearly.

12. If the accelerating effect of gravity be numerically represented by 9660, a yard being the linear unit, find the unit of time.

Result. Half a minute.

13. If a body weighing 30 lbs. be moved by a constant force which generates in it in a second, a velocity of 50 feet

per second, find what weight the force would statically support.

Result. 46·77 lbs. nearly.

14. The wind blowing exactly along a line of railway, two equally quick trains, moving in opposite directions, have the steam track of the one twice as long as that of the other; compare the velocities of the trains and of the wind.

Result. Velocity of the train = 3 times that of the wind.

15. If f_1, f_2 be the measure of the accelerating effect of a force when $m+n$ and $m-n$ seconds are the respective units of time, and a and b feet the respective units of distance,—shew that the measure becomes $\frac{1}{c}(\sqrt{f_1 a}+\sqrt{f_2 b})^2$,—provided $2m$ seconds be the units of time, and c feet the unit of distance.

16. A point, moving with a uniform acceleration, describes 20 feet in the half-second which elapses after the first second of its motion; compare its acceleration f with that of a falling heavy particle:—and give its numerical measure, taking a minute as the unit of time, and a mile as that of space.

Result. (i) $f:g=1:1$ nearly, (ii) $f=21\frac{9}{11}$.

17. A pressure P produces an accelerating effect f on a mass m, determine the relation between P, m and f; the unit of pressure being 1 lb. the unit of mass the mass of a cubic foot of water, and the unit of acceleration the acceleration produced by gravity.

Result. $P=62{\cdot}5.m.f.$

18. If a point be situated at the intersection of the perpendiculars drawn from the angular points of a triangle to the sides respectively opposite to them, and have component

velocities represented in magnitude and direction by its distances from the angular points of the triangle,—prove that its resultant velocity will tend to the centre of the circle circumscribing the triangle, and will be represented by twice the distance of the point from the centre.

19. If a be the distance at any time between two points moving uniformly in one plane, V their relative velocity, and u, v the resolved parts of V in and perpendicular to the direction of a, shew that their distance when they are nearest to each other is $\frac{av}{V}$, and that the time of arriving at this nearest distance is $=\frac{au}{V^2}$.

20. A straight rod moves in any manner in a plane; prove that at any instant the directions of motion of all its particles are tangents to a parabola.

21. A person travelling eastward at the rate of 4 miles an hour, observes that the wind seems to blow directly from the north; on doubling his speed the wind appears to come from the north-east; determine the direction of the wind, and its velocity.

Result. The true direction of the wind is from the north-west—and its velocity is $4\sqrt{2}$ miles an hour.

22. The measures of an acceleration and a velocity when referred to $(a+b)$ ft., $(m+n)''$ and $(a-b)$ ft., $(m-n)''$ respectively, are in the inverse ratio of their measures when referred to $(a-b)$ ft., $(m-n)''$ and $(a+b)$ ft., $(m+n)''$; their measures when referred to a ft., m'' and b ft., n'' are as $ma : nb$, shew that

$$\frac{n^2}{m^2}=1-\frac{b^4}{a^4}.$$

COLLISION. CHAPTER II.

1. What must be the elasticity of two balls A, B in order that A impinging directly upon B at rest may itself be reduced to rest by the impact?

Result. $e = \frac{A}{B}$.

2. A man can pull a boat with three times the velocity of the stream—at what angle to the stream must the boat be rowed in order that he may land at a point directly opposite his starting place?

Result. At an angle with the stream $= \cos^{-1} \frac{1}{3}$.

3. A ship sails N.W. at the rate of 9 knots per hour, and is drifted S.S.W. by the current at the rate of 2 knots an hour—find the actual speed and direction of motion.

Result. Her speed $= \sqrt{85 - 18\sqrt{2 - \sqrt{2}}}$ knots an hour,—her direction makes an angle $\cot^{-1}\left(\frac{9 - 2\cos\frac{3\pi}{8}}{2\sin\frac{3\pi}{8}}\right)$ to the west of north-west.

4. A ball of 9 ounces moving with a velocity of 7 feet a second impinges directly upon a ball of 12 ounces moving with a velocity of 5 feet a second in the opposite direction; find the change in the velocity and momentum of each ball, supposing them inelastic.

5. Under what conditions will the velocities of two balls A, B impinging directly upon each other, be interchanged after impact?

Result. If the balls be equal and the elasticity perfect.

6. Two balls A, B are moving in directions at right angles to each other with the same velocity, the line joining their centres at the instant of impact being in direction of A's motion; find the velocity and direction of motion of each after impact (elasticity $= e$).

Result. In the formulæ of Art. 58 write $\alpha = 0$, $\beta = 90°$, $u = v$.

7. Two bodies of masses $2A$ and $3A$ are moving with the same velocity in directions making angles 45° and 30° with the common tangent at the point of impact. Find the direction and velocity of the centre of gravity.

8. A, B are two equal and perfectly elastic spheres; A moving with a given velocity impinges on B at rest, the direction of A's motion before impact making an angle of 60° with the straight line which joins their centres at the instant of impact; determine the directions and velocities of A and B after impact.

9. Compare the velocity of a place at the earth's equator arising from the earth's rotation, with the velocity of the earth in her orbit about the sun; assuming the earth's radius = 4000 miles, the radius of the earth's orbit = 95000000 miles, and the length of the year = 365¼ days.

Result. 1 : 65 nearly.

10. A ball A impinges directly with a given velocity upon another ball B at rest; if the *vis viva* before impact be n times the *vis viva* after impact, find their common elasticity.

Result. $e^2 = \dfrac{A + B - nA}{nB}$.

11. A ball A moving with a given velocity impinges directly upon a ball B at rest, and B afterwards impinges

upon C at rest; determine the velocity communicated to C. If A and C be of given mass and B variable, shew that C's velocity will be greatest when $B^2 = A \,.\, C$.

Apply the formulæ of Art. 58.

12. A ball A strikes a ball B at rest, the direction of A's motion before impact being 45° inclined to the line AB; find the velocity and direction of motion of each after impact, and the condition that they may move at right angles to each other.

13. A perfectly elastic ball acted on by no force, is projected from the focus of an ellipse and impinges upon the curve; it will return to the focus again in the same time, whatever be the direction of projection.

14. Two planes make an angle of 5° with each other, and a perfectly elastic body is projected against one of them at an angle of 105°; how many reflexions will take place towards the angle where the planes meet?

Result. Three.

15. A ball A impinges obliquely on another ball B at rest, and after impact the directions of motion of A and B make equal angles (α) with A's previous motion: find α, and shew that if the masses of the balls be equal and e the mutual elasticity, $\alpha = \tan^{-1}\sqrt{e}$.

16. A smooth table has a smooth rim in the form of a regular hexagon; shew that an inelastic ball, projected along one side of the hexagon, performs n complete revolutions in $(2^{6n} - 1)$ *time* of describing the first side.

17. Two imperfectly elastic balls, equal in size, but unequal in mass, are placed between two perfectly hard parallel

planes, to which the line joining the centres of the balls is perpendicular,—each ball being initially at a distance from the plane nearest to it, inversely proportional to its mass. The balls approach each other with velocities inversely proportional to their masses; prove that every impact will take place at the same point as the first does.

18. Two balls, of elasticity e, moving in parallel directions with equal momenta, impinge; prove that if their directions of motion be opposite, they will move after impact in parallel directions with equal momenta; and that these directions will be perpendicular to the original direction if their common normal is inclined at an angle $\tan^{-1}\sqrt{e}$ to that direction.

19. A ball of elasticity e is projected along a horizontal plane in an equilateral triangle, and after reflexion at two sides it impinges perpendicularly on the third. Shew that the angle of incidence was $\tan^{-1}\dfrac{\sqrt{3}e(1-e)}{1+3e}$.

* * * * * * *

20. If u, v be the velocities before direct impact of two balls A, B,—u', v' their velocities after impact, shew that

$$Au^2+Bv^2=Au'^2+Bv'^2+\frac{AB}{A+B}(1-e^2)(u-v)^2.$$

21. A body whose elasticity is e is projected from a point in the circumference of a circle, and after three rebounds from the circumference returns to the point from which it was projected; shew that the direction of projection is inclined to the radius of the circle at an angle $=\tan^{-1}(e^{\frac{3}{2}})$.

22. A ball projected from a point in one side of a billiard table returns to the point of projection after striking each side in succession; find the direction of projection, and shew that if it ever returns to its original position it does so after the first circuit.

23. Two equal balls (A, A), moving with equal velocities in directions passing through the centre of a third ball C, impinge upon it and upon one another simultaneously; find the ratio of the masses of the balls, that after impact the directions of motion of the two balls may be perpendicular to that of the third, the coefficients of elasticity being $\frac{1}{2}$.

Result. $C=4A$.

24. A ball A impinges upon a ball B at rest; find the direction of the line joining the centres of A and B, in order that they may after impact move in directions making equal angles with the original direction of A's motion.

Result. With the notation of Art. (58) we must have

$$\tan^2 \alpha = \frac{B - A + 2eB}{A + B}.$$

25. If ABC be a triangle and D, E, F the points where the circle inscribed in it meets the sides BC, CA, AB respectively; shew that if a ball, of elasticity e, be projected from D so as to strike AC in E and then rebound to F,

$$AE = e \, . \, CE.$$

If the ball return to D, $AB = e \, . \, AC$.

26. Two equal balls (of elasticity e) start at the same instant with equal velocities from the opposite angles of a square along the sides and impinge; determine the angle between their directions after the impact.

Result. $\tan^{-1} \dfrac{2e}{1-e^2}$.

27. Three equal smooth balls rest on a horizontal table and each is in contact with the other two; if one of them receive a blow at a given point in the plane passing through the centres of the balls, determine the direction of its motion after impact.

28. Two particles connected by an inextensible string are projected in given directions in one plane with given velocities; determine their motions immediately after the string becomes tight.

29. A body of elasticity e is projected along a horizontal plane from the middle point of one of the sides of an isosceles right-angled triangle, so as after reflexion at the hypotenuse and remaining side to return to the same point; shew that the cotangents of the angles of reflexion are $e+1$ and $e+2$ respectively.

30. The tangents of the angles of a triangle ABC are in geometrical progression, $\tan B$ being the mean proportional; and a ball is projected in a direction parallel to the side CB, so as to strike the sides AB, BC successively. Shew that if its course after the first impact be parallel to AC, its course after the second will be parallel to BA:—and that if e be the modulus of elasticity,

$$e^{\frac{1}{2}} + e^{-\frac{1}{2}} = \sec B.$$

31. A ball is projected from the middle point of one side of a billiard table so as to strike in succession one of the sides adjacent to it, the side opposite to it, and a ball placed in the centre of the table: shew that if a, b be the lengths of the sides of the table, e the elasticity of the ball, the inclination

of the direction of projection to the side a of the table from which it is projected must be

$$=\tan^{-1}\frac{b}{a}\left(\frac{1+2e}{1+e}\right).$$

32. A smooth inelastic ball,—mass m,—is lying on a horizontal table in contact with a vertical wall, and is struck by another ball,—mass m'—moving in a direction perpendicular to the wall, making an angle (α) with the common normal at the point of impact; shew that if θ be the angle through which the direction of motion of the striking ball is turned,

$$\cot\theta\cot\alpha=\frac{m'}{m}+1.$$

33. An elastic ball is projected from a point in one of the sides of a square billiard table so as to describe an inscribed square; prove that if e be the mutual elasticity of the cushions and ball, the time of describing the square is

$$\frac{1-e^{2}}{1-e^{\frac{1}{2}}}\cdot\frac{1}{e^{\frac{3}{2}}}\times$$

time of describing the first side.

34. A particle, of elasticity e, is projected from the middle point of one side of a square, in a direction making an $\angle\,\theta$ with it;—shew that if the ball strike the four sides in order, θ must lie between

$$\tan^{-1}\frac{2e(1+e)}{1+(1+e)^2}\text{ and }\tan^{-1}\frac{2(1+e)}{2+e}.$$

35. Two billiard balls are lying in contact on the table; in what direction must one of them be struck by a third, so as to go off in a given direction?

36. A row of elastic balls A, B, C, ... P, are at rest; if A be made to impinge directly with given velocity upon B, then B on C with the velocity acquired, C on D, and so on, find the velocity of P.

Shew that if A and P be of given magnitude, but B, C... capable of being changed, the velocity communicated to P will be greatest when the masses of the balls are in geometrical progression.

And if the number of balls interposed between A and P become indefinitely great, then the *velocity acquired by* $P = \sqrt{\left(\frac{A}{P}\right)}$. *original velocity of* A.

ACCELERATED MOTION. CHAPTER III.

1. A BODY is projected upwards with a velocity u, and after rising through a space s, has a velocity v; shew that

$$v^2 = u^2 - 2gs.$$

If the velocity of projection is $8g$, find the time in which the body rises through the height $14g$.

2. A particle of elasticity $\frac{1}{2}$ drops through 16 feet, and then rises after impact on a horizontal plane. Find the velocity after rising 3 feet, and the time of this ascent: force of gravity being taken to be 32 feet.

Result. Velocity = 8 feet, and the time = $\frac{1}{4}$ second.

3. A particle moves over 7 feet in the first second of the time during which it is observed, and over 11 and 17 feet in the 3rd and 6th seconds respectively. Is this consistent with

the supposition of its being subject to the action of a uniform force?

Result. Yes.

4. A weight Q is drawn along a smooth horizontal table by a weight P hanging vertically, find (1) the acceleration of P, (2) the acceleration of the centre of gravity of P and Q.

Result. (i) Acceleration of $P = \frac{P}{P+Q}g$. (ii) Of the centre of gravity $= \left(\frac{P}{P+Q}\right)^2 g$ *vertically*, and $= \frac{PQ}{(P+Q)^2}g$ *horizontally.*

5. A constant force (f) acts upon a body from rest during 3 seconds, and then ceases. In the next 3 seconds it is found that the body describes 180 feet. Find both the velocity (v) of the body at the end of the 2nd second of its motion and the numerical values of the accelerating force (1) when a second, (2) when a minute is taken as the unit of time.

Result. $D=40$, (i) $f=20$. (ii) $f=72000$.

6. A force which can *statically* support 50 lbs. acts uniformly for one minute on a body, the weight of which is 200 lbs.; find the velocity and momentum acquired by the body.

7. A body acted on by a uniform force is found to be moving at the end of the first minute from rest with a velocity which would carry it through 10 miles in the next hour. Compare this force f with that of gravity g.

Result. $f : g = 1 : 131$ nearly.

8. If the force of gravity be taken as the unit of force, and a rate of ten miles an hour as the unit of velocity, what must be the units of time and space?

Result. Unit of time $= \left(\frac{11}{24}\right)''$, unit of space $= \frac{121}{18}$ feet.

9. A bullet fired directly into a block of wood will penetrate a inches: find what proportion of its velocity it would lose in passing through a board of the same wood *one inch thick*, supposing the resistance uniform.

10. A particle slides down a rough inclined plane (α); find the acceleration f.

Result. $f = g(\sin\alpha - \mu\cos\alpha)$.

11. If a weight of ten pounds be placed upon a plane which is made to descend with a uniform acceleration of 10 feet per second, what is the pressure upon the plane?

Result. 6·875 lbs.

12. A body falling in vacuo under the action of gravity is observed to fall through 144·9 feet and 177·1 feet in two successive seconds; determine the accelerating force of gravity, and the time from the beginning of the motion.

Result. $g = 32 \cdot 2$, and the first of the two seconds spoken of is the fifth from the beginning of motion.

13. The velocity generated by a gun in a bullet of 1 oz. is 1000 feet per second; supposing that the bullet described the length of the barrel in $\frac{1}{10}$ of a second, and that the force is uniform, find the acceleration and moving force (f, F).

Result. $f = 10000$ feet per second,
$F = 19 \cdot 4$ lbs. nearly.

14. A body falling vertically is observed to describe 112·7 feet in a certain second; how long previously to this has it been falling?

Result. Three seconds.

15. A person drops a stone into a well, and after t'' hears it strike the water; find the depth (x) to the surface of the water (assuming velocity of sound $= 35 . g$ nearly).

Result. Find x from the equation

$$x + 35\sqrt{2gx} = 35gt.$$

16. A balloon ascends with a uniformly accelerated velocity so that a weight of 1 lb. produces on the hand of the aeronaut sustaining it a downward pressure equal to that which 17 oz. would produce at the earth's surface; find the height which the balloon will have attained in one minute from the time of starting, not taking into account the variation of the accelerating effect of the earth's attraction.

Result. 1207·5 yards, taking $g = 32{\cdot}2$.

17. AB is the vertical diameter of a circle; through A the highest point any chord AC is drawn, and through C a tangent meeting the tangent at B in the point T. Shew that the time of a body's sliding down $CT \propto \frac{1}{AC}$.

18. A particle uniformly accelerated describes 108 and 140 feet in the 5th and 7th seconds of its motion:—find the velocity of projection and the numerical measure of the acceleration.

19. Shew how to place a plane of given length in order that a body may acquire a given velocity by falling down it.

20. Prove that the locus of the points, from which the times down equally rough inclined planes to a fixed point vary as the lengths of the planes, is a right circular cone.

21. In a parabola whose axis is vertical, a tangent is drawn at any point P cutting the axis produced in T; shew

that if gravity alone acts, the time of descent down TP bears a constant ratio to the time of descent from T to the focus.

22. APB, AQC are two circles with their centres in the same vertical line ABC, and touching each other at their highest points. If APQ, Apq be any two chords, the times of descent down PQ, pq from rest at P and p are equal.

23. A particle is moving under the action of a uniform force, the accelerating effect of which is f: if u be the arithmetic mean of the first and last velocities in passing over any portion h of the path, and v the velocity gained, shew that

$$uv = fh.$$

24. In what time will a force which would support a 5 lb. weight move a mass of 10 lbs. weight through 50 feet along a smooth horizontal plane, and what will be the velocity acquired?

25. If a body subject to a uniform acceleration describes 36 feet, whilst its velocity increases from 8 to 10 feet per second, how much farther will it be carried before it attains a velocity of 12 feet per second?

26. A heavy body is projected up an inclined plane, inclined at 60° to the horizon, with the velocity which it would have acquired in falling freely through a space of 12 feet, and just reaches the top of the plane; find the altitude of the plane, the coefficient of dynamical friction being $= \frac{1}{\sqrt{3}}$.

Result. 9 feet.

27. Two bodies uniformly accelerated, in passing over the same space, have their respective velocities increased

from 5 to 7 and from 8 to 10,—compare the accelerating forces, and the respective times of describing the space.

* * * * * *

28. AP, AQ are two inclined planes of which AP is rough ($\mu = \tan PAQ$) and AQ is smooth, AP lying above AQ: shew that if bodies descend from rest at P and Q, they will arrive at A, (i) in the *same* time if PQ be perpendicular to AQ, (ii) with the *same* velocity if PQ be perpendicular to AP.

29. An engine whose power is sufficient to generate a velocity of 150 feet a second in a mass m (which is its own mass) is attached to a carriage, mass $=\frac{m}{2}$, by means of an inelastic weightless chain 3 feet long; this carriage again in exactly the same way to another mass $=\frac{m}{2^2}$; this to a third mass $=\frac{m}{2^3}$. The engine and carriages are in contact when the train starts; shew that the last carriage will *begin* to move with a velocity $= 33$ feet per second nearly.

30. A body P descending vertically draws another body Q up the inclined plane formed by the upper surface of a right-angled wedge which rests on a smooth horizontal table; find the force F necessary to prevent the wedge from sliding along the table.

Result. $F = Qg \cos \alpha \dfrac{Q \sin \alpha - P}{P+Q}$.

31. A uniform string hangs at rest over a smooth peg. Half the string on one side of the peg is cut off: shew that the pressure on the peg is instantaneously reduced to two-thirds its previous amount.

32. A smooth wedge (of $\angle \alpha$) on a horizontal plane is moved from rest with a uniform acceleration; find the direction and amount of the acceleration that a heavy particle placed on its inclined plane surface may be in equilibrium relative to it.

Result. The wedge must move in a principal plane with an acceleration $= g \tan \alpha$.

33. Find the locus of points from which inelastic particles may be let fall on a smooth inclined plane, so as always to have the same velocity on arriving at the same horizontal line in the plane.

Result. A plane passing through the given horizontal line.

34. If a body is projected with velocity u in the direction of a uniform force f, and if v be the velocity and s the space described at the end of time t, prove that

$$\frac{v-u}{f} = \frac{2s}{v+u} = t.$$

The velocity of a body increases from 10 to 16 feet per second in passing over 13 feet under the action of a constant force; find the numerical value of the force.

35. Find by geometrical construction or otherwise the line of quickest descent,

(i) From a given straight line to a given point.

(ii) From a given point within a given circle to the circle.

(iii) From a given circle to a given point within it.

(iv) From a given circle to a given straight line or to another circle without it.

(v) From a given circle to another given circle either within it or without it.

36. Two circles lie in the same plane, the lowest point of one being in contact with the highest point of the other; shew that the time of descent from any point of the former to a point in the latter, down the chord passing through the point of contact, is constant.

37. Two equal bodies connected by a string are placed upon two planes which are inclined at angles α, β, to the horizon, and have a common altitude. Prove that the acceleration of their centre of gravity is

$$g \cdot \sin \frac{\alpha - \beta}{2} \cdot \cos^2 \frac{\alpha + \beta}{2}.$$

38. A number of heavy particles start at once from the vertex of an oblique circular cone, whose base is horizontal, and fall in all directions down generating lines of the surface; prove that they will at any subsequent moment lie in a subcontrary section.

39. Two bodies A and B descend from the same extremity of the vertical diameter of a circle, one down the diameter, the other down the chord of 30°. Find the ratio of A to B when their centre of gravity moves along the chord of 120°.

Result. $A : B = \sqrt{3} + 1 : 1$.

40. A series of particles slide down the smooth faces of a pyramid, starting simultaneously from rest at the vertex; shew that after any time t they are in a certain spherical surface whose radius $= \frac{1}{4} gt^2$.

41. P pulls Q over a smooth pully;—and Q in ascending as it passes a certain point A, catches and carries with it

a certain additional weight which makes it altogether heavier than P; and on its descent the additional weight is again deposited at A. Supposing no impulse to take place when the weight is so caught up, and that Q in this manner oscillates through an equal space on either side of A,—find the additional weight.

42. If the weight attached to the free end of the string in a system of pullies, in which the same string passes round each pully, be m times that which is necessary to maintain equilibrium, shew that the acceleration of the ascending weight is $\frac{m-1}{mn+1} \cdot g$, where n is the number of strings at the lower block, and the grooves of the pullies are supposed smooth. What is the tension of the string?

43. A weight W is connected with a weight P by a system of n movable pullies, in which the string passing round any pully has one end fixed and the other attached to the pully next above it—the string to which P is attached passing round a fixed pully, and the strings between the pullies being all parallel:—shew that the acceleration of W *upwards* is $= \frac{2^n P - W}{2^{2n} P + W} \cdot g$.

44. If S be the focus of a parabola whose axis is horizontal and plane vertical, SP the line of quickest descent from S to the curve, shew that SP is inclined at 60° to the axis.

45. Two weights P, Q move on two planes inclined at angles α, β to the horizon respectively, being connected by a fine string passing over the common vertex, in a vertical plane which is at right angles to this common vertex, their

centre of gravity describes a straight line with uniform acceleration equal to

$$g\,\frac{Q\sin\beta - P\sin\alpha}{(P+Q)^2}\sqrt{P^2+2PQ\cos(\alpha+\beta)+Q^2}.$$

46. A heavy particle is projected directly up an inclined plane (α) with velocity u, and is attached to the point of projection by an inextensible string whose length is half the distance a free particle would ascend: determine the time which elapses before the particle returns to the point of projection.

47. Supposing the weights in Atwood's machine to be 7 and 9 pounds and to rest on scale-pans without weight, find the pressure on each scale-pan.

48. A body starts from rest under a uniform acceleration, but at the commencement of each successive second the acceleration is decreased in a geometrical proportion ($r = \frac{1}{2}$) :— shew that the space described in n seconds $= \left(2n - 3 + \frac{3}{2^n}\right) 2s$, —where s is the space described in the first second.

49. Two bodies whose weights are P and Q hang from the extremities of a cord passing over a smooth peg; if at the end of each second from the beginning of motion P be suddenly diminished and Q suddenly increased by $\frac{1}{n}$th of their original difference; shew that their velocity will be zero at the end of $n+1$ seconds.

50. A string charged with $n+m+1$ equal weights, fixed at equal intervals along it, and which would rest on a smooth inclined plane with m of the weights hanging over the top,

is placed on the plane with the $(m+1)^{th}$ weight just over the top;—shew that if a be the distance between each two adjacent weights, the velocity which the string will have acquired at the instant the last weight slips off the plane, will be $= \sqrt{nag}$.

51. A fine inelastic thread is loaded with n equal particles at equal distances c from one another; the thread is stretched and placed on a smooth horizontal table, perpendicular to its edge, over which one particle just hangs; find the velocity of the system when the rth particle is leaving the table.

Hence shew that if a heavy string of length a be similarly placed on a horizontal table, its velocity in falling off will be $= \sqrt{(ag)}$.

Result. $v_r^2 = gc\dfrac{r(r-1)}{n}$.

52. A number n of equal balls connected by a string are laid upon a smooth table, the string being stretched at right angles to the edge of the table; if one ball hanging over the edge draws the others after it, determine the lengths of successive portions of the string, that each may fall over at the end of successive equal intervals of time.

Result. If a_r be the length of string between the rth and $(r+1)^{th}$ balls, we must have $a_r = r^2 . a_1$, and if v_r be the velocity of the system when the rth ball is passing over the edge, $v_r = r(r-1)\sqrt{\dfrac{ga_1}{2n}}$.

PROJECTILES. CHAPTER IV.

1. A particle, acted on by two equal centres of force which vary as distance,—one repulsive and the other attractive,—will, however projected, describe a parabola.

2. A body is projected with a vertical velocity (16·7) and a horizontal velocity (·8); prove that its distance from the point of projection at the end of one second is *one foot* ($g = 32{\cdot}2$ feet).

3. If a body fall down an inclined plane (α), and another be projected from the starting point horizontally along the plane with velocity v, find the distance D between the two bodies (i) after a given time t, (ii) after the first body has descended through a given space s.

Result. (i) $D = vt$. (ii) $D = v\sqrt{\dfrac{2s}{g\sin\alpha}}$.

4. Find the angle which the direction of a projectile makes with the horizon at any point of its path, and determine its distance from a line drawn through the point of projection parallel to this direction.

Result. With the notation of Art. 88, Cor. 3,

$$\tan\phi = \tan\alpha - \frac{gt}{v\cos\alpha},$$

and z = distance required $= v\sin(\alpha - \phi) . t - \frac{1}{2}g\cos\phi . t^2$.

5. If θ, ϕ be the angles which the tangents to the curve at the points P, Q of the path of a projectile make with the horizon, the time of describing the arc $PQ \propto \tan\theta - \tan\phi$.

6. A body slides down an inclined plane of given height, and then impinges upon an elastic horizontal plane; what

must be the elevation of the inclined plane in order that the range on the horizontal plane may be the greatest possible?

Result. 45°.

7. Having given the velocities at two points of the path of a projectile, find the difference of their altitudes above a horizontal plane.

8. If a ship is moving horizontally with a velocity $3g$, and a body is let fall from the top of the mast, find its velocity and direction after 4″.

Result. Velocity $= 5g$, inclination to the horizon $= \tan^{-1}\dfrac{4}{3}$.

9. A body is projected from the top of a tower with a given velocity in a given direction; find where it will strike the ground.

10. A heavy particle is projected from one point so as to pass through another not in the same horizontal line with it; prove that the locus of the focus of its path will be a hyperbola.

11. Particles are projected from the same point in a vertical plane with velocities which vary as $(\sin\theta)^{-\frac{1}{2}}$, θ being the angle of projection; the locus of the vertices of the parabolas described is an ellipse—whose horizontal axis is double the vertical axis.

12. Two heavy bodies are projected from the same point, at the same instant, in the same direction, with different velocities; find the direction of the line joining them at any subsequent time.

Result. It is always parallel to the direction of projection.

13. An imperfectly elastic ball is projected from a point between two vertical planes, the plane of motion being perpendicular to both; shew that the arcs described between the rebounds are portions of parabolas whose *latera recta* are in geometric progression.

14. A body is projected vertically upwards from a point A with a given velocity (u); find the direction (α) in which another body must be projected with a given velocity (v) from a point B in the same horizontal line with A, so as to strike the first body.

Result. $\sin\alpha = \frac{u}{v}$.

15. A ball is projected from a point in a horizontal plane and makes one rebound; shew that if the second range is equal to the greatest height which the ball attains, $\tan\alpha = 4e$: α being the angle of projection and e the elasticity.

16. Particles are projected from the same point in the same direction, but with different velocities; find the locus of the foci of their paths.

Result. The straight line $y + x\cot 2\alpha = 0$ (Art. 88).

17. The greatest range of a rifle-ball on level ground is 1176·3 feet. Find the initial velocity of the ball, and shew that the greatest range up an incline of 30° will be 784·2 feet —neglecting the resistance of the air.

18. If a body be projected at an angle α to the horizon with the velocity due to gravity in 1″, its direction is inclined at an angle $\frac{\alpha}{2}$ to the horizon at the time $\tan\frac{\alpha}{2}$, and at an angle $\frac{\pi-\alpha}{2}$ at the time $\cot\frac{\alpha}{2}$.

19. A body is projected from a given point A with a given velocity and in a given direction. After a lapse of m seconds another equal body is projected from the same point so that the line joining the two bodies always passes through A: shew that the paths of the two bodies and that of their centre of gravity will be equal parabolas.

20. A perfectly elastic particle is projected with a given velocity from a given point in one of two planes equally inclined to the horizon and whose line of intersection is horizontal: determine the angle of projection in order that the particle may after reflexion return to the point of projection, and be again reflected in the same path.

Shew that each plane must be inclined at an angle $\frac{\pi}{4}$ to the horizon.

21. A particle projected with velocity v impinges perpendicularly on an inclined plane drawn through the point of projection at an inclination α,—shew that the range on the plane $= \frac{2v^2}{g} \frac{\sin \alpha}{1 + 3 \sin^2 \alpha}$.

* * * * * * *

22. A body is projected from a given point in a horizontal direction with a given velocity, and moves upon an inclined plane passing through the point. If the inclination of the plane vary, the locus of the directrix of the parabola which the body describes is a horizontal plane.

23. A body is projected horizontally with a velocity $4g$ from a point whose height above the ground is $16g$; find the direction of motion (1) when it has fallen half-way to the ground, (2) when half the whole time of falling has elapsed.

Result. (i) $\phi = 45^\circ$. (ii) $\phi = \tan^{-1} \frac{1}{\sqrt{2}}$.

24. A cylinder is made to revolve uniformly about its axis, which is vertical, while a body descends under the action of gravity, carrying a pencil which traces a curve on the surface of the cylinder: if the surface of the cylinder be unwrapped, what will be the nature of the curve?

Result. A parabola with axis vertical.

25. If a ball of elasticity $\frac{1}{2}$ is let fall through a height h on a plane whose inclination is 30°, shew that it will strike the plane again at a distance $\frac{3h}{2}$ from the first point where it strikes the plane.

26. If the initial velocity of a projectile be given, the horizontal range is the same, whether the angle of projection be $\frac{\pi}{4}+\alpha$, or $\frac{\pi}{4}-\alpha$. Prove this, and compare the times of flight.

27. The velocities at the extremities of any chord of the parabola described by a body projected obliquely and acted on by gravity, when resolved in a direction perpendicular to the chord, are equal.

28. From the top of a tower two bodies are projected with the same given velocity at different given angles of elevation, and they strike the horizon at the same place; find the height of the tower.

29. Having given the velocity and direction of projection of a projectile, determine by a geometrical construction the points where it will strike (i) the horizontal plane passing through the point of projection, (ii) an inclined plane through the same point.

Compare Art. 90.

30. Chords are drawn joining any point of a vertical circle with its highest and lowest points; prove that if a heavy particle slide down the latter chord, the parabola, which it will describe after leaving the chord, will be touched by the former chord,—and that the locus of the points of contact will be a circle.

31. If the plane in Art. 89, *Dynamics*, be a rectangle of given sides, find the velocity with which the particle must be projected from one corner so as to leave the plane horizontally at the other corner: and shew that the ratio of the horizontal range after leaving the plane to that described on the plane is the sine of the $\angle$ of elevation of the plane.

32. The barrel of a rifle sighted to hit the centre of the bull's-eye which is at the same height as the muzzle and distant a yards from it, would be inclined at an elevation α to the horizon. Prove that if the rifle be wrongly sighted so that the elevation is $\alpha + \theta$, θ being small compared with α, the target will be hit at a height $\frac{a \cos 2\alpha}{\cos^2 \alpha} . \theta$ above the centre of the bull's-eye.

If the range be 960 yds., the time of flight 2″, and the error of elevation 1″, the height above the centre of the bull's-eye at which the target will be hit will be nearly $\frac{1}{8}$th of an inch.

33. A ball of elasticity e is projected obliquely up an inclined plane so that the point of impact at the third time of striking the plane is in the same horizontal line as the point of projection. Prove that the distances from this line of the points of first and second impact are in the ratio $1 : e$.

34. If a ball be projected from a point in an inclined plane in a direction such that the range on the plane is the greatest, shew that the direction of motion on striking the plane is perpendicular to the direction of projection.

35. An imperfectly elastic particle falls down an inclined plane of given length, and at the foot impinges on a horizontal plane; shew that the range on this plane will be greatest when the angle of elevation of the inclined plane is $= \tan^{-1}\sqrt{2}$.

36. A body of elasticity e is projected from a point in a horizontal plane. If the distance of the point of nth impact be equal to four times the sum of the vertical spaces described, $\dfrac{1+e}{1+e^n}$ is the tangent of the angle of projection.

37. If α be the angle of projection of a projectile, T the time which elapses before the body strikes the ground, prove that at the time $\dfrac{T}{4\sin^2\alpha}$ the angle which the direction of motion makes with the direction of projection is equal to

$$\frac{\pi}{2} - \alpha.$$

38. If three heavy particles be projected simultaneously from the same point in any directions with any velocities, prove that the plane passing through them will always remain parallel to itself.

39. A perfectly elastic ball is projected from the middle point of one of the sides of an equilateral three-cornered room. It strikes the other two sides and returns to the point of projection. If a be the length of a side of the room and the

velocity of projection be that due to the height $\frac{5a}{4}$, shew that the ball must be projected at an angle $= \frac{1}{2}\sin^{-1}\frac{3}{5}$.

40. An elastic ball is let fall from a given height above a smooth inclined plane; shew that the time of making a given number of hops is the same for all inclinations of the plane.

41. Heavy particles are projected horizontally with different velocities from the same point; shew that the extremities of the latera recta of the parabolas which they generally describe, lie on a cone, of which the axis is vertical and the vertical angle $2\tan^{-1}2$.

42. ABC is a right-angled triangle in a vertical plane with its hypotenuse AB horizontal; a particle projected from A passes through C and falls at B: prove that the tangent of the angle of projection $= 2\operatorname{cosec} 2A$, and that the latus rectum of the path described is equal to the height of the triangle.

43. A perfectly elastic particle dropped from a point P impinges upon an inclined plane at Q. If PN be perpendicular to the plane, shew that the range $= 8 \cdot QN$,—and hence find the locus of P in order that the particle may after one reflexion strike a given point in the plane.

44. A particle A is projected at an angle α to the horizon with velocity V, and is met by a second particle B which is let fall from the directrix at the instant of projection of A,—shew that the distance of the line described by B from the vertical line drawn through the point of projection of A is

$$= \frac{V^2}{2g}\cot\alpha.$$

45. If r_1, r_2, r_3 be three distances of a projectile from the point of projection at which its angular elevations above the point of projection are respectively α_1, α_2, α_3—shew that

$$r_1 \cos^2 \alpha_1 \sin (\alpha_2 - \alpha_3) + r_2 \cos^2 \alpha_2 \sin (\alpha_3 - \alpha_1) + r_3 \cos^2 \alpha_3 \sin (\alpha_1 - \alpha_2) = 0.$$

* * * * * * *

46. From several points of a plane superficies inclined to the horizon bodies are projected simultaneously in different directions, in such a manner that the times of flight along the superficies are the same. Prove that the locus of the bodies at any moment is a plane parallel to the superficies.

47. Tangents at points P, Q in the parabolic path of a particle acted on by gravity, meet in T. If S be the focus, shew that the velocity due to the height ST is a mean proportional between the velocities at P and Q.

48. A plane is inclined at an angle of 45° to the horizon, and from the foot of it a body is projected upwards along the plane, and reaches the top with $\frac{1}{5}$th of its original velocity (v); where will it strike the ground?

Result. At a distance $= \frac{3}{5} \frac{v^2}{g}$ from the point of projection.

49. A perfectly elastic particle is dropped from a point on the interior surface of a fixed smooth sphere: shew that after its second impact on the sphere it will ascend vertically, and will continually pass and repass along the same vertical and parabolic paths, if the horizontal distance of its first vertical path from the centre be $\frac{1}{2}\sqrt{3-\sqrt{2}}\,a$, where a = rad. of sphere.

50. Two inclined planes of the same altitude h and the same inclination α are placed back to back on a horizontal

plane. A ball is projected from the foot of one plane along its surface and in a direction making an ∠ β with its horizontal edge. After flying over the top of the ridge it falls at the foot of the other plane: shew that the velocity of projection is

$$\tfrac{1}{2}\sqrt{gh\,(8+\operatorname{cosec}^2\alpha)}\,.\operatorname{cosec}\beta.$$

51. An imperfectly elastic ball is dropped into a hemispherical bowl from a height n times the radius of the bowl above the point of impact, so as to strike the bowl at a point $30°$ from its lowest point, and just rebounds over the edge of the bowl: shew that the elasticity of the ball is $=\sqrt[4]{3}\,.\,n^{-\frac{1}{4}}$.

52. An imperfectly elastic particle is projected with a given velocity from a point in a horizontal plane from which it continually rebounds; shew that the sum of the areas of the parabolic segments it will describe will be a maximum when the ∠ of projection is $60°$, and that then it is

$$=\frac{\sqrt{3}}{8}\frac{v^4}{g^2(1-e^3)}.$$

53. A ball of elasticity e is projected from a point in an inclined plane, and after once impinging upon the inclined plane, rebounds to its point of projection; prove that, α being the inclination to the horizon of the inclined plane, and β that of the direction of projection to the inclined plane,

$$\cot\alpha\,.\cot\beta=1+e.$$

54. If a projectile can be shot through three points (a, b), (a', b'), (a'', b'') in the same vertical plane, prove that

$$\frac{ab''-a''b}{a''(a''-a)}=\frac{ab'-a'b}{a'(a'-a)},$$

the point of projection being the origin and the axis of x horizontal.

55. If v, v', v'' be the velocities at three points P, Q, R of the path of a projectile, where the inclinations to the horizon are α, $\alpha-\beta$, $\alpha-2\beta$, and if t, t' be the times of describing PQ, QR respectively, shew that

$$v''t = vt', \text{ and } \frac{1}{v} + \frac{1}{v''} = \frac{2\cos\beta}{v'}.$$

56. A body is thrown over a triangle, passing from one extremity of the horizontal base just over the vertex to the other extremity of the base; prove that $\tan\theta = \tan\alpha + \tan\beta$, where θ is the angle of projection, and α, β are the angles at the base of the triangle.

57. From every point in the path of a projectile particles are projected, in the same direction as the projectile at that point, and with $\frac{1}{n}$th of the velocity,—shew that the locus of the foci of the paths described is a parabola.

58. A number of particles are projected in one vertical plane, from the same point P, so that the foci of their paths shall be in a given straight line not passing through P, and making an angle α with a horizontal plane. If v be the velocity, and ϕ the angle of projection of any one, shew that $v^2\cos(\alpha-2\phi)$ is the same for all: and if PS be perpendicular to the given line, S is the focus of the parabola when the angle of projection is $\frac{\alpha}{2}$.

59. If n equal particles be projected from the same point with the same velocity v, and in directions making the angles α, 3α, 5α, &c. with the horizon, and in the same plane,—prove that their centre of gravity will describe the path of a body projected at an angle $n\alpha$ with a velocity $\frac{v\sin n\alpha}{n\sin\alpha}$.

60. From a point P on the ground equidistant between two vertical planes A and B, an imperfectly elastic ball is projected with a velocity $=\sqrt{(2gh)}$ towards A, and reflected by it to B; find c the altitude of the highest point of B the ball can reach, and shew,

(i) That if α be the elevation of the direction of projection which enables the ball to attain that altitude,

$$\tan^2\alpha = \frac{h}{h-c};$$

(ii) That if α', α'' be two elevations such that

$$\tan\alpha' + \tan\alpha'' = 2\tan\alpha,$$

two balls projected in those directions towards A will hit the same point of B.

61. The time of a particle under the action of gravity describing any arc of its parabolic path bounded by a focal chord, is equal to the time of falling from rest vertically through a distance equal to the length of that chord.

62. An elastic ball is projected in a given manner from a point A in a horizontal plane, and at the moment it is moving horizontally it impinges directly upon an equal ball moving in the opposite direction with the same velocity; shew that it will return to A after one rebound if its elasticity $=\frac{1}{2}$.

63. Two elastic balls are projected towards each other in the same vertical plane, v being the velocity and α the angle of projection of each; shew that after impinging on each other they will return to the points of projection if

$$ga(1+e) = ev^2\sin 2\alpha,$$

e being the coefficient of elasticity and $2a$ the distance between the points of projection.

64. Two bodies are projected simultaneously from a point with velocities v, v' at elevations α, α'; shew that the time between their passage through the point common to their path is

$$=\frac{2}{g}\cdot\frac{vv'\sin(\alpha\sim\alpha')}{v\cos\alpha+v'\cos\alpha'}.$$

65. A particle is projected from the vertex of a parabolic tube with velocity due to height h: the axis of the parabola being vertical and vertex downwards; shew that after quitting the tube it will strike the horizontal plane through the vertex in a point whose greatest distance from the vertex is

$$=2\sqrt{ah+h^2},$$

where $4a$ is the latus rectum.

Give a geometrical construction for determining the length of the tube for this maximum range.

Apply the method employed in Art. 92.

66. A ball whose elasticity is e falls through a vertical height h, and is then reflected by a plane inclined at an angle α to the horizon; shew that the range on a horizontal plane passing through the point of incidence is

$$2h(1+e)\sin 2\alpha\,(e\cos^2\alpha-\sin^2\alpha).$$

Interpret the meaning of this expression when $e=0$.

67. Bodies are projected with the same velocity in different directions from the same point A; the locus of the vertices of the parabolas described is an ellipse whose axis minor is the height due to the velocity of projection, and axis major double the axis minor.

68. Planes are drawn in every direction from the point A, and bodies are projected from A with given velocity and

at such angles that the ranges on each of these planes shall be the greatest; shew that the locus of their extremities is a parabola, which touches the parabolic paths of all the bodies.

69. A ball projected from a point on an imperfectly elastic horizontal plane strikes a like vertical plane placed at right angles to its direction at the highest point of its trajectory. After n rebounds on the horizontal plane it returns to the point of projection,—shew that if e be elasticity

$$(1-e)^2 = 2e^n(1-e^n).$$

70. A plane AB inclined at angle α to the horizon leads up to a horizontal plane BC: a particle is projected from the point A directly up AB, with velocity V, traverses the plane AB, and falls upon the plane BC;—if the times of motion from A to B and from B to C be equal, shew that

$$AB = \frac{2V^2}{g}\,\frac{\sin\alpha\,(1+\sin^2\alpha)}{(1+2\sin^2\alpha)^2}.$$

CURVILINEAR MOTION. CHAPTER V.

1. If the length of the seconds pendulum be 39·1393 inches, find the value of g to three places of decimals.

2. A clock loses 5″ per diem; how much must its pendulum be shortened in order that the error may be corrected, the length of the pendulum being 39·14 inches nearly?

Result. ·0045 inches nearly.

3. The force which accelerates a body's motion in a cycloid—whose axis is vertical and vertex downwards—

varies as the arc incepted between the body and the lowest point.

4. What is the length of a pendulum which vibrates, (i) in $\frac{1}{2}$ a second, (ii) in $\frac{1}{4}$ of a second, in the latitude of London?

Result. (i) 9·7846 inches. (ii) 2·4462 inches *nearly*.

5. In a series of experiments made at the Harton coalpit, a pendulum which beat seconds at the surface, gained $2\frac{1}{4}$ beats in a day at a depth of 1260 feet: if g, g' be the force of gravity at the surface and at the depth mentioned, shew that

$$\frac{g'-g}{g}=\frac{1}{19200}.$$

6. How much must a *seconds* pendulum be shortened in order that it may oscillate seconds on the top of a mountain 3000 feet high—assuming the radius of the Earth to be 4000 miles, and the force of gravity to vary as $(\text{distance})^{-2}$ from the centre of the Earth?

7. A railway carriage weighing 12 tons is moving along a circle of radius 720 yards at the rate of 32 miles an hour; find the horizontal pressure on the rails, or what is commonly called the *centrifugal force*.

Result. ·39 tons, *nearly*.

8. A railway train is going smoothly along a curve of 500 yards radius at the rate of 30 miles an hour; find at what angle a plumb-line hanging in one of the carriages will be inclined to the vertical.

Result. $2^0.14'$ nearly.

9. The breadth between the rails in a railway is 4 *ft.* $8\frac{1}{2}$ *in.* Shew that on a curve of 500 *yards* radius, the outer

rail ought to be raised about $2\frac{1}{4}$ *inches* for trains travelling 30 miles an hour.

10. A pendulum is found to make 640 vibrations at the equator in the same time as it makes 641 at Greenwich; if a string hanging vertically can just sustain 80 pounds at Greenwich, how many pounds can the same string sustain at the equator?

Result. About $80\frac{1}{4}$ lbs.

11. The time of oscillation of a particle in a small arc of a circle is *half* the time of oscillation in the cycloid which could be generated by the circle.

12. A seconds pendulum was too long on a given day by a small quantity a, it was then over-corrected so as to be too short by a during the next day; shew that the number of minutes gained in the two days was $1080 \frac{a^2}{L^2}$ nearly, if L be the length of the seconds pendulum.

13. The time of descent to the lowest point in a small circular arc is to the time of descent down its chord $= \pi : 4$.

14. A perfectly elastic ball is projected obliquely, and on reaching its highest point strikes directly another equal ball hanging by a string from the directrix of its path; shew that the struck ball will just reach the directrix.

15. Two particles A, B—of elasticity e—are let fall in opposite directions, at the same instant, from the highest point of a smooth circular tube of very small bore, placed in a vertical position; find the ratio of their masses in order that

the heavier may remain at rest after impact, and determine the height to which the other will rise.

Result. $A = (1 + 2e) B$, and B will rise to a height $= 4e^2$. *diameter*, after the impact.

16. The attractive force of a mountain horizontally is f, and the force of gravity is g; shew that the time of vibration of a pendulum will be $= \pi \sqrt[4]{\dfrac{a^2}{g^2 + f^2}}$: a being the length of the pendulum.

17. A pendulum which would oscillate seconds at the equator, would if carried to the pole, gain 5′ a day; shew that gravity at the equator : gravity at the pole $= 144 : 145$.

* * * * * * *

18. A railway train is moving smoothly along a curve at the rate of sixty miles an hour, and in one of the carriages a pendulum, which would ordinarily oscillate seconds, is observed to oscillate 121 times in two minutes. Shew that the radius of the curve is very nearly *two furlongs*.

Suppose a stone to be dropped from the window of this carriage, find approximately how far from the rail it will fall.

19. A particle is suspended by two equal strings from two fixed points in the same horizontal line, the distance between them being equal to the length of either string; if the particle be raised to one of the fixed points and then dropped, find where it will first come to rest.

Result. When the second string which becomes stretched makes an angle $\theta = \sin^{-1} \dfrac{3\sqrt{3}}{8}$ with the horizon.

20. A groove is cut along the surface of a right cone of height h, so as always to intersect the generating line at a

given angle β; shew that the time in which a heavy particle will arrive at the base is $=\sqrt{\left\{\frac{2(h-h_1)}{g}\right\}}\sec\alpha\sec\beta$: where 2α is the vertical angle of the cone and h_1 the vertical distance of the particle from the vertex at the beginning of the motion.

21. If a heavy particle slide freely from the highest point of a cycloid, of which the axis is vertical and vertex downwards, the angular velocity of the generating circle passing through the point will be constant,—and inversely proportional to the square root of its radius.

22. A number of cycloids are drawn through a given point A and having their vertices situated on a given curve and their axes vertical. Prove that if the given curve be a cycloid whose vertex is at A and whose axis is vertical, the time of descent from A down all the cycloids to the given curve will be the same:—and that whatever be the form of the given curve the cycloid down which a particle will slide in the greatest or least time will have the tangent at A parallel to the tangent drawn to the given curve at the point where the cycloid meets it.

23. Two unequal weights P, Q are connected by a string of given length (c) which passes through a small ring; find how many times in a second the lighter one Q must revolve *as a conical pendulum*, in order that the heavier may be at rest at a given distance a from the ring.

Result. $\frac{1}{2\pi}\sqrt{\frac{Pg}{Q(c-a)}}$. times.

24. Gravity $\propto \frac{\text{mass}}{(\text{distance})^2}$; *mass of the Earth* $= 49$. *mass of the Moon*, and *radius of the Earth* $= 4$. *radius of the Moon*;

prove that a seconds pendulum carried to the moon would oscillate in $\frac{7}{4}$ seconds.

25. A heavy particle being projected horizontally from the lowest point of a smooth spherical cavity of radius r, shew that it will never leave the surface of the cavity if the velocity of projection be either $< \sqrt{2gr}$ or not $< \sqrt{5gr}$.

26. A bead running upon a fine thread, the extremities of which are fixed, describes an ellipse in a plane passing through the extremities, under the action of no external force; prove that the tension of the thread for any given position of the bead is inversely proportional to the square of the conjugate diameter.

27. If a particle start from the extremity of the base of a cycloid (*as in Art.* 102), the velocity at any point will be proportional to the radius of curvature at the point.

28. Two beads of equal weight are sliding down a perfectly smooth circular wire in a vertical plane, and are at the same instant at the extremities of a vertical chord subtending a right angle at the centre; find the velocity and direction of motion of their centre of gravity at that instant, each bead having been started from the highest point with an indefinitely small velocity.

29. A particle is projected from the vertex of a parabolic arc, whose axis is horizontal and plane vertical, up the concave side of the arc with a velocity v, and describes an angle 2θ about the focus before leaving the curve; shew that

$$\frac{v^2}{cg} = \tan^3\theta + 3\tan\theta,$$

$2c$ being the length of the latus rectum—and the length of the latus rectum of the parabola subsequently described is

$$= 2c \tan^2 \theta.$$

30. A smooth parabola is placed with its axis horizontal and plane vertical, and a particle is projected from the vertex so as to move on the concave side of the curve; shew that the vertical space described before leaving the curve is two-thirds of the greatest height attained.

31. A cycloidal arc is placed with its plane vertical, its base horizontal and vertex upwards, and a heavy particle is projected from the cusp up the curve with a velocity due to a height h; shew that the latus rectum of the parabola described after leaving the curve will be $\frac{h^2}{2a}$, a being the length of the axis of the cycloid.

32. A body suspended from a fixed point by a string of length a is projected horizontally from the lowest point with velocity $= (\sqrt{3}+1)\sqrt{\frac{ga}{2}}$; shew that it will pass through the point of suspension, and that its direction of motion at that point will make an $\angle \cos^{-1} \frac{1}{3}$ with the horizon.

MISCELLANEOUS PROBLEMS IN DYNAMICS.

1. If R, R' be the ranges of the two projectiles, which being thrown from the same place, attain the same vertical height, and pass through a common point,—then will

$$RR' = 4\frac{H}{h}\kappa^2,$$

where H is the greatest height attained, and h, κ are co-ordinates of the point common to the two paths.

2. From a number of points, bodies subject to gravity are projected, all directed towards one point with velocities proportional to the distances of the points of projection from that point. All hit another point. Shew that the points of projection lie in a conic section.

3. Two bevilled wheels roll together; having given the angular velocity ω of the first wheel and the inclination (α) of the axes of the cones, find their vertical angles that the second wheel may revolve with a given angular velocity ω'.

Result. If 2θ, 2ϕ be vertical angles of the first and second wheels, we must have

$$\theta+\phi=\alpha, \text{ and } \omega \sin\theta=\omega' \sin\phi.$$

4. The highest point of the wheel of a carriage, rolling on a horizontal road, moves twice as fast as each of two points in the rim, whose distance from the ground is half the radius of the wheel.

5. A ball projected with a velocity v would penetrate into a block of wood m feet; what velocity would it lose in passing through a board n feet thick, the resistance being uniform?

Result. $v\left(1-\sqrt{\frac{m-n}{m}}\right)$.

6. A ball is thrown vertically down on a horizontal pavement, and just rebounds to its original height. Shew that the velocity of projection is to that due to the original height above the pavement as $\tan(\cos^{-1} e) : 1$—e being the elasticity at impact.

7. A particle is projected up a rough inclined plane; shew that if t_1 = time of ascending, t_2 = time of descending, we shall have

$$\left(\frac{t_1}{t_2}\right)^2 = \frac{\sin(\alpha - \phi)}{\sin(\alpha + \phi)},$$

if the coefficient of friction $= \tan\phi$.

8. Two balls are moving in the same straight line, one of them only being acted on by a force; if the force be constant and tend towards the other ball, shew that the times which elapse between consecutive impacts decrease in geometrical progression.

9. A point moves in such a manner that the sum of the squares of its distances from any number of given points in the same plane with it is constant. Prove that if perpendiculars from the points be at any time let fall on its direction of motion, the point itself will be the centre of gravity of the feet of these perpendiculars.

10. The curve $y^2 - y \cdot f(x) + x^2 = 0$ is such that the times down the chords from the origin to any two points in it vertically below each other are the same; the axis of x being horizontal and that of y vertical.

11. Shew that the time of quickest descent from any point of an ellipse to the horizontal axis major down the normal is $= \sqrt{\dfrac{2le}{g}}$, l being the latus rectum, e the eccentricity.

12. Shew that the circumferences of two circles contain all points from which the time of quickest descent to a given vertical circle is the same.

13. A ball whose elasticity is $\frac{1}{2}$ projected from the floor of a room 12 feet high, strikes the ceiling and floor and just rises to the ceiling again,—find the velocity of projection.

Result. $\sqrt{312.g}$.

14. A perfectly elastic ball is thrown into a smooth cylindrical well from a point in the circumference of the circular mouth. Shew that if the ball be reflected any number of times from the surface of the cylinder, the intervals between the reflexions will be equal.

In the last question, if the ball be projected horizontally, making an angle $\frac{\pi}{n}$ with the tangent at the point of projection, it will reach the surface of the water at the instant of the nth reflexion, if the space due to the velocity of projection be

$$=\frac{(\text{radius})^2}{\text{depth}}\cdot\left(n\sin\frac{\pi}{n}\right)^2.$$

* * * * * * *

15. From a point T two tangents are drawn to touch a circle in the points P, Q: given that the velocity acquired by a body sliding down the chord PQ is equal to $1\text{-}n^{\text{th}}$ of the velocity down the vertical diameter of the circle, prove that the locus of T is the curve whose equation is

$$\frac{a^2}{\rho^2}+\frac{1}{n^4\cos^2\theta}=1,$$

the centre of the circle being the pole, and (a) the radius.

16. One end of a string is attached to an angular point of a fixed regular polygon of n sides, its length being equal to the perimeter c; a particle, attached to the other end of the string which is stretched in direction of a side, is projected in

the plane of the polygon perpendicularly to the string with a given velocity V. Determine after what time the string will coinçide with the perimeter of the polygon (the action of gravity being neglected).

Deduce the time when, the perimeter remaining the same, the number of the sides is infinitely increased.

Result. $\frac{n+1}{n} \cdot \frac{\pi c}{V}$.

17. Explain the object and advantages of rifling the barrel of a gun.

18. Find the amount of *work done* in drawing up a Venetian blind. How must the same problem be solved for a curtain?

19. A ship is sailing with a uniform velocity in a southerly direction, and is fired upon at the instant it is due east of a battery; given the velocity of a cannon-ball, determine at what elevation and towards what point of the compass it must be fired that it may strike the ship.

20. Two perfectly elastic balls are dropped from two points not in the same vertical line, and strike against a perfectly elastic horizontal plane; shew that their centre of gravity will never reascend to its original height, unless the initial heights of the balls be in the ratio of two square numbers.

21. A smooth tube of uniform bore and radius a, is bent into the form of a circular arc—$(= 2\pi - 2\alpha)$—greater than a semicircle, and placed in a vertical plane with its open ends upwards, and in the same horizontal line. Find the velocity u with which a ball that fits the tube must be projected along

the interior from the lowest point, in order that it may pass out at one end and re-enter at the other.

Result. $u^2 \pm ga (2 + 2 \cos a + \sec a)$.

22. A body P lying on a table is connected with another Q by a string passing over a pully directly over P; if Q fall through a given height before the string becomes tight, determine the impulsive tension of the string when that takes place, and the change of velocity of Q.

Compare Art. 75, 76.

23. Two particles start simultaneously from the same point and move along two straight lines, the one with uniform velocity, the other from rest with uniform acceleration. Prove that the line joining the particles at any time is always a tangent to a fixed parabola.

24. If C be the centre of curvature corresponding to any point P of the path of a projectile—prove that the vertical velocity of C will be proportional to the time elapsed since P was at the highest point of its path.

25. Several bodies are projected from the same point A in different directions with the same velocity; shew that the locus of them all at any time is a sphere, and find the radius of the sphere and the position of its centre at any time.

26. A given weight descending vertically draws another up a smooth inclined plane by a string passing over the vertex of the plane. Find the path of their centre of gravity when the bodies move from rest.

Result. A straight line.

27. Tangents are drawn to a vertical circle,—find the locus of points in them from which particles would descend in straight lines to the centre in the shortest time.

28. From what height must a perfectly elastic ball be let fall into a fixed hemispherical bowl, in order that it may rebound horizontally at the first impact and strike the lowest point of the bowl at the second?

29. From a given height a perfectly elastic particle is let fall on a perfectly hard inclined plane, so as to strike it at a given fixed point: prove that whatever be the inclination of the plane to the horizon, the vertex of the parabola which the particle describes after impact will lie in a certain ellipse.

30. A perfectly elastic ball is projected from the foot of one of the walls of a room, against the opposite wall, in a vertical plane perpendicular to both the walls; shew that if it be required to hit the ceiling after the rebound, the ball must strike the wall at a point at least $\frac{3}{4}$ths of the height of the room from the floor.

31. A rigid wire without appreciable mass is formed into an arc of an equiangular spiral, and carries a small heavy particle fixed in its pole. If the convexity of the wire be placed in contact with a perfectly rough horizontal plane, prove that the point of contact with the plane will move with uniform acceleration—and find this acceleration.

32. AA', BB' are the axes of an ellipse. A smooth tube is bent into the shape of the portion $AB'A'B$, the ends A, B being open, and the tube is held with B' on a given horizontal plane. A particle is dropped from a certain height

into the tube at A so that after emerging at B it again enters at A. The tube is then held with A' on the horizontal plane and the particle is dropped from the same point so as to fall into the tube at B, and it is found that after emerging at A, it again enters at B. Prove that the eccentricity of the ellipse is $= \dfrac{\sqrt[4]{45}\,(3-\sqrt{5})}{2}$.

33. If two parabolas be placed with their axes vertical, vertices downwards and foci coincident, prove that there are three chords down which the time of descent of a particle under the action of gravity from one curve to the other is a minimum;—and that one of these is the principal diameter and the other two make an angle of 60° with it on either side.

* * * * * * *

34. A ball thrown from any point in one of the walls of a rectangular room after striking the three others returns to the point of projection before it falls to the ground. Shew that the space due to the velocity of projection is greater than the diagonal of the floor.

35. There are three equal and perfectly elastic balls A, B, C. A is let fall from a given point, and at a moment when it reaches a given horizontal plane, B is let fall from the same point, and at the moment when A in returning meets B, C is let fall. Shew that B will meet C for the second time where it first met A.

36. Two planes having a common altitude h are inclined at angles α and $\dfrac{\pi}{2}-\alpha$ to the horizon; two equal, indefinitely small and perfectly elastic balls are projected along them with equal velocities V from their feet, and so that they may im-

pinge at the top; shew that if the ball which ascends along the former plane falls at its foot after impact, then

$$\frac{V^2}{gh} = (1 + \cot a) + (1 + \cot a)^{-1}.$$

37. There are generally two directions in which a projectile may be projected with given velocity from a point A, so as to pass through another point B; and one of these directions is inclined to the vertical at the same angle that the other is inclined to the line AB. Hence shew that the locus of points, for which a given sight must be used in firing with a given charge of powder, is the surface generated by the revolution, about the vertical, of the path of the bullet obtained by aiming at the zenith with the given sight, and the given charge of powder.

See *Solutions of Senate-House Problems for* 1854, Walton and Mackenzie, p. 33.

38. A perfectly elastic particle projected against one side of a plane polygon is reflected at the other sides in succession, the polygon being such that the angle of incidence on each side is the same; find the impulse on the particle at each impact, and deduce the expression for the normal pressure $\left(\frac{v^2}{\rho}\right)$ on a particle moving freely on a curve under the action of no other impressed force.

39. A body falls from rest under the action of an accelerating force which remains constant during certain successive equal intervals of time, but is changed at the expiration of each such interval so that the space described in the nth interval is always $\frac{2^{n+1} - 3}{2^{n-1}}$ times the space described

in the first of them. If the velocity acquired at the end of the first interval be v, shew that after a long lapse of time the velocity approaches a uniform velocity $2v$.

40. Three smooth equal perfectly elastic billiard balls A, B, C are placed with their centres in the angular points of an equilateral triangle; shew that it will be impossible, with another equal ball, to cannon off A on to B,—A itself striking C,—unless the diameter of each ball be equal to half a side of the triangle.

41. A particle of given elasticity e is projected down a smooth vertical cylinder of indefinite length, but terminated by a horizontal plane at its lower end; the particle initially remaining in contact with the cylinder. If it be projected at a height h from the bottom with velocity V at an $\angle\ \alpha$ with the vertical, then after the time

$$\frac{\sqrt{2gh + V^2\cos^2\alpha}}{g} \cdot \frac{1+e}{1-e},$$

it will be moving uniformly with velocity $V\sin\alpha$.

42. Two perfectly elastic balls A and B impinge upon each other. First A impinges upon B at rest and goes off in a direction making an $\angle\ \theta$ with the line joining their centres: then B impinges upon A at rest and at the same angle of incidence, and goes off at an $\angle\ \theta'$. Prove that $\theta + \theta' = 180°$.

Prove also that if the balls be imperfectly elastic, and the angles of incidence in the two cases be α and α', then

$$\frac{\cot\theta}{\cot\alpha} + \frac{\cot\theta'}{\cot\alpha'} = 1 - e.$$

43. Two equal balls, one perfectly elastic, the other inelastic, are dismissed by the same horizontal blow from the

top of a flight of uniform steps, so that each falls just on the margin of the first step: shew that the number of steps cleared by the elastic ball in its successive flights is the series of successive odd numbers,—and that the two balls reach the bottom of the steps simultaneously.

44. From a point in the lower one of two parallel horizontal planes a ball of elasticity e is projected at an angle α,—is reflected by the upper plane, and again reflected by the lower one; the distance between the planes being $\left(\frac{1}{n}\right)$th that due to the velocity V of projection. If v be the velocity of the ball in rebounding for the mth time from the lower plane,

$$v^2 = V^2\left(\cos^2\alpha + e^{4m}\sin^2\alpha + \frac{e^2}{n}\frac{1-e^{4m}}{1-e^2}\right).$$

THE END.

CPSIA information can be obtained
at www.ICGtesting.com
Printed in the USA
LVHW110933160522
718424LV00014B/118

9 783375 008017